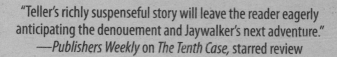

JOSEPH TELLER

DEPRAVED
INDIFFERENCE

MIRA®

MIRA

Recycling programs
for this product may
not exist in your area.

ISBN-13: 978-0-7783-2691-5

DEPRAVED INDIFFERENCE

www.MIRABooks.com

Printed in U.S.A.

To Darcy, Katie, Amy and Rachel, with all my love.
And lest you think that makes me a terrible womanizer,
think again. They are my granddaughters.

1

A VERY BAD D.W.I.

"So," she said, raising herself onto one elbow, just high enough off the bed to reveal a single nipple, still visibly hard. "What do you do for a living, when you're not busy knocking people down?"

She was Amanda. At least that was as much of a name as he'd gotten out of her over the hour and twenty minutes since he'd literally knocked her to the ground by being overly aggressive with a sticking revolving door at the Forty-second Street Public Library. Not that all of their time together since that moment had been devoted to small talk, or any other kind of talk, for that matter. Certainly not the last twenty minutes, anyway.

"I'm a lawyer," said Jaywalker. "Sort of."

"Sort of?"

"I'm not practicing these days," he explained.

"What happened?" she asked. "You get burned out?"

"No," he said, "more like *thrown* out. I'm serving a three-year suspension."

"What for?"

"Oh, various things. Cutting corners. Breaking silly rules. Taking risks. Pissing off stupid judges. The usual stuff."

"They suspend you for those things?"

"It seems so." He left it at that. He didn't feel any particular need to tell her about the juiciest charge of all, that he'd managed to get caught by a security camera in one of the stairwells of the courthouse, accepting—or at least not exactly fending off—an impromptu expression of heartfelt thanks from an accused prostitute for whom he'd just won a hard-fought acquittal.

"What did you say your name was?" she asked.

"I didn't. But it's Jaywalker."

It wasn't just a case of tit for tat, his withholding part of his name because she had. The single name was all he had, actually. Harrison J. Walker had years ago elided into Harrison Jaywalker, and not too long after that, the Harrison part had disappeared altogether. So for years now, he'd been known to just about everyone simply as Jaywalker.

"You're that guy!" exclaimed Amanda, suddenly and self-consciously covering up her wayward nipple with a pillow. "I *knew* you looked familiar. I saw you on Page Six. You were dating that…that *billionaire heiress murderer!*"

Jaywalker winced painfully. Three years ago, had someone asked him to describe his own personal vision of what hell might be like, he might well have replied, "Showing up on the Entertainment Channel," or "Landing on Page Six of the *New York Post*." And thanks to a brief, torrid and not-so-discreet romance with a client named Samara Tannenbaum, he'd managed to accomplish not one but both of those distinctions, and in the short space of a single week.

"Yup," he acknowledged meekly now, "that would be me."

Amanda laughed out loud and threw her head back, her stylishly short blond hair framing her face, in what could easily have been a fashion model's pose. In the process, both of her breasts came completely free of the sheets, causing a decided swelling in Jaywalker's appreciation of her.

"So tell me, mister famous lawyer man," she said. "How much do you charge for a drunk-driving case?"

"I don't," said Jaywalker. "I'm suspended, remember?"

"Right, but for how much longer?"

Jaywalker shrugged. "I don't know, seven months, maybe eight." The fact was, he hadn't exactly been counting the days. If anything, he'd lately been giving some serious consideration to "re-upping" for another three years. Although even as he'd been enjoying his estrangement from the legal profession, his checking account balance was rapidly approaching zero, making such a choice problematic.

"And if you *weren't* suspended?"

He shrugged again. "I don't know. I used to get twenty-five hundred, thirty-five hundred, something like that." And in spite of everything, he found himself already contemplating the variables, just as he used to do. First of all, it would depend on whether they were talking about a plea or a trial. After that, where the case was. A D.W.I. in Manhattan, the Bronx or Brooklyn was no big deal. If there'd been a blood-alcohol test and Amanda's reading hadn't been too high, there was a good chance he could get her a plea to driving while impaired, maybe even a reckless. A couple of appearances, and the case would be done. Queens and Staten Island tended to be a bit tougher. And as you worked your way out into the neighboring counties—Westchester, Nassau and Suffolk, where there was a lower volume of cases—the D.A.s got noticeably more hardassed and could afford to insist upon a plea to the full charge. Not that it mattered all that much, though. What they were talking about here was a fine, a license suspension, or at very worst a revocation, a court-ordered one-day safe-driving course and a substantial increase in her insurance premiums. In other words, a slap on the wrist and a smack on the wallet.

"Where were you arrested?" he asked her. "And did you take a test?" He couldn't help himself.

"Oh, no," said Amanda, shaking her head from side to side, with the inevitable ripple effect it caused to the, uh, rest of her. "It's not me."

"Oh?" said Jaywalker. "So who are we talking about?"

"My husband."

Jaywalker sat up, reflexively reaching around for his pants. His level of appreciation had suddenly shrunk dramatically. Funny how that happened.

"Don't worry," said Amanda. "It's not like he's about to walk in on us or anything."

"How do you know?"

"Because he's in jail, on five million dollars' bail. That's how."

Jaywalker relaxed ever so slightly. "Five million dollars," he echoed. "It must have been a very bad D.W.I."

"It was," said Amanda. "Nine people died."

2

Which, of course, immediately changed everything.

A drunk-driving case is only a drunk-driving case. Until someone dies. When that happens, it blossoms into a vehicular homicide. When *nine* someones die, it can become a full-blown murder case, especially when the victims are incinerated after the van in which they're riding gets forced off the road, flips three times and explodes.

Jaywalker knew the case. Who didn't? It had led off the evening news, even made the front page of his beloved *New York Times,* about three weeks ago. The driver of a passenger van had been literally run off the road and down a steep embankment by an oncoming Audi sports car speeding in the wrong lane. It had happened just north of Congers, New York, right before Route 303 ended and joined up with Route 9W. A witness in a pickup truck had seen the whole thing. He'd thought briefly about giving chase to the Audi as it sped off, before deciding instead to stop to see what he could do for the victims.

The answer was nothing.

Within minutes, the van had burned so badly that the

newspaper photographs of it revealed only a portion of the lettering painted onto its side. All that remained visible was —MAZ—ESHI—, a fact that quickly gave birth to a rumor that the occupants had been Muslim terrorists who'd accidentally blown themselves up before reaching their intended target. That rumor was soon replaced by another one, that the van had been overcrowded because it had been carrying migrant Mexican farmworkers, who were no doubt illegal aliens.

The right-wing radio talk-show hosts lost no time in picking up the story. To them and their call-in listeners, it didn't seem to matter too much whether the dead were terrorists or illegals; whichever turned out to be the case, the consensus was that they'd pretty much deserved their fate. "Good for that Audi guy!" said one caller. "Maybe that'll teach them criminal alien bombers a lesson!" Before the hour was up, one host was referring to the driver of the car as the "Audi Avenger."

It was only after emergency responders had succeeded in putting out the fire and extricating the bodies that the grim truth was discovered. Eight of the nine dead, the van's driver being the sole exception, were young children whose ages would eventually be determined to range from six to eleven. All had been students at the Ramaz Yeshiva, a Jewish school located fifteen miles from the site of the impact. They'd been heading to a groundbreaking ceremony for a new synagogue over in Haverstraw.

Just like that, the Audi Avenger became the Audi Assassin.

If the driver of the pickup truck had been unable to help the occupants of the van, at least he'd accomplished something that day. Turning to watch the fleeing Audi, he'd managed to not only note the model but read its license plate, and although he'd forget the complete registration before being interviewed by state troopers, he'd distinctly remembered that it ended with the numbers 724. That happened to be his wife's birth date, July 24.

The following day, even as computers were busy searching data files for all Audis and Audi look-alikes in the tristate area with registrations ending in 724— there were only six, it would turn out—a man by the name of Carter Drake III, accompanied by his business attorney, turned himself in to the New York State Police in Nyack. Drake was forty-four and had no prior arrests. That said, he'd allowed his driver's license to lapse over parking tickets he'd accumulated several years ago, along with the insurance on the Audi.

Congers is a one-stoplight village in Rockland County, a half an hour north of the George Washington Bridge, on the Jersey side. The county seat is New City, which means that all felonies end up there for trial. But New City has another distinction. It happens to be home to one of the largest concentrations of Orthodox-Jewish populations in the western hemisphere.

Like his wife, Amanda, Carter Drake happened to be blond, good-looking and decidedly not Jewish, let alone orthodox.

Not exactly the best fit for New City.

"So," said Amanda, "will you represent my husband? I'm pretty sure we can afford your fee."

Jaywalker was pretty sure that was an understatement. "You're forgetting my suspension," he reminded her.

"No, I'm not," Amanda assured him. "You told me yourself you like to cut corners, break silly rules, take risks. What's a little suspension between friends? Besides which, doesn't it take months and months for a case to go to trial? By that time, you'll be relawyerized."

"Reinstated," Jaywalker corrected her.

"Whatever. And Carter's no dummy. He can always get sick or something, if the case needs to be slowed down. If you know what I mean."

Jaywalker nodded. Of course he knew what she meant. It was the kind of delaying tactic he himself had resorted to more than once. A bit devious, to be sure. But deviousness had its place in Jaywalker's bag of tricks. So it certainly wasn't Amanda's suggestion that was bothering Jaywalker at the moment. Still, something was. And he decided it was the nagging feeling that he was being set up.

Because the thing was, long before their revolving-door encounter, Jaywalker had noticed that he was being followed. Not by a car; his ancient beat-up Mercury, the one he'd bought himself for six hundred dollars several years back as a reward for winning a brief but serious bout with the bottle, was rusting away in a parking lot over on Twelfth Avenue. No, on foot. Someone had been tailing him, lingering back in the shadows, walking when he walked, stopping when he stopped, crossing the street when he crossed.

Had it not been for his days as a DEA agent, it's likely Jaywalker never would have picked it up. But so many of his colleagues had been doing something wrong back then, whether that meant something as minor as a little bit of creative writing on the hours entered on their Daily Activity Logs, all the way up to outright stealing or selling the very narcotics they were paid to keep off the streets. Whatever it was, they were constantly *checking for a tail,* as they used to call it. Over time, Jaywalker had found himself gradually adopting their paranoia as his own, almost unconsciously looking over his shoulder as he walked and glancing in the rearview mirror as he drove. Even after he'd left the job, the habit had proved a hard one to kick, and now, years later, it still stayed with him to a certain extent.

So yesterday afternoon, when he thought he'd spotted someone eyeing him through sunglasses from outside the plate-glass window of the Korean grocery where he was buying pretzels, cheese and other essentials, he'd decided to conduct a little experiment. He'd proceeded to walk two full avenues out of his way, all the way from West End to Amsterdam, before abruptly stopping in the middle of the intersection, slapping his head in an exaggerated fashion as though he'd forgotten something and suddenly doubling back toward Broadway.

And he'd been right.

Somewhat to his surprise, it had turned out to be a woman, a thirtysomething blonde almost as tall as he was. Though it was an overcast day, she was wearing sunglasses. And as soon as he looked her way, she averted her glance, turned away and crossed the street, disappearing into the midafternoon crowd.

He'd looked for her again this morning and had actually been disappointed when he'd failed to spot her. But soon enough, there she was again. More careful this time, wearing a large hat pulled down over her forehead, hanging back a little farther, even following him from across the street at one point. But Jaywalker had tricks of his own. In order to get a better look at her, he'd stopped in front of a stationery store and pretended to study the items on display. In fact, he was able to angle himself so that in the reflection of the glass he could see her slow down and then stop on the opposite sidewalk, pretending to be looking into a shop herself. But it was unlikely: the shop she was staring into bore the name, at least in Jaywalker's mirrored view, ᗡƎHSAƆ ƧꓘƆƎHƆYAꟼ . In unmirrored English, that would be PAYCHECKS CASHED, and she definitely didn't look like the type who needed her paycheck cashed.

He could have lost her right then, had he wanted to. But by that time he was curious. For starters, unlike his old DEA cronies, Jaywalker knew he wasn't doing anything wrong. He'd faithfully abided by the terms of his suspension. He'd given up his law office, which had never been more than a desk, a phone, an answering machine and a computer in a tenth-floor suite. He'd stayed away from 100 Centre Street, Foley Square and all the other courthouses of the city. He'd stopped giving out business cards, refrained from offering legal advice to the few friends and family members he had, and quickly corrected anyone who addressed him or referred to him as a lawyer, attorney, counselor-at-law, or anything else that suggested he was still practicing. Beyond taking those precautions, he lived a life that was almost boring in its adherence to the law. With his car in dry dock, he accumulated no speeding or parking tickets. Without an income, he had no taxes to cheat on. If he broke the law at all, he excused his transgressions as the inevitable by-product of his name: as a pedestrian he continued to pay little heed to hatched crosswalks, traffic lights, and WALK and DON'T WALK signs. But those offenses were hardly the stuff that called for the authorities to go out and recruit Mata Hari types to conduct clandestine surveillance on him.

So who *was* this blonde who was following him, if rather amateurishly? Jaywalker had been determined to find out. So he'd gradually led her, looking back only surreptitiously, and only often enough to make certain she was still there, all the way to the main branch of the public library. There he'd mounted the outer flight of steps and entered through one of the revolving doors. From the darkened interior, he'd watched as she'd climbed the steps in pursuit. Then, as soon as she'd stepped inside one of the four sections of the door, he'd gotten in opposite her and jammed the thing with his foot. Only after he'd gotten a good look at her from up close—and liked what he saw—had he given the door a good shove to get it going again. Unfortunately, she must have been pushing at the same time, and their combined efforts, as he released his foot, had literally knocked her to the ground. Which meant that, being a gentleman, Jaywalker had had no choice but to come around to her side and help her to her feet.

Her hat had somehow stayed in place, but the force of her fall had knocked the sunglasses from her face. He picked them up and held them up to his eyes for inspection.

"No damage," he assured her.

What he'd really been doing, of course, was checking to see if they were prescription and therefore necessary on a day that was, if anything, even more overcast than the previous one. They weren't, meaning they were nothing but a prop. Still, Jaywalker hesitated a bit longer before returning them to her, getting an even better look at her.

That had been an hour and a half ago. The chat on the library steps, the cup of coffee in a nearby luncheonette and the cab ride to her place had taken less than an hour. The rest, as they say, was history. Yet at no point had Jaywalker confronted her about having followed him. Instead, he'd allowed her the fiction that they'd met only because he'd happened to knock her down.

He decided she must have known who he was all along. Her *"You're that guy!"* epiphany had been nothing but an act, meant to convince him that it had been pure serendipity that she'd ended up in bed with just the man she wanted to defend her husband.

Why had she gone to such elaborate lengths to meet him? If the answer to that question still went begging,

Jaywalker could come up with a pretty plausible explanation. Immediately following his suspension, he'd
vacated his office, disconnected his phone, canceled his
e-mail account and all but ignored whatever showed up
in his post office box. His home phone number, as it
always had been, remained unlisted. In other words, he'd
become a phantom, a very difficult man to find. Had
Amanda Drake—now that he knew her real name—used
more traditional means to try to meet with him and hire
him, she no doubt would have failed. So she'd somehow
hunted him down and then resorted to the old *follow-
him-until-he-catches-me* trick. Then she'd lured him into
her bed and, coming up for air, innocently asked him
what he did for a living. So while Jaywalker was forced
to deduct one point for her having been less than forth-
right, he gave it back to her for sheer cleverness.

A woman after his own heart.

Even though he was pretty much satisfied with his explanation of why Amanda had been following him, he
was tempted to come right out and ask her. Not so much
to test his hypothesis as to show off his own superior
instinct and skill at having spotted her. But he resisted
the urge. Some cards are better played early on in the
game; others are best held on to. Who knew if an oppor-
tune moment might arise when confronting Amanda
would pay a dividend? So he'd settle for having made
the tail, in more ways than one.

He kept quiet, therefore, and turned his thoughts to
the notion of getting back into the business of defending criminals—okay, *accused* criminals. And the love-
hate relationship he'd long carried on with the way he'd
been making his living for the past twenty-some years.

As much as he'd been enjoying his extended sabbati-
cal from the law, Jaywalker could feel the pull of getting
back into the trenches. He missed the courthouse, that

filthy place of long lines, broken elevators and peculiar smells. He missed the people, the camaraderie—defense lawyers and prosecutors he'd grown middle-aged with; judges who itched to hold him in contempt every time he stepped across some foolish line they'd drawn, but would have hired him in a New York minute if they themselves had gotten into trouble; court officers, corrections officers, clerks, court reporters and translators he'd come to feel he'd known forever. He missed even the defendants, often initially surly or even hostile, invariably self-destructive, but almost always deeply appreciative by the time he parted ways with them. He missed the battle, that matching of wits, that take-no-prisoners struggle they called a trial but might just as well have called a war. He missed opening statements, cross-examination, summing up. He missed sitting on the edge of his seat and feeling his heart pounding in his chest as the jurors filed into the courtroom one last time to deliver their verdict. He missed the incredible high that lifted him into the stratosphere with each acquittal. He even missed, in some strange way, the depths of despair into which he plunged following a conviction.

What's more, Jaywalker found himself intrigued by the case against Carter Drake. Should the act of driving, no matter how poorly or even recklessly, ever be a sufficient predicate for a murder charge and the mandatory sentence of life imprisonment it carried? Was Jaywalker being old-fashioned by thinking that before accusing a man of murder, the state ought to first be required to demonstrate that he'd set out to harm somebody? Was that asking too much?

But beyond Jaywalker's interest in that legal issue, there was a much more mundane reason for wanting to get involved. And that was the worst invention Homo sapiens had ever managed to come up with. Money. A

murder case, even one predicated upon the faulty opera-
tion of a motor vehicle, meant a five-figure fee. God
knew he could use the money, which would be his first
income in more than two years. And since Carter Drake
was apparently willing to do whatever it would take to
drag the case out until Jaywalker's suspension was over,
things might actually work out. He'd have to be careful,
of course. He'd have to steer clear of the New City courthouse, refrain from saying anything about the case that
might find its way into the newspapers and avoid any
conduct that might arguably constitute *practicing law.*
And if he were to accept any money, he'd have to do it
in such a way as to make it look like something other
than a legal fee. But that could be done, he was pretty
sure.

Then there were the secondary drawbacks and benefits of getting involved. On the negative side was the
sheer notoriety of the case. Taking on Carter Drake as
his comeback act would mean that Jaywalker would be
returning to the scene of his past transgressions with a
considerable bang. Right off the bat, he'd be representing a high-profile murder defendant in what was sure to
be a media-circus trial. The prospect of that kind of free
publicity would no doubt have delighted every one of
Jaywalker's colleagues, but in that respect he stood apart
from them. In fact, the thought of it brought him dangerously close to gagging.

Finally, there was the chance that one of the benefits
of representing Carter Drake might be Amanda Drake.
Then again, what a conflict of interest *that* would be!
Jaywalker allowed himself a chuckle as he imagined a
slew of new charges from the disciplinary committee. He
could picture the presiding justice snarling down at him
with righteous indignation. "So, Mr. Jaywalker, we conclude that you deliberately made certain that your client

would remain locked up for as long as possible, just so you could continue to have an affair with his wife."

Well, that was one benefit that might just have to be curtailed. But what a shame.

That night, in the privacy of his own place, Jaywalker thought things over. Unlike Amanda Carter's four-bedroom triplex just off Fifth Avenue, Jaywalker's apartment wasn't much more than a furnished room. What it was, was a fourth-floor walk-up studio in what real estate agents tend to write off as a *developing neighborhood,* much the same way economists might refer to a *developing nation.* Implicit in both terms is the suggestion that the entity being described still has a long way to go before qualifying for actually being *developed.* So as he pondered the advisability of getting involved in Carter Drake's case, Jaywalker stretched out on his sofa, which doubled as his bed, and also served from time to time as his laundry sorter, work surface and exercise mat.

A criminal case begins, as Jaywalker well knew, with an investigation, followed by an arrest. Or sometimes it's the other way around, an arrest followed by an investigation. By the time a defense lawyer gets contacted, selected, and either hired by the family or appointed by the court, that lawyer already finds himself playing catch-up. It had already been three weeks since Carter Drake's arrest, and based upon the little that Jaywalker remembered from the newspaper accounts, the only representation Drake had had in that time was from the business lawyer who'd surrendered him, followed by some local guy who'd stood up for him when he got to court. It would be another seven or eight months before Jaywalker would be allowed to practice again. That would mean an eight-month head start for the prosecution, an all but insurmountable advantage.

So what was Jaywalker to do in the meantime? He couldn't contact the D.A.'s office or the state police, or risk calling either of the lawyers who'd been representing Drake; any one of them could turn him in for doing so. Yet he couldn't just sit on his hands and watch his future client languish in the hands of a couple of incompetents while the prosecution perfected its case, could he?

He found a half-smoked joint, fired it up and inhaled deeply. Ever since he'd given up drinking, Jaywalker had resorted to the old devil weed for occasional inspiration. It soothed him, relaxed him, helped him see things a bit more clearly, and brought on a moderate case of the "munchies"—an indispensable aid to a man who, to the envy of most men and every woman he knew, had serious trouble keeping his weight up. With no known adverse side effects and no possibility of a lethal overdose, it was, as Martha Stewart might have put it, *a good thing*. Little wonder, thought Jaywalker, that the government had criminalized it, or that the last administration had chosen to make it the primary target of its war against drugs.

It didn't take long for Jaywalker to hatch a plan. What he'd do would be to have Amanda hire him as a private investigator for her husband. That would allow Jaywalker to go into jail and talk with Drake, gather police reports and other documents, locate and interview witnesses, and generally snoop around. His DEA background more than prepared him for the job, and his law degree qualified him, much the same way it permitted lawyers to act as real estate brokers and notary publics without having to undergo additional training or licensing. It was all part of the genius behind the scheme of having laws that are written by lawyers, enforced by lawyers who've become judges, for the benefit and protection of lawyers.

Now, did the little matter of Jaywalker's suspension disqualify him from availing himself of those benefits and protections? No, he decided; that would be over-thinking it. He was still a lawyer, albeit one who was temporarily incapacitated. Kind of like how a baseball player who was on the disabled list was still a baseball player, no? A perfect analogy. So as long as Jaywalker were to stick to investigating, he wouldn't really be *practicing law*, would he be?

He allowed himself another hit of the joint.

Yeah, investigating would be just fine.

He broke the news to Amanda two days later. They met at the same luncheonette they'd gone to from the library. She looked every bit as stunning as he'd remembered her, and he found himself powerless to keep his eyes off her. He managed somewhat better when it came to his hands, but it was hard. Keeping his hands off her, that is.

This time they had lunch instead of just coffee, she a fancy wrap of some sort, he a tuna-fish sandwich. As they ate, he outlined his plan, and Amanda was quick to approve it. And that was pretty much it. Unlike the events of two days earlier, they didn't follow things up with a cab ride to Amanda's apartment. And if Jaywalker was disappointed in that nondevelopment, and surely he was, he was at least consoled by the fact that he came away from the meeting with a check in the pocket of his jeans in the amount of five thousand dollars, exactly twice what he'd asked Amanda for. He'd instructed her to make it out to "Harrison Jay Walker, Private Investigator," and had made her fill in the Memo blank with the words "*Not for legal services*."

You could never be too careful.

But even if he was only an investigator for the time being, Jaywalker knew better. He was back in the game.

3

FIVE TINY FINGERS

The very first thing Jaywalker did the following morning was to pay a visit to his bank. There he endorsed and deposited the five-thousand-dollar check Amanda Drake had given him. As soon as the teller had completed the transaction, he asked her for his current balance. She tapped some keys on her computer and handed him a slip of paper. There were a bunch of numbers on it, showing which funds were available, which weren't, and when they would be. But he chose to ignore the qualifiers, and went right to the bottom line, which included Amanda's check: $5,176.24

It had been that close.

After that, Jaywalker the Investigator got to work. He started off by making a visit to the scene. Not the scene of the crime—or *accident*, as he preferred to call it— where the van had been run off the road. That would come, but for now it could wait. Instead, he returned to the scene of his first meeting with Amanda, the Forty-second Street branch of the New York Public Library. There he went to the newspaper archives room and pulled up on a microfiche screen all the articles he could find on the crash, the surrender and arrest of Carter Drake, and the developments that had occurred since. Had he been a better navigator of the Internet, he probably could have found them on his computer. But he was stubbornly old-fashioned at times, Jaywalker was, and besides, he loved the archives room. He figured it was as good a place as any to get an overview of things, a starting point before he began to dig for details and tried to get first-person accounts.

As overviews go, it turned out to be pretty devastating stuff for the home team.

The photos of the burned van, and of the immediate area where it had come to rest, were hard to look at. Jaywalker could only guess at the ones that had been kept out of the papers, that the editors had deemed too graphic to print. He'd see those later, no doubt, with the police reports. There'd be charred bodies, charred *tiny* bodies. He shuddered at the thought, shuddered again at the jurors' reactions to the carnage.

Several of the papers had run with the early rumors of a terrorist cell and the premature detonation of an explosive device, or of a van overcrowded with undocumented migrant apple pickers. Only with the following day's editions had the truth come out, that eight of the nine dead were young children enrolled at one of New City's several *yeshivas,* or Jewish religious schools. There were interviews with the driver of the pickup truck who'd stopped to offer assistance, including his account of the car that had run the van off the road. Looking for the public's help, the police had released the partial license plate ending in 724 and were imploring other witnesses to come forward. Then, in the next day's accounts, there was the surrender of Carter Drake and his arrest, as well as some brief comments by his "business attorney." Jaywalker paused to smile at the phrase. There were business attorneys, patent attorneys, corporate attorneys, trust and estate attorneys, even admiralty attorneys. But when things got truly nasty, you were well advised to go out and get yourself a criminal lawyer. All of a sudden, it was a *lawyer* you needed. Down in the trenches, there was no room for *attorneys.*

"Mr. Drake is guilty of absolutely nothing," the business attorney had said. "He hadn't been drinking, and he wasn't speeding. He momentarily lost control of his vehicle. As unfortunate and tragic as the results were— and our hearts go out to the victims and their families— it was an accident, pure and simple. An accident."

The judge who'd set Carter Drake's bail at five million dollars had apparently begged to differ.

The newspaper stories had continued for almost a week. There were interviews with grieving parents and outraged school officials. There were calls for tighter seat-belt laws and looser seat-belt laws, the proponents of the latter camp arguing that some of the children might have escaped the fire had they not been restrained, though a look at the extent of the damage shown in the photos strongly suggested otherwise. And there were the funerals, the terrible funerals, accompanied by snapshots of tiny faces smiling out at the camera in happier times.

After that, the coverage dwindled and all but stopped. The exception was the *Rockland County Register,* which ran editorials daily for nearly three weeks, demanding restoration of the death penalty, "complete with excruciating suffering" for the "cold-blooded killer" of the community's "most treasured and vulnerable citizens."

It was midafternoon by the time Jaywalker emerged from the library. He found himself startled by the sudden brightness of the sunshine, and it took his eyes a few moments to make the adjustment. It reminded him of coming out of the movies after a matinee, something he hadn't done since his wife's death, a dozen years ago.

He found a phone booth, no mean feat in the Age of the Cell Phone. But Jaywalker had long resisted the ads that promised a powerful network, five bars, and unlimited nighttime and weekend minutes with family and friends. He figured that if he lived long enough, he might just be the last holdout on the planet. Sure, going phoneless meant being inconvenienced from time to time, but that was a small price to pay for the retention of his privacy. Besides, now was no time to *get connected,* or whatever it was they called it, not while he was still suspended and trying to fly beneath the radar.

Jaywalker had gotten the name of Carter Drake's business attorney from his newspaper research and found a phone number for him on the Internet. Now he dropped a Samoan penny into the coin slot—they just happened to be the same size as U.S. quarters, so he'd ordered a hundred of them through a Times Square coin dealer for three dollars—and dialed the number.

"PetersonKellnerWhiteandTayler," said a woman's voice, as if it were all one name. "How may I direct your call?"

"I'm trying to reach Chester Ludlow," said Jaywalker.

"Please hold for his administrative aide."

Jaywalker held, wondering where he'd been while secretaries had turned into *administrative aides.*

"Mr. Ludlow's office," said another female voice.

Jaywalker identified himself and stated his business. If he'd thought doing so might open doors, he was in for a surprise. Over the next fifteen minutes, he sparred first with the administrative aide, and then with a young man who described himself as Ludlow's *executive assistant.* Yes, Mr. Ludlow would be more than happy to take a meeting with him, but he *billed out* at seven hundred and fifty dollars an hour, payable in advance.

"How about six minutes?" Jaywalker asked. He'd neglected to discuss expenses with Amanda, and wasn't about to spend seven hundred and fifty dollars of his own money, or hers, either—at least not without checking with her first. On the other hand, he figured shelling out seventy-five bucks for a tenth of an hour…

The executive assistant was evidently not amused.

Eventually they settled on a five-minute phone conference, *pro bono.* Jaywalker was instructed to call *Chet* back the following day, at 10:15 a.m. "Not any earlier, not any later."

Fuck you! Jaywalker wanted to say. *And fuck Chet, too.* Instead he said, "Thank you very much," and hung up.

Maybe it wasn't going to be such a picnic after all, this investigator gig.

Next he called Carter Drake's current lawyer up in New City, a man named Judah Mermelstein. The Samoan pennies were too cumbersome for the job, not to mention too precious, so he used a calling card.

Mermelstein answered his own phone, a sure sign that he was user-friendly and a good indication that he worked on a shoestring budget. Both were attributes that Jaywalker was quite familiar with. As he had with Chester Ludlow's staff, he explained his business and said he'd like to meet with Mermelstein.

"Sure, sure. C'mon up."

They agreed on one o'clock the following day. Jaywalker didn't want to jeopardize his five-minute phone conference with Chet, after all.

The following morning's five-minute phone conference with Chester Ludlow went pretty much as Jaywalker had expected. Ludlow was brusque, dismissive and completely uninformative. Carter Drake, for whom he'd been doing some complicated mergers-and-acquisitions work—the implication being that it was well beyond Jaywalker's understanding—had phoned the office and said he was the "Audi Assassin," and that he wanted to turn himself in before the police figured out he was the one they were looking for and came to arrest him. Ludlow had agreed and had accompanied him to state police headquarters. He'd had no idea where it was, he added, "So I set the GPS on my car. We got there, and they took him into custody. And that was pretty much it. Now," he said, clearing his throat loudly, "if you'll excuse me, I have a meeting—"

"I still have nineteen seconds," Jaywalker pointed out. Actually, he had no idea how long they'd been talking, but he doubted that Ludlow did, either. "What was the basis of your comment to the press," he asked, "that Drake hadn't been drinking or speeding prior to the accident?"

"I'm not sure what you mean."

"I mean," said Jaywalker, "did Drake actually tell you those things?"

"Drake? No, of course not. As a matter of fact, I never discussed that with him. I had our media department draw up a statement. They're real pros at that sort of stuff. It's what they do."

Great, thought Jaywalker, *trial by sound bite.* He wanted to ask Ludlow if he had any idea of the damage such a remark could do to Drake's chances down the line. But he knew he was already into overtime. "Thanks for your time," he said, and hung up.

The good news was that Ludlow had given him the five minutes *pro bono.* The bad news was that Jaywalker had pretty much gotten his money's worth.

* * *

The meeting with Judah Mermelstein went somewhat better. It had taken Jaywalker only forty-five minutes to get to Mermelstein's office, if you didn't count the two hours spent locating his ancient Mercury in its parking lot, finding a set of booster cables ($14.95), getting a jump start from an obliging cabbie ($10), and coaxing the relic out onto the West Side Highway (priceless).

The first thing Jaywalker noticed about Mermelstein wasn't his boyish good looks, his black suit, white shirt and conservative tie, or even his firm handshake. It was his yarmulke.

"Do they let you wear that?" Jaywalker asked. "I mean, in court? At trial?" He'd once known a legal aid lawyer in Brooklyn who was also a Catholic priest, and they'd let him wear his clerical collar in court. But all the guy ever did was arraignments; he never went to trial.

"Absolutely," said Mermelstein. "U.S. Supreme Court, First and Fourteenth Amendments. Freedom of religion, freedom of speech, expression, association, wardrobe, warmth. Not to mention the little-known but all-important freedom to cover one's bald spot."

"Cool," was all Jaywalker could come up with. It was something his daughter might have said, back when she was, oh, seven or so. But it *was* cool, and he couldn't help picturing himself delivering a summation before a home-crowd New City jury, two rows of black-dressed ortho-dox Jews. Jaywalker was half-Jewish himself, after all, even if he hadn't seen the inside of a synagogue in a good twenty years. But that gave him the right, didn't it? And if he were to dig through the side pockets of his suit jackets, chances were pretty good he'd find a yarmulke or two, left over from a long-ago funeral, or a bar mitzvah he hadn't been able to get out of.

"I understand Mrs. Drake has hired you as a private investigator in her husband's case," said Mermelstein, once the two of them had taken seats facing each other across his desk. That experience itself had been momentarily unsettling for Jaywalker, who'd spent twenty-some years sitting in the lawyer's chair, not the client's.

"Yes, she has," said Jaywalker. "But I think you also ought to know that it's her hope that if the case has to be tried, I should be the one to try it. If the court doesn't force it to trial before my, uh, suspension is up, that is."

"Thank you for being up front about that," said Mermelstein.

Jaywalker shrugged, his way of saying, *Hey, it was the right thing to do.*

"Actually," said Mermelstein, "Mrs. Drake told me herself. And I have no problem with it. Not that I couldn't use the publicity. But the truth is, I've never tried a murder case. Or even a felony, for that matter. So not only will I bow out gracefully when the time comes, but in the meantime I'll appreciate all the help you can give me, until you're—"

"Kosher?"

"I couldn't have said it better."

"Don't plan on bowing out," said Jaywalker. "I'm an outsider here, in more ways than one. You're local, and you seem to have your head on straight. I'm pretty sure Amanda can be convinced of the virtues of a co-counsel arrangement."

Mermelstein didn't respond one way or the other, and they talked about the case for the next forty minutes. Jaywalker learned that the Drakes had found Mermelstein through an ad in the local Yellow Pages that touted him as an expert in criminal law, divorce, real estate, immigration matters, slip-and-fall cases, product liability, medical malpractice and dog-bite injuries. He'd tried and failed to get Carter's bail reduced from the five million set at arraignment. The Rockland County D.A., a tough-on-crime Republican named Abraham Firestone, intended to make an example of Drake, hoping that sending him away for life would deter others from killing vanloads of children. And according to Mermelstein, Firestone intended to try the case himself, if there had to be a trial, rather than assigning it to one of his assistants, as was the customary practice.

"I notice Drake's charged with drunk driving," said Jaywalker, "in addition to murder." He didn't mention the leaving-the-scene charge, or the unlicensed operator, or the uninsured vehicle. Those charges ranged from the mundane to the serious. Leaving the scene of an accident resulting in death, for example, was itself a separate felony. But all of those acts or omissions were either after the fact or merely incidental to the murder charge. Drunk driving, on the other hand, especially when combined with indications of recklessness, could be used to show a *depraved indifference to human life,* a necessary statutory element of proving murder in a vehicular homicide case in New York State.

"That's right," said Mermelstein.

"But Drake didn't surrender until sometime the following day, did he?"

"Right again," said Mermelstein. "And his big-shot business lawyer issued a press release announcing to the world that his client hadn't had anything to drink before the accident."

"So help me out here," said Jaywalker. Early on in his career, he'd had occasion to wonder why anyone would leave the scene of an accident, when doing so was a crime and sticking around to face the music wasn't. The answer, he soon learned, was pretty simple. The ones who fled did so because they were drunk, unlicensed or uninsured, or because they'd just robbed the bank around the corner and had the money on the front passenger seat and a loaded gun on the floor. Getting away, even for a limited period of time, gave them an opportunity to hide the evidence. And part of that evidence was the alcohol in their blood. Ted Kennedy may or may not have been testing his swimming ability that night long ago at Chappaquiddick, but by the time he turned himself in the following day it was too late for the police to draw a meaningful, or admissible, blood sample from him. And even if it hadn't been, he could have claimed that the incident had so upset him that he'd poured himself a couple of stiff drinks as soon as he got home. Exactly as the captain of the *Exxon Valdez* had maintained after his little mishap up in Prudhoe Bay.

"It seems Abe Firestone has done his homework," said Mermelstein. "He had the troopers trace Drake's movements over the twelve hours preceding the crash. Apparently they can put him in a *sports club* over in Nyack. And the *sport* he and his buddies were engaged in seems to have consisted of seeing who could throw back the most shots of tequila before falling on the floor."

"Wonderful," said Jaywalker.

They talked for another twenty minutes, following which Mermelstein made Jaywalker copies of whatever documents he had in his file. There wasn't much: the felony complaint, Drake's rap sheet, a summary of an accident report prepared by the state police and a couple of other pieces of paper.

"Firestone hasn't exactly flooded you with discovery," Jaywalker observed.

"Abe?" said Mermelstein. "He's so tight his ass squeaks when he walks."

They exchanged goodbyes and promised to share anything either of them found out.

"And give my best to Amanda," said Mermelstein.

"I will," said Jaywalker, noticing that she was suddenly no longer *Mrs. Drake,* and wondering if she'd followed Judah Mermelstein around for two days and then slept with him, too, before hiring him.

Nah, he liked the Yellow Pages story better.

From Judah Mermelstein's office, Jaywalker headed west and then north, toward the site of the accident that had claimed nine lives. He drove carefully, not because he was afraid of becoming a tenth victim, but because his Mercury was pretty much on life support. Owning a car in the city was something of a double-edged sword. You didn't need one to get around, and with parking impossible and garages charging a fortune, you were better off without one. Until you had to get somewhere else.

So Jaywalker had compromised. He'd bought the cheapest car he could find, a '57 Mercury with no extras and, so far as he knew, the last remaining three-speed manual transmission in America. Then he'd found an open-air parking lot so far over on the West Side that you had to hike halfway to New Jersey just to get there. He'd bargained the manager down from the usual hundred and twenty-five a month to seventy-five dollars cash, no tax, explaining that since he almost never used the thing, they could bury it way in the back, where it would take about a week and a half to get it out. And because he started it up so rarely and drove it even less, it performed, well, about like a neglected '57 Mercury with 185,000 miles under its belt. So when he did drive it, he tended to creep along. But even creeping, it took him less than twenty minutes to get from Judah Mermelstein's office to the spot marked with a black X on the accident-report summary.

It was nothing but a bend in the road, where the northbound lane had little room for a shoulder. About all that separated it from the drop-off was what remained of a low guardrail, its metal twisted grotesquely and torn away where the van had breached it. There were a handful of makeshift memorials marking the spot— flowers, candles, other stuff. Jaywalker found a place to pull over a hundred yards or so past it, and shut off the Merc's engine. From there he walked back to the site.

There were eight memorials. One, he guessed, for each child that had died there. He'd seen others like them often enough before—arrays of crosses, flowers and jars containing candles—but only from the cocoon of a car, as he sped by on the highway. Though he'd known what they signified, they hadn't really touched him. Now, up close, they were something very different. There were Bibles—Old Testaments, no doubt. There were hand-written notes from classmates. There were framed color photographs of smiling children who would never smile again. There was a tiny pink party dress with matching shoes, possibly never worn. There were a couple of stuffed animals, a bear and something that looked like a cross between a small rabbit and a large mouse. There was a leather baseball glove, complete with five impossibly tiny fingers.

The earth leading downhill from the torn-away guard-rail was still scarred, and down the embankment there were a couple of trees with fresh damage visible. And then a large, circular charred area, where new grass was just beginning to sprout through the blackness. And there were boulders, big enough, jagged enough and numerous enough to insure that the tumbling van had never had a chance of finding a safe landing spot.

There was a reason why they'd called it Rockland County.

He'd brought a camera along, an old Nikon his

daughter had given him years ago when she'd gone digital. As far as he knew, it was the last one left in the world that still took a roll of real film. He snapped a few photos of the scene. Not that there was much of a reason to do so. The police would have taken dozens, and the defense would get copies in due time. But Jaywalker was an investigator today, and it seemed like an investigator-like thing to do.

Then he walked back to the Merc and headed south, to the city.

That night Jaywalker went over his notes and took stock of his investigation. Over two days, he'd familiarized himself with the newspaper accounts of the case, conferred with both of the lawyers who'd represented Carter Drake so far, gotten hold of a few sheets of paper and visited the scene of the crime. Even if it was a good beginning, it had turned up nothing really useful. Still on his checklist were subpoenaing police reports, locating and interviewing witnesses, and researching the law on precisely what it took to elevate a motor vehicle accident into a murder case.

But all of those things could wait a day or two. The next order of business would take Jaywalker back up to New City. Knowing that, and figuring he'd be using the Mercury on a more or less regular basis, he decided he might as well park it on the street. But that was a momentous decision, given that he lived in Manhattan. He spent the next forty-five minutes searching for a legal parking place. Every empty spot turned out to be a fire hydrant, a bus stop or the private driveway to some building. Twice he had to get out and squint at the fine print on the alternate-side-of-the-street parking signs, which were obviously intended to entrap the unwary motorist. Did NO PARKING 10 AM TO 11:30 AM MON AND

THURS mean you could park there at other times? Or was that sign subject to the one above it that said NO STANDING 4 PM TO 7 PM? And since both of them included the red-letter warning TOW-AWAY ZONE, it appeared to matter.

Back up in his apartment, more or less legally parked, Jaywalker had made a dozen phone calls just to find out what credentials he'd need and what procedures he'd have to follow for what he was planning to do. Next, he'd gone onto his computer and, using a mix of type fonts, print sizes and images, and about two hours of unbillable trial-and-error labor, had managed to create a rather impressive-looking identification card.

> Private Investigator
> in the *STATE OF NEW YORK*…
>
> ### HARRISON J. WALKER
>
> HEIGHT: 5'11"
> WEIGHT: 175
> EYES: Blue
> SEX: Male

In the lower right-hand corner, Jaywalker glued a photograph of himself. He looked younger in it, and a lot less gray. Then again, it had to be at least a dozen years old. He knew that because he'd clipped it out of a photograph of him and his wife, after silently begging her forgiveness. Now, as he admired the laminated and trimmed results of his handiwork, he thought of her again and decided she'd be understanding about it.

Not that he believed in any of that afterlife stuff.

He'd avoided the temptation to fill in the blank following "Sex" with "Yes" or "Hoping" or anything else stupid. He'd been equally careful to omit the modifier "licensed" right before "private investigator." Other than the one that permitted him to drive, the only license Jaywalker had was currently suspended, so using the term could easily get him into trouble. Make that *more* trouble. Since he was already on probation of a sort, all he needed was to commit one more transgression. And this one would have been a whopper, a felony, in fact. *Criminal Impersonation,* they called it, and it carried four years. Not that they'd have given him all of that. But he certainly could have wound up in jail.

Which struck him as just a bit ironic, since that was precisely where he intended to wind up next. Because tomorrow morning, at ten o'clock sharp, Jaywalker had an appointment at the Rockland County Jail to have a face-to-face with Carter Drake.

4

JIMMY CHIPMUNK

"What the fuck is *this* supposed to be?"

For a moment there, it seemed that the corrections officer at the outer gate wasn't nearly as impressed with Jaywalker's identification card as Jaywalker himself had been the evening before. But after twenty minutes' worth of calls to the man's supervisor and his supervisor's supervisor, as well as to Amanda Drake and Judah Mermelstein, Private Investigator Jaywalker was finally buzzed in, to begin another half hour of being searched, signing forms and waiting.

When he was finally escorted through a long underground corridor and up a flight of steps to the visiting room, Jaywalker discovered that his meeting with Carter Drake would be a face-to-face one in only the most literal sense. In order to actually speak and be heard through the three-quarter-inch, wire-reinforced, bulletproof glass separating them, they'd have to use a pair of black phone receivers with frayed cords and exposed wires, things that had likely been around since the days of Alexander Graham Bell.

"Hi," said Jaywalker.

"Hello," said Drake over the static. He was an athletic-looking man with blond hair that was just beginning to turn gray. A good match for Amanda, thought Jaywalker. And he was seeing Drake outside his element. He tried picturing him propped up behind a big mahogany desk, or at the end of a long boardroom table, instead of inside a cubicle at the Rockland County Jail, but it wasn't easy to do. Jail had a funny way of making you look like you belonged there.

"My name is Jaywalker. I'm a private investigator at the moment. Seven or eight months from now I expect to be a lawyer again, and your wife would like me—"

"My *estranged* wife," said Drake.

"Oh?"

"We've been separated for five months now."

Jaywalker considered the implications of that for a moment. It might make Amanda a more credible witness if he were to put her on the stand. She could come off as hostile enough to Carter to have left him, but at the same time she could back him up on any factual or character matters. And for another thing—

"So it's okay if you're sleeping with her."

"Who said I'm sleeping with her?" asked Jaywalker, doing his best to summon up an appropriate measure of righteous indignation at the idea.

"Nobody," said Drake. "All I said was, it's okay if you are."

Jaywalker shifted his weight in his chair. "What I was about to tell you," he said, "was that your wife, estranged or not, would like me to take over for Mr. Mermelstein at some point."

"So she told me."

"So how about we discuss your case?" Jaywalker suggested.

"Here?"

Jaywalker looked around. "I suppose we could reserve a table at the Oyster Bar," he said.

"That's not what I meant," said Drake. "Everyone says these phones are monitored."

Jaywalker was about to explain that while that was no doubt true, the guards knew enough not to record or listen in on lawyer-client conversations, which were privileged. Then he realized: he wasn't Drake's lawyer, or a lawyer at all, for that matter. So this wasn't a lawyer-client conversation. And even though he was arguably there on behalf of Mermelstein, who *was* a lawyer, he could hardly count on the corrections officials who ran the place to grasp such nuances. "You're right," he agreed.

"Can you get me out?" Drake asked. "I mean, five million dollars' bail on a drunk-driving case? Not that I couldn't have come up with it. But the lawyers for the families have gone into civil court and frozen all my assets."

"It's not really a drunk-driving case," said Jaywalker. "Nine people died."

"I know that," said Drake. "But it was still an accident. I mean, I never *meant* to kill them. Everyone knows that."

He had a point there. Jaywalker had long marveled at the courts' schizophrenic attitude toward drinking and driving. If you got pulled over at a checkpoint with six or seven drinks in your system, you paid a fine and got your license suspended for ninety days. The second time, the fine got a little bigger, the suspension a little longer. You got what, maybe four or five bites of the apple before they got serious and actually *revoked* your license, and one or two more before they slapped you in the local jail for thirty days.

But God help you if you had those same six or seven drinks and got into the same car and drove at exactly the same speed, but were unlucky enough to broadside a school bus, or run a vanful of kids off a road and into a fireball. Then suddenly you were a murderer, front-page stuff, Public Enemy Number One. And you were looking at twenty-five years to life.

Where had this institutional hypocrisy come from? Jaywalker—who, if asked, had a theory for most things—had a pretty good idea.

Judges were lawyers, after all. They'd come from privileged-enough backgrounds to have been able to afford to go off first to college and then law school. They were financially able to have bankrolled their own campaigns, or to cough up enough political contributions to the campaigns of others who, once elected, had appointed them to the bench. In other words, they weren't street people. They didn't go around committing robberies, burglarizing apartments or selling drugs, and they had little natural empathy for those who did. But they drank, some of them, and they drove. And occasionally they even combined the two endeavors. *That* was something they could empathize with. So they were ready to look the other way or apply an understanding slap to the wrist of anyone who happened to get caught doing what they themselves had done more than once.

But *kill* someone? Kill *nine* someones? Including eight innocent little Jewish kids? That was a different story altogether. For one thing, *they'd* never done that, had they? And sitting there in the glare of publicity, with the families of the victims, the media and the rest of the world screaming for blood, those very same judges all of a sudden became the toughest *lock-'em-up-and-throw-away-the-key* law-and-order types that ever lived. Murder? You bet! Five million dollars' bail? Not a penny less! We'll show those vicious drunk-driver menaces that we mean business!

"No," he told Drake, "I can't get you out of here. But

I'll talk to Mr. Mermelstein, see if he can do anything about getting some of your assets untied. In the meantime, I'd like you to do something for me."

"What's that?"

"Get a hold of some paper and a pen, and write out, *in as much detail as you possibly can,* everything that happened over the twenty-four-hour period preceding the accident, the accident itself and everything afterward, up to the time you were brought to court. At the top of each page, write the words 'Confidential, For My Lawyer Only.' I'll be back in a few days to pick it up. Can you do that for me?"

"I guess so."

"Good," said Jaywalker. "And remember, I want *as much detail as you can possibly give me.* Understand?"

"I understand."

"I want a *book.*"

Drake nodded.

"Okay," said Jaywalker. "I hate doing it this way, and I'm sorry to have to give you a homework assignment like this. But I'm afraid you're probably right about these phones."

It was the truth. Not just the part about the phones being less than secure, but the part about being sorry, as well. It was what lazy lawyers did, had their clients write out statements instead of drawing the facts out of them in a cooperative process. Left to their own, people tended to summarize, Jaywalker had learned over the years. They omitted the myriad of tiny details that, when included and uttered from the witness stand, fleshed out a narrative and gave it the hallmark of truth. Having a witness testify that "it wasn't quite dark out," for example, wasn't going to convince anyone. But were the same witness to add, "At one point I had to check my directions, and it turned out there was still just enough daylight for me to read them," the jurors would come away with a concrete image burned in their minds. Not only would they *remember* what the witness said about the lighting, they'd also *believe* him. Why? Because his narrative had been so detailed and so specific, and so consistent with the jurors' own everyday experiences. Still, despite the admonition to include as much detail as possible, Jaywalker knew that Carter Drake would summarize the facts to a certain extent. Everyone did. But it would be a start, at least, something to work with for the time being.

That night, Jaywalker reported to Amanda what he'd done so far on the case. Which didn't sound like much, once he heard himself run down the list out loud. But she seemed to think otherwise.

"I'm impressed," she said, sipping a martini. Both of her nipples were covered this time, but only because they were in a restaurant. An hour earlier that had decidedly not been the case.

"Above all else," the angel perched on Jaywalker's left shoulder had whispered, *"you must avoid conflicts of interest."*

"Schmuck!" had shouted the devil on his right shoulder, who was not only louder and far more persuasive, but apparently Jewish. *"They're separated!"*

And so it had come to pass that once again Jaywalker had succumbed to human frailty, primal instinct and Amanda Drake. And had he been forced afterward to take the stand and defend himself under oath, the very best he could have come up with was that the devil had made him do it.

"Seriously," Amanda was saying, "I'm surprised Carter would speak to you at all."

Jaywalker managed to raise his eyebrows while sipping his Coke. His drinking days were behind him. He hoped.

"I mean, he wouldn't talk to the police, he wouldn't talk to Chet Ludlow, and he barely says a word to Judah Mermelstein. Except to keep asking him when he can get the bail reduced. And now he's going to write the whole thing out for you, and in detail. That's progress, isn't it?"

"Why the silent treatment?" Jaywalker asked.

Amanda shrugged. "Guilt, I guess. I mean, it was a pretty bad accident. I think he's horrified by it and wants to be punished."

Jaywalker was tempted to say, *He's going to get his wish.* But he didn't want to come across as too pessimistic. Not yet, anyway. There'd be plenty of time for that down the road, when Carter Drake would wake up one morning to the reality that they were aiming to give him twenty-five years to life in state prison. He wouldn't feel he deserved *that* kind of punishment.

They ordered dinner, Amanda a steak, medium-rare, Jaywalker a burger and another Coke. When the check came, he reached for his wallet, but she'd already picked it up. Instead of arguing the point, he thanked her. He figured if he tried hard enough, he could get used to being kept. Especially while he was on an investigator's salary.

Way back in his DEA days, Jaywalker had worked with a fellow agent named James Chippamunga, whom everyone referred to, naturally enough, as Jimmy Chipmunk. Law enforcement was similar to the military in that respect, or sports teams. Pretty much everyone got a nickname. It was at the DEA, in fact, that Harrison J. Walker had become Jaywalker.

Jimmy Chipmunk was what they called a *stand-up guy.* That designation described somebody you could trust to watch your back and not rat you out. And Jaywalker had done both of those things for Jimmy one night in East New York, which at the time—along with Bed-Stuy, Brownsville and Red Hook—had made parts of Brooklyn more dangerous than Manhattan's Harlem. These days, Red Hook was an up-and-coming yuppie neighborhood. Go figure. Jimmy had half stupidly and half drunkenly gotten himself into a shoot-out. Jaywalker had gotten him out of it, and together they'd made Jimmy come out like a hero on paper. Which meant Jimmy owed Jaywalker big-time, and always would.

It was time to call in the acorns.

Chippamunga had left the DEA not too long after Jaywalker did. But while Jaywalker was learning how to try a case at Legal Aid and then building a law practice of his own, Jimmy had moved over to the NYPD and risen through the ranks to his present assignment as a high-ranking Commander in the office of the Chief of Detectives.

They met in a bar in midtown, shortly after Jimmy's four-to-midnight shift was over. Over Jack Daniel's and Cokes—the former Jimmy's, the latter Jaywalker's—they reminisced about old times. Old times always included the East New York adventure, now well past the five-year statute of limitations. It wasn't until the fourth round of drinks, and the third round of men's-room visits, that Jaywalker handed Jimmy the envelope.

To the untrained eye, it might have looked as if Jimmy was a cop on the take, accepting a payoff of some sort from a civilian. But the untrained eye would have been fooled. There was no money inside the envelope. What was in it were half a dozen subpoenas *duces tecum,* demands for copies of all the police reports that had been generated in the case against Carter Drake III. They were attorney's subpoenas, rather than court-ordered ones, which put them pretty much into the same category as Jaywalker's Samoan pennies: they weren't quite as good as the real thing, but they tended to get the job done. And that was especially true when placed in the hands of Jimmy Chipmunk. On the couple of times Jaywalker had asked the same favor of Cippamunga, Jimmy had returned a couple of days later, both times with copies of just about every document Jaywalker had requested. Of course, both of those cases had been in Manhattan. And on both occasions, Jimmy had explained afterward, it turned out he didn't even have to actually serve the subpoena. "But," he'd added, "it's a good idea just the same. Keeps the both of us covered. Know what I mean?"

Jaywalker had known exactly what he'd meant.

Chippamunga polished off Jack Daniel's Number 4 before opening the envelope. "Rockland County, huh? A little bit outta my bailiwick."

Only a veteran law-enforcement type would use a term like *bailiwick,* the same way he'd refer to a suspect's girlfriend as his *paramour,* or say "I did proceed to exit my vehicle at that particular point in time," instead of *"Then I got out of my car."*

Jaywalker, despite the severe handicap of being a lawyer, liked to keep things as brief as possible. Short words, simple sentences. Right now, he needed neither. He simply shrugged his shoulders. It was his vote of confidence, his silent but overt expression of complete faith that Jimmy would somehow work his magic and overcome all obstacles, bailiwick related or not. After all, they weren't talking the niceties of *jurisdiction* here, or *venue*; they were talking *clout.*

"I suppose…" Jimmy's voice trailed off. "Gimme a coupla days, willya?"

"You got it," said Jaywalker, throwing back the last of his fourth large Cokes. God, they were huge. The bartender, a former NYPD lieutenant who'd worked under Cippamunga at one time, was either an extremely generous soul, or else he'd somehow mixed up the flower vases with the soda glasses. Jaywalker took a wet paper napkin off the bar and lifted it to his mouth, not so much to wipe anything, but to stifle what otherwise might have proved to be a belch of room-clearing proportions. All the while he kept his thighs tightly crossed, desperately trying to forestall a fourth trip to the men's room for as long as possible, or at least another thirty seconds.

That had been Friday night, or, technically, early Saturday morning. Until he had Carter Drake's written account of his actions, or whatever Jimmy Chipmunk could turn up in the way of police reports, there wasn't much more for Jaywalker to do on the case. So he slept late Saturday morning—the real Saturday morning— late being somewhere in the neighborhood of seven o'clock. Then he downed his usual breakfast, which consisted of a couple of pretzels and a glass of iced tea. The pretzels were the old-fashioned sourdough kind, big enough to choke a horse and hard enough to break a tooth on. The iced tea was a homemade concoction, with enough sugar to kill a diabetic, and a generous squeeze of fresh lemon juice that, to Jaywalker's way of thinking, balanced the sugar by acting as a sort of natural insulin. And right there he had all of what he considered the four essential nutrition groups—salt, sugar, caffeine and crunchiness.

With nothing else to do, Jaywalker spent the afternoon hitting the books. It wasn't just a matter of needing a refresher course to shake off the accumulation of more than two years of rust. The fact was, in his twenty-plus years of defending criminals, Jaywalker had never handled, much less tried, a case even remotely similar to Carter Drake's. Under New York law, 99.9 percent of murder cases fall into two categories. There are *intentional murders,* and there are *felony murders,* and Jaywalker had had his share of both. An intentional murder, simply put, is one where the defendant intended to kill someone. Gone are such archaic notions as *premeditation* or *malice aforethought.* Nowadays in New York, you kill someone while intending to kill someone, it's murder.

Jaywalker had tried dozens of intentional murders. He'd tried one where the defendant, intending to kill a suspected informer, had aimed poorly and mistakenly killed a man standing next to him. Murder nonetheless. He'd defended a serial murderer who'd killed six almost randomly selected victims over as many weeks, but when asked why, could offer no better rationale than "I found out it was something I could do." Still, at the time he'd shot each of them, he'd intended to kill them.

Felony murder was a bit different. There the legislature has decreed that under a certain specific combination of circumstances, there can be murder even in the absence of an intent to kill. How? If a defendant is engaged in the commission of any of several enumerated serious felonies—think robbery, kidnapping or arson, for good examples—and if he's armed with a deadly weapon or knows that an accomplice is, he can be convicted of murder if someone dies in the process. Those crimes are deemed so dangerous, and so likely to lead to a death, that the lawmakers have substituted the defendant's participation in them for his actual intent to kill anyone.

Again, Jaywalker had tried his share of felony murders, though the number was far fewer. And there was an interesting reason for that. Caught after a robbery-gone-bad, perpetrators invariably rush to distance themselves from the resulting death. They'll readily implicate an accomplice as the planner or the one who put the tape over the victim's mouth, insisting that their own role was minor and in no way related to the fatality. "We were just after his money and his watch, was all. And I stayed in the car the whole time. I never meant for him to *die* or anything like that." Felony murder.

But the list of crimes that could trigger a felony murder didn't include drunk driving or speeding or being in the wrong lane of a two-lane highway, or anything remotely like those offenses. How then, assuming that Carter Drake hadn't run the van off the road in order to intentionally kill its occupants, could the prosecution possibly charge him with murder?

Jaywalker knew the answer, but he still had to look it up in order to remind himself of the precise wording of the statute. And there it was, sandwiched in between intentional murder and felony murder, buried in paragraph 2 of section 125.25 of that perennial bestseller and summer-reading favorite, the New York State Penal Law.

A person is guilty of murder when...under circumstances evincing a depraved indifference to human life, he recklessly engages in conduct which causes a grave risk of death to another person, and thereby causes the death of another person.

From there, Jaywalker leafed back a few pages to section 125.10, entitled "Criminally Negligent Homicide."

A person is guilty of criminally negligent homicide when, with criminal negligence, he causes the death of another person.

And down the page to sections 125.12 and 125.13, "Vehicular Manslaughter," which was subdivided into two parts, each premised upon the degree of intoxication of the operator of a motor vehicle. If the driver was drunk, it was second-degree vehicular manslaughter; if he was *really* drunk, it was first degree.

But the big difference wasn't in the titles of the various sections. The big difference was in the penalties they carried. Criminally negligent homicide and vehicular manslaughter in the second degree were class E felonies, with maximum sentences of four years each and no mandatory minimum. For first-degree vehicular homicide, the maximum went up to seven years, but there was still no minimum. In other words, a defendant could be convicted of any of those crimes and still end up with a fine, or thirty days in jail, or probation.

Murder was a different story.

Murder sentences *began* at fifteen years to life, and went up to twenty-five to life. That meant a convicted defendant would have to serve the minimum—fifteen or twenty-five, or something in between the two extremes—before even being eligible to see the parole board.

Which meant that the wording of the statute became crucial.

What, for starters, did *depraved indifference to human life* mean? Jaywalker checked the two definition sections of the penal law, first the general one near the beginning of the volume, and then the specific one that related only to homicides. But neither section made any reference to *depraved indifference to human life,* or, for that matter, *depraved indifference, depraved, indifference,* or *indifferent.* Nowhere was there the vaguest of clues what any of those terms was supposed to mean. Yet even now, Jaywalker could see with absolute clarity that whether Carter Drake got his wrist slapped or his head handed to him it was eventually going to come down to whether twelve rather randomly selected citizens of Rockland

County would believe that those five words, *depraved indifference to human life,* fairly described Drake's state of mind the night of the incident.

So Jaywalker couldn't afford to sit around and congratulate himself on his clairvoyant powers. Well, perhaps the investigator Jaywalker could. But the once-and-future lawyer Jaywalker couldn't; he had some work to do. The problem was that legal research had never been his favorite pastime, or even on his top-ten list, for that matter. He'd found that out as early as law school, marveling at how some of his classmates could spend hours—hell, *days*—holed up in the library, reading cases that dated back hundreds of years. Those same classmates invariably had all the answers when called upon in class the next day, while Jaywalker hid out in the back row, avoiding eye contact with the professor. They got A's on midterm and final exams, while Jaywalker struggled to get B's and C's. They passed the bar exam with flying colors, while Jaywalker squeaked by on the second try. And they landed jobs with the top firms or clerkships with prominent judges, while Jaywalker strapped on a gun and went to work for the DEA. Now, almost thirty years later, he had no idea what his former classmates were up to. He didn't bother checking the "Class Notes" section of his alumni bulletin and hadn't heard that any of them had become president or attorney general yet. He assumed they were all making tons of money and was pretty sure that none of them was currently riding out a three-year suspension from practice. But he seriously doubted that any of them had tried more criminal cases than he had, or won a larger share, or had more fun along the way.

Yet like it or not, Jaywalker knew the time had come to get down to some serious research. So he made himself a grilled-cheese sandwich, watched a few innings of a Yankee game and took a long walk by the river. Tomorrow, after all, was another day.

5

BAD NEWS INDEED

When a statute uses a term without defining it—as the penal law had done in the case of *depraved indifference to human life*—there's a rule of statutory construction that says the words are to be given their ordinary, everyday meaning.

Which means you start with a dictionary.

So sometime around nine o'clock Sunday morning, Jaywalker did just that. Not for the *human life* part; thanks to the fact that neither the driver of the van nor any of the children occupants in it had been pregnant, those words turned out to be pretty unambiguous.

He looked up *indifference* first, figuring it would be the simpler of the two terms to pin down. And so it was.

> **in·dif·fer·ence**, *n.* lack of interest or concern, apathy, insensibility, lack of feeling.

Not much help there.

> **de·praved**, *adj.* Corrupt, wicked, or perverted— Syn. Evil, sinful, iniquitous, debased, reprobate, degenerate, dissolute, profligate, licentious, lascivious, lewd. See immoral.

Was Carter Drake any or all of those things? If you read the editorials in the *Rockland County Register,* or listened to the press releases issued by Mothers Against Drunk Driving, the answer was an unqualified yes. But none of the definitions seemed more than minimally helpful. Was Drake *corrupt, wicked* or *perverted* because his actions had led to the deaths of nine innocent people? Wasn't that too facile, too much an after-the-fact analysis? Suppose for a moment that Drake had been equally drunk and momentarily had found himself on the wrong side of the road, but had managed to pull back over before encountering any other vehicles? Could his conduct nevertheless be said to have risen to the level of *evil, sinful* and *debased?* Would the state still want to empanel a jury of his peers and call upon them to decide whether or not he was *immoral?*

It took you full circle back to the same old quandary, the double standard that had little to do with the act of drunk driving and everything to do with the outcome. But for the presence of the van, Drake would be looking at a stiff fine; *because of* the presence of the van, he was a *debased reprobate degenerate,* staring at life in prison.

So much for the dictionary, with all of its ordinary, everyday meanings. On to the case law, just as Jaywalker had expected and feared, and procrastinated over since the day before in a futile attempt at avoidance.

Case law is a term used to describe the enormous body of opinions written by judges whose job it is to interpret laws—be they as lofty as constitutional amendments or as mundane as parking regulations—and determine if those laws have been adhered to or broken. The average trial generates no written opinions at all. It is only the unusually erudite trial judge, or the politically ambitious one, who bothers to commit his rulings to paper. Far more typical at the trial level is the one-word oral pronouncement: "overruled" or "sustained," "granted" or "denied," "guilty" or "not guilty."

It is, for the most part, at the appellate level that the writing takes place. And it takes place only if there's been a conviction after trial. If there's been an acquittal, the prohibition against double jeopardy prevents the prosecution from appealing. What's sauce for the goose isn't always sauce for the gander.

The defendant who's been found guilty *below* is permitted as a matter of right to appeal his conviction to a *higher court,* and from there to a succession of even higher courts, all the way up to—in the words of one of Jaywalker's phrase-making jailhouse lawyers—"the Supremes," if the judges of those courts deem the issue or issues involved sufficiently worthy of their attention. And at each step of the appeals process, those judges spell out the reasons behind their decisions in black and white. A single case can therefore generate dozens of written opinions, including separate concurrences and dissents, as it works its way up the appellate ladder, occasionally sidestepping from state court to federal court and back again. And just about every one of those opinions is collected, published and preserved for all eternity between the covers of some *reporter,* those standard-size, handsomely bound books that fill the shelves and form the backdrop of every photograph taken of a lawyer since the invention of the camera.

For the practitioner—or anyone else concerned enough or foolish enough to care—any one of those opinions can be found at a law library. All that's needed is a *citation,* something that might be expressed as 6 NY3d 207, 211 (2005). Translate those hieroglyphics into English and you'd know to look for Volume Six of the New York Reporter, containing the decisions of the

Court of Appeals, New York's highest court, third series. You'd also know that while the opinion itself begins on page 207, the particular point you're looking for is discussed four pages later, and that the case was decided in 2005.

With the advent of the computer, the task has been rendered even easier. Gone are the days when a trip to a distant law library was required, not to mention the sheer strength to lug fifty or sixty pounds of books to a reading table. All that's needed now is that little coded citation, or the name of a case or the number of a statute, or even a particularly vexing phrase lifted verbatim from the language of that statute.

Depraved indifference to human life, for example.

So Jaywalker could be an armchair researcher right in his own apartment, allowing himself snacks, bathroom breaks and even an occasional check of a ball-game score whenever he liked.

It turned out that the phrase *depraved indifference to human life* was no newcomer to the language and hardly an invention of the legislators up in Albany. It had been around for centuries, in fact. One contributor to the Internet dated it as far back as 1762, tracing it to a court-martial judge's condemnation of troops unnecessarily firing upon civilians, particularly women and children.

In 1965 it found its way into New York's penal law as a means to extend the reach of maximum punishment to offenders who caused the deaths of others, but whose actions fell outside the scope of the previous murder statute, which required either an intent to kill or the commission of an underlying felony during which a death occurred.

An early example, from 1974, took up the case of a driver and passenger who picked up a severely intoxicated hitchhiker on a cold, snowy night. After robbing him and removing both his eyeglasses and boots, they forced him out of the car and onto the highway, where he sat helplessly for the next half hour, in temperatures near 32°F and near-zero visibility, until he was struck and killed by a speeding pickup truck. The New York Court of Appeals affirmed the robbers' murder conviction under the depraved indifference theory.

Next was a 1983 incident in which a man walked into a bar with a loaded gun. For a moment, Jaywalker thought that might be the beginning of a joke. But then the man announced that he was going to kill someone that night. And true to his word, he proceeded to fire his gun, killing another customer. He, too, was found guilty of depraved indifference murder. While the Court of Appeals affirmed his conviction, years later the same court, by then made up of different judges, would overrule the case, holding that it had misapplied the law. The defendant's actions had either been intentional murder or not murder at all, said the later court; in no event had they constituted *reckless-ness*.

Nor, said an intermediate appellate court, could the driver of a car be convicted of depraved indifference murder, even though he'd been racing another driver at speeds approaching a hundred miles per hour when he rear-ended a third car, killing two of its occupants and seriously injuring five others.

Yet in 2003, the Court of Appeals affirmed the de-praved indifference murder conviction of a defendant who'd pushed a twelve-year-old boy into the water and walked away, leaving the boy to drown.

Most recently, and most relevantly, a twenty-five-year-old Valley Stream, Long Island, man had gotten behind the wheel of his pickup truck with what was later determined to be a .28 blood alcohol reading, more than three times the .08 legal limit. He somehow managed to get onto the highway, but in the wrong direction. Ignoring the beeping horns and flashing lights of oncoming cars, he continued for two full miles, before crashing into a limousine returning from a wedding, killing two people, one of them a seven-year-old girl, who was decapitated. After a hard-fought trial, the jury found him guilty of murder, concluding that his actions revealed a depraved indifference to human life. And although the appellate courts hadn't yet begun to review the case, Jaywalker was pretty sure they'd find a way to affirm the conviction.

There's an old saying among lawyers that goes, "Bad cases make bad laws." What that means is that when the facts are truly egregious, not only do juries tend to convict even in the absence of compelling legal evidence, but judges then strain to uphold those convictions. And it was Jaywalker's guess that the Valley Stream case, and a few others like it, signaled a new trend in the law as it applied to drunk drivers.

Over the decade preceding the Valley Stream conviction, Jaywalker had been able to find only a handful of New York cases in which depraved indifference murder had been used successfully in the context of motor vehicle accidents. And that was despite the fact that, according to MADD statistics, upward of sixteen thousand people die from drinking-related driving accidents nationally *every year*.

But it seemed all that was about to change.

Why?

Because *bad cases make bad laws*.

When a seven-year-old girl gets decapitated and the jurors are forced to hear a mother's sobbing account of having held her daughter's severed head in her hands, legal niceties have a way of yielding to raw emotions—

not only in the jury box, but later on, as well, in the conference rooms of appellate judges. And once a verdict such as the Valley Stream one is upheld, it becomes precedent and gets applied to other cases that follow it, cases in which the facts aren't nearly as extreme. But precedent is precedent, and subsequent defendants would invariably be more likely to be convicted of murder, and have their convictions affirmed, because of the Valley Stream driver and the young mother cradling her daughter's head in her hands.

Bad cases make bad laws.

And to Jaywalker, there could be no doubt about the impact that cliché would have on the case of Carter Drake. Instead of causing merely two deaths, Drake had caused nine. Instead of having killed a single child, he'd killed *eight* of them. And in place of the image of a severed head was the specter of eight tiny bodies, charred almost beyond recognition. Whether the legislature had ever intended the depraved indifference section of the murder statute to apply to motor vehicle accidents no longer mattered. The Valley Stream verdict now served as an exclamation point following the handful of earlier cases that had expanded the application of the law in that direction, and short of a highly unlikely reversal by the appellate courts, there'd be no turning back.

Which was good news for prosecutors, Mothers Against Drunk Driving and all the sober, law-abiding users of the state's roads and sidewalks.

But bad news indeed for Carter Drake.

6

THE WASP ON THE WINDSHIELD

On Monday, Jaywalker got a call from James Chippamunga. Not that Jimmy would say much over the phone; he never did. In that respect, he exhibited all the paranoia of an international terrorist, a high-ranking member of organized crime, or a cop on the take—none of which he was. He simply didn't trust phones—*fuckin' landlines,* he called them—and preferred to do his talking in person.

"We need a meet," said Jimmy. Not a meeting, a *meet.*

"Where?" asked Jaywalker.

"The usual."

"When?"

"Hour from now."

And that was it.

The usual was as far west as you could go on 125th Street without getting wet, right by the banks of the Hudson River, if the Hudson River still had banks. What it had instead was a parking area, or at least a place where you could sit in your car and watch to see if anyone was watching you.

It suited Jimmy Chipmunk just fine.

As soon as Jaywalker had climbed out of his Mercury and into the passenger seat of Chippamunga's Ford Crown Victoria, Jimmy handed him a large manila envelope.

"Turned out I didn't need the subpoena after all," he said. "Soon as they saw it, they decided to make things easy."

Vintage Jimmy Chipmunk. Jaywalker had no real idea how he'd gotten the stuff, whether it had been through force, threats, bribery, extortion or what. Then again, he didn't care. He'd done his part legally, by filling out the subpoenas. How Jimmy served them, or if he served them at all, was strictly Jimmy's business.

He peeked into the envelope. Inside were maybe twenty or thirty sheets of paper, some loose, some stapled or paper-clipped together. Just by thumbing the edges of them, Jaywalker could see that they were police reports, diagrams of the crash scene, photocopies of photographs, and other documents relating to Carter Drake's case.

"You're the best," he said.

"Nuthin to it," said Jimmy Chipmunk.

Back in his apartment, Jaywalker spent a couple of hours reviewing the documents, organizing them into subject headings and making handwritten notes. But he was no more than five minutes into the process when it became readily apparent to him that District Attorney Abraham Firestone had done his homework.

First, he'd had his investigators thoroughly go over the crash sight. They'd been able to backtrack the path of the van, beginning at the end, where it had come to rest and ended up in flames. As it had gone over the embankment, it had not only torn up the grass, but it had uprooted shrubs and even left marks on rocks and trees that it had bounced off of after leaving the highway. But perhaps most telling were the skid marks the van's tires had left on the pavement.

Skid marks, Jaywalker knew, could tell a story all by themselves. They were created by a driver hitting the brakes hard enough to lock up the vehicle's wheels on a dry, or relatively dry, surface. From the rubber left on that surface, a trained observer could tell exactly where the vehicle had been when the wheels first locked, in what direction it had been heading and how it continued once the brakes were applied. Furthermore, from measuring the length of the marks and adjusting for the coefficient of friction—a fancy way of describing the stickiness of the road surface at the time—it was possible to compute the speed the vehicle had been traveling.

And the results were telling.

The van had been right where it was supposed to be when its brakes locked up, squarely in its northbound lane and a good two feet from the double yellow center line. Its brakes had engaged and begun to slow it without any noticeable "fishtailing" or "drift" to either the left or right. Then there'd come a point where, still standing on his brakes, the van's driver had steered to his right, no doubt attempting to evade the southbound vehicle in his lane. Only when he'd left the pavement altogether and was on the narrow cinder shoulder of the road had the driver tried to correct back to the left. But it had been too late. A twelve-foot stretch with a complete absence of skid marks or tracks of any sort indicated that the van had taken off at that point, literally becoming airborne, before touching down again on the downslope of the embankment. The rest, as they say, was history.

The posted speed limit on that stretch of highway was fifty miles per hour. Allowing for a margin of error of 5 mph either way, Firestone's investigators had been able to conclude that at the time the driver hit the brakes and locked up the wheels, the van had been moving at approximately forty-seven miles an hour.

As for the oncoming vehicle, there was no way to estimate its speed because it had left no skid marks at all. Which meant that its driver had never tried to stop—either before, during or after the incident.

What Firestone had done next was to have his investigators—and he'd assigned at least four of them to the task, on a full-time basis—go even further back in time, in an attempt to track Carter Drake's movements over the twelve hours that had preceded the crash. What they'd done was to interview witnesses, people who'd been with Drake the previous afternoon and evening. And although the names of those people had been blacked out in the copies of the documents Jimmy Chipmunk had dug up, a number of tantalizing clues emerged from the interview reports. There was, for example the "Sports Bar." And there were "Bartender A" and "Bartender B," along with the occasional unredacted pronoun revealing that one was male and the other female. And there were "Customers 1, 2, 3, 4 and 5." Finally, there was a word that kept popping up in the investigators' conversations with those bartenders and customers, a single pesky word that Jaywalker lost count of after the tenth repetition or so.

And that word was *tequila.*

Since Carter Drake hadn't bothered to stop and stick around after running the van off the road, it followed that he'd gone home, or at least someplace else. He hadn't turned himself in for another fourteen hours, no doubt figuring that any alcohol he'd consumed the night before would no longer be detectable in his system. And he'd been right about that. What he hadn't counted on was that the authorities could nevertheless show that he'd been drunk, by proving it circumstantially. In other words, if the prosecution could reconstruct the previous evening and put, say, ten drinks into Drake, they wouldn't need a blood test or a Breathalyzer; they could prove his intoxication through a combination of eyewitness accounts and expert testimony. It was an unusual way of doing it, but a creative one. And as far as Jaywalker was concerned, there was nothing legally objectionable about it.

Which meant he had some interviewing of his own to do.

That evening, Jaywalker got a call from Judah Mermelstein. Drake had called him from jail, he said.

"He told me he's finished writing out some statement you asked him to do."

"Good," said Jaywalker.

"What kind of statement?" Mermelstein asked.

"Facts," said Jaywalker. "I want his account of everything he can remember, starting twenty-four hours before the accident and continuing all the way up to his arraignment."

"Aren't you afraid it'll get read on the way out?"

"Of course I am," Jaywalker admitted. "But I was also afraid to talk on their phones. I'm not exactly covered by lawyer-client privilege. And even if I was, I wouldn't trust law-enforcement types to play by the rules."

"Really?"

Over the phone, it was hard to tell if Mermelstein was truly shocked or was putting Jaywalker on.

"Really," said Jaywalker, deciding to play it safely down the middle. "I used to be one of them, in a previous life."

"How about I go in and visit Drake tomorrow?" Mermelstein suggested. "It's a schlep for you, but it's right around the corner from here. And it'll probably be easier for me to get the papers from him. You'd probably have to sign your life away, wait two weeks for approval, and submit to a body-cavity search."

"Good idea," said Jaywalker.

"The body-cavity search?"

"I think I'll take a pass on that, thanks." But the exchange brought a smile to Jaywalker's face. Not only was Mermelstein offering to save him time and aggravation, but he'd demonstrated that he understood how dysfunctional bureaucracies operated, or failed to operate. And that he possessed a sense of humor, without which a lawyer was definitely in the wrong business.

Or was Mermelstein's offer his way of saying he wanted to see Carter Drake's statement for himself? Perhaps Jaywalker's little homework assignment for Drake had somehow ruffled Mermelstein's feathers. Then again, he *was* Drake's lawyer, at least for the next seven or eight months or so, which made the statement every bit as much his business as it was Jaywalker's. No doubt Jaywalker was being paranoid in attributing an ulterior motive to Mermelstein. But he couldn't help it; paranoia was one of the occupational hazards of being a criminal defense lawyer. Sooner or later you learned to suspect absolutely everyone and everything. Giving fellow human beings the benefit of the doubt and presuming innocent motivation on the part of others were noble enough concepts, but they were concepts best left for juries.

True to his word, Judah Mermelstein went in to see Carter Drake on Monday, and on Tuesday an Express Mail envelope arrived at Jaywalker's apartment. In it was a second envelope, bearing the hand-printed words

From Carter Drake III. Privileged Communication For My Lawyers Only. The gummed seal of the inner envelope was still intact; Mermelstein hadn't even opened it before forwarding it to Jaywalker.

One of the good things about being paranoid was how often you got to be pleasantly surprised by people.

STATEMENT OF CARTER DRAKE III

The day before the accident I had a meeting scheduled for 10:00 a.m. in Nyack, N.Y. The client I have there owns a bunch of real estate holdings, and he wanted to go over certain things with me. We worked straight through, and then we went to a nearby restaurant to get something to eat, since we had skipped lunch. From the restaurant, which was a sort of a sports bar with lots of TV sets tuned to ESPN and other sports channels, the client called his girlfriend and suggested she come over and meet us.

About an hour later, she showed up with 2 of her girlfriends. By the time they got there, I had already had some appetizers and a couple of drinks. I was drinking martinis, but when the girls joined us they started drinking tequila, so I switched over. I never did get around to eating a real dinner. Instead I had maybe 3 shots of tequila, for a total of 5 drinks, no more.

By the time I left it was just dark outside. I was able to drive okay, but somehow I missed the entrance for Route 9W heading south to NYC. When I reached Route 303, I decided to take it instead. I knew it would eventually take me to the Palisades Parkway and the G. Washington Bridge to the city. As I was heading south, I noticed that a wasp was flying around inside my car. That worried me, because I'm highly allergic to insect bites. My eyes close up, my mouth gets all swollen, and I have trouble breathing. I've ended up in emergency rooms a couple of times. I know I should have stopped the car and gotten out, but just when I was getting ready to, the wasp landed on the inside of my windshield, toward the middle but closer to the driver's side. I took a folded newspaper and I reached over and tried to kill it. In the process I must have swerved over the center line, because when I looked up, a white van was right in front of me, coming at me. I cut back sharply into my lane, and I thought the van passed safely by me on my left, so I continued on my way.

I made it all the way home without any other problems, getting there about 9:00. I was pretty exhausted, and I went right to bed.

The next morning, listening to the news, I heard about the accident and that the police were looking to question the driver of an Audi with a partial license plate the same as mine. So I contacted my lawyer Chet Ludlow and turned myself in. I wanted to explain everything that happened, but Chet insisted that I remain silent, so I did.

When I went before the judge, I thought he'd let me go. Instead he set 5 million dollars' bail. And to make sure I couldn't post it, they froze all my accounts and other assets. So here I am.

And that's all I know. Honest to God.
Carter Drake III

Jaywalker read it from start to finish, three times. As statements went, it wasn't bad. Sure, there could have been more detail, but that was to be expected, and would come over time. But substantively, it was fine. Drake's version of the events laid out the makings of a pretty good defense. Under federal law imposed upon the states, with the cost of noncompliance being the denial of billions of dollars in highway funding, there is now a nationwide limit on the amount of alcohol a driver of a motor vehicle can legally have in his blood. That limit is .08 percent, or eight hundredths of a percentage point, calculated by weight. A good rule of thumb is that for every drink consumed by the average adult male, there's a corresponding blood alcohol elevation of .02 percent. Women, for some reason other than a lower average body weight, experience a slightly higher elevation per drink, closer to .03 percent. And it doesn't seem to matter whether that drink is a twelve-ounce bottle of beer, a four-ounce glass of wine or a single shot of something far stronger. Nor does it depend upon whether that shot is served straight-up, over ice, or diluted with soda, juice, water or anything else, so long as the anything else is nonalcoholic.

The math was easy enough. Five drinks would have put Drake at about .10 percent over the limit, to be sure, but only by a bit. Hell, Jaywalker had seen readings in the .20s and .30s in his day. He'd even had a murder case where the deceased's blood had read out at .45 percent on autopsy, or almost one part in fifty. Miraculously, the guy had still been standing, at least up to the point when his stepson had conked him on the head with a bottle. But that was an extreme case. Most people will pass out before they reach .30 percent, lapse into a coma around .35 percent, and die of acute alcohol poisoning around .40 percent.

Compared to those numbers, Carter Drake had been a model of sobriety.

And the business about the wasp was terrific. It explained how Drake had ended up in the wrong lane. Even the part about not realizing the van had gone off the road was good. Not only did it provide a defense for knowingly leaving the scene of an accident, it also negated the inference that Drake had fled because he knew how far over the limit he'd been. And it made him less of a villain for not stopping to help or turning himself in more quickly.

Of course, all that depended upon whether Drake's version of the events—regarding his drinking, the accident, and his failure to stop—was to be believed. If he was lying about any or all of those things, it was a different story.

And that, Jaywalker knew, was one of the problems with the written statement. Writing his account at his leisure had given Drake time to ponder, to choose his words carefully, to sanitize things, emphasizing the good stuff and editing out things he thought might work against him. In short, to lie. Jaywalker would have much preferred hearing Drake describe the events orally and extemporaneously. He would have liked to be able to interrupt him, challenge him, even cross-examine him as to certain details. But that opportunity hadn't been his.

It was one of Jaywalker's pet peeves about the legal system. The rich got out on bail and were free to meet with their lawyers behind closed doors in plush offices. The poor had to settle for whispered conversations over ancient telephones in communal visiting rooms, or for opaque written statements, totally devoid of the usual indicia of credibility. Not that Carter Drake was poor, by any standard. It was just that he'd been rendered poor, or the functional equivalent of it, by the combination of a five-million-dollar bail and an order freezing his assets.

There had to be some poetic justice, Jaywalker decided, to that particular set of circumstances. Or at least some economic justice. The rich-and-powerful financier suddenly finding himself reduced to the status of an indigent defendant, no better than a pauper in the eyes of the law. The bleeding-heart liberal in Jaywalker found he kind of liked the idea. But the defense lawyer in him hated it, just as he'd always hated it on behalf of his truly indigent clients.

For consolation, he knew that sooner or later he'd get a chance to sit down with Carter Drake in a secure setting, and have a face-to-face conversation with him, a conversation in which all of Drake's little *tells* would become apparent to Jaywalker's trained eye—the tiny tics, the involuntary traveling of the hand upward to the mouth, the sudden breaking off of eye contact, the unnecessary repetition of the question to buy time before composing an answer, the pregnant pauses at inappropriate moments, the almost comical pulling back at the first mention of the word *polygraph*.

But all that would have to wait. For now, Jaywalker would have to settle for trying to locate a particular unnamed sports bar somewhere in the vicinity of Nyack, and seeing if Bartenders A and B, and Customers 1, 2, 3, 4 and 5 would verify Carter Drake's account or put the lie to him.

Tomorrow.

7

THE END ZONE

The sports bar, it turned out, was a place called the End Zone, located on the outskirts of Nyack, if one was willing to grant Nyack the benefit of doubt in terms of worthiness of outskirts. It struck Jaywalker as a sort of Hooters for not-quite-yet-beer-bellied ex-jock wannabes in their thirties and forties who'd happened upon the True Meaning of Life: since God had given each of them two eyes, He must've intended one for watching tits and the other for watching football on a screen the size of Connecticut. Though not necessarily in that order.

He'd found the End Zone by going undercover—if you wanted to stretch things again. He'd dug out an old New York Giants jacket, pleased to discover it still fit him. He'd matched it up with an even older Yankees cap, and had completed the outfit with dirty sneakers and a pair of faded jeans. Then he'd headed up to Nyack and started stopping total strangers and asking them if they happened to know where a guy could find a nice place to sit, have a beer or two, and maybe watch a ball game. A few folks seemed put off by the ancient Mercury, but one or two actually admired it. "Cool wheels," said one young man. "*Retro,* huh?" And not only did Jaywalker receive near unanimity in advice to try the End Zone, but he even got company, a fellow who answered to the name Bubba, who'd been thinking of heading that way himself, and allowed that he'd be more than happy to climb in and navigate. Bubba had a baby face and an easy grin. He could have been twenty-five or forty-five, or just about anything in between. But either way, his best years were clearly behind him. To Jaywalker, he was a perfect case study in what happens when muscle meets malt and converts to marshmallow.

Between the Giants jacket and Bubba's first-name familiarity with the End Zone's late-afternoon regulars, Jaywalker had little difficulty locating one bartender and two customers who'd been in the place nearly a month ago, when Carter Drake had been throwing back shots of tequila.

"Might not'a remembered him," said the bartender, a large woman whom everyone referred to as Twiggy, irony apparently being no stranger at the End Zone. "But a few weeks back, a coupla detectives came in with a picksher of him, askin' a lotta questions. But the guy you wanna talk to is Riley. He kept the tab on the table the guy was at, and they had him testify at the whatchacallit, the grand union."

"The grand jury?" Jaywalker asked.

"Yeah, that's it."

"Any idea where I might find him?"

"Yeah," said Twiggy. "Stay put. He comes on at eight."

So Jaywalker stayed right where he was, drinking Cokes, eating salted peanuts, and leaving a couple of twenties on the bar in front of him, the way he'd seen big tippers do it. And sure enough, just before eight o'clock, a second bartender materialized in front of him, a wiry Irishman who couldn't have gone more than five foot four, but looked like he could take anyone in the place.

"You Riley?" Jaywalker asked him after a bit.

"Who wants to know?"

Jaywalker slid one of the twenties a few inches toward the back edge of the bar. "I'm a P.I.," he said, immediately regretting it. It made him sound like a bit player in a Raymond Chandler movie.

Riley said nothing, but he didn't turn away, either. Jaywalker had made sure that he'd noticed the bit with the twenty. Not that he'd had to; he was pretty sure this was a guy who didn't miss much.

"I understand the D.A.'s people talked with you," said Jaywalker. "And I was hoping you could tell me what you told them."

Riley began drying glasses with a towel. "Who you workin' for?" he asked.

It was a fair question. "Guy's wife," he said.

Riley kept drying glasses. He was good at it.

"The thing is," said Jaywalker, "they're looking to throw the book at him. Want to give him twenty-five to life."

"Maybe he's got it comin'."

"Maybe," said Jaywalker. "I'm not saying he doesn't. I'd just like to know, one way or the other. That's all."

Riley glanced down at the bar. Jaywalker took it as a cue, and slid the second twenty toward the first one, until the two of them were touching.

"He was drunk," said Riley, "if that's what you want to know."

"How drunk?"

"I cut him off, made him call home."

This was news. Drake certainly had made no mention of it. Then again, maybe Riley was making it up, to cover his own butt. Jaywalker decided to call him on it. "Anyone show up to drive him home?" he asked.

"Yeah," said Riley, "as a matter of fact. A kid showed up, maybe eighteen or nineteen, young enough looking that I woulda carded him. But even before they was out the door, your guy was startin' in with him, saying he was okay to drive hisself."

More news.

"Tell me," said Jaywalker, "before they took you into the grand jury, did they make you sign any papers?"

"Papers. What kinda papers?"

"Something called a Waiver of Immunity."

"Nah," said Riley, "I didn't sign no papers. I'da remembered if I did."

They talked for a little while longer. Drake and the other people at his table had not only been doing shots of tequila, they'd been downing a "designer brand" that went for fifteen bucks a shot. Riley reached behind him at that point and produced a bottle. Jaywalker paid little attention to the name, other than spotting the word *oro,* which he was pretty sure meant "gold" in Spanish. Instead he looked for, and found, the alcohol content. According the label, the stuff was 120 proof.

As for the bar bill, the detectives had taken that, then had Riley decipher it during his grand jury appearance. There'd been no way for him to tell from it exactly how many of the shots had found their way into the man whose photo Riley recognized, but Riley had estimated the number at eight to ten.

Walking through the End Zone's parking lot, Jaywalker replayed the conversation in his mind. According to Riley, not only had Carter Drake had more to drink than he'd admitted to in his written statement, but the shots had been stronger. Ordinary tequila ranged from 86 proof to 100, with proof being the alcohol content doubled. Drinking 120-proof tequila changed the formula a bit, and pushed Drake's blood alcohol content even higher, up around the .20 percent range.

The other noteworthy piece of information to come out of the discussion was that the D.A. hadn't asked Riley to waive his own immunity from prosecution before putting him into the grand jury. A bartender who continues to serve an intoxicated customer commits a crime, and if that customer drives off and kills some-body—as Drake had done—that crime becomes a very serious one. But by having Riley testify without a waiver, Abe Firestone was giving him a pass: he was now immune from prosecution for whatever law or laws he may have broken. Evidently Firestone had made a decision as to his priorities. He didn't want some bar-tender minimizing how much he'd served a customer in order to protect his own ass.

Firestone had apparently wanted truthful answers out of Riley, even if they came at the expense of never being able to charge him for his contribution to the nine deaths the tequila had led to. It was a reasonable trade-off, Jay-walker knew. After all, Riley might have been guilty of serving his customers too much and too long, but he hadn't killed anyone. So, forced to choose, Firestone had decided he didn't want Riley.

He wanted Drake.

Jaywalker found his Mercury, unlocked it and got in. He would have liked to revisit the scene of the crash—he figured it couldn't be more than fifteen or twenty minutes away—but knew it would be too dark to make the detour worth it. He started the engine, put the car in Reverse, and had just backed out of the spot he'd been in, when the driver of another vehicle, off to his right, evidently decided he was taking too much time doing it. The headlights of the vehicle headed straight toward him, or at least straight toward the side of his car, and for an instant Jaywalker braced for a collision. Then, at the last possible moment, the other driver veered off sharply and, without ever braking, pulled out of the parking lot, noisily spraying gravel behind him.

"Goddamn drunken idiot!" Jaywalker yelled, by that time to no one but himself. He waited a moment for the adrenaline rush to subside, then pulled the Merc carefully out onto the highway.

It was a full two miles and five minutes later that the true significance of the event dawned on him. Back in the parking lot, Jaywalker had briefly thought about calling 9-1-1 and reporting the other driver before the jerk killed somebody. Then he'd realized that not only had he failed to get the guy's license-plate number, he couldn't even say what make or model the car had been—if indeed it had been a car, rather than a pickup truck or an SUV—or what color it was.

All he'd seen had been headlights.

Yet in his written statement, Carter Drake had recounted how he'd looked up from trying to swat a wasp, only to see an oncoming vehicle about to hit him head-on. Yet he'd been able to tell *not only that it had been a van, but that it had been white.*

That, Jaywalker now knew for a fact, would have been totally impossible. In the dark, all Drake would have seen would have been a pair of headlights, coming straight at him and just about blinding him.

He'd made up the rest.

But why?

8

OUT FOR BLOOD

The following day was a court day, Carter Drake's arraignment on murder charges in New City. That the charges would include murder—as well as a laundry list of lesser crimes—should have been a secret, known only to the grand jurors who'd voted to indict him and the prosecutor's office that had presented the evidence to them. But nine people had died, and this was a big case. And the bigger the case, and the more media and public interest it generated, the more leaks it tended to spring.

Not that Abe Firestone, the Rockland County district attorney, had held a press conference or called the editor of the *New York Times* or anything like that. What he'd done instead was to give Judah Mermelstein a "courtesy call," designed to prepare him and his client for the worst. Or so the D.A. had phrased it. More likely, Firestone had had an ulterior motive in mind. While he was prohibited by law and ethics from divulging the specific charges contained in the indictment, no such prohibition extended to the defense. To Jaywalker's cynical way of thinking, Firestone was counting on Mermelstein to go public, thereby doing Firestone's work for him.

It wasn't a matter of the two adversaries working

together, though. Firestone, Jaywalker guessed, wanted the added publicity a murder indictment would generate. He was an old-school politician, a law-and-order former sheriff up for reelection in November. The community had been outraged by the incident, and the sentiment on many lips was that, short of a slow and painful death, no sentence handed out to Carter Drake could possibly be enough. There'd been an early rumor, stoked by a column in the *Rockland County Register* and fanned by local radio talk-show hosts, that because Drake had turned himself in so long after the accident, after he'd likely sobered up, he might not be able to be charged with anything more serious than leaving the scene of an accident. Abe Firestone was eager to put that rumor to rest.

Judah Mermelstein, on the other hand, was interested in defusing the drama from the situation. Short of coming right out and announcing that Firestone had told him there'd be a murder charge, Mermelstein could say pretty much whatever he wanted to. And he did. Constantly hounded by reporters intent on keeping the story on the front page and the evening news, he took advantage of every opportunity to tell them that he fully expected his client to be indicted for murder. "Yes, *murder*," he'd add solemnly. "Nine counts of it." Then he'd paused a moment for dramatic effect.

"Now, is this really a murder case?" he'd ask them rhetorically. "Of course not. But given the very understandable anger of the good people of Rockland County, there's been a tremendous amount of pressure brought to bear on the authorities. The D.A. happens to be a friend of mine, and a good man. But he's also a politician. I can absolutely guarantee you he's going to overreact and make a point of showing everyone how tough he is. If I were in his shoes, I might even do the same thing. I'd be dead wrong to do it, of course. But that's our system for you."

If politics makes for strange bedfellows, so too does criminal law, at least occasionally.

Amanda had phoned Jaywalker the night before and asked him if he was going to be present in court for the arraignment. "I'm not too confident in Mr. Mermelstein," she'd confided. "And since eventually you're going to take—"

"I'll be there," Jaywalker had told her. "But I'll be in the audience, just like you." Being suspended meant he wasn't permitted to *pass the bar.* The bar in this case was a literal one, a solid railing, waist high and usually fashioned out of dark wood. It had a break in the middle, where either a swinging gate or a chain, often wrapped with ceremonial red velvet, divided the spectator section from the *well,* the front area where the judge and other court officials sat, facing the lawyers and the defendant.

"Do you need a ride?" Amanda had asked.

"That'd be nice," Jaywalker had said. No need to overtax the Mercury, which was in a legal parking spot for the next two days, nothing to sneeze at.

"Do you need me to bring my son along?" Amanda asked. "Or can I leave him home?"

"Your son," echoed Jaywalker. That would be the kid described by Riley the bartender, the one who'd showed up at the End Zone after Drake had called home. "How old is he?"

"Eric is seventeen," she'd said, "going on twelve."

"Meaning?"

"Meaning he's in his rebellious stage. One day it's blue hair, the next it might be a nose ring. He likes to keep us guessing."

"Why don't we leave him home this trip," Jaywalker had suggested. "Or in school."

"Fat chance of that."

After he'd hung up, Jaywalker hadn't quite been able to decide if he'd excluded the son because he was afraid his appearance might work against Carter Drake, or because he wanted Amanda Drake for himself.

Even before they reached the courthouse, it became clear to Jaywalker that they were heading into a circus of sorts. There were a dozen television vans, their telescoping antennae reaching skyward. Hundreds of people surrounded the building, spilling out into the streets and across the way. Many chanted and carried signs. A representative sampling of the ones Jaywalker could read from inside Amanda's Lexus included "MURDERER!" "DEATH PENALTY FOR DRAKE," "HOLOCAUST II," "KILL THE KILLER," and "IT WAS NO ACCIDENT, IT WAS A POGROM!" Cops were everywhere, many of them sporting riot helmets and plastic shields. Blue wooden barricades cordoned off the crowd and kept the courthouse steps clear. Jaywalker was able to count more than two dozen still cameras and almost as many video recorders, most bearing the logos or numbers of national networks or their local affiliates, or the cable news channels. Off to one side, MADD had set up a booth where volunteers were busily handing out flyers decrying the menace of drunk drivers. And some guy with a pushcart had set up shop, and was selling coffee and doughnuts. Jaywalker half expected to spot a lion tamer next, or a dozen clowns climbing out of a Volkswagen.

So much for Judah Mermelstein's efforts to *defuse the drama from the situation.*

Once inside the building, Jaywalker stood in a long line with Amanda, waiting to go through the metal detectors and the briefcase searches that had become standard since September 11, 2001. Afraid to take a chance with his homemade ID card at the Court Personnel, Police Officers and Attorneys Only line, Jaywalker opted for the All Others line, which was about ten times longer. But he didn't resent the delay. Although he was pretty confident that few Mideastern terrorists were listing the Rockland County courthouse as their next big target, he was less certain about the "Death-Penalty-for-Drake" crowd. Not to mention the Mothers Against Drunk Driving.

They found seats toward the rear of what soon became a standing-room-only courtroom, even though it was the largest in the building. But if getting to sit was the upside of their early arrival, getting to wait was the downside. Jaywalker passed the time people-watching. That, and drinking in the perfume of Amanda Carter.

Finally, at ten-thirty, a court officer shouted "All rise!" and the judge entered, dwarfed by a pair of uniformed state troopers on steroids. "Be seated!" shouted the court officer, and everyone sat.

"The People of the State of New York versus Carter Drake Three," the same officer intoned, quickly demonstrating that his reading comprehension was no match for his volume.

So they meant to get right to the main attraction, Jaywalker realized. No lounge-act crowd warmers here. And as he and everyone else watched, an orange-jump-suited Carter Drake was led into the well from a side door. Not only was he, too, flanked by a pair of large troopers, but he was handcuffed behind his back, and a set of leg irons restrained his ankles with a short chain.

Judah Mermelstein rose from his seat at the defense

table and greeted his client. The two of them huddled for a moment.

"If the court please," said Mermelstein, "may my client's restraints be removed for this proceeding?"

"No," said the judge.

Jaywalker winced. Such things never happened in Manhattan. In Brooklyn or Staten Island, maybe, but only if the prisoner had earlier proved that he was a security risk. Up here, either it was s.o.p. or it was going to be for Drake.

The arraignment itself took less than five minutes. The court clerk announced that the defendant had been indicted for murder and related crimes, and asked him how he pleaded, guilty or not guilty. The courtroom fell stone silent as spectators leaned forward to hear.

"Not guilty," said Drake in a voice that was still barely audible. Though standing right next to his lawyer and surrounded by a phalanx of large men, to Jaywalker he looked absolutely alone.

"Forty-five days for defense motions," said the judge. "Anything else?"

"Yes, Your Honor." It was Mermelstein's voice, not much louder than Drake's had been. "My client is currently being held on five million dollars' bail. It seems to me—"

"This is a murder case," said the judge. "He's lucky there's any bail at all."

An approving murmur bubbled up from the audience, quickly silenced by the judge's gavel.

"People's position?"

Abe Firestone rose from the D.A.'s table. In New York State–court parlance, the prosecution gets addressed and referred to as "the People." The terminology had always infuriated Jaywalker, with its implication that the defendant and his lawyer were something else, something less. *Non-people* of some sort.

"The People oppose," boomed Firestone in a deep, practiced baritone. Again there was an approving murmur, quickly silenced by another bang of the judge's gavel. After a beat, Firestone began recounting the horror of the deaths Drake had caused. As soon as he realized it was going to be a stump speech, all about community outrage and totally unrelated to the facts of the case, Jaywalker tuned out. He'd been up against adversaries like Firestone in the past, usually when he'd ventured outside of Manhattan. The general rule of thumb was that the farther you got from the city, the more politicized prosecutors' offices became. And a corollary to that rule was that not only did the volume increase in direct proportion to the distance, but the competence decreased.

"…and for those reasons," Firestone was concluding, more loudly than ever, "the People request that bail be raised to the amount of *fifty* million dollars."

This time the judge was able to quiet the courtroom by simply lifting his gavel. "I'm going to split the difference," he said, "and deny both of your applications. The bail will remain exactly as it is. The case is assigned to Judge Hinkley for trial. Next case."

It wasn't until they were filing out of the building that Jaywalker was recognized by a couple of reporters he knew. Courthouse regulars, they were, guys who used to hang around 100 Centre Street and cover the juicy cases. On slow days, when they'd had nothing better to do, they'd sit in on a Jaywalker trial, if one was going on. Then again, a lot of people used to do that. One was from the *Post*, as he recalled, the other from the *Daily News,* but he could never remember which was which. It didn't help that one of them stood about 5'4" and the other 5'2".

"How ya doon?" the short one asked.

"Not bad," said Jaywalker. He could see them staring

at the beautiful blonde next to him, but he was pretty sure they didn't know who she was. And he wasn't about to introduce them.

"You gonna take this one over?" asked the shorter one. "Mumbles Mermelstein seems pretty overmatched."

"No comment," said Jaywalker.

"Off the record," promised the short one, lifting his right hand in a solemn oath of silence.

"Yeah, right," said Jaywalker, and all three of them laughed out loud.

"I'm hungry," said Amanda.

Great, thought Jaywalker. Not twenty minutes ago, her husband—okay, *estranged* husband—had been told that his bail would stay at five million dollars, virtually guaranteeing that he wouldn't get out before his trial. And getting out *after* his trial might well take fifteen to twenty-five years, if the parole board threw him a break. So what was her first reaction? She was *hungry*.

They walked to a nearby diner and found a booth. Amanda ordered an omelet of some sort, and an order of home-fried potatoes. Jaywalker stuck with a cup of tea with lemon, sipping it as he watched her down her food. She ate the same way she made love, throwing herself into it with no hint of self-consciousness. Halfway through the meal, Short and Shorter came into the place. Jaywalker spread his jacket out onto the seat next to him, a move intended to preempt the two reporters from joining them. But it turned out not to be necessary: they had a third man with them, a taller guy who wore a camera around his neck.

"So how do things look?" Amanda asked, wiping a bit of egg from one corner of her mouth. "And who's this Judge Hinkley that's going to try the case?"

"Never heard of him," said Jaywalker. "I'll check with

Mermelstein, first chance I get. As far as the case…" He finished the sentence with a shrug of his shoulders.

"That doesn't sound so good."

"You were there," he told her. "You saw how they're all out for blood."

Amanda nodded.

"There's one thing that's bothering me," said Jaywalker.

"What's that?"

He leaned forward so he could keep his voice low. They were in a public place, after all. "Carter claims that in the instant he saw the van in front of him, he could not only tell it was a van, but he could see that it was white."

"So?"

"So that couldn't have happened," said Jaywalker. "For some reason, he's making that up."

"Maybe you misunderstood him," said Amanda. "Or misheard him."

"No," said Jaywalker. "I had him write it out. Those were his words."

She looked away at that point, as though her attention had been suddenly drawn to something off to one side of the booth. Jaywalker looked, too, but there was nothing going on there, nothing but the wall, the jukebox selector, their menus, and the salt and pepper shakers.

What am I missing here? he asked.

But he formed the words silently, asking only himself.

9

BACK IN THE BALL GAME

SUSPENDED LAWYER SPOTTED STEPPING OUT WITH KID-KILLING DRIVER'S WIFE

…read the caption beneath the photo. And there he was again, back on his least favorite place in the western world, Page Six of the *New York Post*.

Not that he ever would have known about it, had it not been for a call from his daughter. A friend of hers had spotted it and phoned her, exclaiming, "Is that your father?" And there was no missing him. There he was, in perfect profile, sitting in the booth of the diner he'd taken Amanda to the previous morning. Only it didn't look like a diner in the photo; it looked like a bar. And Jaywalker wasn't really sitting at all; he was bent halfway across the table, his lips parted and within inches of Amanda Drake's, their eyes locked on each other. He remembered the moment. It had been when he'd leaned forward and dropped his voice so that he could ask her, without being overheard, about Carter's claim that he'd been able to tell that the oncoming headlights belonged to a white van.

"Shit," he muttered. "Shit, shit, shit!"

There was an inch or two of text farther down the page, and Jaywalker could see his own name and Amanda's, both in bold print. He didn't bother reading it. There'd be phrases like "romantically linked," "husband in jail," and "drove off together in a beige Lexus." And needless to say, there'd be no mention that it had happened to be around noon when the photo had been taken, and in a perfectly respectable diner right around the corner from the courthouse, where Amanda had dutifully shown up as the defendant's family and Jaywalker had appeared as a private investigator working on the case.

"Shit," he muttered again. Would he never learn?

The letter from the Disciplinary Committee arrived two days later, by certified mail, return receipt requested. Jaywalker's right hand shook visibly as he signed for it.

What had he done *now?* It had been *lunch.* No, not *even* lunch. He'd had a goddamn cup of *tea,* was all.

All morning, phrases kept drifting back to him from his previous go-round with the committee. Phrases like *overzealous...utter contempt for long-established rules...open defiance of members of the judiciary... pushing the ethical envelope almost to the breaking point...conduct totally unbecoming a member of the bar...* And finally, the only one Jaywalker didn't consider a personal badge of honor, *a well-documented sexual indiscretion that took place in this very courthouse.*

Over the next two days, as he prepared for the Status Review Hearing the letter had informed him of, Jaywalker reviewed the transcripts of his prior appearances before the committee, researched the law, and even reached out to a colleague or two for advice—something he hadn't done for years. None of them was able to help him any more than Jaywalker was able to help himself. So far as he could tell, he'd broken no law, breached no canon of ethics, and done nothing to bring shame to the bar. Nor, most to the point, had he "engaged in the practice of law," the cardinal sin that he knew could cost him his ticket, not to mention his freedom. And if he'd partaken in a bit of *sexual indiscretion,* he'd done so only behind closed doors, with a very consenting adult. Or did Page Six have a photo of that, too, which they'd slipped to the judges before running it in tomorrow's edition?

"Welcome back," said the presiding judge, the one sitting in the middle. The three of them peered down like vultures from their perches behind the dark mahogany bench that separated them from him. Or maybe it was oak, stained to look like mahogany. Jaywalker bit his lip and fought to concentrate on the business at hand, but it was hard. After two full days of worrying, he still couldn't figure out what he'd done to land himself back here.

"Good morning, Your Honors." A little show of respect couldn't hurt, he figured.

"We've received a report," said the presiding judge, "that you were present at the county court arraignment of one Carter Drake. Is that correct?"

"Yes, Your Honor. I was in the spectator section."

"Is that so?"

"Yes, sir."

The judge raised his eyebrows in an exaggerated parody of disbelief. Then he adjusted his reading glasses and began leafing through what appeared to be a thick set of documents in front of him. But by standing on his tiptoes, Jaywalker could see that what the judge was really doing was flipping through the pages of a copy of the *New York Post*.

"Tell me," said one of the other judges, "is it your hope to substitute as counsel for Mr. Drake at some point?"

"It is indeed," said Jaywalker. "But certainly not until my suspension has run its full course." He'd been practicing that statement for a day and a half now, knowing the question would be asked sooner or later. Though the soonness kind of surprised him. *Soonification? Soonth?* He bit his lip again.

"So hope springs eternal?" The third judge.

"Yes."

"In the two and a half years since your suspension took effect," asked the P.J., "have you engaged in the practice of law—*even once?*"

Jaywalker could spot a trap from a mile away. It was the sort of question that could have been lifted from his own playbook. All the witness had to do was say no, and the jaws would spring shut on him. Obviously they'd discovered that he'd done *something,* even if he himself couldn't remember what. Still, there was only one way to answer. Jaywalker took a deep breath, fixed the judge's eyes with his own, and said "Absolutely not" in as strong and steady a voice as he could muster.

"Good," said the P.J. "Do you have a motion?"

"A motion?"

"Yes."

Jaywalker had absolutely no idea what sort of motion the judge had in mind. Early in his career, when a criminal court judge had said, "Let's see your motion," Jaywalker had obliged him with an elaborate demonstration of his pitching motion, the no-men-on-base, full-windup version. That stunt had earned him a fifteen-second outburst of laughter, a standing ovation—and a contempt citation. He was pretty sure the presiding judge didn't have that particular kind of motion in mind. Still, he'd made it clear he expected *something*.

"I move that we, uh, adjourn for lunch?"

"How about," suggested the judge dryly, "a motion to terminate your suspension early?"

For once, Jaywalker was speechless. It was his turn to raise his eyebrows in disbelief.

"This court," the judge was saying, "finds that the respondent has, for the past two years and several months, comported himself admirably. He appears to have refrained from practicing law and, except for this recent bit of notoriety, from bringing embarrassment to his profession. Additionally, we have been advised by Justice Travis Hinkley, of the Rockland County Court, that this case will be put on a fast track for trial, and that no applications for lengthy adjournments will be granted. We are well aware of your, shall we say *creativity,* Mr. Jaywalker. We have no doubt that you're fully capable of coming up with some clever strategy to delay the trial until you're able to practice again. Now that won't be necessary. Your suspension is hereby terminated forthwith, Mr. Jaywalker, and you are reinstated as a member of the bar in good standing. This court is in recess."

"Thank you," Jaywalker managed to say, but he had to settle for saying it to the three judges' backs. It seemed as though they were every bit as anxious to get out of there as he was.

So just like that, he was back in the ball game, without so much as a demonstration of his stretch with runners on base or his pick-off move, which had always been pretty good, at least for a righty.

Didn't they even want to see *that?*

10

DRIVER'S ED

Under different circumstances, Jaywalker might have spent the rest of the day celebrating his good fortune. But he knew he didn't have that luxury. So as long as he was downtown, he found a camera store with a PASSPORT PHOTOS $5 sign in the window, where he traded a Korean woman a twenty-dollar bill for four one-by-one-inch Polaroid mug shots of himself. ("For five dolla," she explained, "you get only one photo, no good.") Two of the four he took back to the courthouse, where an obliging clerk updated his Attorney Identification Card. No more sneaking around with his homemade private investigator's ID. The other two he took to the legal office of the NYC Department of Corrections, then emerged an hour later with an official Get-Out-of-Jail card. Not that it was valid in Rockland County, technically speaking. But he figured between the two pieces of ID, he'd be able to bypass the All Others line at the New City courthouse. And more important, he'd get to sit down and have a real conversation with Carter Drake in the counsel visit room, rather than having to settle for talking with him over staticky phones, or reading his written statements. Next he called Amanda and told her the news of his reinstatement.

"That's *wonderful*," she said. "Should I fire Mr. Mermelstein?"

"No," said Jaywalker, "I think we should keep him. You know, as local counsel, if you can afford us both. He knows the players, the court officers, maybe even some of the prospective jurors. And besides…"

"Besides?"

"His name can't hurt us."

"His name?"

"I'm half-Jewish," said Jaywalker, "but you wouldn't know it from my name. And to an orthodox Jew, Carter Drake the Third might as well have GOY stamped on his forehead."

"Goy?" said Amanda. She wasn't getting this.

"Gentile," explained Jaywalker. "Christian. In other words, not a Member of the Tribe. A name like Judah Mermelstein, on the other hand, could go a long way toward diffusing some of that insider-outsider bias."

"Okay," said Amanda, "if you say so. What else?"

"What else," said Jaywalker, "is we have to meet, settle on a fee and draw up a retainer agreement." The rules had changed since his suspension had begun. Handshake agreements, once commonplace between criminal defense lawyers and their clients, were no longer permitted. Apparently there'd been too many after-the-fact disputes about who'd agreed to what.

"Where do you want to meet?" Amanda asked. "My place, or your office?"

His *office?* In his haste to renew his credentials, meet with his client and formalize his retainer agreement, Jaywalker had completely forgotten that he was a lawyer without an office. Yet as he thought about it, he decided he kind of liked the ring of it. If there could be Doctors Without Borders, surely there was room on the planet for Lawyers Without Offices, wasn't there?

"Your place is fine," said Jaywalker.

* * *

That afternoon, Jaywalker put in a call to Nicky Legs. With his brief career as a private investigator suddenly at an end, he figured he was going to need the real thing. And Nicolo LeGrosso, a retired NYPD detective, was definitely the real thing.

"Hey, howya doon?" said Nicky as soon as he recognized Jaywalker's voice.

"Good, I think. They gave me my ticket back."

"No shit? It's been tree yeahs awready?"

"Something like that," said Jaywalker. "Look, I need some work done on a case."

"That Rockland County thing?"

Word traveled fast. "Yeah," said Jaywalker, "that Rockland County thing."

They met an hour later, over coffee in a midtown luncheonette. Nicky looked good; he'd been playing a lot of golf. "Yaughta take it up," he said.

Jaywalker wrote out a list of half a dozen things he wanted LeGrosso to do on the case, and pushed the list across the table. Nicky read it without bothering to turn it around, nodding six times. Jaywalker had no idea how he could do that. If *he* tried to read upside down, he'd bring on a migraine, or at least get dizzy.

"Is this like the last case?" LeGrosso asked. "You know, the ex-hooker with the big bucks? Or am I doon it on the arm?"

On the arm was coptalk for *out of the goodness of my heart.* On several occasions Jaywalker had asked Nicky to do things for defendants who had little or no money— repeat customers who'd fallen on bad times, referrals from friends or family members, and others to whom Jaywalker hadn't been able, for one reason or another, to just say no. And Nicky had always obliged.

"No," he said, "there's money here. You need something up front?"

"Nah," said Nicky. "I'm good."

He met with Amanda that evening, and although she answered the door wearing a man's oxford shirt and, so far as he could tell, nothing else, he made her put on a robe. "Business," he told her.

"I think I liked it better," she said, "when you weren't a lawyer."

Jaywalker ignored the remark, sat her down and pulled out a retainer agreement he'd printed out earlier. For fee purposes, it broke the case down into three stages: pretrial investigation and motions; evidentiary hearings; and trial. It was how he'd always charged, though he'd rarely bothered to spell it out in black and white, as the new rules now required. He handed the agreement to Amanda, and waited while she skimmed it.

"The dollar amounts are blank," she said.

He nodded. "We have to reach an agreement on what's fair."

Jaywalker had been toying with the idea of asking for fifty thousand, if the case had to be tried. It would be his largest fee ever, but he knew he'd earn it. Hell, he'd read of cases where lawyers had charged upwards of a million dollars and complained about it not being enough. No doubt they had expensive offices, huge payrolls and vast overheads. He had no office, no payroll and an answering machine. So he was fully prepared to negotiate, and settle for somewhere between twenty-five and thirty-five thousand, still a pretty good payday.

"How about an even hundred thousand?" Amanda suggested. "Do you think that would cover you?"

Cover him?

Jaywalker did his best imitation of someone thinking, but it was impossible. "Sure," he said, trying to look like a grown-up. It reminded him of a morning thirty years ago, when he'd found out he'd passed the bar exam on the second try. He'd spent the rest of the day walking around with a dumb smile he couldn't wipe off his face. A *shit-eating grin,* his brother had called it, and Jaywalker had been afraid to ask what that meant. "Sure," he told Amanda again, "I think I can live with that." And fought to keep his hand steady as he inked in the amounts on the retainer agreement. From the way Amanda treated the numbers, he sensed it was nothing but small change to her, or a few months' interest from a bottomless trust fund. But to Jaywalker, it was like winning the lottery.

Okay, a small lottery.

"Is business over?" she asked, crossing her legs so that the two sides of her robe fell apart.

"No," said Jaywalker, trying to look away. "Did Carter phone you from the bar that night?"

"Yes," she said.

"And?"

"And we drove up to get him."

"We?"

"I picked up Eric at his father's place," she said. "I figured he could drive Carter's car."

"You told me he's only seventeen. What does he have, a learner's permit?"

"Yes, but he's a good driver. Like his father. Too fast, but a good driver."

In Jaywalker's book, no seventeen-year-old was a good driver. Not even those who had licenses.

"Anyway," Amanda added, "it was short notice, and I didn't have time to get anyone else."

"And what happened when you got there?" Jaywalker asked.

"I waited outside in my car and sent Eric in to get his father. I was pissed at Carter, and I didn't want to have to deal with him, especially if he was drunk. A few minutes later the two of them came out, and they were arguing. Carter said, 'I'm not going to allow Eric to drive.' So Eric got back into my car, and we drove home. Carter was supposed to be following us, but at some point we got separated. I pulled over and waited for him, but he must've gone a different way or something. So I drove Eric to his father's and dropped him off. I told him to call me and let me know when his father got there. And by the time I got home, there was a message from him that Carter had made it, safe and sound."

"And the next day?" Jaywalker asked.

"The next day the accident was all over the news. Carter called me to tell me that it must be him the police were looking for. He knew his license plate by heart—I didn't—and he recognized the digits they were broadcasting on all the news reports. He said he was going to call his lawyer. I said okay, good. I figured if he came forward, they'd give him a break. The next I knew was when he called me from jail and told me it had turned into a murder case."

"So much for the break," said Jaywalker.

Amanda nodded. "Is business over *now?*" she asked, uncrossing her legs.

"Yes," said Jaywalker, who never had succeeded in looking away. "Business is over."

Afterward, she asked him to stay, but he said no. "You're paying me a shitload of money," he told her. "I've got to start earning it, first thing in the morning."

"You mean you've been faking it up till now?"

"No," said Jaywalker. "It's just that not being Carter's lawyer, or *anyone's* lawyer, for that matter, my hands have been tied."

He noticed Amanda grinning. "What?" he asked her. "Why are you looking at me like that?"

"I was trying to picture you," she said, her voice dropping an octave, "with your hands tied."

Jaywalker stood up. "Amanda," he said, "you remember when business was over?"

"Yes."

"Well, now pleasure's over." He bent down, kissed her, and said, "Good night."

The following day was indeed a busy one for Jaywalker. He surrendered his good parking spot and drove up to New City, stopping first at Judah Mermelstein's office. He caught Mermelstein as he was getting ready to go to court.

"I don't know if you heard," said Jaywalker, "but I wanted to let you know I've been reinstated—"

"I did hear," said Mermelstein, "and congratulations. You have my permission to substitute as counsel for Carter Drake."

"Thanks," said Jaywalker, "but if you have no objection, I'd prefer to join you as co-counsel."

Mermelstein seemed to think about it for a moment before answering. Then he said, "I appreciate the offer, but I think I'm going to decline. This is a pretty tight community we've got up here, in case you haven't noticed. I'd say ninety percent of my clients are orthodox or conservative Jews. My livelihood, and my family's, depends on their goodwill. I've already heard from a number of them that they're, shall we say, uncomfortable with my representing a…" His voice trailed off at that point, leaving Jaywalker to finish his thought for him.

"…Non-Jew? Gentile? *Goy?*"

Mermelstein shook his head slowly, from side to side. "I'm afraid it gets worse than that," he said.

"How much worse?"

"Try *Hitler?* Or *Mengele.*"

"That's worse," Jaywalker agreed.

So Judah Mermelstein was bailing out. Not exactly a Profile in Courage. Then again, could Jaywalker really blame him? Was Mermelstein supposed to risk losing his entire practice, and with it his ability to feed his kids, just so he could hang on to a piece of a case with a radioactive client?

"I'm sorry," Mermelstein said.

"Me, too," said Jaywalker.

But as was the case with so many things in the strange world of criminal law, it was a development that had an upside to it. It had been Jaywalker's intention to have Mermelstein second-seat him at trial. If doing so accomplished nothing else, it would send a message to the jurors that here was one of their own, not only willing to sit next to the defendant and whisper back and forth with him from time to time, but maybe even grasp his arm at some point, or lay a comforting hand on his shoulder. Now that dynamic was gone. But in its place, Jaywalker was already calculating, the same jurors would now look over at the defense table and see only two people, the accused and his defender. That would provide a nice contrast with the scene at the prosecution table, where Abe Firestone— who rarely if ever had tried cases himself—would no doubt surround himself with several assistant district attorneys, and possibly even an investigator from his office. Sure, Jaywalker knew, jurors find it a lot easier to empathize with people like themselves. But they also tend to like underdogs, outcasts, long shots. And representing long shots was what Jaywalker did best.

From Mermelstein's office, Jaywalker walked to the courthouse, this time entering via the short line, the one

reserved for POLICE OFFICERS, COURT PERSON-
NEL AND ATTORNEYS ONLY. He proceeded to the
clerk's office, where he filled out three copies of a Notice
of Appearance, formally declaring that he was the new
lawyer for Carter Drake. From there he went to the
district attorney's office, stopping at the reception desk.

"My name is Jaywalker," he told the uniformed
trooper, handing him a business card. "I'm substituting
as counsel for Carter Drake. I was hoping to introduce
myself to Mr. Firestone, if he has a moment."

The trooper eyed the card, then pressed a button on
an intercom. "There's a Mr. Jaywalker here," he said.
"Says he's the new lawyer in the Drake case. Wants to
meet your boss."

"I'll let him know," said a woman's voice over the
intercom.

Jaywalker waited, passing the time studying the por-
traits of former Rockland County district attorneys on the
wall behind the desk. The only face he recognized was
that of Kenny Gribitz, who'd been a young A.D.A. in
Manhattan way back when Jaywalker had been with
Legal Aid. Then Gribitz had gotten himself elected
Rockland County D.A. A short while later, he'd gotten
himself into trouble. Over a woman, if Jaywalker remembered correctly. His kind of guy.

"The boss says this Jaywalker guy has got to file a
Notice of Appearance," said the woman's voice, "before
he'll talk with him."

Jaywalker held up his copy of the notice. There was
a bright red FILED stamp across it, complete with the
date and time.

"Done," said the trooper.

Another thirty seconds went by. Then the woman's
voice could be heard again, but barely. "Tell him the boss
isn't in," she was saying.

Jaywalker and the trooper exchanged glances. Jaywalker pointed at his wristwatch and held two fingers in the air.

"He only wants a minute or two," the trooper told the machine.

This time it was a full minute before there was a voice on the other end. Only it was a man's voice now, gruff and combative. And it said, "Tell him anything. Tell him he can go shit in his hat, for all I care."

Jaywalker smiled. "Mr. Firestone, I presume?"

The trooper nodded, returning the smile.

The attorney's visiting room at the Rockland County Jail was everything the regular visiting room hadn't been. Jaywalker was able to sit across a real table from Carter Drake, with no wire-reinforced bulletproof glass separating them, and no staticky phones to talk over.

Drake looked like somebody who'd been locked up a month would be expected to look. Jaywalker recognized the signs, the things that incarceration did to a person—some subtle, some not so subtle. There was the pallor, the waxy complexion that came from being indoors twenty-three hours a day, or twenty-four, if it happened to be raining when "yard time" was scheduled. There were the extra pounds that accumulated from a high-carb, low-protein, no-exercise diet. They tended to show up around the midsection, but in Drake's case, there was also a noticeable slackness to his cheeks, the beginning of Nixon-like jowls. There was the not-quite-clean-shaven look, the slightly unkempt hair and the faint odor suggesting that today—and perhaps yesterday, as well—had not been a shower day. But most of all, there were the eyes. Not only did they appear sunken and framed by dark circles, but a dull film had begun to spread over the pupils themselves, producing a listless, faraway expression. It was just one more symptom, Jaywalker knew, of a larger malaise, a gradual sinking-in of the reality that, contrary to early hopes and unrealistic expectations, these walls were going to be home for the foreseeable future.

So how did Jaywalker greet his new client?

"You look good," he said, the same way he might have said it to a cancer patient, or a mother who'd just delivered after a forty-eight-hour labor.

Drake smiled sheepishly. He had to know better.

"Thanks for writing out that statement for me," said Jaywalker.

"Was it what you wanted?"

"Yeah, pretty much."

"Not long enough?"

"It was a good starting point," said Jaywalker. "I'm here today so we can fill in a few blanks, get a little more detail. Then we'll go from there."

Drake leaned back in his chair. He struck Jaywalker as a man who was used to running things, and running them his own way. Having to answer questions and follow directions was going to be something of a new experience for him.

"How's my wife?" he asked in a way that might or might not have been accusatory.

"She's okay," said Jaywalker. "Worried about you."

Drake's smile was as enigmatic as his question had been. "Worried about me?" he asked. "Or worried about herself?"

Jaywalker shrugged. He had no desire to get into their marital dynamics, and every reason to steer clear of the subject. "Why don't we get to work," he suggested, thumbing through his file until he found Drake's statement. "For starters, I'd like you to tell me everything that happened at the End Zone that evening."

"Again?"

"Again."

Reluctantly, Drake complied. His memory was still fresh enough that he was able to recall the couple of martinis he'd started off with, the food he'd done no more than nibble at, and the two or three shots of tequila that had followed.

"And that's all?" Jaywalker fixed him with his most skeptical stare.

"That's all."

"I spoke with the bartender," said Jaywalker.

"I figured you had," said Drake, "since you came up with the name of the place."

They exchanged smiles.

"According to him," said Jaywalker, "it was more like eight or ten drinks, total."

Drake said nothing.

"Who's right?" Jaywalker asked him.

"It wasn't ten," said Drake. "That much I know. It might have been six, seven at the most."

Jaywalker rubbed his eyes. "Look, Carter, I'm your lawyer, not your dentist. This shouldn't be like pulling teeth."

"Maybe eight. No more, honest."

Eight would have given Drake a b.a.c. of around .16, double the legal limit. Factor in the 120-proof tequila, and you were still at .20, maybe a bit higher. Enough to get him convicted of drunk driving, to be sure, but hardly the stuff to turn it into a murder case.

"What made you leave the place?" Jaywalker asked. He wanted to know if Drake was going to admit that the bartender had cut him off and made him call home, or if he was going to leave that little detail out, as he had in his written statement.

"My son showed up."

"How come?"

"I'd called my wife earlier," said Drake. "The two of them drove up. I guess Amanda didn't want to walk into the place. She was pissed off at me, I guess. For a change."

"And?"

"And what?"

"And I left," said Drake.

"Who drove?"

"I did. Amanda stayed in her car, and my son got back into it. I drove my car."

"How come you drove?" Jaywalker asked.

"My son only has a permit," Drake explained. "It's not good after dark. I wouldn't allow him to drive. Besides, I really thought I was okay."

With eight drinks under your belt? But Jaywalker only thought the words. Now wasn't the time for lectures, he knew. He wanted honest answers, even if they were stupid ones. If Carter Drake had truly thought he could drive home safely in the dark in an unfamiliar area, after knocking back two martinis and six tequilas, Jaywalker wanted to hear that. Even if a jury wouldn't.

"What happened next?" he asked.

"I got into my car, started it up and drove off."

"And?"

"And I guess I must've missed the entrance for Route 9W heading south to the city. When I reached Route 303, I decided to take it, instead. It connects up with the Palisades Parkway, which brings you to the George Washington Bridge."

"Okay," said Jaywalker. He didn't want this to be a Q and A. He wanted Drake to ramble, to describe the events in his own words. Sometimes, for example, what a person left out from a story could be every bit as telling as what he included. "What next?"

"At some point," said Drake, "I became aware of a wasp flying around inside the car. That concerned me because I'm very allergic to insect bites. My mouth blows up, my eyes become all puffy, and I feel like my throat's— you know, like I'm not going to be able to breathe. Anaphylaxis, they call it, and it's pretty scary. Life threatening. Emergency-room stuff. You can verify it all through my physician, if you like. Do you want his name?"

"Sure," said Jaywalker, and he took notes for a few minutes as Drake supplied details.

"Where was I?" Drake asked.

"You'd just noticed a wasp flying around in your car."

"Right," said Drake. "A wasp. I had a newspaper on the console, between the front seats. I rolled it up and took a good swat at the thing. It was on the inside of the windshield, toward the middle, but more on the passenger side. I guess as I reached over to try to kill it, I must've pulled the steering wheel to the left. You know, to keep my balance?"

Jaywalker nodded, scribbling a word or two. "Did you get it?" he asked.

"I'm not sure," said Drake. "All I know is, when I straightened up, I must've been in the wrong lane, because I was looking directly at a pair of headlights. I cut back to the right as fast as I could. I never hit anything, and never heard anything but tires screeching. I assumed the other vehicle got by me safely, on my left. So I continued on home."

Jaywalker thought for a long moment before saying anything. When finally he spoke, it was to say, "You talk about 'the other vehicle.' When did you realize it was a van?"

"I didn't," said Drake. "Not till I heard the news the next morning."

"Or that it was white?"

"Maybe when I saw the photos in the *Times*. I'm not sure."

Jaywalker had seen the photos in the *Times,* too. He'd had to read the story to know it had been a van. And in the photos, it had been charred black. Just about all of it, except for some of the lettering on one side.

"How come," he asked, "when you wrote out your statement, you said you saw a white van in front of you?"

"I didn't say that."

Jaywalker handed him a copy of the statement, and waited while Drake read it.

"What I meant was," Drake explained, "is that it must've been the same white van that was in the news. And the photos. I see what you mean, though. My fault for not being clear. Sorry about that, but this is all new to me. I've never been asked to write out a statement like that before. I should have been more precise."

They spoke for another hour, covering a range of topics. But Jaywalker found himself oddly distracted. And as he drove home that afternoon, he found himself trying to reconcile Drake's two stories, the one contained in the written statement and the oral account he'd come up with today.

It hadn't been the first time a defendant had minimized his wrongdoing, or even lied about it outright. Hell, in Jaywalker's business, which was dealing with criminals, those things were pretty much the norm, especially in the early stages of the lawyer-client relationship. The five drinks instead of eight or ten, for instance. That one was certainly easy enough to understand.

But how about Drake's backtracking on whether or not he'd been able to tell it had been a white van in front of him? His explanation—that he'd simply been trying to acknowledge that it had to have been *the* van—was tortured and lame. The only possible reason Jaywalker could come up with for Drake's correcting himself was that Amanda had gotten to him, had told him that Jaywalker had picked up on the implausibility of the version in the written statement. But if that explained why Drake had corrected himself, it still left the more important question unanswered: Why had he lied in the first place?

And there was more.

Why had Drake left out the whole business about the bartender's making him call home, and Eric's walking into the place, explaining that Amanda was outside waiting? And why, in explaining how he'd rejected the idea of letting Eric drive one of the two cars home, had husband and wife managed to use the identical phrase, that Carter "wouldn't allow" his son to drive? Was that simply coincidence, or was Jaywalker's paranoia working overtime?

Then there was the business about the wasp, and the accidental swerve into oncoming traffic. Jaywalker had no doubt that Drake was seriously allergic to insect stings, and that his doctor would be able to back him up with all sorts of medical records and emergency-room documentation. What left him puzzled was the physics of Drake's account, repeated almost verbatim in both versions. According to Drake, he must have unconsciously steered to the left while reaching to the right in his attempt to swat the wasp. He'd even moved the critter farther away from him in his recent telling of the incident than he'd had it in his original written statement. There the wasp had been closer to the driver's side of the windshield; now he'd pushed it over to the passenger's side, in what seemed to Jaywalker like an attempt to exaggerate the distance he'd had to reach.

Way back in high school, Jaywalker had signed up for an elective after-school safe-driving course. Because the school had been a small one that couldn't afford to buy a dual-control car, the course had been nothing but a combination lecture and discussion group. It had been taught by a pleasant, bald man named Ed Shaughnessey, whom everyone had, naturally enough, called Driver's Ed. One of the things Driver's Ed had taught them was that while driving along, if you reached to your right— or even *looked* to your right, for that matter—you'd invariably pull the steering wheel to your right also. And over the years since, Jaywalker had found it to be true. You turned your head one way, or reached for something to one side of you, and as soon as you returned your attention to the road in front of you, you would find that you'd steered in the same direction you'd looked or reached, sometimes dangerously so. Drake's claim that he'd unconsciously steered left while swatting at something to his right was preposterous. Which was nothing but a fancy way of saying he'd been lying about that, too.

There'd been no wasp, no swat with a rolled-up newspaper. And Jaywalker knew that for another reason, as well. When he'd asked if Drake had succeeded in killing the thing, the only answer he'd gotten had been "I'm not sure." Hardly what you'd expect from someone who'd been scared to death of being stung.

So Drake had to have made the whole thing up. And Jaywalker, who'd certainly made up more than his share of things over his fifty years, had to grudgingly give his client a certain amount of credit, if only for inventiveness. It was a good story, as stories went, and with a bit of tweaking here and there, it might fool a jury into believing that even if he'd had as much to drink as Riley the Bartender was going to claim, Carter Drake's drunkenness hadn't been the cause of the accident at all.

In other words, they should blame the wasp, not the WASP.

11

PANNING FOR GOLD

The media was out in force again for Carter Drake's next court appearance. This time Jaywalker drove up to New City by himself, in the Mercury. He wanted to distance himself from Amanda as much as possible. One photo of the two of them together had been more than enough. He had asked her to make the trip, though, since this would be Carter's first appearance before Travis Hinkley, the judge who, at least according to the Disciplinary Committee, intended to put the case on a fast track to trial. And Jaywalker had suggested Amanda bring her son along this time. Not only was a little show of family solidarity in order, but he wanted to meet Eric and get his recollection of the evening of the accident. But Eric, it turned out, had an exam of some sort at school, and given his already spotty attendance record, he couldn't afford to miss it.

But if he'd driven up alone, Jaywalker had hardly arrived empty-handed. He'd brought along a set of motion papers, as well as a written Demand to Produce. Neither he, nor Judah Mermelstein before him, had so far received a shred of discovery material from the D.A.'s office. True, he had the reports that Jimmy Chipmunk had dug up, and the fruits of his own brief turn as a private investigator. But he wanted to force the prosecutors to pony up everything the law required of them. Not just to give them a hard time, but to preserve for appellate review their withholding of anything, in case of a conviction.

Because even this early on, those words, *in case of a conviction,* had become something of a silent mantra for Jaywalker. While he continued to think he had a fighting chance of beating the murder count, he had no illusions about some of the lesser charges in the indictment. A jury might conceivably buy Drake's account that he'd never been aware of the van's going off the highway and acquit him of leaving the scene of an accident. But given the testimony of Riley the Bartender, they were going to have to convict him of driving while intoxicated, and most likely of vehicular manslaughter, too. So *appellate review* was something he had to be very much keeping in mind.

For several days Jaywalker had been trying to conjure up an image of Travis Hinkley. The last name, he'd decided, was a giveaway. Definitely Irish, never a good omen for a defendant. Conventional wisdom had it that judges of Irish ancestry were among the toughest you could draw, unless you were *really* unlucky and landed in front of a judge with a German name. And for once, Jaywalker subscribed to the conventional wisdom. So he started with a ruddy-faced, blustering, law-and-order ogre. On the positive side, maybe the guy drank. And drove.

It was the *Travis* part that intrigued him. Travis was a cowboy. Travis was a country-western singer who, when he wasn't riding his horse, drove an American-made pickup truck, a Chevy Silverado, Dodge Durango or Ford F-500. He ate meat and potatoes, chewed Red

Man tobacco, and drank Budweiser straight from the bottle. But he was also something of a romantic, with a feel for the underdog.

With a little luck, Travis Hinkley might just turn out to be a regular guy.

The real Travis Hinkley turned out to be just a wee bit different from the one of Jaywalker's imagination. She might well have been Irish, given her flaming-red hair and piercing green eyes, but her face showed no signs of ruddiness, and there was no bluster to her. She was a small woman, short and stylishly thin, fiftyish. Her mouth was tightly pursed, and she opened it just enough to spit out a generic "Good morning," before retracting her tongue. Nothing about her suggested the possession of even a rudimentary sense of humor. To Jaywalker, who'd still been thinking country-western when she'd walked into the courtroom, she was the personification of a rather pretty rattlesnake.

Unlike the judge at the appearance several weeks ago, Hinkley had her clerk call all of the other matters on her calendar before Carter Drake's. Jaywalker had no way of knowing whether the order reflected the age of the cases, deference to the media, a flair for the dramatic, or a perverse desire to keep him waiting as long as she could. Some judges welcome "visiting" lawyers warmly; others seem threatened to the point of open hostility. Travis Hinkley made no secret as to which camp she belonged to.

As he waited, Jaywalker took the measure of his adversary. Jaywalker's expectations and the real thing matched up pretty well. Abe Firestone was a human bowling ball, barely five feet tall and nearly as wide. He squinted out at the world through thick glasses. What was left of his hair was gray. His suit was a three-piece relic from the previous millennium. And he had *feisty* written all over him.

"Call the murder case," the judge finally said, around a quarter of twelve, when there was nothing else left to call.

They brought Drake in through a side door. Again he was handcuffed behind his back, though the leg irons had disappeared. Still, Jaywalker made no complaint. This was the judge's courtroom, after all, and he wasn't about to hand her any easy victories.

"I have your motion papers," she said. "You'll receive my decision within ten business days. May I assume there has been an adequate exchange of discovery between the parties?"

In a criminal case, an *exchange of discovery between the parties* is a misnomer. The defense is required to notify the prosecution of only two things—any alibi witnesses it intends to call at trial, and whether it plans on raising a psychiatric defense—neither of which had any application to Drake's case. The prosecution, on the other hand, is obligated to turn over all sorts of things: scientific reports, photographs, diagrams, drawings, maps and sketches, as well as exculpatory material, anything tending to demonstrate the defendant's innocence.

"I'm afraid," said Jaywalker, "that that would be an unwarranted assumption."

"Well, why don't you serve a Demand to Produce on Mr. Firestone's office?" said the judge, the way you might tell a recalcitrant toddler that he has to finish his string beans if he has any hope of getting dessert.

"I did," said Jaywalker. "Two weeks ago."

"And? Are you certain you haven't received Mr. Firestone's reply?"

Not "How about that, Mr. Firestone?" or "Why

haven't you given the defense even the bare minimum it's entitled to?" Instead, she was continuing to grill Jaywalker, as though he was the one who'd been dragging his feet. And when Jaywalker did nothing but smile at the absurdity of the judge's misplaced anger, her face reddened visibly.

"Well?" she demanded.

"To be truthful," said Jaywalker in a matter-of-fact voice, without the least edge to it, "the only reply I've received from Mr. Firestone is that for all he cares, I can go shit in my hat."

There are quiet courtrooms, and there are quiet courtrooms. For a full ten seconds it was as though everyone assembled—and counting court officials, interested onlookers and the media, the number had to be well over a hundred—fully expected a bolt of lightning to pierce the vaulted ceiling and strike Jaywalker dead on the spot.

But nothing happened.

Except that Justice Hinkley rolled her eyes upward, almost imperceptibly. Had he not been looking directly at her, in fact, Jaywalker would never have noticed.

"Please come up," she said.

Up at the bench, Jaywalker fully expected to be held in contempt. Not that it would be the first time, or the last. Still, even he would be forced to admit it was a bad start, even if all he'd done was to tell the truth.

"You're lucky," said the judge. She kept her voice low and under control, so that those in the audience couldn't hear. But the result, whether intentional or inadvertent, was that her words came out more softly, and not merely in terms of decreased volume. "I might not have believed you," she continued, "but over the years, I've become familiar with some of Mr. Firestone's, shall we say, more charming expressions."

Jaywalker exhaled.

Judge Hinkley turned to the D.A. "What's the problem here, Abe?"

"The problem," said Firestone, barely able to disguise his anger, "is that this son-of-a-bitch defendant murdered eight of our innocent kids and one adult, for good measure. The problem is that because of our goddamn bleeding-heart Court of Appeals, we no longer have a death penalty for the likes of him. So here's what I'm going to do. I'm going to convict him of nine counts of murder, and then you're going to give him... What's nine times twenty-five?"

"Two hundred and twenty-five," said Jaywalker, having done the math himself some time ago.

"Two hundred and twenty-five years to life."

"And the way you propose to do that," said the judge, "is to withhold discovery from the defense, so Mr. Jaywalker here, who they tell me is a pretty smart lawyer, can go to the Appellate Division and get all those convictions reversed?"

Firestone emitted what was either a grunt or the last remains of something he'd eaten for breakfast.

"Give him what he's entitled to," said the judge. "And do it today, okay?"

Grunt.

"Now," she continued, "are we going to need any pretrial hearings?"

"There were no statements made by the defendant," said Firestone, "and no physical evidence seized from him. But there was a lineup."

This came as news to Jaywalker, something else Drake hadn't bothered to mention. "People from the End Zone?" he asked the D.A.

"Do I have to tell him?" Firestone was looking at the judge for help.

"Abe."

Grunt, grunt.

Evidently one was for yes, two for no.

"Abe."

"No, I said. Not the End Zone witnesses. The *eye*witness, the guy in the pickup truck." Then, turning to Jaywalker for the first time, he snarled, "And you're not entitled to his name until trial."

Which was technically true, but a curious battle to pick. The guy's name had been all over the newspapers. He'd been interviewed by Matt Lauer, for God's sake. Even now, Nicky Legs, Jaywalker's investigator, was out looking for him, in order to pin him down on his story.

"Positive ID?" the judge was asking Firestone.

"Absolutely."

"So we'll have a Wade hearing," said Hinkley. "I've read the minutes of the grand jury testimony, and it was more than legally sufficient to sustain the indictment. And as far as your motion for a change of venue, Mr. Jaywalker, you can renew that during jury selection if you like. But off the record, we're trying this case right here in Rockland County, where it happened. We'll let a few weeks go by so everyone can calm down. When can you gentlemen be ready?"

"The People are ready for trial today," boomed Firestone, loud enough to reach the far corners of the courtroom.

"No, you're not," said the judge, motioning the lawyers to step back. "Not until you've given the defense everything it's entitled to. Understood?"

Grunt.

"Anything else?"

"Yes," said Jaywalker. "I have an application."

"If it's about a bail reduction," said the judge, "forget about it. This is a murder case, and bail is discretionary. If you ask me—"

Jaywalker raised a hand high enough to get her attention, but no more. That red hair scared him.

"—your client's lucky to have *any* bail."

"It's not about bail," said Jaywalker. Not anymore it wasn't, anyway. But there was still his second application.

"What is it, then?"

"My application is for what's commonly called a gag order. I'm sure the court and both sides want a fair trial, uninfluenced by any outside comments made or leaked by the parties."

"Mr. Firestone?" said the judge. They were standing back from the bench now, and *Abe* had given way to *Mr. Firestone.*

"I take that personally!" he shouted. "And I oppose it vigorously. The press has a right to report the facts, and the people of Rockland County and the world have a right to know the facts."

Jaywalker had to hand it to the guy, getting all wound up over a gag order. Even if he had managed to exclude his county from the rest of the planet.

"Facts—" Jaywalker began, but this time it was the judge who raised a hand.

"Facts they may report," she said, completing Jaywalker's sentence for him. "I have no power over the press, or the people of the world you mentioned in your little speech, Mr. Firestone. But that speech is precisely the reason I'm going to grant Mr. Jaywalker's application. Effective immediately, neither side—and that includes any and all police agencies involved in the case—shall issue or permit the issuance of any statement, comment, remark or leaked material of any sort. Do I make myself clear?"

"Yes," said Jaywalker.

"Yes," muttered Firestone.

"Anything else?"

There was nothing else.

"The case is adjourned to September 5," said Justice Hinkley, "for hearing and trial. Nice meeting you, Mr. Jaywalker."

"Nice meeting you, too, Your Honor."

So Jaywalker left the courthouse that day with a trial date, three cartons of discovery material and a few new insights into how justice would operate in New City.

For starters, Abe Firestone, once you got to know him, was even worse than imagined. Despite Justice Hinkley's order, he still refused to meet with Jaywalker, instead delegating a low-level assistant to turn over the cartons of material. Worse yet, whether by design or not, he picked an octogenarian woman assistant with a bad back, so Jaywalker had to make three separate trips from the D.A.'s office to the parking lot.

But Jaywalker had hardly been surprised by the D.A.'s antics. When somebody starts off a professional relationship by suggesting that you should go shit in your hat, your expectations tend to be modest, at best. Not that Firestone had disappointed. Pretty much everything out of his mouth, grunts included, had been gruff, angry and obnoxious. Jaywalker had been up against old-school street brawlers before. It was never fun, but it did have one saving virtue. It would allow Jaywalker to take off the gloves and fight back. Allow it? It would *require* it. And sometimes that could be fun.

But no, Abe Firestone had been no surprise.

Travis Hinkley had been the surprise. Smart, quick-witted, focused on the issues and, above all, strong enough to keep from getting steamrolled by the likes of Firestone. In an absurd hurry to move the case to trial, but Jaywalker would figure out a way to slow her down.

He was good at stuff like that. The question of whether they could get a fair trial from her, given the hugely lopsided equities of the case, remained to be answered. Jaywalker hadn't much cared for her little speech about bail, which had been an almost verbatim reprise of the previous judge's comments. But he could only imagine what would have happened if she'd lowered the bail, and Drake got out and killed another nine people. Forget her judgeship; there'd be no place on earth safe for her. So he could understand that, and he'd already told his client to accept it and get used to his new home.

"Can you get me a quick trial?" Drake had asked him some time ago, prompting Jaywalker to give him a short tutorial on the magical healing powers of delay. But at least for the moment, it looked as though Drake might well get his wish.

The morning's court appearance had been brief but instructive. In addition to serving as an introduction to the major players, it had produced a good ninety pounds of reading material, which, it turned out, the D.A.'s office had boxed up several days ago, apparently figuring that single act fulfilled their obligation to turn it over to the defense. And Jaywalker had even learned a few things about the case. As he'd expected, because Carter Drake had turned himself in, there'd been no physical evidence seized from him, and following his lawyer's advice he'd made no admissions or confessions. But there had been a lineup, at which the driver of the pickup truck, the same guy who'd recognized the make of Drake's Audi and remembered part of its plate number, had picked him out. That was a surprise in itself, given Jaywalker's own recent experience with headlights and night blindness. But equally surprising was the fact that neither Drake nor either of his previous lawyers had mentioned it. Chester Ludlow had surrendered Drake. That meant there was a lawyer in the case, a lawyer who had a right to be notified by the police or the prosecution that a lineup was going to be held, and provided a reasonable opportunity to attend and observe it. Had Judah Mermelstein taken over from Ludlow by the time the lineup took place? If so, had he been alerted? Had he witnessed it? Did he even know about it?

The discovery material would no doubt provide Jaywalker with some answers, or at least give him a few clues.

What the discovery material actually provided Jaywalker with was a monumental headache, and an awareness that Abe Firestone, for all his bluster and buffoonery, had a shrewd side to him.

Despite the fact that it had taken Jaywalker three trips to load the cartons into his car, and another three to haul them up to his apartment, he'd been consoled by the fact that there was such a volume of material. New York law carefully spelled out the things the prosecution was required to turn over to the defense at this early stage of the proceedings, and the list excluded not only the names of witnesses Firestone intended to call at trial, but any prior statements those witnesses had made regarding the substance of their testimony, whether written, recorded, or uttered in front of the grand jury. Those statements, which normally made up the vast majority of discovery material, didn't have to be turned over until the trial had actually begun, with the selection of a jury.

Yet here Firestone had put together no less than three full cartons of stuff. To Jaywalker, that had to mean one of two things. Either the D.A. didn't know the law and had included witnesses' statements through ignorance, or there was an awful lot of other relevant stuff for Jaywalker to sift through and exploit.

Neither turned out to be the case.

Barely twenty minutes into the process, he realized what Firestone had done. He'd crammed the boxes full of multiple copies of wordy documents that bore little or no relevance to the case. He'd included, for example, more than five hundred photocopied pages of excerpts from the Vehicle and Traffic Law, pages that Jaywalker could have read from his own copy. Then there were lengthy accounts of the nine funerals of the victims, copies of every newspaper item that even mentioned the case, as well as many that didn't. There were redundant printouts of the penal law sections charged in the indictment, and long court decisions that touched only tangentially on some of the issues likely to be raised at trial.

Even worse, none of these documents were bound, stapled or even paper-clipped together. Instead, their pages had been stuffed into the boxes almost haphazardly, as if the only concern had been making them fit. There'd been absolutely no regard to keeping them in order, or to separating them from the pages of other documents.

Jaywalker had been bombarded with garbage.

But why?

Was Firestone so perverse that he took delight from a schoolboy's dirty trick? Would he spend his weekend laughing at the thought of his adversary poring over mounds of paper, only to discover that every last sheet of it was totally worthless?

Jaywalker thought not. *Dumb like a fox* was the expression that kept coming back to him. So he gritted his teeth, cleared as large a section of his floor as the dimensions of his apartment allowed, and began sorting. It infuriated him and took him well past midnight, but in the end he was left with twelve piles of pages stacked against one wall. Eleven of the stacks were taller than they were wide, and were largely worthless. But then there was the twelfth stack, though in its case, *stack* would have been a misnomer, since it contained only four sheets of paper.

Once, more years ago than he cared to admit, Jaywalker and his wife and daughter, who'd been a toddler at the time, had panned for gold. They'd done it as a lark, stopping at a roadside tourist attraction by a Colorado creek and paying fifty dollars against a promise that they could keep all the gold they found. The operator had known what he was doing, of course. At the end of two hours, their backs ached and their sifting pans had yielded maybe a dozen tiny grains of what might or might not have been the real thing. Had they lumped them all together, they might have had enough for a dental filling, provided the cavity was a small one. The only certainty, in fact, was that they were fifty bucks poorer.

Except for one thing.

Jaywalker's daughter, now a grown woman with children of her own, had every one of those grains to this day. She'd kept them in a tiny glass vial, absolutely convinced they were treasure. She'd found them panning for gold in the Rockies, after all, with her mother, who was now long gone, and her father, who'd been absent too often, off in a place they called Court.

The four sheets of paper were Jaywalker's treasure. He'd panned for them as surely as he and his little family had panned for gold that long-ago afternoon in the Colorado sun. Abe Firestone and his staff had gone to considerable lengths to hide them, burying them deep among the mud and silt. The only conceivable reason they would have done that was to keep Jaywalker from discovering them and realizing that they were pure gold.

12

NIRVANA

Over the next two weeks, Jaywalker busied himself preparing for Carter Drake's hearing and trial. Not that he expected it to begin the first week of September, or any week of September, for that matter. No judge, not even Travis Hinkley, would push a murder case to trial within three months of the arrest over the objection of the defense. Maybe in Yemen or Bangladesh or Texas. But not in New York. Not even in Rockland County.

Then again, there was a first time for everything.

He started by checking in with Nicolo LeGrosso. Nicky reported that he'd located Firestone's eyewitness, the guy who'd been driving the pickup truck.

"Guy's name is Concepción Testigo," said Nicky. "He's a P.R." Which, Jaywalker was pretty sure, meant neither public relations nor press release. "I made like I was Spanish myself, and we hit it off pretty good. By the way, you'll never guess what his name means in English."

"I give up," said Jaywalker.

"Get this," said Nicky. "*Born to testify*. Cool, huh?"

Jaywalker, who knew enough Spanish to know Nicky was stretching things, chose not to argue the point. "So what did he say?" he asked.

"Guy says he didn't get that good a look at the driver. He couldn't describe him at the scene or anythin' like that."

"According to the D.A.," said Jaywalker, "he picked Drake out in a lineup."

"Yeah, but that was like a week after the arrest. By that time, the guy's face was all ovuh the news."

"And had Testigo seen it?"

"Oh, yeah," said Nicky. "Though before he tole me that, he looked around all suspicious like, an' ast if we was talkin' off the record."

"And you said?"

"I said sure, off the record."

Jaywalker smiled. Not the most ethical tactic on Nicky's part, perhaps. But when you were defending someone on a murder charge, there were ethics and there were ethics. "How about the accident itself?" he asked. "Did he see what happened?"

"You betta believe it," said LeGrosso. "Says our guy was goin' way ovuh the limit, right smack in the middle'a the wrong lane. Van nevuh had a snowball's chance."

"Like *steady* in the wrong lane, or just for a moment?"

"He din' ezzackly use the word *steady*," said Nicky. "But he made it pretty clear that it was no momentary thing."

LeGrosso had also tried to interview Eric, the Drakes' seventeen-year-old son. Jaywalker wanted Eric's take on just how drunk his father had seemed that night before driving off. But Eric had apparently been avoiding Nicky.

"Kid's a ballbuster," he explained. "I set up three meets wid him. Two of 'em he cancels, an' the third time he's a no-show."

"Probably doesn't want to rat out his old man," said Jaywalker. "Leave him alone. I'll see if I can work on his mother."

"I bet you will," said Nicky.

* * *

Twice Jaywalker cranked up the Mercury and drove up to New City to spend some more time talking with his client. Yes, Drake confirmed, he had been placed in a lineup. It had taken place a week or so after he'd surrendered. No lawyer had been present. The fill-ins had all been cops, all white guys, but almost all of them were considerably younger than he was. He had no idea who'd been on the other side of the mirrored glass they were told to face, and had no way of knowing if he'd been identified or not.

"Have you put in a speedy trial motion for me?" Drake wanted to know.

"We've got a trial date less than a month away," Jaywalker reminded him. He didn't mention that that was still much too soon, as far as he was concerned.

"Have you ever been in jail?" Drake asked pointedly.

"Yes, as a matter of fact. Several times."

"What was the longest?"

Jaywalker caught himself trying to remember, then decided it was none of Drake's business. "What's the problem?" he asked. "Specifically. Other inmates? The guards?"

It was nothing like that, said Drake. It was boredom, extreme boredom. "What am I supposed to do, *read* all day?"

Heaven forbid.

"Look," said Jaywalker. "I feel for you, I really do. But the next twenty-five years of your life are hanging in the balance here. Your wife didn't hire me just to try your case. She hired me to *win* it, if that's possible. So if it takes another six months of your sitting in this place to give us a fighting chance, you're going to sit."

"There's no way I can do another six months."

Which reminded Jaywalker of the old story about the

judge who's just finished sentencing a defendant to seventy-five years in prison. "There's no way on earth I can do seventy-five years," moans the defendant.

"Do as much as you can," says the judge.

And on one of his trips to New City, Jaywalker actually sat down with Abe Firestone and had something that vaguely resembled a civil conversation. He wanted to know if there was any chance the case could be resolved with a plea bargain.

Not that Drake had pushed for the meeting or anything like that. The truth was, he didn't even know about it, and no doubt would have objected to it had he been consulted. But Jaywalker had long felt that one of his many obligations as a defense lawyer was to explore the subject of an offer, a plea to a lesser charge that carried a lighter sentence. Then he'd convey that offer to his client, along with his own recommendation. The defendant, of course, was free to accept it or reject it. It was his case, after all, and his time to serve.

Jaywalker had phoned Firestone's office two days earlier and made an appointment, an act that all by itself took twenty-five minutes. Once he showed up at the designated time and place, he got to wait another forty minutes, filling the time thumbing through ancient issues of *People* magazine, the *Rockland County Pennysaver* and the *New York State Police Bulletin*. Then he was ushered into a conference room where, after an additional ten minutes of waiting, Firestone and two aides finally joined him. One was a nerdy-looking guy who took notes, the other a pretty, young woman who smiled a lot. Neither of them said a word the entire time.

"What can I do for you?" Firestone asked. No "Hello," no "How are you?" No handshake, no introductions, no small talk. Just, "What can I do for you?"

"Hello," said Jaywalker. Sort of like the way he'd say "You're welcome" when someone he'd held a door open for neglected to thank him.

Grunt.

Noted.

Smile.

"I was wondering," said Jaywalker, "if you intend to make my client an offer of any sort."

"An offer. You mean like a *plea bargain?*" Firestone spat out the words as though he were talking about a plague, or an unmentionable body function.

Jaywalker nodded.

"Yeah," said Firestone. "He can plead to the murder count, and we won't oppose the minimum, if the judge wants to be a pussy."

This was ice in the winter. The minimum on the murder charge was fifteen to life, and the judge was free to impose it, with or without the D.A.'s opposition.

"That's it?"

"Yeah, that's it. And after trial, all bets are off, and I'll be demanding twenty-five to life. And I'll get it, too. You'll see."

Jaywalker stood up and kindly thanked the three of them for their time.

Justice Hinkley's decision arrived in the mail. As expected, she'd found the evidence presented to the grand jury sufficient, and had ordered a Wade hearing to test the fairness of the lineup. When it came to Jaywalker's motion for a change of venue to someplace other than Rockland County, she'd been smart enough not to deny it outright, a ruling that might have been questioned on appeal. Instead, she'd reserved decision, stating that she'd wait until they were into jury selection to see if it was possible to find people unaffected by the publicity the case had instigated.

If that sounded promising, it wasn't. It was a time-honored dodge. Even though the community had been inflamed by the loss of its children and infected by calls for their killer's scalp, there'd be more than enough prospective jurors who would insist they could still give him a fair trial. Some of them would be flat-out lying, of course, while others would be guilty only of vastly overestimating their capacity for objectivity. A few might even be up to the task, but only a few. Getting an impartial jury for Carter Drake in Rockland County was going to be something like getting an impartial jury for Adolf Eichmann in Tel Aviv.

In mid-August, with the hearing and trial scheduled to begin in three weeks, Jaywalker sat down at his computer and composed a one-page letter to Justice Hinkley. In it he stated that despite his very best efforts, there was no way the defense could possibly be ready by September 5, or any time in September, for that matter. He sent the letter off by Priority Mail, and a copy of it to the district attorney's office. That one he sent by regular mail. As far as Jaywalker was concerned, forty-four cents was already far too much to spend on Abe Firestone.

It took only a day and a half for a response. It came in the form of a phone call from Hinkley's law clerk, an earnest-sounding young man. "The judge would like to meet with the lawyers as soon as possible," he said. "She wants to know if you can be at her chambers tomorrow morning, at nine o'clock sharp."

"Let me check," said Jaywalker.

A glance at his calendar revealed that the only date circled other than September 5 was January 14 of next year, his granddaughter's birthday.

"I believe I can make it," he said.

* * *

They met around a polished wooden table in the library that was part of the judge's chambers. It put anything Jaywalker had ever seen at 100 Centre Street to shame. As he had been at their meeting, Firestone was flanked by his twin bodyguards, Nerd Man and Smile Woman. The judge began the meeting by reading Jaywalker's letter aloud so that a court reporter could take it down on a stenotype machine. As soon as she got to the part about the defense not being able to be ready, Firestone shouted, "I object!" and followed it up with, "The People are ready for trial."

"Relax, Abe," she said. "There's no audience here."

"There should be," said Firestone. "This should be done in open court."

"The People's objection is noted," said Hinkley. "Mr. Jaywalker, would you care to tell the court precisely why you won't be ready to proceed?"

"I'd be delighted to," said Jaywalker, who'd actually come armed with a list of reasons scribbled on a crumpled sheet of paper. While none of them was terribly persuasive standing by itself, there were no less than eleven of them, twelve if you wanted to count *Come on, this a murder case, for crying out loud.* "But I'll only do so *ex parte.* My explanation will reveal confidential material and defense strategy, neither of which I'm either required or willing to share with the prosecution."

"Objection!" shouted Firestone, a vein throbbing visibly in his forehead.

"Sit down, Abe. You're going to hurt yourself."

"I want this all on the record!"

As the judge rose, she pointed at Jaywalker and the court reporter. "Come with me," she said. "The rest of you relax, chat among yourselves."

As soon as they were in Justice Hinkley's private

office, she took off her robe and lit a cigarette. "Terrible habit," she said, inhaling deeply. "Amy, you take a break," she told the court reporter, and the young lady took a seat, pulling a copy of *O Magazine* from her handbag.

So much for *on the record.*

The judge took another long drag of her cigarette before stubbing it out in an ashtray. "Disgusting," she muttered.

Jaywalker fought back a snort.

"So," she said, "I gather you need the witness."

"Excuse me?"

"You heard me."

"I heard you," said Jaywalker. "I just didn't think you were old enough to know the expression." *He* was, though. He'd heard it early on in his career, almost always from an old-timer. He *needed the witness,* he'd tell the judge, when he couldn't go to trial because he hadn't been paid the balance of his fee yet. And if the judge was too young or too slow to catch on, the lawyer would clue him in him by supplying the witness's name, which almost always turned out to be Mr. Green. Though Jaywalker had heard Mr. Franklin's name come up once or twice, as well as Mr. Grant's.

"I'm a lot older than you are," said the judge.

"I'll bet you're not," said Jaywalker, fishing into his pocket for a Samoan penny. He had more than his share of vices, but high-stakes gambling wasn't among them.

"I'm afraid you're going to have to take my word on this one," said the judge. "My *husband* doesn't know how old I am, and we've been married...a long time. Anyway, why didn't you just tell me what the problem was? I was in practice once myself."

Jaywalker hesitated for just a moment. The truth was, he didn't need the witness at all. Amanda Drake had already paid him more than half his fee, and he had no worries about the balance. And he hated the idea of being lumped together with a bunch of incompetent hacks whose chief concern was collecting their fees. But he knew that judges were lawyers, and that this particular judge had just gone out of her way to tell him that she understood his predicament. In other words, it was easier for her to empathize with a lawyer who needed to be paid than it was for her to understand a lawyer who needed to win.

A Jaywalker.

So he swallowed his pride and let it go.

"Look," she was telling him, "we both know the Appellate Division wouldn't have let me force you to trial over your objection. I was simply testing you. A lesser lawyer would have whined like a baby in court when I set the date. You didn't do that. You did it the right way." And here she picked up the letter he'd sent her and waved it in the air.

"We're going to have a fun trial, Mr. Jaywalker, you and I. And when it's over, and the jury has convicted your client, I'm going to give him twenty-five to life. Not a day less. You I like. Him, he's a worthless piece of shit. Now, when can you be ready for trial?"

"I've got a commitment January 14," he said. "I can be ready anytime after that."

"Fair enough," said the judge, glancing at a wall calendar. "January 20, hearing and trial. And…"

"Yes?"

"That's it. Before I grant the defense another adjournment, I'll need a certified copy of a death certificate, with your name on the top of it. Do we understand each other?"

"We do."

Jaywalker would have loved to see the look on Abe

Firestone's face when he learned of the new date, but the pleasure was not to be his. Justice Hinkley instructed him to leave by a side door. "You go home," she told him. "I'll deal with Napoleon."

Still, he sang halfway home, and when he ran out of voice, he whistled the rest of the way. Even to a normal person, receiving permission to put off an unpleasant ordeal for five months is welcome news. For a certified procrastinator, it's nothing short of Nirvana.

13

But Jaywalker's reprieve would prove short-lived.

It had been one thing to put off working on a case back when he'd had others to turn his attention to. But this time there weren't any others. Still, there was everything else to distract him. There were his daughter and her family to visit in New Jersey. There was the baseball season, suddenly getting interesting with the Yankees and the Red Sox battling it out in the Eastern Division. Football was right around the corner, and the Giants were considered a likely contender for a playoff spot. Meanwhile, the days were still warm, and long walks in the park beckoned. There were a couple of books he'd looked forward to reading, and some writing of his own he wanted to get back to. And chances were there'd be some good movies on late-night TV.

Yet it took him only two days to realize that none of those things, nor all of them combined, were going to fill the void created by the postponement Justice Hinkley had granted him. His daughter was busy with other stuff, and his granddaughters barely knew him. The Yankees were slumping, and the Giants were already suffering from training camp injuries. The park, he found, had been taken over by children, nannies, dog walkers and lovers. Reading made him fall asleep. Writing went badly. And every movie on TV seemed targeted at an audience of fourteen-year-olds. So who was he trying to kid with this *Thank-God-I've-got-all-this-free-time-on-my-hands* routine? The truth was, not only did he have no other cases to occupy his attention, he had no life, either.

Well, he had Amanda, a night or two a week. But while the sex was good, the guilt hovered over him like a stranger in the room. If she sensed it, and she must have, she never spoke of it, so neither did he. And while he never quite ended his visits to her apartment—for they never dared go outside—they became less frequent, and less fulfilling.

When he caught himself reaching for a bottle of Kahlúa one night, he pulled his hand back no less quickly than if he'd reached into a live fire. "Enough!" he shouted, the sound of his own voice echoing in his empty apartment startling him. "Enough," he repeated, more softly, but every bit as firmly. Then he took a deep breath, walked the length of the room, and stopped when he got to the door of his closet.

Procrastination might temporarily have had him in her grasp, he knew. But when it came right down to it, she was no match at all for her rival. That rival didn't have a grasp, she had a death grip. Growing up, Jaywalker had had an older cousin on his father's side, a scary-looking woman named Dorothy, who spent her days sweeping up invisible dust and rearranging the books on her shelves by color, size, alphabetical order or copyright date. He thought of her whenever he was forced to take stock of his demons. "Old Cousin Dorothy's got a hold of me," he used to tell his wife. Since her death, it had become his own private joke, one he never explained to anyone. The joke was in her initials, which stood for an undiagnosed but nevertheless full-blown case of obsessive-compulsive disorder. Jaywalker's particular strain of OCD was like no one else's he knew. It didn't force him to wash his hands fifty times a day, or vacuum his apartment incessantly, or repeatedly check the locks on the doors of his car before he could walk away from it. It didn't compel him to make sure each letter he inserted into a mailbox actually obeyed the laws of gravity and dropped safely downward. It would not have required him to line up the knives, forks and spoons separately and just so in a dishwasher, had he happened to own one.

No, Jaywalker's OCD manifested itself in a unique and singular way. It drove him—and *drove* doesn't even begin to tell the story here—to prepare and overprepare and over-overprepare, until he knew everything there was to know about a case, forwards and backwards, inside out and upside down. One colleague, who'd tried a six-week multiple-defendant case alongside him, had come away from the experience shaking his head in wonderment and disbelief. "It's not like he walks into court better prepared than anyone else, myself included. He walks in *a hundred times* better prepared."

Now Jaywalker turned the knob of the closet door, reached into the darkness and withdrew the file. It was only three inches thick at this point, and light enough to lift easily with one hand. But over time it would double in size and weight, and then spawn another dozen like it. He looked down at the label, read his own carefully printed words. *The People of the State of New York vs Carter Drake III.* It was time to get to work.

His procrastination had lasted all of four days.

Although he'd done little more than spend a couple of hours reading and rereading the file, the exercise had served to break the ice, always the hardest part. The rest would fall into place, Jaywalker knew; it always did. The next morning he took a drive up to New City, for another meeting with his client.

He found Drake sullen and uncommunicative. The reason soon became clear.

"Not only didn't you press for a speedy trial, you went and put my case off for five months!"

"Four and a half," said Jaywalker. "Actually, even a bit less than that."

"Don't you get it? I'm going *nuts* in here. I've got nothing to do. And I can't make a living sitting in a *cage*."

"Sorry," said Jaywalker. He decided to spare Carter the lecture about the need for preparation and the importance of the passage of time in calming the community's anger. He realized he was beginning to truly dislike the man, and that was bad. Not in and of itself, there being no requirement that he and his client be buddies. No, it was bad because if Jaywalker didn't like Drake, chances were the jurors wouldn't, either. And a jury that disliked a defendant would find it that much easier to convict him.

"I met with the D.A.," said Jaywalker.

"That clown?"

"He refuses to offer you anything less than the murder charge. Though he says he'd be okay with the minimum sentence."

"Which is…?"

"Fifteen to life."

Drake laughed. But it was a bitter, snorting laugh. A dislikable laugh. "Who told you to ask him?" he wanted to know.

"Nobody," said Jaywalker. "It's part of my job. Just as it's part of my job to communicate his response to you."

"Do me a favor?"

Jaywalker nodded tentatively.

"Don't go begging for me. Not to the D.A., not to the judge. I want a trial, *T-R-I-A-L.* Is there any part of that word you don't understand?"

Dislikable? Try *loathsome.*

"Okay," said Jaywalker, doing his best to ignore the sarcasm. "And at that trial, would you like to take the witness stand?"

"Of course I would. Who else is going to explain what caused the accident?"

"You mean the wasp?"

"Exactly," said Drake.

Jaywalker filled him in on what Concepción Testigo had told Nicolo LeGrosso, that the car had stayed in the wrong lane for quite some time. "The wasp, in other words, may not fly."

"He's lying," said Drake. "It was a momentary thing. I was there."

"What about your wife?"

"What about her?"

"Would you like her to testify?"

"About what? What could she say?"

"That you didn't seem drunk to her? That you were able to start your car without any apparent difficulty, and pull out of the parking lot smoothly? That for as long as she followed you, you weren't speeding or weaving or anything like that?"

"I guess so."

"And your son?" Jaywalker asked.

"Leave him out of it."

"Why?"

"What could he add?"

"That he offered to drive your car, but you wouldn't let him."

"He's only seventeen," said Drake. "All he's got is a learner's permit that's no good after dark."

"Exactly," said Jaywalker. "You were protecting him. The jurors may find it in their hearts to like you a little bit for that."

"What is this, a personality contest?"

"In a way."

"Can't I explain those things myself?"

"You can," Jaywalker conceded. "But we call that kind of testimony *self-serving*. It means more when someone else says it."

"Even my son?"

"Especially your son."

Drake seemed to think about that for a few seconds, before saying, "No, leave Eric out of it. He and I, we have issues. I don't trust him to be able to pull it off."

Jaywalker shrugged. There'd be plenty of time to revisit the matter, he knew. Still, it was a curious position for Drake to take. Here he had two witnesses who were in a position to help him, if only tangentially. One he was lukewarm about, the other adamantly negative.

Was it possible, Jaywalker found himself wondering on the drive home, that Carter Drake was in a hurry to go to trial and not looking for help because he was so consumed with guilt that he wanted to be convicted? If so, that would be a first for Jaywalker. Sure, back in his Legal Aid days he'd stood up for a wino or two who'd requested a couple of nights in jail to dry out, and a homeless guy who'd copped out to ninety days one December, just so they'd send him to Rikers Island and give him "three hots and a cot" till the worst of winter was over. But twenty-five to life? Nobody wanted that kind of time. Nobody but a total lunatic.

"I need to talk with Eric."

"I thought Carter said to leave him out of it."

"He did," said Jaywalker. "That's why I need to talk with him."

They were sitting in her hot tub, or Jacuzzi, or whatever the thing was called. It took up half her bathroom, held about fifty thousand gallons of water, and had more jets than Boeing. But it did wonderful things to Amanda's nipples, which in turn did wonderful things to Jaywalker.

"He's off at school," said Amanda. She explained that Eric was on his sixth high school in as many years. This particular one was a boarding school up in Massachusetts. It was what they called an *alternative* school, she said, leaving it at that.

"It's still August," Jaywalker pointed out.

"They start early."

"When will he be home next?"

Amanda shrugged. "*Home* is something of a flexible concept for Eric," she said. "At any given time, it might mean here, or his father's apartment, or his grandmother's, or any of several friends with kindhearted parents."

"What I mean is, when will he be physically in the city, so I can meet with him?"

"Thanksgiving? Christmas, more likely."

Which would be three weeks before trial. "How long does it take to drive up there?" he asked.

"Two and a half, three hours. But they don't allow visitors."

Jaywalker frowned. "Just how alternative is this school?" he asked.

"Let me put it this way," said Amanda. "It was that or a secure juvenile facility until his twenty-first birthday. Okay?"

"Okay."

"Now *I* have a question," said Amanda.

Jaywalker waited.

"Is that some kind of periscope you've got there? Or are you trying to tell me you're in the mood again?"

A week later, Nicolo LeGrosso showed up at Jaywalker's apartment with a thick packet of medical records. He'd subpoenaed three physicians, two emergency rooms, a walk-in clinic and a pharmacy. They in turn had supplied him with over a hundred pages of documents attesting to the fact that Carter Drake III was indeed highly allergic to insect stings and would go into full anaphylactic shock unless treated promptly with epinephrine, better known as adrenaline. One of Drake's doctors had prescribed an EpiPen for him, a self-contained device he was to keep with him at all times in case of emergency.

"Good stuff," said Jaywalker. "Anybody willing to testify?" Getting a doctor to show up in court, he knew, was a little bit like getting a cat to show up for a bath.

"Yeah," said LeGrosso. "The guy who wrote the scrip for the works."

Nicky tended to talk like the ex-detective he was, at least when he was in the company of a former DEA agent. A *scrip* was a prescription, a *set of works* a junkie's tools for injecting himself.

"Said he'll need three large for half a day," LeGrosso added.

And *three large* was what it sounded like, three thousand dollars. Not too shabby for a few hours spent in court. But even at that rate, it would be worth it. There were times when it paid to be rich, Jaywalker knew, and standing trial on a murder charge was definitely one of those times.

The following day Jaywalker received an envelope containing a written solicitation from a firm that specialized in assisting lawyers—*attorneys,* it called them—with jury selection. For a "reasonable fee," which worked out to just under twenty-five hundred dollars a day plus expenses, the firm promised to create a profile of the "ideal juror" Jaywalker should be looking for to sit on Carter Drake's trial, and then to supply an "experienced consultant" to sit with him at the defense table during jury selection, also at twenty-five hundred dollars a day.

Jaywalker had by that time given considerable thought to just what kind of jury he wanted, and the answer was as alarming as it was elusive.

Normally he looked for racial minorities, blacks and Hispanics. Over the years he'd found them to be distrustful of cops and prone to identify with defendants. But there were precious few of either group in Rockland County, and fewer still who voted, owned a home or registered a vehicle there, the three things that would qualify them for jury service.

His other favorite demographic was young people. They tended to be idealistic, and not yet cynical about crime and criminals. But Abe Firestone—who, like Jaywalker would have twenty peremptory challenges to play with—wasn't going to let anyone under forty on the jury if he could help it.

Next came Jews, whom Jaywalker considered compassionate and forgiving. Maybe it was something about their collective history of persecution. Whatever it was, all things being equal, he'd take a Jew any day over an Irishman, a German or an Asian. Except in this case, of course, where the victims were Jewish, the prosecutor was Jewish, and the defendant had already been unfavorably compared to Hitler.

Women, he'd found, were generally preferable to men. They tended to be softer, more sympathetic, less prone to anger. But in this case, women were actually problematic. Every one of those eight dead children had a grieving mother, and in a close community like New City, there would hardly be a woman who wouldn't know someone directly affected by the tragedy.

Teachers, social workers and nurses made up another good group. They'd sacrificed big paychecks in order to join the ranks of the helping professionals, dedicating their efforts to the young, the needy and the ailing. But here again, the nature of the case stood conventional logic on its head. Young, needy and ailing didn't describe the defendant. It described the victims and their loved ones.

Carter Drake was a rich, unlikable, forty-four-year-old, non-Jewish man whose reckless conduct and depraved indifference had led directly to nine deaths, eight of them young Jewish children. There simply *was* no ideal juror for him. Chances were, there weren't even any *acceptable* jurors for him. But Jaywalker didn't need to pay anybody twenty-five hundred dollars a day to sit next to him and tell him he should be looking for young, childless, black Muslim soup-kitchen volunteers who'd just arrived in New City on a spaceship from Mars. He put the solicitation back into its envelope and tossed it into the trash.

Which was right around when a thought occurred to him. How about no jurors at all? What if he—with Drake's agreement, of course—were to waive a jury altogether, and take his chances with a bench trial?

He'd done so before, with almost uniformly good results. But in many of those cases he'd been prompted by a judge who'd let on that he or she didn't think much of the prosecution's case. Or he'd known the judge well enough to peg him or her as someone who'd be inclined to give the defendant the benefit of the doubt. While that was something the law actually demanded of all *finders of the facts,* meaning jurors and judges alike, there were plenty of judges out there who'd convict their own mothers, and then sentence them to the maximum.

So which category did Travis Hinkley fall into?

On the plus column, she'd struck Jaywalker as both smart and fair. She'd come right out and said she liked him, always an important consideration. And she seemed to have a limited tolerance for Abe Firestone. Finally, she wasn't Jewish, a fact that might insulate her just a tiny bit from the community's wrath.

But there was plenty in column B. She was Irish, and in Jaywalker's book, going non-jury in front of an Irish judge created a *prima facie* case of ineffective assistance of counsel. Next she'd not only expressed her dislike of the defendant, she'd promised to throw the book at him after he was convicted. Not *if* he was convicted, but *after*. Then there were the pure mathematics of the calculation: it would take twelve jurors to convict Drake, but only one judge. With a jury, Jaywalker could hope for a weirdo who'd hold out and hang the jury. But there was no such thing as a *hung judge,* so long as one were to discount the rumors about "Long John" McGrath. Finally, there was an appeal to consider. In a jury trial, all sorts of things could go wrong and lead to reversible error. But after a bench trial conviction, the appellate courts had little to look at, and less to second-guess.

So even without consulting his client, Jaywalker discarded the idea, just as he'd discarded the notion of a jury selection expert. Carter Drake would have a jury and, for better or for worse, Jaywalker would be the one to pick that jury.

Though exactly how, he had no idea.

September 5, which had once been their trial date, came and went. Jaywalker busied himself preparing for the Wade hearing, for jury selection, and for the trial itself. He drew up long lists of questions for potential jurors, aimed at disqualifying those who'd known the victims or were friendly with their parents, or were otherwise too close to the case to be impartial. He revisited the scene of the crash, taking photographs and measurements, from which he constructed poster-size blowups and diagrams. He met half a dozen times with his client, wrenching details from him and shaping them into a coherent direct examination, which Drake mastered effortlessly, yet somehow unconvincingly. Then Jaywalker would change his voice and do his best Abe Firestone imitation, putting Carter through a series of mock cross-examinations. He was alternately folksy, sarcastic and belligerent, but it didn't seem to make much of a difference. No matter which approach Jaywalker adopted, Drake did as poorly on cross as he did on direct. He met sarcasm with sarcasm, belligerence with belligerence, and folksiness with contempt.

"Carter," Jaywalker would point out, "you're going to make it very hard for the jurors to like you."

"I don't give a damn whether they like me or not," Drake would counter. "As long as they acquit me."

"And why should they do that?"

"Because I'm innocent!" Drake would shout. "Because I didn't murder anybody."

And Jaywalker would be forced to point out that even though he was inclined to agree, that left half a dozen other charges, from drunk driving to vehicular manslaughter to leaving the scene of an accident, any one of which would send Drake off to state prison, even if not for quite so long.

"I'm still pissed off at you," Drake would say.

"At me?"

"Yes."

"For what?"

"For postponing the trial without my permission."

And then they'd fight that battle all over again.

Amanda, on the other hand, would be a good witness. Jaywalker found her an easy study, quick to pick up hints without making him spell things out for her. There's a fine line between telling a witness what to say and telling her how to say it. The former is not only unethical, but can become downright criminal, as in *subornation of perjury*. The latter, teaching a witness how to best express herself, is not only permissible but is an important part of the defense lawyer's job. And anyone who doubts that needs to wake up and understand that across town—or, in this case, up in Rockland County— it's precisely what the prosecutors were no doubt already doing.

Although not nearly as well as Jaywalker.

September gave way to October, and October to November. Thanksgiving came, and Christmas, though for a very large segment of New City, it came early, lasted eight days, and went by the name Chanukah. With the crush of the holidays, the almost biblical commandment to shop, and the first flakes of snow, the case at last vanished from the newspapers and the airways. It would come back, Jaywalker knew only too well, but not with quite the same urgency and drive for vengeance. Carter Drake might not like the idea of spending New Year's Eve locked up in the Rockland County Jail, and he might hate Jaywalker for his role in ensuring that he did. But in the meantime, delay was quietly going about her business, applying salve to raw wounds and giving new tissue a chance to begin forming over deep scars.

14

HEADS I WIN, TAILS YOU LOSE

"Call your first witness on the Wade hearing, Mr. Firestone."

Firestone stood up, as best as Jaywalker could tell. At an even five feet, it was sometimes hard to be sure. "Mr. Kaminsky will be conducting the hearing," said the D.A., gesturing toward the nerdy assistant seated immediately to his left. David Kaminsky, Jaywalker had come to learn, had been recruited from the Appeals Division, just as Julie Napolitano, to Firestone's right, had been drafted from Special Victims. Kaminsky was what trial lawyers referred to as a "law man," someone short on presence but long on precedents. With no jury around to play to, it made perfect sense that for the hearing, Firestone would yield center stage to someone who actually had some idea of what he was doing.

"Mr. Kaminsky?" said Justice Hinkley.

The young man stood, pushing a bony finger against the bridge of his glasses so that they rode up his nose a bit, but just a bit. It was a gesture he would repeat a thousand or so times over the next three weeks. "Yes?" he said uncertainly.

"Call. Your. First. Witness."

"I only have one witness," he said.

"Call him!" shouted the judge. "Or her, or it."

"The People call Investigator Alan Templeton."

And with that, the hearing began.

Having derived its name from a U.S. Supreme Court case decided dozens of years ago, a Wade hearing is triggered by a motion made by the defense—as Jaywalker had made on behalf of Carter Drake—to suppress, or exclude from the trial, the identification of the defendant by an eyewitness. The theory is that the witness has made a previous identification of the defendant under circumstances that were so fraught with suggestiveness caused by the police or prosecution that permitting a courtroom identification at trial would now deprive the defendant of the due process of law and, with it, a fair trial.

In practice, the inquiry at the hearing becomes a two-pronged one. First, was the conduct of the law enforcement authorities so suggestive, either in the words they said or the things they did, as to render the prior identification so suspect that any mention of it must be kept from the jury? And second, if so, has that impermissible suggestiveness resulted in a situation where the witness, if now permitted to identify the defendant at trial, either by pointing to him as the perpetrator or testifying that he is, will be remembering him not because of his recollection of him from the crime scene, but from the subsequent police-arranged viewing of him, or from some inseparable mingling of the two prior sightings of him? If the answer to the second question is also yes, then not only must any reference to the improper police-arranged confrontation be excluded, but the witness will be barred altogether from making an identification of the defendant at trial.

By indicating that they intended to call only a single witness at the hearing, and choosing a law enforcement official rather than the eyewitness himself, the prosecutors were following a time-honored strategy. Jaywalker immediately recognized Investigator Templeton's name from the documents Firestone had bombarded him with. Templeton had conducted the lineup at which Concepción Testigo, the driver of the pickup truck, had picked out Carter Drake. Not only would Templeton swear that the lineup was a model of fairness in every respect, but by calling him to describe it, the prosecution could shield Testigo from having to testify at the hearing, saving him instead for trial. As much as Jaywalker wanted to get a preview of the state's only true eyewitness, the D.A.'s office intended to deprive him of that free look.

KAMINSKY: By whom are you employed, Investigator Templeton?

TEMPLETON: The New York State Police.

KAMINSKY: In what capacity?

TEMPLETON: I'm a senior investigator. That's roughly the equivalent of a detective in a municipal police department.

KAMINSKY: Did there come a time when you conducted a lineup in this case?

TEMPLETON: Yes, there did.

KAMINSKY: When was that?

TEMPLETON: It was on the evening of the same day that the defendant surrendered.

KAMINSKY: Was the defendant represented at that point?

TEMPLETON: Represented?

KAMINSKY: Did he have a lawyer yet?

TEMPLETON: Yes. *(Refers to his notes)* He'd been accompanied by an attorney named Chester Ludlow at the time he surrendered and was taken into custody.

Good, thought Jaywalker. At least the witness wasn't going to pretend that he wasn't aware there was a lawyer in the picture. That meant they'd had an affirmative duty to notify counsel and give him an opportunity to attend.

KAMINSKY: Prior to conducting the lineup, did you notify Mr. Ludlow that you were about to do so?

TEMPLETON: Yes. I placed three calls to Mr. Ludlow's office, the first at 1705 hours, the second at 1845, and the third at 1901. In civilian time, that would be 5:05, 6:45 and 7:01 p.m.

KAMINSKY: And did you ever get to speak with Mr. Ludlow?

TEMPLETON: Yes. Mr. Ludlow finally called me from his home at 2014, or 8:14 p.m. He said he didn't expect to stay with the case, and had no intention of driving back up to New City for any— May I quote him?

KAMINSKY: Yes.

TEMPLETON: For any fucking lineup.

Great, thought Jaywalker. The guy bills at seven hundred and fifty dollars an hour, but he's too lazy to hop in his car, take a drive and watch what goes on. Or to get some paralegal or first-year associate to show up for him. Then again, it's just the only eyewitness we're talking about here, and it's nothing but a run-of-the-mill, nine-victim murder case.

God, how he hated lawyers.

KAMINSKY: Did you conduct the lineup anyway?

TEMPLETON: Yes, I did.

KAMINSKY: Please tell us how you went about it.

Templeton described how he'd been unable to round up "civilians" at that time of evening. So he'd recruited five fellow troopers. He'd had them remove their hats, holsters and weapons, and change out of their uniform shirts into civilian shirts or jackets. Then he'd placed them in the "suspect room," in front of a one-way viewing mirror. Once the defendant had been brought into the suspect room by another trooper, Templeton had directed him to select whichever position he wanted to stand in, from 1 to 6. When Drake had picked 5, he'd been given a large placard with that number on it, to hold against his chest. The five fill-ins had been given similar placards, 1 through 4, and 6.

KAMINSKY: What did you do next?

TEMPLETON: I left the suspect room and went around to the viewing room, where I met Mr. Testigo, the witness.

KAMINSKY: Was this the first time you'd met him?

TEMPLETON: Yes.

KAMINSKY: What time was it?

TEMPLETON: It was 2033, or 8:33 p.m.

KAMINSKY: Did you have a conversation with him?

TEMPLETON: I did.

KAMINSKY: What did you say, and what did he say?

TEMPLETON: I told him that when the shutters were opened he'd be looking at a lineup of six individuals. That he'd be able to see them, but they wouldn't be able to see him. That he could take as much time as he needed to look at them. And then I'd be asking him two questions. Did he recognize any of them? And if so, where did he recognize him from? I asked him if understood, and he said yes.

It was textbook stuff, Jaywalker knew. First, in allowing the suspect to pick his own number, Templeton had eliminated the appearance that the lineup had been rigged. Then, by keeping Templeton and Testigo isolated from each other until the lineup, the troopers had avoided the possibility that the investigator might infect the witness's choice, either intentionally or inadvertently. Next, by limiting the questions that Testigo would be asked, Templeton had eliminated any suggestiveness that might otherwise have seeped in. ("Are you sure?" "Take a good look." "Remember, the guy might be dressed differently now, or have shaved since the other day." And, all else failing, good old "How about number five?")

Finally, although a few controlled studies had shown that sequential lineups—in which the witness looked at only one individual at a time—produced fewer false identifications than old-fashioned simultaneous lineups, they also produced fewer true identifications. Shown six people, one after the other, witnesses often failed to pick out any of them. Shown the same six together, they were more willing to choose the one who most resembled the perpetrator. Give the average person a multiple-choice question, and he'll take a guess, educated or not. But in spite of those studies, the vast majority of police departments still clung to the old model. And judges, who are never to be confused with innovators, uniformly went along.

KAMINSKY: What happened next?

TEMPLETON: I opened the shutters and gave Mr. Testigo an opportunity to view the lineup. After a second or two, he said, "Okay." I asked him if he recognized anyone, and he said, "Yes, number five." I asked him where he recognized him from, and he said, "He was the guy who was driving the Audi."

On cross-examination, Jaywalker spent a few minutes getting some more specificity from Templeton regarding Chester Ludlow's refusal to show up for the lineup. He'd already dispatched Nicolo LeGrosso to serve a subpoena on Ludlow, more out of spite than anything else. It wasn't that he doubted Chet had opted out. That, Jaywalker knew, was fully in character. But he wondered if Ludlow's sheer indifference might not have risen to the level of ineffective assistance of counsel, an issue for an eventual appeal. Beyond that, there was the poetic justice of it. Eight months ago, Ludlow couldn't be bothered to make the trip, even though it would have meant picking up a couple thousand dollars for his time. Let him see how he liked doing it now, for nothing.

From there, Jaywalker turned to the composition of the lineup itself.

JAYWALKER: Let's talk about the fill-ins you selected, okay?

TEMPLETON: Okay.

JAYWALKER: You say they were all fellow troopers?

TEMPLETON: That's right.

JAYWALKER: And that's because it was too late in the day to find civilians?

TEMPLETON: Correct.

JAYWALKER: What time was it when you were first told to conduct the lineup?

TEMPLETON: May I check my notes?

JAYWALKER: Sure.

(Witness reviews report)

TEMPLETON: It was 1645 hours, 4:45 p.m.

JAYWALKER: And the streets were empty?

(No response)

JAYWALKER: Where did you go to look for civilian fill-ins?

TEMPLETON: Where did I go?

JAYWALKER: Yes.

TEMPLETON: Nowhere.

JAYWALKER: Nowhere?

TEMPLETON: Nowhere.

JAYWALKER: And despite going nowhere over the next four hours, you still weren't able to find anyone?

KAMINSKY: Objection.

THE COURT: Sustained. I get the point, Mr. Jaywalker. Let's move on.

JAYWALKER: All right. Can you tell us the ages of the troopers you used as fill-ins?

TEMPLETON: I'd have to read from my notes.

Jaywalker, who by this time had copies of the witness's notes, photos of the lineup and several pounds of additional documents, invited him to read away.

TEMPLETON: Their ages were twenty-four, twenty-three, thirty-one, twenty-five and twenty-seven.

JAYWALKER: And the defendant was how old at the time?

TEMPLETON: Uh, forty-four.

JAYWALKER: In other words, thirteen years older than the oldest fill-in, eighteen years older than the average of their ages, and twenty-one years older than the youngest.

TEMPLETON: If you say so.

JAYWALKER: Would you like a moment to do the math?

TEMPLETON: No.

JAYWALKER: I ask that this photograph be marked for identification as Defendant's Exhibit A at the hearing.

(Exhibit marked for identification)

JAYWALKER: Do you recognize the photo?

TEMPLETON: I do.

JAYWALKER: How do you recognize it?

TEMPLETON: I took it.

JAYWALKER: Does it fairly and accurately depict the lineup that Mr. Testigo viewed?

TEMPLETON: It does.

JAYWALKER: I offer it into evidence.

KAMINSKY: Objection.

THE COURT: You're objecting to a photo of the lineup?

KAMINSKY: Yes.

THE COURT: On what basis?

KAMINSKY: I'll withdraw the objection.

THE COURT: Received as Defendant's A.

(Exhibit marked in evidence)

JAYWALKER: Taking a look at Defendant's A if you need to, do you recall the colors of the pants the men in the lineup were wearing?

TEMPLETON: Five were wearing gray pants, and one was wearing tan pants, I guess.

JAYWALKER: And the name of the one wearing tan pants?

TEMPLETON: Carter Drake.

JAYWALKER: And those five pairs of gray pants. Did they by any chance have a pair of contrasting stripes running down the full outer length of them?

TEMPLETON: Yes.

JAYWALKER: All five of them?

TEMPLETON: Yes.

JAYWALKER: Ten stripes?

TEMPLETON: Yes.

JAYWALKER: How about the shoes?

TEMPLETON: The five troopers are wearing regulation dress boots.

JAYWALKER: What color?

TEMPLETON: Black.

JAYWALKER: And Mr. Drake?

TEMPLETON: Looks like brown loafers, with tassels.

THE COURT: Anything else, Mr. Jaywalker?

There were times when such an interruption by a judge would anger him to the point where he'd not only say "Yes, as a matter of fact," but continue for another twenty minutes, long after he was out of questions. But this interruption was different. It meant Justice Hinkley had heard enough and was prepared to suppress the lineup.

"No," said Jaywalker. "I have nothing else."

But David Kaminsky did. Smart enough to realize where things were going, he excused Investigator Templeton and called Concepción Testigo to the stand, in order to redirect his focus to the second prong of the hearing, whether or not the taint from the suggestive lineup would infect the witness's identification of the defendant at trial, requiring that to be excluded, as well.

But in the process, he'd be forced to give Jaywalker the free look at the eyewitness he so wanted.

Testigo strode into the courtroom easily. He was a construction worker by trade, a guy who made his living with his hands, framing walls. He didn't strike Jaywalker as a man with an agenda, or one who was overly impressed with his role in the drama. In other words, he was likely to be a good witness.

Kaminsky spent only a few minutes on preliminaries, knowing that the less ground he covered, the less Jaywalker would be permitted to go over. Then he got to the point.

KAMINSKY: Tell me, Mr. Testigo. As you sit here now, looking at Mr. Drake, where do you remember seeing him from, the lineup or the scene of the crime?

JAYWALKER: Objection.

THE COURT: Overruled. There's no jury here. I assure you, I'm not going to be swayed by the phrase *scene of the crime*.

JAYWALKER: That's good to know, Your Honor. But that's not the basis of my objection.

THE COURT: What is it, then?

JAYWALKER: May we approach?

THE COURT: Come up.

(At the bench)

JAYWALKER: Counsel has improperly made the question an either-or exercise. By doing so, he's committed the logical fallacy called *excluding the middle*. The witness's recollection might be based upon neither the lineup nor the accident scene, but upon something else entirely. Or upon both of those things, in combination. Or upon—

THE COURT: The objection is sustained. Rephrase the question, Mr. Kaminsky. Leave out the choices.

(Back in open court)

KAMINSKY: Exactly where do you remember Mr. Drake from?

TESTIGO: I remember him from the crash site, where I saw him force the van off the road.

KAMINSKY: Is there any doubt in your mind?

TESTIGO: As to what?

KAMINSKY: That he was the one who forced the van off the road.

TESTIGO: No.

KAMINSKY: Or that that's where you remember him from?

JAYWALKER: Objection. Leading.

THE COURT: Overruled. You may answer.

TESTIGO: No, no doubt at all.

As soon as Jaywalker heard the answer, he knew he could forget about any victory celebration. Justice Hinkley would hang her hat on Testigo's answer and permit him to point Drake out at trial as the one who'd run the van off the road. Still, he was determined to make it as hard as he could for her, and in the process nail the witness down on some details. He started where Kaminsky had left off.

JAYWALKER: Tell me, Mr. Testigo. That question that Mr. Kaminsky put to you, about where you remember my client from. Is this the first time you've heard it asked?

TESTIGO: Yes.

JAYWALKER: Are you sure?

Even as he asked the question, Jaywalker was fishing through one of the three cartons Abe Firestone had dumped on him five months earlier, and extracting a document. It happened to be a photocopy of an obscure subsection of the Vehicle and Traffic Law, something about a right turn being permitted at a steady red light after a full stop outside a municipality with a population not in excess of a million people. But the witness had no way of knowing that.

TESTIGO: Yeah, I'm sure. I mean, we may have talked about it.

JAYWALKER: We?

TESTIGO: Me and Mr. Kaminsky. And Mr. Firestone, I guess, once or twice.

JAYWALKER: So you talked about it on a number of occasions. Right?

TESTIGO: I guess so.

JAYWALKER: And did you ever say it was a combination of things that you remembered the driver from?

At that point Kaminsky interrupted and demanded a copy of whatever document Jaywalker was using. "But of course," said Jaywalker. And with that he hoisted the carton, all thirty pounds of it, onto one shoulder and lugged it over to the prosecution table, where he dropped it with a courtroom-shaking thud. "Actually, you'll find *twelve* copies of it in there, along with several tons of other garbage you folks dumped on me."

KAMINSKY: May we have a page reference?

JAYWALKER: Yes. Page one. How about it, Mr. Testigo? In addition to the "crash site," as you call it, what were some of the other places you'd seen my client, either in person, on television, or in photographs?

KAMINSKY: Objection.

THE COURT: Overruled.

TESTIGO: I'd seen him on TV earlier that day.

JAYWALKER: How about in photographs?

TESTIGO: No. Not unless you count a photo of him that they showed on the news.

JAYWALKER: You saw that?

TESTIGO: Yes.

JAYWALKER: Before the lineup?

TESTIGO: Not right before it.

JAYWALKER: But before it?

TESTIGO: Yes.

But when Jaywalker tried to get him to admit that his present recollection of Drake was based upon a combination of those various sightings plus the lineup itself, Testigo balked, insisting that his memory was based solely upon the first time he'd seen Drake, behind the wheel of his Audi. And although Jaywalker tried his hardest to undermine that insistence, suggesting that the confrontation had been nothing but a split-second glimpse, Testigo wouldn't budge.

In the end, it was good enough for Justice Hinkley. "I'm going to grant the motion to suppress," she announced, "with respect to the lineup. Although it was procedurally conducted without flaw, I find that it was indeed overly suggestive in its composition. The People are therefore barred from introducing it or referring to it in any way at trial, unless the defense opens the door first. As to the proposed courtroom identification of the defendant by the witness, I find that it has an independent basis in fact, untainted by the shortcomings of the lineup. What the witness may have seen or not seen on TV is irrelevant to the issue before me, because what was broadcast was in no way due to any impropriety on the part of the police or prosecution. While you are free to raise it on cross-examination, Mr. Jaywalker, it has no impact on my ruling with respect to suppression.

"Now," she continued, "are both sides ready for trial?"

"The People are ready!" The voice was unmistakably Firestone's.

"The defendant is ready."

"Good. Nine-thirty tomorrow morning."

"Excuse me, Your Honor."

All eyes turned to a junior court clerk sitting behind a desk in the corner. He was holding a telephone receiver aloft.

"Yes?" said the judge.

"There's an urgent phone call for Mr. Jaywalker. A Chester Ludlow, Esquire. And," he added, covering the mouthpiece with his free hand, "he sounds *very* upset."

Jaywalker chuckled. He'd completely forgotten that he'd dispatched Nicky Legs to subpoena Ludlow. "May I?" he asked the judge.

"Be my guest."

Jaywalker took the receiver from the clerk. "Hi, Chet," he said.

"I'm ten minutes away," said the voice on the other end. "I hope you know this is going to cost your client seven-fifty an hour, plus the limousine charges, plus—"

"Wrong, Chet. This isn't going to cost my client a cent. You're coming up here as a subpoenaed witness, not a lawyer."

Silence.

"But maybe I can save you a few minutes," said Jaywalker. "When an Investigator Templeton from the state police invited you to attend a lineup, did you by any chance tell him that you had no intention of driving back up to New City for—let me check the transcript of the call so I get it right—quote, 'any fucking lineup'? Was that you?"

"He *recorded* that conversation?"

"Of course he recorded it." It was Jaywalker's turn to cover the mouthpiece. He didn't want Ludlow hearing the laughter in the courtroom, a good portion of which was coming from the bench.

"Well," said Ludlow. "I may have said something to that effect. It was late, I was tired, and—"

"Not something to that effect," said Jaywalker. "Were those your words?"

"I guess they were."

"Good night, Chet." And with that, Jaywalker slammed down the phone. Then, in the interest of completing the sign-off, he turned to Kaminsky and said, "Good night, David."

But Kaminsky couldn't have been much over thirty, if that. All he could come up with was a glance at his watch and a confused "Good night?" After all, it was three-fifteen in the afternoon.

Driving back to the city that afternoon, Jaywalker took stock of the day's proceedings. His victory in getting the lineup suppressed had not only been fleeting, but Pyrrhic as well. Concepción Testigo would be permitted to identify Carter Drake at trial. True, the jurors wouldn't hear that he'd picked him out at a lineup six months ago. But that meant they wouldn't hear how flawed that lineup had been, and how it now might be contributing to Testigo's recollection. Jaywalker was free to introduce the lineup in order to show those things. But if he did so, he'd be *opening the door,* as the judge had put it, to the results of that lineup, and to the rigorous way Investigator Templeton had conducted it.

In other words, it was a classic *heads-I-win, tails-you-lose* proposition. With Jaywalker and Drake as the *you.*

No, he quickly decided, he couldn't bring it up without hurting their chances even more. Luckily, the case wouldn't turn on it. It wasn't a whodunit, after all. Carter

Drake had been driving the Audi. He was going to testify to that. That and the wasp.

Jaywalker turned on the radio, an ancient staticky AM thing with old-fashioned push-button settings. Jewish klezmer music came on from a local station.

Not a good omen.

15

ABSOLUTELY FAIR AND IMPARTIAL

"Good morning, jurors, and welcome to Part Two." The judge was standing, the better to project her voice and be seen by the two hundred people who filled the seats in front of her and, when they'd run out of seats, lined the walls of the courtroom. A hundred of them were jurors, or at least potential jurors. The rest were court personnel, troopers, lawyers, reporters, sketch artists and the just plain curious, provided their curiosity had been enough to prompt them to get out of their beds on a subfreezing morning and stand on line for two hours.

"My name is Travis Hinkley," she continued, "and I'm going to be presiding at this trial. The name of the case that you've been called in on is *The People of the State of New York versus Carter Drake.* And as most of you, if not all of you, know, it's a case that has been the subject of some publicity."

Some publicity? Jaywalker smiled at the understatement. For the past half hour there'd been an audible buzz in the courtroom as people mumbled to each other that they'd been right, that this was really it. This was The Case, the one about the rich goy from the city who'd gotten drunk and forced a vanful of kids from the yeshiva off the road and to their deaths.

Jaywalker had long ago lost count of how many jury trials he'd had, but the number had to be up in the hundreds. Never before, though, had he seen a jury so white, so devoid of minorities of any sort, and so openly hostile toward him and his client. "I'm *half-Jewish*," he wanted to jump up and tell them. "I'm one of you!"

Justice Hinkley introduced the participants, asking all four lawyers and the defendant to stand in turn, so that the jurors could get a good look at them and see if they knew any of them. As Carter Drake rose from his seat, the room fell absolutely quiet. Drake had rejected Jaywalker's advice and overdressed in a gray suit, white shirt and red tie. A power tie, they used to call it. Not smart.

Eventually seventeen people acknowledged that they knew or were related to Abe Firestone, another two knew David Kaminsky, and one was engaged to Julie Napolitano. When a list of likely prosecution witnesses was read off, three jurors admitted knowing Alan Templeton, and one worked or had worked with Concepción Testigo. Every single one of them, however, insisted that he or she could be absolutely fair, and the judge excused only one of them for cause. "Being engaged to one of the lawyers could be a problem," she allowed. The young man rose and stormed out of the courtroom, obviously upset that his objectivity had been called into question. At the prosecution table, Miss Napolitano thrust her lower lip forward and pouted cutely, to warm laughter.

No one said they knew Jaywalker, or Carter Drake.

Justice Hinkley spent the morning describing her own function and that of the jury, explaining basic principles of law, and excusing those jurors who claimed they couldn't serve because of one hardship or another.

Jaywalker thought he'd heard just about every excuse there was, from the young child at home to the bedridden elderly parent to the dog that needed walking or the cat that needed feeding. He'd learned about long-planned vacations and short-interval bladders. He'd seen letters from doctors, dentists, priests, astrologists and drug counselors. He'd listened to people who couldn't be locked up during deliberations, feared retaliation at the hands of the mafia, and took instructions only from God. He'd heard native-born New Yorkers with names like Smith and Jones swear they couldn't understand English.

But this day he heard none of these things.

Everyone, it seemed, was willing to endure whatever hardship jury service might entail, for however long the trial might last. Had civic duty, a virtue nearly extinct everywhere else, somehow managed to flourish and thrive in Rockland County? Jaywalker had his doubts. What he was witnessing, he knew full well, was just another manifestation of the community's outrage. For once, those called to jury duty weren't just willing "to set all other business aside," as the court clerk had asked them to repeat in their preliminary oaths. They *wanted* to serve. They *couldn't wait* to serve.

Something else to worry about.

It was midafternoon by the time the judge turned the questioning over to the lawyers. Abe Firestone took the stage. He soon showed that he was capable of checking his combativeness at the door. He talked to the jurors with a folksy, good-humored ease. They listened to his concerns, followed his analogies, laughed at his corny jokes, and promised to convict the defendant if the evidence established his guilt beyond a reasonable doubt. "As I'm confident it will," Firestone added.

"Objection," said Jaywalker.

"Yes," said the judge. "Sustained. The jurors will disregard it."

As if.

"Sorry," said Firestone.

Right.

Five o'clock came, and Jaywalker still hadn't had a turn at questioning the panel. The judge broke for the evening, directing everyone to return at nine-thirty the following morning, and wishing them a safe trip home.

"How does it look?" Amanda asked him on their way to the parking lot.

How does it look? The evidence wouldn't begin until the following week, most likely. So far they hadn't picked a single juror. Jaywalker had yet to ask a question. Yet here was Amanda, wanting to know how things looked. What bothered Jaywalker wasn't the fact that her question was at worst stupid and at best premature. What bothered him was that he could answer it anyway.

"Terrible," he said. "It looks terrible."

Jaywalker got his turn the next morning, although an overnight snowfall made for a delayed start. January was a dumb month to be driving the Mercury back and forth to Rockland County. It had rear-wheel drive, bald tires and a heater/defroster that was temperamental, if one wanted to be charitable. He should have tried the case back in September, he told himself, as his client had wanted him to. Sure, he'd done a lot of preparing since then, and a lot of obsessing. But nothing he couldn't have crammed into three weeks' worth of forced labor. And as far as defusing the passions of the community, it now appeared that the additional time had only solidified the outrage. He read that in the morning newspaper, heard it on his AM radio and saw it in the set faces of the jurors as he rose to question them.

It had long been Jaywalker's practice—and it was a practice that set him apart from just about every one of his colleagues—to settle on a game plan early, and then to stick to it. Other lawyers approached a trial with a let's-see-what-shakes-loose attitude. They played things close to the vest, asserting little, conceding nothing and waiting for weak spots to appear in the prosecution's case. In other words, they played conservatively, defensively, careful to keep their options open.

Jaywalker subscribed to that old overworked sports adage, *the best defense is a good offense.* He prepared as hard and as thoroughly as he could, so that even before the trial began, he *knew* what was going to happen. He knew the strong spots, the weak spots, and everything else there was to know about the prosecution's case. On the basis of that knowledge, he committed to a single, cohesive view of the case, a unified strategy he'd stick to, come hell or high water. And so far, precious few of his clients had either burned or drowned. In a business where other defense lawyers were forced to boast about partial acquittals, hung juries and even lengthy deliberations, Jaywalker never boasted. He never had to. Almost without exception, after the verdict sheet had been read and filed, his client would stand up and walk out of the courthouse with him, through the public entranceway. It was all the boasting he needed.

A natural extension of committing to a unified strategy was sharing it with the jurors early on. That meant telling them about it at the first available opportunity. That meant during jury selection. That meant now.

"A terrible, terrible thing happened back in May of last year," he began. "Eight innocent little children died, and one equally innocent adult. The man whose actions led to those deaths, the man whose actions caused their van to swerve and go off the road, sits here in this courtroom, right over there. He will tell you that, when the time comes." And at that point Jaywalker moved from the lectern to stand over his client, placing his hands on Drake's shoulders while still facing the sixteen people who filled the jury box. "What's more," he said, "my client had been drinking that day. He will tell you that, too."

There's an expression that goes, *So quiet you could hear a pin drop.* At that moment, the courtroom was so quiet you could have heard a pin *rusting.* You could have heard a pin *thinking about rusting.*

"Okay," said Jaywalker, back at the lectern. "Who's heard all they need to hear? Who's ready to convict my client right now?"

Silence.

"Come on, folks. Remember that oath you took yesterday, to answer all questions to the best of your ability? These are the questions. Forget about what you do for a living, how many kids you have, what magazines you read, and all those other softballs Mr. Firestone lobbed at you. That was the easy part. Now comes the tough stuff. You've just heard the defense lawyer concede that this defendant was indeed the driver of the Audi. That he did in fact cause the van to go off the road, leading directly to nine deaths. And that he'd been drinking. Be honest with me. Raise your hand if, as far as you're concerned, that's all you need to know."

It took about ten seconds, which might as well have been ten minutes. But finally a woman in the second of the two rows tentatively raised her hand, though no higher than her shoulder. Just in case anyone had missed it, Jaywalker pointed to her and asked her why.

"I mean, if that's all there is," she said uncertainly. "Unless he's going to tell us something else."

By that time, several of the jurors in the front row had

turned their heads to see the woman who'd dared to speak their own thoughts. They seemed to be waiting for Jaywalker to bite her head off, or worse. Instead, all he did was smile, thank her, and say, "Of course."

The effect was almost comical. Before long another hand was raised, and another after that, until five of the eight jurors in the second row looked as though they were ready to pledge allegiance.

Epidemiologists have a term they use in describing how a pathogen that has previously been confined to one host species, such as mice, suddenly and inexplicably begins to spread to another, like monkeys or humans. The way they say it is that it *jumped*.

And there in that courtroom, right before everyone's eyes, the hand-raising jumped. It jumped from the back row to the front, and from there it spread out to either side. By the time the outbreak had peaked, no fewer than eleven of the sixteen people were sitting with one hand raised in the air. There was a veritable epidemic of jurors who were willing to admit they'd heard enough.

"All right," said Justice Hinkley. "Let me explain a few things."

The twelfth hand in the air was Jaywalker's.

"Yes?" said the judge.

"May I give it a try?"

She seemed to think for a moment, before nodding and saying, "Go ahead. But the first time you misstate the law, you're done."

To Jaywalker, no green light ever looked better.

He spent the next forty-five minutes explaining to the jurors why their reactions, as understandable as they might be, would unfairly deny his client a fair trial. Not that he lectured them. The rules, and his own better judgment, prohibited him from doing that. Instead, he wove his points into a question-and-answer format that eventually had them nodding their heads and agreeing with him.

There were three distinct reasons why, in spite of the things Jaywalker had earlier conceded—that his client had been the driver, that his actions had led directly to nine deaths, and that he'd been drinking—the case was far from over. The first was the presumption of innocence, which remained with a defendant throughout the trial and up to the moment a unanimous verdict was reached. Certainly none of the jurors were for dispensing with that, were they? The second was the burden of proof, which never, ever shifted from the prosecution to the defense. No argument about that, was there? And finally, the constitutional right to remain silent, and its logical corollary that a defendant's silence was proof of nothing and could never be used against him in any way. No one was for stripping away that protection, were they?

Halfway into the discussion, most of the hand-raisers were trying to apologize for their haste to judge the case. "Don't be silly," Jaywalker told them. "I would have answered the question the same way. But now we see how I would have been wrong, too."

"Might this be a good time," the judge asked, "to take our midmorning recess?"

"It would be a perfect time," Jaywalker agreed.

"Now," said Jaywalker, once they'd resumed, "I want you to forget about everything I said before."

There was a bit of uncertain laughter in the jury box, and a lot of confused expressions. But nobody looked bored. Every eye was on Jaywalker, waiting to see what he had in store for them next.

"Not *really* forget about, of course. Presumption of innocence, burden of proof never shifting from the prosecution, and no inference to be drawn from a defendant's not testifying. That's all the law, as Justice Hinkley has explained to you and will explain again at the end of the case. And it's all terribly, terribly important. But just for now, just for a few moments, I want you to forget about it.

"Remember," he said, singling out the timid-voiced woman who'd been the first to raise her hand. "Remember when you said the case would be over for you unless he—" and here he pointed at Carter Drake "—were to tell you something else?"

She nodded, and opened her mouth to defend herself. But Jaywalker held up a hand to stop her. He wasn't looking for apologies.

"Well," he said, "you're going to get your wish. Forget the presumption of innocence. Forget who has the burden of proof. Forget that the defendant doesn't have to testify or call a single witness, and that his not doing either of those things can't be used against him in any way. Because here's the thing. He *is* going to testify. We *are* going to call witnesses. And if you can just keep your mind open, you're going to learn *exactly* what happened in the seconds leading up to the crash, and *precisely* what caused it. Because you know what?"

"What?" came a collective murmur.

"Because he's the only one who knows. He's the only one who can tell you. Will you keep an open mind and wait for that?"

Sixteen prospective jurors promised they would.

Not that it meant much. But at least he'd given them something to think about, something to wait for. And if he'd accomplished anything, it was to drive out into the open the notion that drinking, driving and death were enough. They weren't. There had to be more. There had to be causation. Which left a tiny bit of daylight. Just enough for a bug to crawl into. A wasp, say.

Before it was over, jury selection took four full days. Because it was a murder trial, each side was allowed the maximum number of peremptory challenges, twenty, to eliminate jurors for no particular reason. Jaywalker ended up using every one of his, Firestone only fourteen. In addition, the court removed another thirty-some for cause, as she had earlier for Ms. Napolitano's fiancé. No less than six times, Jaywalker renewed his motion for a change of venue, pointing to the large number of jurors familiar with the case and ready to convict the defendant.

"This case made the *New York Times,*" said the judge after the jurors had been excused once again. "Hell, I'm told it made the *London Times.* Where would you propose we try it?"

No, she told him, Saskatchewan was out of the question. "Besides which, I think you handled that very well in your *voir dire.*"

"Flattery will get you everywhere with me," said Jaywalker. "But it won't get my client a fair trial."

"Why don't you leave that to me," said the judge. "Haven't I given you plenty of leeway so far?"

Jaywalker could only smile. Leeway became a funny thing in a criminal trial, he'd learned. About the only time a judge gave a defense lawyer leeway was when she was confident there'd be a conviction and wanted to make sure it would stand up on appeal.

It was nearly five o'clock on Tuesday when Jaywalker muttered a final "Satisfactory to the defense" for Alternate Juror Number 4, completing the selection process. Not that Alternate 4 was really satisfactory. She was a retired parole officer, her husband a retired FBI agent, her son a state trooper. But he'd run out of challenges.

The clerk swore in the juror, and the judge excused everyone until the following morning.

Carter Drake's jury would have twelve regular jurors and four alternates. Of the twelve, seven were women, five men. There were two computer technicians, two schoolteachers, a psychologist, an accountant, a teacher's aide, a bank teller, an unemployed actress working as a barmaid and three homemakers. There were no racial or ethnic minorities of any sort represented. None. Six of the twelve were identifiably Jewish from their names, with at least three others Jaywalker considered likely. The youngest was twenty-seven, the oldest sixty-eight. The average age came out to just under fifty-five. All twelve had not only heard about the case but had followed it "closely or with some significant degree of attention" on television, in the newspapers, or both. Eight of them subscribed to, or were regular readers of, the *Rockland County Register,* the local paper that had crusaded against the "Audi Assassin" in the weeks following his arrest.

All twelve promised that they could be absolutely fair and impartial.

Jaywalker had picked a lot of juries in his day. With the possible exception of a case over in Cayuga County, where several farmers had showed up for jury duty chewing tobacco and wearing overalls but no shirts, this one had to rank as his worst ever.

16

If the media circus had died down a bit for the Wade hearing and jury selection, it was back up to three rings Wednesday morning, with Carter Drake's trial about to begin for real. Outside, an extra parking lot had been opened to the public, and three enormous trailers set up in front of the courthouse to accommodate the press, additional security personnel and a makeshift first-aid station. Across the street, the vans were back, with their satellite dishes and telescoping antennae bearing the logos and numbers of all the major networks and several cable channels.

In the lobby, despite the addition of extra banks of metal detectors, the line waiting to go through them backed up and snaked out the door and around the corner. Several food vendors had set up their trucks and were doing a brisk coffee and doughnut business, and one enterprising young man quickly sold out his stock of battery-operated hand warmers to early-morning shiverers.

By nine o'clock, Justice Hinkley's courtroom was filled to capacity. Anticipating as much, the administrative judge had ordered all other cases in the building postponed for the duration of the trial, and had set aside not one but two additional courtrooms to accommodate the overflow. Those rooms had been fitted with coatracks, extra rows of seats and oversize screens and speakers, so that those who'd failed to make the cut could still follow the proceedings via closed-circuit television.

Jaywalker took it all in as he entered, making mental notes and smiling bitterly at the environment in which his client was expected to get a fair trial, free from outside influences. Just prior to opening statements, he renewed his motion for a change of venue for the fifteenth time, and for the fifteenth time Justice Hinkley denied it.

Abe Firestone delivered his opening in workmanlike fashion, surprising Jaywalker with both his restraint and his command of the facts. He drew the obligatory comparison between his remarks and the table of contents of a book. Mercifully, he refrained from reading the indictment from start to finish, settling instead for listing the specific crime charged in each of its ninety-three counts. He told the jurors which witnesses he would call, and briefly summarized what each of them would contribute to his case. Finally, as all prosecutors apparently feel compelled to do, he predicted with confidence that at the end of the case, after all the evidence was in, he would address them again, at which time he would ask them to convict the defendant on all charges, including nine counts of murder. Why? Because the defendant's own behavior would prove not just beyond a reasonable doubt, but beyond *all* doubt, that he'd acted in a reckless manner, evincing a depraved indifference to human life.

With that, he thanked the jurors for their attention and sat down, exactly forty minutes after he'd begun. If his opening had been less than riveting, it had certainly done its job. Had Jaywalker been sitting in the jury box, he would have been more than ready to vote guilty right then.

But Jaywalker was sitting at the defense table. And he kept sitting there, just long enough to force Justice Hinkley to inquire if he, too, wished to make an opening statement. "Unlike the People," she reminded the jurors, "the defendant has no burden of proof, and therefore no duty to open."

Just as he'd counted on.

"Yes," he said.

Jaywalker had been debating for weeks—for months, actually—whether to include the wasp story in his opening. On the plus side was his belief that it was generally best to get his client's side of the facts in front of the jury as soon as possible. And then there was his conviction that his own telling of the story would be better than Carter Drake's version. Drake, he felt, was likely to come off as a decent storyteller, but hardly a great one. Jaywalker, on the other hand, was one of the best. Not that he came by it naturally. It was more of an accidental by-product, he figured, of having spent his adult life first posing as a drug dealer, then defending criminals, and lately writing fiction.

Lying, others might call it.

In the end, he'd decided against including the wasp incident in his opening statement. To do so would put it out there *too* early, where the jurors would have it, but would have nothing but Jaywalker's word for it, nothing to corroborate it. It would be better, he'd convinced himself, to have it come from Drake's mouth, however imperfectly, and then to quickly back it up with the medical records Nicolo LeGrosso had dug up.

The problem was that such a tactic would limit what Jaywalker could say in his opening. He hated the standard *Keep-your-minds-open-until-you've-heard-all-the-evidence* approach that so many of his colleagues hid behind, and hated even more the *Don't-rush-to-judgment* mantra that Johnnie Cochrane had used to such success in a certain West Coast trial some years back.

So he compromised.

He conceded, as he had during jury selection, that his client had been driving the Audi that swerved across the dividing line and forced the van off the highway. "By doing that, Carter Drake's actions were the direct cause of nine deaths. And eight of those deaths ended the lives of this community's most prized treasure, its children." Furthermore, he again confessed, his client had been drinking earlier that afternoon, and by his own admission, drinking more than he should have, considering that he was going to have to drive home.

Jaywalker left out the business about Amanda and Eric's having shown up, and Drake's refusal to let Eric drive illegally. Let the jurors hear that, too, from the defense witnesses. Let them hear firsthand Drake's regret over that fatal bit of miscalculation.

Then he got to the point.

"Once the prosecution finishes calling witnesses to tell you what they saw and heard and assumed and calculated from outside the Audi, we're going to put on the stand the one witness who can tell you what happened *inside* the Audi. Because he was there. He was in the driver's seat. He's the defendant, Carter Drake. The prosecution's witnesses may tell you the absolute truth, they may exaggerate a little, and some of them might even tell a lie or two. It doesn't much matter. Because until you hear Carter Drake's testimony, you're going to have no way of knowing what really caused him to swerve. And once you hear why, you're going to know immediately, and you're going to understand everything."

Looking into their eyes, he searched for a spark, a glimmer, a sign that they were finally with him at that moment. Was that a nod coming from Number 3, or just a stiff neck she was stretching? Was Number 6 leaning forward in his seat because he was buying it, or because his hemorrhoids were bothering him? And there in the back row, Number 10. Did her hint of a smile mean Jaywalker had her hooked, or was she seeing right through his act?

And the thing was, as with so many things that came up at trial, he had only a split second to decide. Did he go on, and begin talking about the rest of his witnesses? Did he take Firestone to task for having predicted what he'd be asking for in his summation before they'd heard a word of testimony or seen a single shred of evidence? He'd even settled on a term for that display of arrogance, and for two days now had been working on his pronunciation of *chutzpah*. Did he thank the jurors for their attention, as Firestone had made a point of doing? Or did he leave it right where he was, while he had them. In his dreams, at least.

He sat down.

"Call your first witness, Mr. Firestone," said the judge a little too quickly, to Jaywalker's way of thinking. Had she deliberately cut short his moment of drama? Was she that smart? That worried?

Along with everything else he did during the course of a trial, Jaywalker had a habit of asking himself an awful lot of questions.

"The People call Hannah Weintraub."

Jaywalker reached to the very back of a folder he'd marked Other Prosecution Witnesses. The files it contained were arranged alphabetically, so he wouldn't have to waste precious time searching for them as their names were called. Old Cousin Dorothy had been at work. A lot of prosecutors he'd tried cases against told him in advance the order of the witnesses they intended to call. Not Firestone, though. When Jaywalker had asked him for the same courtesy, Abe had responded with a sneer and a gruff "Show me where it says I gotta do that."

What Firestone *had* been required to do was to turn over another carton of reports to the defense, this one containing the prior statements of his witnesses. True to form, he'd waited to the last possible moment, meaning that Jaywalker had been up half the night reading the stuff, making notes from it, and arranging it into files. Hannah Weintraub, he therefore knew, was one of three individuals who'd been driving on Route 303 shortly before the crash and had seen a red car either speeding, in the wrong lane of traffic, or both.

Had Jaywalker been prosecuting the case, he'd decided some weeks ago, he would have started off with the witnesses from the End Zone, to show how many drinks Carter Drake had downed prior to the incident. Then he'd have followed up with an expert to translate those drinks into an estimate of Drake's blood alcohol content. That way the jurors would have had an explanation for his driving even before they heard the details of it, and would have had ample reason to be hostile toward him. Then again, they looked hostile enough as it was. Perhaps Firestone had figured as much when he'd decided to start with the driving and then backtrack to the reason for it.

Now, as Hannah Weintraub entered the courtroom, dwarfed by a state trooper, Jaywalker got his first look at her. Shorter even than Firestone, she had to be in her seventies. And judging from the thick glasses she wore, she had to have the eyesight of an aging mole.

This, thought Jaywalker, was going to be easy.

FIRESTONE: Where do you reside, Mrs. Weintraub?

WEINTRAUB: Reside?

FIRESTONE: Live.

WEINTRAUB: Right here in New City.

FIRESTONE: Do you recall where you were on the evening of May 27, at about nine o'clock?

WEINTRAUB: Yes, I do.

FIRESTONE: And where were you?

She'd been driving her friend Bessie Katz home from a mah-jongg game in Pearl River. Bessie had recently undergone a hip transplant, Hannah explained, and wasn't yet able to drive herself. A case of the blind leading the lame, thought Jaywalker, reminding himself to be gentle on cross-examination.

FIRESTONE: And did something unusual happen?

WEINTRAUB: I'll say.

Jaywalker noticed a couple of tentative smiles in the jury box. Not good.

FIRESTONE: Tell us what happened.

WEINTRAUB: A little red car, like a sports car, zoomed past us. It had to be going about a million miles an hour.

The smiles broadened, and there was even some muffled laughter. Not good at all.

FIRESTONE: Did it pass you on the left, or on the right?

WEINTRAUB: How could it pass me on the right? I was on the right.

FIRESTONE: So it passed you on the left?

WEINTRAUB: Right.

That took a few minutes to sort out, but with Justice Hinkley's help, the *Who's-on-first?* routine was soon resolved. The red car had come up from behind them, passed them, and then stayed in the left lane, the one meant for oncoming traffic.

FIRESTONE: Did you see what it did after it passed you?

WEINTRAUB: Sure I saw. It kept zooming, and it stayed in the lane it didn't belong in.

FIRESTONE: Did you lose sight of it?

WEINTRAUB: Naturally.

FIRESTONE: Did you ever see it again?

WEINTRAUB: Only in a picture you showed me.

Firestone produced a photograph and had it marked in evidence. Mrs. Weintraub identified the car depicted in it as the one that had zoomed past her. Then, with a little coaching from Firestone, she more or less pointed out on a large map the spot where she'd been on the highway when that had happened.

On cross-examination, Jaywalker established that, even corrected, the witness's eyesight left a lot to be desired. Asked to tell him the time by looking at a clock on the rear wall of the courtroom, she was unable to.

"But I can tell it's a clock," she said. "Just like I could tell it was a red car."

Jaywalker smiled indulgently. But when he shot a glance over at the jury box, he saw only love. The jurors were eating up every word of Hannah's testimony. They absolutely *adored* her. So did he try to get her estimate of the red car's speed down from a million miles an hour to, say, a more plausible thousand? Did he ask her how fast she herself had been going when the car seemed to speed by, figuring her answer might well be in the single digits? Did he underscore the fact that Firestone hadn't even tried to have her identify the defendant as the other driver?

"No further questions," said Jaywalker.

Julie Napolitano took over for Firestone and called Moishe Leopold. Jaywalker had been aware of Leopold for several months. He'd discovered a one-page report in the three cartons of stuff Firestone had given him, referring to an interview way back in July. It had been one of the four gold nuggets hidden among the mud and silt. Leopold, too, had been out driving on that evening in May. He, too, had seen a red car speeding in the wrong lane. But unlike Hannah Weintraub, Leopold had been going in the opposite direction and would have been run off the road himself, had he not managed to swerve onto the shoulder.

Not that Firestone had turned over the report so early out of the goodness of his heart, assuming he had one. No, the report constituted exculpatory material, because it contained several things that could reasonably be considered favorable to the defendant. Years ago, in a case called *Brady v. Maryland*, the Supreme Court had ruled that any such material had to be turned over to the defense at the earliest possible moment.

The first of these exculpatory matters was Leopold's misidentification of the car. Not content to call it a "little red sports car" and leave it at that, as Hannah Weintraub had been willing to do, Leopold had stated with certainty that it had been a "late-model Porsche." The second mistake Leopold had made was to tell the trooper who'd interviewed him that there'd been not one but two people in the car.

To Jaywalker's way of thinking, neither of those errors had been particularly significant, given the fact that Carter Drake was going to admit that it had been he, in his Audi, who had forced the van off the road, and that he'd been alone at the time. But of course Firestone hadn't known that back in July. Back then, he'd had to assume that the defense would make him prove who the driver of the red car had been, and prove it beyond a reasonable doubt. And because Moishe Leopold's inaccuracies might undermine his credibility, Firestone had acted properly, for once. Even if he'd then tried to bury the evidence.

As Firestone had with Weintraub, Julie Napolitano had Leopold recount the events of May 27. He described with some detail how he'd almost lost his life that evening. Then, on the same map Firestone had used, he pointed out the spot where he'd encountered the red car. It was almost a quarter of a mile from where the driver of the van had been considerably less fortunate. The implication was clear. The red car had stayed in the wrong lane for a considerable period of time.

NAPOLITANO: Tell me, Mr. Leopold. Back when you first saw the car coming towards you in your lane, what did you do?

LEOPOLD: I beeped. I flashed my lights, my high beams. But it kept coming right at me—fast.

NAPOLITANO: Then what did you do?

LEOPOLD: I pulled to the right, onto the shoulder. And I, I—

NAPOLITANO: Yes?

LEOPOLD: And I…soiled my trousers. That's how scared I was.

Nobody laughed at that.

Napolitano then took the trouble to preemptively bring out the errors Leopold had made in his statement to the troopers. She even produced photos of a late-model Porsche, red, and had them marked in evidence so that the witness could compare them with Carter Drake's Audi.

"I see I was wrong," said Leopold. "But they sure do look similar." And even Jaywalker had to agree.

NAPOLITANO: And when you said you thought there might have been two people in the red car…?

LEOPOLD: I could have been wrong about that, too. As I said, it all happened very fast, and it scared the—

THE COURT: Yes, okay. I think we get the idea.

Jaywalker had jotted down a dozen questions or so for Mr. Leopold. He could have played around with the misidentification of the car or the existence of a phantom passenger in it. But Julie Napolitano had already covered both of those things for him, and neither was worth over-emphasizing. When it came right down to it, Jaywalker realized, Moishe Leopold was telling the truth as he knew it. No amount of cross-examination was going to get him to change his testimony or unsoil his trousers. As far as Jaywalker was concerned, the sooner he got rid of Leopold the better.

"I have no questions of the witness," he said, trying to sound as though the reason was obvious, that his testimony hadn't hurt the defense at all.

Just in case there were any idiots on the jury.

Following Moishe Leopold's testimony, the judge broke for lunch. Amanda was a bit put off when Jaywalker explained that he wouldn't be joining her at the diner. This time it wasn't just Pagesixaphobia that made him decline her offer. Never much of a breakfast eater, unless you wanted to count pretzels and iced tea, it had been Jaywalker's long-standing habit to skip lunch when he was on a trial. Adrenaline seemed to have a way of trumping appetite, and there were the afternoon's witnesses to prepare for. Not that he wasn't ready to cross-examine Concepción Testigo, the truck driver, whom he figured would be next up for the prosecution. But there was ready, and then there was Jaywalker ready, which didn't leave time for silly distractions like food. So he found an empty windowsill, hopped up onto it and spent the hour reviewing reports and revising notes that he'd already reviewed and revised a hundred times earlier.

Why was it again that he'd been in such a hurry to get back to this love-hate business they called trying a case, and had been so happy when the Disciplinary Committee judges had given him the green light? Oh, yeah. The money. That was it.

* * *

Abe Firestone was back at the podium for the direct examination of the first of what, as Jaywalker saw things, would be his three star witnesses. First would be Testigo, the pickup-truck driver who'd seen the accident and managed to remember the three critical numbers off the Audi's license plate. Then there'd be Riley, the bartender from the End Zone. And finally, an expert in alcohol metabolism, to convert drinks into drunkenness.

FIRESTONE: By whom are you employed, Mr. Testigo?

TESTIGO: ABC Construction, over in Nanuet.

FIRESTONE: And prior to working for ABC, where were you employed?

TESTIGO: For eleven years I worked as an auto mechanic for Rockland Foreign Cars.

FIRESTONE: In the course of your work, did you become familiar with different makes and models of imported cars?

TESTIGO: Yes, I did.

FIRESTONE: Are you by any chance familiar with the Audi TT?

TESTIGO: I am.

FIRESTONE: Have you worked on one?

TESTIGO: Yes. Several.

FIRESTONE: Did you happen to see one back on May 27 of last year?

TESTIGO: Yes, I did.

FIRESTONE: What color was it?

TESTIGO: It was red, bright red.

Firestone had his witness describe the time and locate the exact place on the map. He'd been heading home, Testigo stated, coming from a construction site where he'd put in a twelve-hour day. Other than a single bottle of Corona Light with his lunch eight hours earlier, he'd had nothing to drink.

FIRESTONE: Did you see something?

TESTIGO: Yes. I seen a red Audi TT driving in the wrong lane, very fast.

FIRESTONE: How fast would you estimate it was traveling?

JAYWALKER: Objection. No foundation.

THE COURT: Overruled. You may answer.

TESTIGO: Seventy, seventy-five.

FIRESTONE: Do you know what the posted speed limit is on that stretch of highway?

JAYWALKER: Objection.

THE COURT: Overruled. Do you know?

TESTIGO: Fifty or fifty-five. I'm not sure.

FIRESTONE: What happened?

TESTIGO: Like I said, the Audi was in the wrong lane, facing oncoming traffic. I seen a van come around a bend, a white van. And the Audi never pulls over. It stays in the van's lane, heading straight at it.

FIRESTONE: What happened next?

TESTIGO: The driver of the van must have braked, 'cause I hear his tires laying down rubber, squealing like. Then I seen him veer off to the right, to get out of the Audi's way. For a second or two I thought he was going to make it, but then he lost it like, an' took off in the air.

FIRESTONE: The van became airborne?

TESTIGO: Yeah.

FIRESTONE: And then?

TESTIGO: And then I seen him come down hard, bust right through the metal fence there—

FIRESTONE: The guardrail?

TESTIGO: Yeah, the car rail.

FIRESTONE: And?

TESTIGO: And he flips over an' goes down the hill, hitting things.

FIRESTONE: Things?

TESTIGO: Trees, rocks, whatever was in the way.

FIRESTONE: What did you do?

TESTIGO: I looked at the Audi, to see if it was going to stop.

FIRESTONE: Did it?

TESTIGO: No.

FIRESTONE: When you looked at the Audi, what were you able to see?

TESTIGO: I got a quick look at the driver. But I got his license plate.

FIRESTONE: Front plate, or rear?

TESTIGO: Rear.

FIRESTONE: Do you see the driver in court?

TESTIGO: I think that's him, over there.

(Witness points)

FIRESTONE: Indicating the defendant.

TESTIGO: I remember his jello hair.

FIRESTONE: Excuse me?

TESTIGO: I could see his hair was jello.

Jaywalker raised his notepad to hide his smile. He'd represented his share of Hispanic clients over the years, and had learned that a number of them had difficulty when it came to pronouncing certain letters. J and Y, for example, proved especially hard, no matter which one they were trying to say. So just as he'd had to get used to being called Mr. Yaywalker, or the more familiar Mr. Yay, so too did he have to learn not to take offense when told by one of his clients, "I really like jew." Therefore he now knew exactly what Mr. Testigo was trying to say, even if he was the only one in the courtroom who seemed to. And since the identity of the driver wasn't what the case was all about, he decided he might as well solve the mystery for the rest of them.

JAYWALKER: The defense will stipulate that the witness is referring to the color of my client's hair, which is blond or yellow, as in *Y-E-L-L-O-W.*

That drew a collective "Aaaah" from the jury box, a thank-you from the judge, and even a grunt of approval from Firestone.

Firestone had his witness describe how, at the time, he had been able to read the entire plate, but could later on remember only the numerals 724. He was absolutely certain of them, though, because they were the same as his wife's birthday, July 24. But that was the last he ever saw of the Audi, which continued on without ever slowing down or stopping.

FIRESTONE: Did you see what happened to the van?

TESTIGO: Yeah. I stopped my truck and jumped out, and

I was climbing down to help. There was like a little bit of fire coming out from underneath it. Then all of a sudden it blew up like, exploded. And I had to back off. It was so hot I couldn't get close.

(Witness crying)

THE COURT: Do you need a minute?

TESTIGO: No, no. I'm okay.

FIRESTONE: What happened next?

TESTIGO: It kept burning, but I couldn't do nothing, I couldn't get anywhere near it. Other people stopped, too. One guy had a fire 'stinguisher in his car, but it didn't work, nothing came out of it. Somebody with a cell phone called 9-1-1. And after a while the police came, and the fire trucks and ambulances. But it was too late, it was too late.

Firestone was smart enough to leave it right there, on an emotional high point. Jaywalker briefly considered asking no questions at all. Testigo really hadn't hurt the defense too badly. The Audi's speed was bad, but Hannah Weintraub had already established that. The wrong-lane business would have to wait until Carter Drake took the stand and told his wasp story. And his continuing on without slowing down or stopping could be explained by his belief that the driver of the van had recovered control of his vehicle and managed to keep it on the road. In an ironic way, Drake's speed might even work in his favor there. By the time the van had gone over the edge, he'd been too far away to be able to see. Though that might be a tough sell to the jury.

Still, Jaywalker had to ask Testigo *something*. Suppose the jurors were to get into deliberations and decide they wanted to hear his testimony again. A readback ending with a dramatic description of the van engulfed in flames, followed by no cross-examination whatsoever by the defense, could prove devastating. So he stood up, walked to the podium and gave it a shot.

JAYWALKER: When you first saw the red Audi in the wrong lane, did you beep your horn or flash your lights, or did it all happen too fast?

It was a trick question, of course. If Testigo *hadn't* beeped his horn or flashed his lights, chances were he'd now feel guilty, or at least sorry, about not having done so. In offering him an out, that it had all happened too fast for him to do either of those things, Jaywalker was just about putting words in his mouth. Not coincidentally, they were precisely the words he wanted the jurors to hear.

TESTIGO: No, I didn't have time. It happened too fast.

JAYWALKER: Is it fair to say that the whole thing, from the time you first saw the van until it disappeared, took only seconds?

TESTIGO: Yeah, that's fair to say.

It had been another trick question. Because the incident *had* to have taken only seconds. The key was leaving out the number of them. Come summation time, Jaywalker would remind the jury that even according to the prosecution's star eyewitness, the event had taken *only seconds,* which everyone thinks of as *only a few seconds.*

But Jaywalker wanted more.

JAYWALKER: I'm going to ask you to close your eyes, Mr. Testigo, and try to visualize, to see in your mind, what you saw that evening. I'm going to say, "Start," and that'll mean you first see the Audi coming along. I want you to say, "Stop," as soon as the Audi disappears, and you can't see it anymore. Do you understand?

TESTIGO: You mean, to see how long it took?

JAYWALKER: Exactly. Okay, you ready?

TESTIGO: Yeah.

JAYWALKER: Start.

He kept one eye on the witness, the other on his watch. It was no mean feat, and definitely the stuff that migraines were made of.

TESTIGO: Stop.

According to Jaywalker's calculation, the interval had been about seven seconds. Short enough, he knew, to be explained by Drake's leaning over to swat at the wasp. Still, he would have liked it to have been even shorter.

JAYWALKER: May the record reflect that the interval between the end of my "Start" and the beginning of the witness's "Stop" was precisely five and a half seconds.

THE COURT: So noted.

That word "precisely" got them every time. That, along with the inclusion of the half second. The implication was that he'd been looking at a sophisticated stopwatch, capable of breaking seconds down to fractions. The truth was, Jaywalker's watch didn't even have a second hand. It was a knockoff he'd bought on Canal Street for five dollars. "Movado," the Korean woman had told him, the same one who sold fake Gucci handbags and disposable three-dollar umbrellas. "Very good watch."

Jaywalker spent only a few more minutes on his cross-examination. He established a period at the beginning of the incident where Testigo could see the approaching Audi but couldn't yet see the driver. That would dovetail nicely with Drake's account that he'd been bent over to his right, trying to swat the wasp. Then he chipped away at the witness's estimate of the Audi's speed, getting him to concede that it might have been as low as sixty or sixty-five. Which would bring it down to ten or so miles an hour above the limit, something most drivers would be comfortable with, and few would be shocked by.

With that he thanked the witness and sat down.

Abe Firestone had evidently counted on Testigo's cross-examination lasting a lot longer than it had. He'd no doubt expected Jaywalker to contest not only the length of the incident and the speed of the Audi, but the make and model of the car, the identification of Carter Drake as the driver, his being in the wrong lane, and his failure to stop or even slow down after running the van off the road. But Jaywalker hadn't even touched on those subjects.

"May we approach?" Firestone asked.

"Yes," said Justice Hinkley.

"My next witnesses won't be here until the morning," he confessed. "I assumed—"

"Don't assume," said the judge. "Who's up next?"

Firestone looked over at Jaywalker. "Do I have to tell *him?*" he asked.

"Oh, grow up, Abe, for God's sake. What's he going to do, go out and kill the guy?"

"The intoxication witnesses."

Jaywalker had guessed as much, but it was good to know for sure. If nothing else, it would mean lugging fewer files to court tomorrow.

They stepped back from the bench and returned to their tables. "I understand we may get a little snow this evening, or some freezing rain," the judge told the jurors. "For that reason, I'm going to let you go early. I'll see you tomorrow morning, at nine-thirty sharp."

For some reason, judges love to lie.

It hadn't been a terrible day, Jaywalker admitted to Amanda outside the courthouse. As a witness yet to testify, she was prohibited from being in the courtroom during testimony. But he'd insisted on her showing up every day, even though that meant spending most of her time sitting on a bench in the hallway. The jurors would see her there as they came and went, and her presence was therefore important. She was *doing the Hillary thing,* he'd explained, standing by her man.

"How's Carter holding up?" she asked him.

It was a good question. What had struck Jaywalker most about his client over the past several days was his emotional detachment, his almost total disconnect from the goings-on. Here was a man who was looking down the loaded barrel of a twenty-five-year-to-life sentence, and it didn't seem to faze him in the least. Didn't he *get* it? Didn't he understand that the best he could possibly hope for was double-digit time on some of the lesser charges? And that was only if they got lucky and beat the murder count. Yet with all that, he just sat there, watching the jury selection, listening to the testimony, as though it was someone else's trial he was observing.

"He's okay," said Jaywalker. The last thing he wanted to do was to start psychoanalyzing Carter for Amanda. He was into their marriage deep enough as it was. So to speak.

"What happens tomorrow?" she asked.

"The shit hits the fan," he told her. "They're going to put on the bartender from the End Zone, and probably a couple of people who drank with Carter. Then an expert to estimate how drunk he was."

"Can they do that? I mean, legally?"

"I'm afraid so," he said. "It's not going to be a very good day. If you know what I mean."

"Would a very good *night* help? If you know what *I* mean."

He laughed out loud at the pure absurdity of it all. First Carter, who didn't seem to care about anything. And now Amanda, who seemed to care about only one thing.

"Not tonight," he said.

But not without smiling.

17

A TOTAL SLEAZEBAG

Thursday morning brought a light freezing rain to the Northeast. Maybe, Jaywalker decided, Justice Hinkley hadn't been lying after all. Maybe she'd just gotten her timing wrong. Which wasn't to say she might not make it in a future life as a weather forecaster, one of those daring souls who were forever putting their reputations on the line by boldly predicting a fifty percent chance of showers.

Thursday morning also brought the End Zone witnesses. First up was a man named Frank Gilson. Gilson was the client Carter Drake had worked with in Nyack earlier on the day of the incident. Jaywalker had known Gilson would be called, not only from the reports turned over to him by Firestone, but from a letter of apology Gilson had sent Drake, through Amanda. He felt terrible about testifying against his business associate and friend, but he had been given little choice by the prosecutors, who'd said he could either take the stand or thirty days for contempt. He'd decided to take the stand.

Julie Napolitano did the honors.

NAPOLITANO: Did you have a meeting with the defendant on May 27 of last year?

GILSON: I did.

NAPOLITANO: Where was that meeting?

GILSON: At my office in Nyack.

NAPOLITANO: What time did that meeting begin?

GILSON: About ten, ten-thirty in the morning.

NAPOLITANO: And when did it end?

GILSON: Maybe four-fifteen.

NAPOLITANO: What did you do at that point?

GILSON: We'd skipped lunch, and we were both hungry and thirsty. So I suggested we go get something to eat and drink, and Carter agreed.

NAPOLITANO: Where did you go?

GILSON: We went to a place called the End Zone, also in Nyack. It's what they call a sports bar. Good food, good drinks, nice crowd. We found a table, sat down and ordered.

NAPOLITANO: Was it just the two of you?

GILSON: At first it was. After a while, I called up a friend of mine and suggested she come over and join us.

NAPOLITANO: Can you tell us her name?

GILSON: Trudy, Trudy Demarest.

NAPOLITANO: By the way, Mr. Gilson, are you married?

GILSON: No, I'm not.

Gilson described how Trudy, along with two of her girlfriends, had joined them at the End Zone. As the evening wore on, they gradually switched from martinis and buffalo wings to shots of tequila.

NAPOLITANO: Over the course of the afternoon and evening, did you have an opportunity to observe how much the defendant had to drink?

GILSON: I certainly wasn't keeping count, if that's what you mean.

NAPOLITANO: We've discussed this before, haven't we, Mr. Gilson?

JAYWALKER: Objection.

THE COURT: Sustained. Please rephrase the question.

NAPOLITANO: What is your best recollection as to the number of drinks the defendant had at the End Zone?

GILSON: I would say he had two or three martinis. After the girls showed up, well, there were a lot of glasses on the table, and honestly, it was hard to tell who had how many.

NAPOLITANO: Do you recall testifying before the grand jury in June of last year?

JAYWALKER: Objection.

THE COURT: Overruled.

GILSON: Yes.

NAPOLITANO: Do you recall Mr. Firestone asking you how many shots of tequila you saw Carter Drake drink?

GILSON: Yes.

NAPOLITANO: Do you recall answering, "I'm not sure. Five, six, seven. Something like that"? Do you recall saying that, under oath?

GILSON: Yes.

NAPOLITANO: Was that testimony accurate then?

GILSON: Yes.

NAPOLITANO: Is it accurate today?

GILSON: I guess so.

NAPOLITANO: You guess so?

GILSON: Yes, it's accurate.

If Gilson had been trying to avoid hurting Drake, and Jaywalker was pretty sure he had been, his reticence had had precisely the opposite effect. It was bad enough to be damned by your enemies. When your friends testified against you, it got much worse. And ironically, it was Gilson's genuine reluctance—based on his obvious loyalty to Drake, trumped only by the threat of jail—that branded his testimony with a capital *T* for Truth.

Julie Napolitano spent another twenty minutes with Gilson. He admitted that he'd had almost as much to drink as Drake had that day, and that neither of them had eaten anything other than a few buffalo wings, and that had been early on. Yes, he had to admit, he would have considered himself drunk.

He remembered a young man showing up to drive Drake home, or so he assumed. But he was unable to describe the young man. Shown a photograph of Eric Drake, the most that he could state was, "That looks sort of like him."

"I'll stipulate," said Jaywalker, "that it was indeed my client's son who showed up." No use making a mystery of it. He didn't need the jurors speculating that the young man was some gay teenage lover, or something like that. Drake had enough strikes against him as it was.

Nicky Legs had interviewed Gilson months ago, and Jaywalker knew there was little to be gained from cross-examining him. Still, he couldn't very well ask *nothing*. Gilson had hurt Drake too much.

JAYWALKER: The two young women who showed up with Trudy. Do you happen to remember their names?

GILSON: Yes. One was Rachel Harper. The other was Amy Jo something, a redhead. I don't recall her last name. I'd never met her before.

JAYWALKER: Does the name Amy Jo O'Keefe refresh your recollection?

It had actually taken both Jaywalker and Nicky Legs an awful lot of work to come up with the last name. Way back at the time of Firestone's three-carton-discovery bombardment, it had been apparent that three women had joined Drake and Gilson at their table that evening. But for some reason, only two of them—Trudy Demarest and Rachel Harper—seemed to have names. Stuff like that tended to make Jaywalker suspicious, so suspicious that he'd not only made a written note of the fact, but had deemed the omission worthy of gold-nugget status. Eventually, Nicky had succeeded in identifying the woman as Amy Jo O'Keefe, but he'd gotten no further; she hadn't agreed to talk to him. So at that point, Jaywalker still considered her important, though if asked, he couldn't have said why.

GILSON: That might have been it. I'm not sure. They did call her "Irish," though. You know, as a nickname.

JAYWALKER: Okay. And you say the five of you sat around talking and doing shots of tequila?

FIRESTONE: I object. There's no evidence they were talking.

JAYWALKER: I object to Mr. Firestone's objecting. It's not his witness.

THE COURT: Yes, sustained.

NAPOLITANO: Objection.

JAYWALKER: I'll withdraw the question. Mr. Gilson, did the five of you talk?

GILSON: Yes.

JAYWALKER: And were you sitting around while you did that?

GILSON: Yes.

JAYWALKER: Thank you. Is it fair to say that as the evening wore on, there were a number of glasses on the table.

GILSON: Yes.

JAYWALKER: And it was difficult to tell which glasses belonged to which people?

GILSON: Yes.

JAYWALKER: And who had had how many drinks?

GILSON: Yes, very difficult.

JAYWALKER: So the number you gave Miss Napolitano earlier was more like an estimate or a guess than an accurate recollection?

GILSON: Correct.

JAYWALKER: Do you recall the actual number of drinks Mr. Drake had?

GILSON: No.

JAYWALKER: Was he talking loudly?

GILSON: No.

JAYWALKER: Acting boisterously?

GILSON: No, not at all.

JAYWALKER: Having trouble speaking or walking?

GILSON: No.

JAYWALKER: Did he at any time strike you as reckless, depraved, indifferent, wicked, perverted, immoral, degenerate, lewd, licen—

FIRESTONE and NAPOLITANO: Objection, objection.

THE COURT: Sustained.

GILSON: No, not at all.

THE COURT: I said sustained. That means you don't answer the question.

GILSON: Oh. Sorry.

Napolitano called Gilson's girlfriend, Trudy Demarest, to the stand. Her testimony turned out to be pretty much a carbon copy of Gilson's, at least from the point she'd arrived at the End Zone. Nicky Legs had interviewed her, too, so Jaywalker had expected as much. On crossexamination, he focused on the two friends she'd brought along.

JAYWALKER: Rachel Harper. Do you happen to know where she is now?

DEMAREST: She's in California. L.A. She moved out there in September. Couldn't stand the cold.

JAYWALKER: How about Amy Jo? Is her last name O'Keefe, by the way?

DEMAREST: Yes.

JAYWALKER: Do you know where she is?

DEMAREST: Right over there.

(Witness points)

THE COURT: Would counsel approach, please?

Jaywalker was joined by all three prosecutors at the bench. He loved it when that happened. It highlighted the mismatch.

"Why is she sitting in the audience?" Justice Hinkley wanted to know.

"I didn't know she was here," said Firestone. "But it *is* a public courtroom."

"Thank you for the civics lesson," said the judge.

"We don't intend to call her," explained Kaminsky, the law man. "Her testimony would be merely cumulative."

Bingo, thought Jaywalker. The prosecution had listed among its witnesses no fewer than twenty-one individuals prepared to testify about the identities of the nine victims, none of which were in question. Yet they were reluctant to call one of the four people who'd been drinking with the defendant, because it would be *merely cumulative?* Not likely. Amy Jo O'Keefe, who had for some reason refused to talk with Nicky Legs, had to have something to hide.

"Why don't we exclude her," suggested Jaywalker. "I might just call her."

"Step back," said the judge. Then, to the jurors, "I think this might be a good time to take our midmorning recess. We'll resume in fifteen minutes. Don't discuss the case."

* * *

When they reconvened, Firestone asked to approach the bench again. But it was Kaminsky who spoke once they got up there. "We've decided to call Miss O'Keefe after all. Because we failed to exclude her from the courtroom during prior testimony, we wanted to give Mr. Jaywalker an opportunity to be heard, in case he objects."

"Mr. Jaywalker?" said the judge.

Again, it was one of those moments when he had to think fast. There were three things he could do. First, he could oppose her testifying at all. But he'd already decided that Firestone must have had a reason for not calling her in the first place. Second, he could ask for a *sanction* against the prosecution, such as the judge's instructing the jurors to regard her testimony with additional scrutiny, since she'd had the benefit of hearing earlier witnesses describing the same events she'd be asked about. But if it turned out that Miss O'Keefe's version of the facts was more favorable to Drake, as Jaywalker strongly suspected it might be, that instruction would boomerang and come back to hurt the defense.

Having set enough traps of his own over the years, Jaywalker recognized one when he saw it. So he picked Door Number Three. "I appreciate the prosecution's looking out for me," he said. "But I have no application regarding the witness."

"You know I'll issue a cautionary instruction," said Justice Hinkley, "if you request it."

"No, thank you," said Jaywalker, unable to suppress a wink. "And I'll assume Mr. Firestone has fulfilled his *Brady* and *Rosario* obligations."

The prosecutors looked at each other blankly. *Brady* required them to turn over any exculpatory material. *Rosario* dealt with reports containing prior statements of witnesses.

"Of course," said Firestone.

"Yes," said Kaminsky.

"Naturally," said Napolitano.

Jaywalker couldn't help picturing the three monkeys, See No Evil, Hear No Evil, and Speak No Evil.

"You may step back," said the judge. And once they had, "Call your next witness, Mr. Firestone."

In describing that witness in its next day's edition, the reporter for the *Rockland County Register* would put it this way:

Barely five feet tall in heels, Amy Jo O'Keefe weighs 99 pounds, by her own admission. With flaming-red hair, bright green eyes, a button nose and an absolutely irrepressible smile, she's as cute as a firecracker.

What the paper delicately refrained from pointing out was the fact, obvious to everyone in the courtroom, that either Amy Jo had been spectacularly endowed by her Creator, or that a good portion of those ninety-nine pounds consisted of silicone, or at least some material not naturally found in the human body.

FIRESTONE: Is it Miss O'Keefe, or Mrs? Or Ms.?

O'KEEFE: It's Miss.

FIRESTONE: Are you employed, Miss O'Keefe?

O'KEEFE: Yes, I'm a sales rep for Pfizer. That's a pharmaceutical company.

FIRESTONE: Do you recall the late-afternoon and early-evening hours of May 27 of last year?

O'KEEFE: Yes, I do.

FIRESTONE: Where were you at that time?

O'KEEFE: I was at the End Zone.

FIRESTONE: Who were you with at the End Zone?

O'KEEFE: Rachel Harper, Trudy Demarest, Frank Gilson, and that man over there.

(Points)

FIRESTONE: Indicating the defendant.

THE COURT: Yes.

FIRESTONE: Prior to that date, had you ever met him?

O'KEEFE: No.

Firestone had her recount how the five of them had taken turns downing shots of tequila. Amy Jo had lost count around the fifth round, she said. Yes, she was pretty sure Drake had kept up. She confessed that the two of them had flirted. "He wasn't wearing a wedding band," she explained. "I didn't know he was married till I read about him in the papers, two days later. Honest."

Great, thought Jaywalker. One more reason for the jurors to dislike Drake.

FIRESTONE: Who left the End Zone first, you or the defendant?

O'KEEFE: He did. His son showed up to drive him home. I remember, 'cause I'd given him my phone number earlier, and when I found out he had a son who was almost as old as I was, I took back the napkin with my number on it.

FIRESTONE: How did he react to that?

O'KEEFE: He seemed angry, or more like embarrassed, I guess.

FIRESTONE: But he did leave?

O'KEEFE: Yes.

FIRESTONE: Have you had any contact with him or his lawyer since?

O'KEEFE: No. Please forgive me for saying this, but I think he's a total sleazebag.

FIRESTONE: We can strike that, Your Honor.

THE COURT: Mr. Jaywalker?

JAYWALKER: She said it.

THE COURT: Do you wish it stricken?

JAYWALKER: No, thank you.

Jaywalker had learned long ago that the lesson of the Trojan horse applied to courtroom battles as well as historical ones. It was one thing when an honorable prosecutor offered to strike something that threatened to give his side an unfair advantage. When an Abe Firestone did it, it was time to beware of Greeks bearing gifts.

THE COURT: We'll let it stand, then. But please confine your answers to the questions, Miss O'Keefe.

O'KEEFE: Yes, ma'am.

Whatever had been the source of Firestone's reluctance to call Miss O'Keefe continued to remain unclear. Certainly it hadn't been Drake's drinking or flirting, or the fact that his son had showed up to drive him home. Or even her personal opinion of him. So it had to be something else.

Every once in a while, Jaywalker knew, cross-examination could turn into a treasure hunt.

JAYWALKER: You say the defendant matched you, shot for shot. Is that correct?

O'KEEFE: Yes.

JAYWALKER: And you matched him?

O'KEEFE: Yes.

JAYWALKER: How many drinks did you have after he left?

Not "Did you have any more drinks?" That would have been the proper form of asking the question, instead of assuming a fact not in evidence, as Jaywalker's version had. But that would have allowed Amy Jo to answer "No." Firestone was asleep at the switch, however, and didn't think to object, at least not until it was too late.

O'KEEFE: Two or three.

Which would make up for Drake's earlier martinis and put them pretty much at the same count. If anything, hers were bunched more closely together.

JAYWALKER: Tequilas?

O'KEEFE: No, I switched over to Jägermeister.

He'd have to check the proof of that. Not as strong as 120-proof tequila, no doubt. But probably the equivalent of a martini.

JAYWALKER: Fair to say you can hold your own when it comes to drinking?

O'KEEFE: Hey, they don't call me "Irish" for nothing.

THE COURT: Careful.

(Laughter)

JAYWALKER: But you can hold your liquor?

O'KEEFE: You could say that.

JAYWALKER: It doesn't count if I say it. Would you say it?

O'KEEFE: Definitely. I can hold my liquor with the best of them.

JAYWALKER: Forgive me for asking, but how much do you weigh?

FIRESTONE: Objection.

THE COURT: Overruled. It may have some relevance.

O'KEEFE: Ninety-nine pounds.

JAYWALKER: About the same as you weighed last May?

O'KEEFE: Yes.

JAYWALKER: Do you by any chance recall what time you yourself left the End Zone that evening?

O'KEEFE: Nine, nine-thirty. Something like that.

Okay, thought Jaywalker. It was now or never. Sometimes you played things close to the vest, and sometimes you said fuck it and took your shot. This, he'd decided, was one of those times.

JAYWALKER: Would you say you were drunk when you left?

O'KEEFE: No.

JAYWALKER: I noticed you didn't hesitate before answering. Does that mean there's no question in your mind?

O'KEEFE: There's no question in my mind.

Here goes, Jaywalker told himself. And muttering a silent prayer to a God he didn't believe in, he asked the question. If it worked, it worked. If it didn't, no big deal. He'd have the rest of the day to wipe the egg off his face.

"How'd you get home?" he asked her.

This time Amy Jo did hesitate before answering, and Jaywalker fully expected to hear an objection from Firestone. Technically speaking, how she'd gotten home was irrelevant to the charges against Carter Drake, and Jaywalker wasn't sure how he'd go about arguing otherwise. But Firestone, who'd been quick to object to letting the jurors hear Amy Jo's *weight,* of all things, let it go.

"I drove," she said.

And there it was.

He spent the next fifteen minutes having her describe her drive home. How capably she'd managed it, how fully she'd been in control, and how she'd arrived safely, without incident.

JAYWALKER: By the way, where is your home?

O'KEEFE: Ramapo.

JAYWALKER: Ramapo, New Jersey?

O'KEEFE: Yes.

JAYWALKER: Same as last May?

O'KEEFE: Yes.

JAYWALKER: How long a drive was that?

O'KEEFE: About forty minutes.

JAYWALKER: No problem driving it?

O'KEEFE: Nope, no problem.

JAYWALKER: Did you consider it reckless on your part?

FIRESTONE: Objection.

THE COURT: Overruled. You may answer.

O'KEEFE: No, I did not.

JAYWALKER: Did you think you were acting with a depraved indifference—

FIRESTONE: Objection!

JAYWALKER: —to human life?

FIRESTONE: Objection! Objection! Objection!

THE COURT: I'll allow it. And then we'll move on, Mr. Jaywalker.

O'KEEFE: Could you repeat the question?

JAYWALKER: Let me rephrase it. Did you think at the time, Miss O'Keefe, that you drove those forty minutes with a depraved indifference to human life?

FIRESTONE: Objection!

THE COURT: Sit down. I've ruled.

O'KEEFE: No, I did not.

JAYWALKER: And as you reflect upon it now, would your answer be any different?

O'KEEFE: No, not at all.

And there it was, Jaywalker's summation.

Amy Jo O'Keefe was a woman, meaning a given amount of alcohol would affect her nearly fifty percent more than it would a man of equal body weight. She weighed maybe half what Carter Drake did. Over a slightly shorter period of time, she'd consumed roughly the same amount of alcohol as he had. Yet she'd been able to get into her car, start it up, and drive forty minutes without incident *to another state*.

And Carter Drake? In getting into his car and driving himself home, had he acted one bit more recklessly than Amy Jo? One bit more *depravedly indifferent to human life?*

Of course he hadn't. He'd just been unlucky, that was all. *Terribly* unlucky.

Under our system, jurors, a good argument can be made that both Amy Jo O'Keefe and Carter Drake broke the law that night. She drove while intoxicated. So did he. She got away with it, as do thousands, if not millions, of motorists, year in and year out. He didn't. But ask yourselves this. Should dumb luck mean that one of them should be able to walk away free, to joke about her Irish heritage and say "No problem," while the other one should spend the rest of his days locked up in a cage? Even if he does happen to be a no-good, cheating son-of-a-bitch sleazebag?

Okay, so it needed a little polishing. But there it was, the utter hypocrisy of the law, laid bare. All because Firestone and his team had initially decided against calling a witness whose testimony, they'd explained, would be *merely cumulative*. Jaywalker would have been willing to bet his entire fee—okay, a pocketful of Samoan pennies—that they'd known full well that

O'Keefe had driven home safely, that they'd chosen not to call her precisely because they'd been afraid that fact might come out, and that they'd shredded any police reports mentioning her, in violation of both *Brady* and *Rosario.*

On redirect, to his credit, Abe Firestone brought out a few differences in the way Amy Jo had driven home and the way Carter Drake had.

FIRESTONE: Did you speed on the way home?

O'KEEFE: No, I drove under the speed limit.

FIRESTONE: Did you drive on the wrong side of the road?

O'KEEFE: No.

FIRESTONE: Did you run any vans off the road?

O'KEEFE: No.

FIRESTONE: Did you kill eight little kids and—

JAYWALKER: Objection.

THE COURT: Sustained.

On second thought, maybe he had to rethink that part of his summation just a bit.

They broke for lunch.

That afternoon Firestone called Riley the Bartender. Riley, who actually turned out to have a first name, Daniel, showed up in a faded blue suit, a white shirt two sizes too big at the collar and a one-inch-wide black tie. It was an outfit straight out of the 1950s, and it made him look as though he was auditioning for a bit part in a retro movie. Had he been Jaywalker's witness, he would have worn his bartender vest, with a white towel thrown over one shoulder. Jaywalker would never understand what possessed other lawyers to try to dress up their witnesses.

Firestone established that Riley had thirty-six years of bartending experience, the last nine of them at the End Zone. He'd come on duty around five-thirty the afternoon of May 27, just in time for the evening rush. Yes, he remembered the defendant, who'd been seated at a table with Frank Gilson, a "sort of regular" customer. And yes, they'd been joined a few minutes later by three attractive young ladies, all of whom Riley recognized.

FIRESTONE: What were they drinking?

RILEY: Martinis, at first. Once the young ladies joined them, they switched over to tequila.

FIRESTONE: Any particular type of tequila?

RILEY: Yeah. They asked for what we in the business call a designer brand. This particular one was a dark amber, 120 proof instead of the usual 90 or 100, and said to be very smooth going down.

FIRESTONE: What do you mean by "said to be smooth"?

RILEY: Well, I wouldn't really know. I don't drink.

(Laughter)

RILEY: It also happens to be very expensive.

FIRESTONE: How expensive?

RILEY: They were doing shots. It was costing them fifteen dollars a shot.

FIRESTONE: How much tequila was there in each shot?

RILEY: About an ounce and a half.

FIRESTONE: At this time, are you able to tell us how many martinis and how many shots of 120-proof designer tequila the defendant consumed that evening?

RILEY: I'd have to look at the tab.

   At that point Firestone produced a check and showed it to his witness, who identified it as the one that had been turned over to state troopers back in June. With no objection from Jaywalker, it was received in evidence.

FIRESTONE: Does looking at that exhibit refresh your recollection?

RILEY: Yeah. All told, they had six martinis and, let me see, twenty-four shots of tequila. Of those, I'd say the defendant personally had three martinis and maybe six or seven tequilas.

FIRESTONE: Did there come a time when you had a conversation with the defendant?

RILEY: Yes.

FIRESTONE: What did you say, and what did he say?

RILEY: I asked him if he had a ride home. He pointed at himself, like he was his own ride. I said, "No good." I handed him a phone, a cordless one we keep behind the bar, and I asked him to call somebody to come pick him up. He protested for a moment or two, but then he agreed and made a call.

FIRESTONE: Why did you say "No good" and make him call somebody?

RILEY: Because I didn't think he was in any condition to drive.

FIRESTONE: Over your thirty-six years of experience as a bartender, have you seen a number of people who were intoxicated?

RILEY: More than you can imagine.

FIRESTONE: In your opinion, was the defendant intoxicated?

RILEY: Yes.

FIRESTONE: Do you happen to know who he called?

RILEY: Not for sure. But about forty-five minutes later, a kid showed up, maybe nineteen or twenty years old. And after the defendant settled up with Mr. Gilson, he and the kid left the place together.

Firestone thanked the witness, collected his notes, and started walking away from the podium. "Oh, yeah," he said as if he'd suddenly remembered, in his best Peter Falk impersonation. "One more thing. What did the check come to?"

Riley said he had to look at it to remember. "Let's see. Four hundred and ninety-two dollars and seventy-five cents."

"Thank you very much," said Lieutenant Colombo.

Following the midafternoon break, Jaywalker began his cross-examination of Riley where Firestone had ended his redirect.

JAYWALKER: Four hundred and ninety-two dollars and seventy-five cents, huh?

RILEY: Yeah.

JAYWALKER: Not all of that was for drinks the defendant had, was it?

RILEY: No. Like I said, there was five of them at the table. So all you got to do is divide it by five.

JAYWALKER: So all five of them were drinking?

RILEY: Yup.

JAYWALKER: And I see there's some food items included on the bill?

RILEY: Right.

JAYWALKER: And some tax?

RILEY: Got to give the governor his cut.

JAYWALKER: Right. Now these fifteen-dollar shots of tequila. Toward the end, were you watering them down just a bit? You know, to keep folks from getting drunk?

RILEY: No way. I couldn't have, even if I'd wanted to. It would have made them look lighter.

JAYWALKER: So you can only get away with that if they're drinking gin or vodka. Right?

RILEY: Right.

JAYWALKER: And you've done that once or twice in your thirty-six years of bartending. Haven't you?

RILEY: No.

JAYWALKER: Never?

RILEY: Well, maybe once or twice.

JAYWALKER: But that's impossible to do with an amber-colored drink.

RILEY: Right.

JAYWALKER: Unless, of course, you were to add a drop or two of caramel food coloring along with the water. Right?

RILEY: I suppose so.

JAYWALKER: That's the stuff that gives Cokes and

Pepsis and root beer and all sorts of other drinks their nice amber color. Right?

RILEY: I guess so.

JAYWALKER: Tell me. Do you by any chance keep a little caramel food coloring behind the bar?

RILEY: Yes.

Jaywalker hadn't just gotten lucky there. He'd worked his way through law school tending bar, out in Ann Arbor. He knew all the dirty little tricks. Including telling the State Liquor Authority inspectors that the stuff was for making the soda coming out of the tap look darker when there wasn't quite enough syrup in the mix.

JAYWALKER: And these Jägermeisters on the bill. I assume they were ordered after my client had already left?

RILEY: Right.

JAYWALKER: You saw him leave, as a matter of fact. Didn't you?

RILEY: Yup.

JAYWALKER: He didn't stagger out, did he?

RILEY: Nope.

JAYWALKER: Didn't fall down?

RILEY: Nope.

JAYWALKER: Didn't require assistance?

RILEY: Nope.

JAYWALKER: And you never cut him off, did you?

RILEY: Cut him off? Well, I made him call for a ride.

JAYWALKER: But you never refused to serve him?

RILEY: No.

JAYWALKER: You would have done so if you thought he was intoxicated, wouldn't you?

It was one of those win-win questions Jaywalker loved so much. The law prohibited a bartender from serving an intoxicated person. So either Riley would have to admit committing a crime that made him complicit in nine deaths, or he'd have to vouch for the defendant's sobriety. Firestone saw the trap immediately, and was on his feet objecting.

THE COURT: Overruled.

JAYWALKER: Wouldn't you have cut him off?

RILEY: Yes.

JAYWALKER: Do you remember Mr. Firestone asking you about an hour ago for your opinion, based upon your thirty-six years of experience as a bartender, whether my client was intoxicated or not? Do you remember that?

RILEY: Yes.

JAYWALKER: And you said yes?

RILEY: Well…

JAYWALKER: Well? Did you say yes, in your opinion he was intoxicated?

RILEY: Yes.

JAYWALKER: Was that a lie?

RILEY: No, it was…

JAYWALKER: I'm sorry, I couldn't hear you.

RILEY: I'm not sure what it was. I was confused.

JAYWALKER: But whatever it was, it wasn't the truth. Was it?

RILEY: No, not exactly.

JAYWALKER: As you observed my client back on May 27 of last year, it was actually your opinion that he wasn't intoxicated. Right?

RILEY: Right.

JAYWALKER: No question about that?

RILEY: No question about that.

God, how Jaywalker hated himself at times like this. He had every reason to believe that Carter Drake had not only been drunk, but had been obviously drunk. Riley had seen that and known it. His making Drake call for a ride proved it. Yet he'd continued to serve him. Abe Firestone had tried to do everything in his power to allay Riley's fear of what might happen to him if he admitted the inconsistency. First he'd immunized Riley from prosecution by putting him into the grand jury and having him testify without requiring a waiver of immunity from him. That meant Riley could never be prosecuted for what he'd done, never. Then he'd no doubt given Riley all sorts of assurances that he was safe, no matter what he were to say at the trial. Finally he'd popped the question, and Riley had passed the first test by saying yes, in his opinion Drake had been intoxicated. So far, so good. But as soon as Jaywalker had zeroed in on the implications of that opinion, that the bartender had continued to serve an intoxicated person, Riley had caved and said no, that hadn't been true.

Mothers, Jaywalker had said more than once, don't raise your sons to be prosecutors. But if you must, at least teach them to know that their witnesses will screw up every time they're backed into a corner and accused of breaking the law.

Now Jaywalker had to nail things down a bit.

JAYWALKER: Tell me, Mr. Riley. Did you consult with a lawyer in connection with this case?

RILEY: Yes. My manager provided a lawyer for me.

JAYWALKER: Did it ever occur to you that that lawyer might have a conflict of interest?

RILEY: What do you mean?

JAYWALKER: I mean that he might have been more concerned about protecting the business and its liquor license than protecting you.

RILEY: That's possible, I guess.

JAYWALKER: Well, did that lawyer explain to you that by his actions, Mr. Firestone had made it impossible, legally impossible, for you to be charged, even though you continued to serve my client? Did he explain that to you?

RILEY: Yes.

JAYWALKER: And you understood that, didn't you?

RILEY: Yes.

JAYWALKER: And you believed it, didn't you?

RILEY: Yes.

JAYWALKER: So as you sit there now, you're immune from prosecution, right?

RILEY: Immune from prostitution?

JAYWALKER: They can't charge you, can they?

RILEY: No.

JAYWALKER: So did your lawyer instruct you, therefore, to go ahead and tell the absolute truth?

Pretty safe there.

RILEY: Yes.

JAYWALKER: And did Mr. Firestone tell you the same thing?

RILEY: I don't remember him saying that.

FIRESTONE: I said it.

JAYWALKER: Objection.

THE COURT: Sustained. The comment is stricken, and the jury will disregard it. Consider yourself warned, Mr. Firestone. Please continue, Mr. Jaywalker.

JAYWALKER: Thank you. In any event, Mr. Riley, you took an oath earlier today, did you not?

RILEY: Yes.

JAYWALKER: And that oath was to tell the truth, the whole truth, and nothing but the truth. Correct?

RILEY: Correct.

JAYWALKER: And when you testified a little while ago that in your opinion my client was not intoxicated, and that there was no question about it, was that in fact the absolute truth?

RILEY: Yes.

JAYWALKER: Thank you.

As he had with Amy Jo O'Keefe, Abe Firestone tried

to rehabilitate Daniel Riley. He had some success, for example getting Riley's assurance that he hadn't watered down the tequila that evening, despite the knowledge and wherewithal to do so. But when it came to his opinion as to whether or not Carter Drake had been intoxicated, Riley wouldn't budge. Jaywalker had by that time so cemented the reversal of Riley's first answer that the poor guy was now unwilling to re-reverse himself, even if it meant going back to the truth.

FIRESTONE: And yet you insisted that he call somebody to come pick him up and get him out of there. Didn't you?

RILEY: I did.

FIRESTONE: Why did you do that?

It was a good point. That said, any question that begins with the word *why* has the potential of drawing a totally unintended, not to mention totally undesired, response. No doubt Firestone fully expected to hear his witness—for it was his witness, after all—say that he at least had harbored reservations about Drake's sobriety and his ability to drive home safely. But for once, he didn't get what he'd asked for.

RILEY: To tell you the truth, because I didn't like the way he was hitting on Amy Jo.

Splat!
It was as good a way to end the day as Jaywalker could have hoped for. Firestone could have chosen to leave well enough alone, and then argued in summation that Riley's actions had spoken louder than his words.

Despite his denials, he had, after all, made Drake call for a ride. There's a legal expression, encrypted in ancient Latin to keep ordinary mortals from understanding it, that goes *res ipsa loquitor.*

The thing speaks for itself.

Instead, by asking the *why* question, Firestone had seized defeat from the jaws of victory. He'd managed to inject an ulterior motive into Riley's testimony: that the bartender had been overly protective, and perhaps even jealous of the defendant's obvious interest in Amy Jo O'Keefe.

All this from a witness who should have been able to walk into court and say in plain English that Drake was drunk as a skunk, that he should have cut him off an hour before, and that he'd done the next best thing by making him call for a ride home.

"I hear you did great," said Amanda, who once again had been forced to spend the day on a bench in the corridor outside the courtroom. "The families were all muttering about the 'dumb Irish bartender.' And I overheard two of the jurors on the way out talking about how impressed they are with you."

"That's nice," said Jaywalker. "But today meant nothing. Tomorrow we're going to get clobbered."

"What happens tomorrow?"

They were standing out in the parking lot. Jaywalker had refused to say anything until they were well clear of the building, and out of range of jurors, reporters and anyone else with ears. Even then, he leaned forward to answer her question, close enough to breathe in the smell of her neck. And as smells went, it was a good one. Musk and a trace of lilac, he would have guessed.

"Tomorrow," he said, "we get the expert, the guy who's going to convert all those martinis and shots of tequila into a blood alcohol reading, and tell the jury that your husband was bombed out of his mind and had no business getting anywhere near the wheel of a car. That's what happens tomorrow."

That night he stayed up well past two, knowing that the weekend was just around the corner, and he'd be able to catch up on sleep then. He read the latest edition of Peter Gerstenszang's tome on drunk driving cover to cover for the third time in as many months. He reviewed the expert witness's reports and calculations and rough notes until he all but had them memorized. He composed long lists of questions for cross-examination. But none of it mattered, he knew. They were going to get worse than clobbered tomorrow. They were going to get massacred.

And he had to admit to himself that there was a certain justice to that. Carter Drake had tanked up on gin and vermouth and tequila on an almost empty stomach, and then he'd gotten behind the wheel of his car. Whether there was any truth to the wasp-on-the-windshield story was beside the point. Drake had driven far too fast and, at the very best, far too carelessly. As a direct result, nine people had died.

So why was Jaywalker so bummed? Certainly not for Drake, whom he totally despised. For Amanda, who was already separated from Drake and no doubt better off without him? Hardly. But for whom, then?

And the thing was, he knew the answer. He always did. It wasn't about the client, not when he dug down deep to the core and was willing to be totally honest about it. It wasn't about the family, in this case the woman who'd sought him out and put her faith and money in his hands. And it certainly wasn't about Justice. Justice, in this particular case, was squarely on the side of the victims. She might have been blindfolded, but that didn't mean she couldn't hear. And if she'd been listening to the testimony, chances were she was rooting for a conviction on all charges, and a sentence to match.

No, it was all about him and his stubborn pride, his absolute unwillingness to lose. It was what had driven him from the trenches in the first place, along with a little assist from the Disciplinary Committee judges. But it was also what had brought him back. It was what made him obsessive and compulsive and certifiably insane. And it was what made him the very best at what he did.

But come tomorrow, he knew, it wouldn't be good enough.

18

DOUBLE-SECRET PROBATION

Jaywalker had long felt that the prosecution's expert on alcohol metabolism would be the most important witness of the trial, with the possible exception of the defendant himself. His testimony might not prove to be the most exciting, or the most colorful, emotional or dramatic. But in terms of the sheer damage he could, and no doubt would, inflict upon the defense, the expert promised to have an impact on the outcome far greater than anyone else the prosecution would put on the stand.

It therefore came as something of a surprise to Jaywalker when he learned on Friday morning that it wouldn't be Abe Firestone handling the direct examination, but David Kaminsky. Then again, it made a certain amount of sense. This was a technical world they were about to enter, a world of academic credentials, hypothetical questions and expert opinions. It was a world where Firestone's bluster and bravado would be of little advantage compared to Kaminsky's knowledge of the rules of evidence and the laws of biochemistry.

"The People call Dr. Malcolm Rudifer," Kaminsky

announced, and a tall bald man who might have been anywhere from fifty to seventy strode into the courtroom. He wore a hound's-tooth checked jacket over a patterned wool vest and striped tie, complemented by a pair of faded tan corduroy slacks. If the outfit harkened back to an earlier millennium, it also threatened to bring on an acute case of vertigo in the beholder.

Despite the fact that Jaywalker rose to state that he was fully prepared to stipulate to the witness's expertise, Kaminsky spent a good twenty minutes questioning Rudifer about his credentials. They included a master's degree and two doctorates, a teaching fellowship at Columbia University, a stint at the National Institutes of Health, the publication of six books and forty-some articles, and over thirty years spent studying the changes that occur in the human body and brain when ethyl alcohol is introduced to the equation.

KAMINSKY: The People now offer Dr. Rudifer as an expert in the metabolism of alcohol.

JAYWALKER: As I tried to say half an hour ago, we're more than happy to concede that he is.

Justice Hinkley spent a few minutes explaining to the jurors what that meant and didn't mean. While it didn't mean that they'd have to accept his testimony as true, or regard it as any more or less important than that of any other witness, it did mean that he would be permitted to offer his opinion on matters that fell within his particular area of expertise.

KAMINSKY: Dr. Rudifer, are you familiar with a cocktail known as the martini?

RUDIFER: I am. A martini comprises mostly gin, although occasionally vodka is substituted for the gin. To the gin is added a small amount of dry vermouth, a white wine. Often a garnish is added, typically a green olive, a small onion or a twist of lemon peel.

KAMINSKY: How much alcohol is contained in the average martini?

RUDIFER: Roughly an ounce. Gin and vodka tend to be 86 or 90 proof, meaning they're forty-three to fifty percent alcohol. The typical martini glass holds three ounces of liquid, or a bit more. Half of that comes out to roughly an ounce and a half of pure alcohol.

KAMINSKY: And are you familiar with tequila?

RUDIFER: I am. Tequila is made from an extract of the agave plant. Tequilas can range anywhere from 80 proof to 150 proof. That translates to forty percent pure alcohol all the way up to seventy-five percent.

KAMINSKY: If the particular tequila in question happened to be 120 proof and undiluted, how much pure alcohol would you expect to find in a one-and-a-half-ounce glass?

RUDIFER: Well, again 120 proof means sixty percent. So I'd expect to find six-tenths of an ounce of alcohol in each ounce of liquid. Multiply that by one and a half, and you get point-nine-oh, or nine-tenths of an ounce of pure alcohol.

Kaminsky asked some questions about variables, including the gender of the drinker, his body weight, what he'd had to eat, and the amount of time over which he'd consumed the alcohol. Then he took a deep breath and asked the first of his hypothetical questions.

KAMINSKY: Dr. Rudifer, I'm going to ask you to assume that a two-hundred-pound male has had nothing to eat since breakfast time. Beginning about five o'clock in the afternoon, and continuing to about eight-thirty in the evening, he consumes a small amount of fried chicken wings. Over that same period of time, he drinks three martinis and six or seven one-and-one-half-ounce glasses of 120-proof tequila. First of all, are you able to give us your expert opinion, to a reasonable degree of scientific certainty, as to how much pure alcohol he would have ingested during that time?

JAYWALKER: Objection.

THE COURT: Come up, Counsel.

Up at the bench, Jaywalker explained his unease with the vagueness of the terms *breakfast time* and *small amount.* And were buffalo wings actually fried? Having managed to steer well clear of them his entire life, he had no idea. But the things were so small. Wouldn't it take a ridiculous amount of them, flapping like crazy, to get a full-size buffalo off the ground?

"Anything else?" the judge asked.

"Give me a minute. I'll think of something."

"Objection overruled."

As well it should have been. And Jaywalker had expected as much. All he'd really been interested in doing was to interrupt, to break the flow of Kaminsky's direct examination, and to see if he could ask the question all over again. If he changed it in any material way, Jaywalker planned on objecting again.

But the judge was on to his game. "Read back the question," she instructed the court reporter.

When finally given an opportunity to answer, the witness stated that in his opinion, the hypothetical man would have ingested somewhere between 9.9 and 10.8 ounces of pure alcohol, depending on whether it had been six or seven tequilas that he'd had.

KAMINSKY: And based upon the same set of assumptions, do you have an opinion, again to a reasonable degree of scientific certainty, as to the percentage of alcohol, by weight, that that same man would have in his bloodstream some thirty to forty-five minutes after consuming the last of those drinks?

Again Jaywalker objected. Again his objection was overruled, this time without the courtesy of an invitation to approach the bench.

RUDIFER: I do. Taking the lower figure, the 9.9 ounces of pure alcohol, to give the man the benefit of the doubt, it is my opinion that he would have a blood alcohol content of .20, or twenty one-hundredths of a percent.

KAMINSKY: Can you tell us how you arrive at that figure.

RUDIFER: Yes. It's quite simple. Studies conducted over many years, with many thousands of subjects, tell us that for the average male, the ingestion of one ounce of alcohol raises the amount in his blood by two-hundredths of a percentage point. The 9.9 ounces would therefore have produced a percentage by weight of .198. I then rounded that figure off to two decimal places, as is customary, and came up with .20.

KAMINSKY: Are you familiar with the expression "the legal limit"?

RUDIFER: I am. It refers to the maximum amount of alcohol one may have in his blood before he reaches the level prohibiting him from driving in New York State, as well as in the other forty-nine states.

KAMINSKY: What is the legal limit?

RUDIFER: It is .08, eight one-hundredths of a percent.

KAMINSKY: The .20 you came up with for our hypothetical man. Is that more or less than the legal limit of .08?

RUDIFER: More.

KAMINSKY: By how much?

RUDIFER: By a factor of two and a half, or two hundred and fifty percent.

KAMINSKY: In other words—

This time Jaywalker's objection was sustained. But it was cold comfort. Had it been a chess match they were competing in rather than a trial, it would have been the equivalent of capturing a pawn after losing your queen, two rooks and a bishop.

Next, Kaminsky had the witness describe the effects

of such an amount of alcohol on one's ability to operate a motor vehicle.

RUDIFER: Again, we have a huge body of studies and literature on the subject. We know from hundreds of controlled experiments that perception, motor coordination, hand-eye coordination, response and reaction time, and judgment all become impaired. And we know that the degree of impairment increases in direct proportion to the increase in blood alcohol content. We also know this, unfortunately, from the vast number of motor vehicle accidents in which alcohol has been confirmed to have been a contributing cause, if not *the* cause, of the accident.

Jaywalker looked around. Not at the jurors, who—he'd long ago noticed—were listening to Dr. Rudifer with rapt attention. Not at the judge, who'd been taking notes at every damning response. And surely not at Carter Drake, who, though he still pretended to be unfazed by what he was hearing, had to be shitting bullets. Or was it *sweating* bullets? He could never remember, and neither one made any sense.

No, what Jaywalker was looking around for was a hole, a hole big enough to climb into and hide in until this witness would disappear and it would be safe to come out again.

But there was no hole in sight.

Jaywalker had done enough reading to know that Dr. Rudifer's calculations were pretty much on the money. He cross-examined him for twenty-five minutes, trying to create a little wiggle room on his numbers. First, he had Rudifer concede that at two hundred pounds, Carter Drake was significantly heavier than the "average male" of a hundred and seventy-five pounds that the statistical models were based on.

JAYWALKER: Wouldn't that additional body weight dilute the alcohol in the bloodstream?

RUDIFER: Yes, but he's not far from average. The difference would be a few percentage points, no more.

JAYWALKER: Well, correct me if I'm wrong, but two hundred minus a hundred and seventy-five equals twenty-five. That's one-seventh of a hundred and seventy-five pounds. No?

RUDIFER: I'd need paper and pencil.

JAYWALKER: Here.

(Hands item to witness)

RUDIFER: Yes, you're correct.

JAYWALKER: And that's more than fourteen percent over the model your figures are based on. Isn't it?

RUDIFER: Yes.

JAYWALKER: Not just, quote, "a few percentage points, no more." Agreed?

RUDIFER: Agreed.

JAYWALKER: If we were to take that into account and adjust that .20 blood alcohol estimate downward by 14.3

percent, we'd be down to an estimate of below .17. Agreed again?

(Witness making calculations)

RUDIFER: Yes, agreed again.

JAYWALKER: Thank you. Suppose for a moment that those tequilas were watered down. Say that each ounce and a half contained a half an ounce of water with a few drops of nonalcoholic caramel food coloring. Would that fact, if true, affect your results?

RUDIFER: Yes.

JAYWALKER: Substantially?

RUDIFER: Yes, but it's my understanding that they weren't watered down.

JAYWALKER: I see. And from whom did you get that understanding?

RUDIFER: From Mr. Kaminsky and Mr. Firestone.

JAYWALKER: And is it your understanding that they were present at the End Zone?

KAMINSKY: Objection.

THE COURT: Overruled.

RUDIFER: The what zone?

JAYWALKER: How about individual tolerance? Do you

agree that even without regard to gender, food intake or body weight, different individuals metabolize alcohol at different rates, resulting in varying degrees of impairment?

RUDIFER: Yes.

JAYWALKER: Have you had an opportunity to study how Mr. Drake's system, in particular, metabolizes alcohol?

RUDIFER: No.

JAYWALKER: Have you ever met a young lady named Amy Jo O'Keefe?

(Laughter)

RUDIFER: Who?

JAYWALKER: Amy Jo O'Keefe. Ninety-nine pounds, red hair. Claims she can hold her liquor with the best of them.

RUDIFER: Not that I remember.

JAYWALKER: Oh, you'd remember.

(Laughter)

KAMINSKY: Objection.

THE COURT: Yes, the remark will be stricken.

JAYWALKER: And as I understand it, again disregarding body weight, alcohol effects women almost fifty percent more than it affects men. Agreed?

RUDIFER: Agreed. But these are all averages, and—

JAYWALKER: Exactly.

RUDIFER: —you have to allow for individual variations.

JAYWALKER: So at best, we're working with estimates here?

RUDIFER: Yes.

JAYWALKER: And those estimates are subject to individual variations?

RUDIFER: Yes.

JAYWALKER: And you don't really know what was in those drinks, other than what the prosecutors asked you to assume. Correct?

RUDIFER: Correct.

JAYWALKER: And if those assumptions are off, so are your results. Correct?

RUDIFER: Correct.

JAYWALKER: Just as they were off because of the defendant's body weight. Correct again?

RUDIFER: Correct again.

It seemed as good a place as any to stop, so he did. Kaminsky gave it a shot on redirect, and managed to undo some of the damage Jaywalker had inflicted. By the time Dr. Rudifer stepped down from the witness stand, his testimony had been weakened a bit, but by no means seriously undercut. If the jurors chose to believe Daniel Riley's account that had he hadn't watered down the drinks, there were still three martinis and six or seven tequilas between Carter Drake and sobriety.

It was also time for the lunch break.

The afternoon session brought to the witness stand two of the first responders to the scene of the crash. The first of these was a baby-faced state trooper named Adam Faulkner. Faulkner had been on routine patrol, meaning he'd been on the lookout for speeders and other miscreants, when a broadcast had come over the air directing any troopers in the area to respond immediately to the accident site. He'd gotten there, lights flashing and siren wailing, in under four minutes.

NAPOLITANO: What did you find?

FAULKNER: I found a van, down the hill from the shoulder of the highway. It was still smoldering. I would say it was ninety, ninety-five percent destroyed.

NAPOLITANO: What did you do?

FAULKNER: I searched for signs of life.

NAPOLITANO: Did you find any?

FAULKNER: No, no. Absolutely none.

NAPOLITANO: Are you okay?

FAULKNER: Yes. No. It was pretty bad.

NAPOLITANO: Take your time. What did you do next?

FAULKNER: I emptied my unit's fire extinguisher on the wreckage. I was afraid there might be an after-explosion. I radioed my supervisor to tell him what I'd found. And I tried to keep people from getting too close. A lot of motorists had stopped. And pretty soon EMS showed up, and other units.

NAPOLITANO: EMS?

FAULKNER: Emergency Medical Services. The EMTs and paramedics.

NAPOLITANO: Were you there when the bodies were removed from the wreckage?

FAULKNER: At first I was. Then, when I saw they were bringing out kids, children, I had to leave. They were black, like charcoal. Some of them had smoke still coming from them. I couldn't stay there. I, I had to get away. If I close my eyes today, I can still—

THE COURT: I think we'll move on, Ms. Napolitano.

NAPOLITANO: Yes, Your Honor.

Miss Napolitano may have moved on at that point, but the jurors weren't about to. Jaywalker noticed out of the corner of his eye that several of them were shaking their heads slowly from side to side. He didn't dare look directly at them. Nor did he intend to ask Trooper Faulkner a single question.

Next up was Tracy D'Agostino, one of two EMTs who'd arrived within minutes of Faulkner. A twelve-year veteran on the job, Ms. D'Agostino looked far more hardened than the youthful Faulkner.

KAMINSKY: What was the first thing you did upon arriving?

D'AGOSTINO: I put on a pair of heavy gloves.

KAMINSKY: Why did you do that?

D'AGOSTINO: I needed to get into the van, just to make sure there were no survivors that needed assistance. I put on the gloves because I figured the van was too hot to touch bare-handed.

KAMINSKY: Were you able to get inside?

D'AGOSTINO: Yes. A trooper and I were able to pry open one of the doors, using a crowbar. But he was shaking too much, so I climbed in.

KAMINSKY: What did you see?

D'AGOSTINO: I saw several rows of small children, most of them still belted into their seats, and the driver, who was crushed under the dashboard. All of them were charred. Some of them were still smoldering. All of them were dead.

KAMINSKY: What did you do?

D'AGOSTINO: I climbed out of the van, walked twenty yards and, if you must know, I vomited my guts out.

So much for hardened.

Again, Jaywalker asked no questions. It would be part of his summation to concede how gruesome the crash scene had been, and how horrible the results of his client's actions. But for now, the sooner he could get Tracy D'Agostino off the stand and out of the courtroom the better.

Firestone called William Sheetz.

Like Faulkner, Sheetz was employed by the New York State Police. But in place of a baby face was a weathered mask of experience and resignation, topped by a shock of almost white hair. And instead of appearing in his gray patrol uniform, as Faulkner had, Sheetz showed up wearing a blue suit, a white shirt and a conservative tie. Evidently the prosecution team had decided to present him as the cerebral expert he was, setting him apart from the rank-and-file troopers the jury had grown accustomed to, both on the witness stand and in the courthouse. It was a shrewd move, Jaywalker had to admit, something he might have pulled himself.

FIRESTONE: By whom are you employed?

SHEETZ: The New York State Police.

FIRESTONE: How long have you been so employed?

SHEETZ: Thirty-one years.

FIRESTONE: What is your current assignment?

SHEETZ: I'm a senior investigator. I head up the AIS, the Accident Investigation Squad.

FIRESTONE: How long have you been doing that?

SHEETZ: Nine and a half years, give or take a month.

JAYWALKER: The defense stipulates that the witness is an expert in motor vehicle accident reconstruction.

THE COURT: Thank you, Mr. Jaywalker.

Sheetz had a nice way about him. He was laid-back and soft-spoken, but his voice had a rich, baritone resonance to it. His pale blue eyes squinted out from a deeply lined and weathered face. He reminded Jaywalker of John Wayne, without the hat and horse. He guessed it was no accident that Abe Firestone intended on sending the jurors home for the weekend after hearing from him.

FIRESTONE: What sort of accidents do you and your squad investigate?

SHEETZ: All fatalities. Also any accidents that result in serious bodily harm, or where alcohol or drugs appear to have played a significant role.

Firestone had the witness describe how he'd responded to the site of the crash back on May 27, and what he'd found. Mercifully for the defense, by the time of Sheetz's arrival, the van and its occupants were no longer smoldering. In fact, by then the county medical examiner and his deputies were already on the scene, directing the removal of bodies.

Sheetz had begun examining the scene, working

backward from the van's final resting place, up the embankment, through the guardrail, and finally along the road surface to the spot where fresh skid marks had first appeared on the blacktop. The pavement had been dry, he explained, addressing his remarks directly to the jurors. That had allowed the van's brakes to lock up its wheels, leaving a trail of rubber behind. Because the van was an older one, it hadn't had antilock brakes, and the skid marks were therefore solid bands rather than broken lines. There had come a point, however, where, according to Sheetz, the driver must have realized that braking alone wasn't going to be enough to enable him to avoid whatever was in front of him.

FIRESTONE: What, in your opinion, did he do at that point?

SHEETZ: Continuing to brake, he turned the van's steering wheel clockwise, to the right.

FIRESTONE: With what result?

SHEETZ: The result was that the van began to drift, then fishtailed—

FIRESTONE: What do you mean by "fishtailed"?

SHEETZ: Imagine a fish with a vertical tail. In other words, one that is constructed up and down *(Demonstrates),* rather than, say, sideways, like the flukes of a whale *(Demonstrates).* The fish propels itself forward by thrusting its tail back and forth, to the left, then the right *(Demonstrates).* "Fishtailing," as I use the expression, occurs when the rear of a vehicle swings back and forth in much the same fashion. But instead of occurring as the vehicle is being propelled forward, it occurs because the vehicle's rear wheels have lost traction with the road surface. Next there'd come a point where the skid marks had ended altogether, indicating that the van had literally become airborne. When it had touched down again, it had done so briefly, on the shoulder of the road. From there it had bounced and gone through the guardrail and over the embankment, flipping over several times before landing, exploding, and bursting into flames.

FIRESTONE: In your opinion, what caused it to explode?

SHEETZ: It's not possible to know precisely, but in all probability a spark occurred, created by the rubbing of metal against metal, or perhaps metal against rough dry pavement. And that spark ignited gasoline fumes, which are extremely volatile.

Sheetz had taken a number of photographs of the skid marks, the embankment and the charred remains of the van. Firestone had them marked in evidence, and had his witness describe what was depicted in each photo, and the significance of it in understanding the actions of the van's driver. In this way, Firestone was able to have his expert describe what had happened a second time. And just in case that wasn't enough, Sheetz had taken measurements and created a rough diagram, which he'd subsequently converted into a large, full-color, professional-quality exhibit. That, too, was now received in evidence and then explained in detail by the witness. So the jurors were treated to yet a third version of the events. But if any of them seemed to mind, their faces weren't showing it.

Every one of them continued to give John Wayne their rapt attention.

Next, Firestone turned to the issue of speed. Was it possible, he wanted to know, to determine how fast the van had been moving when its driver had first hit the brakes? Yes it was, replied Sheetz. By measuring the length of the skid marks, factoring in the coefficient of friction of the road surface, and referring to charts that had been developed from thousands of hours of testing, one could come up with the speed of the van within a margin of error of five percent.

FIRESTONE: And what answer did you come up with?

SHEETZ: According to my observations and calculations, when the van's wheels first locked up, it was traveling at a speed of forty-six miles per hour, give or take two and a half miles an hour either way, at most.

FIRESTONE: In other words, under the speed limit?

SHEETZ: Yes, sir.

FIRESTONE: Now assume for a moment that the object that the van's driver had been attempting to avoid hitting was an oncoming car, directly in the van's lane. Are you able to tell us how fast that oncoming car was traveling?

SHEETZ: No, I'm not.

FIRESTONE: Why not?

SHEETZ: Because I found no skid marks at all coming from the opposite direction. So I had nothing to measure, nothing to start with.

FIRESTONE: Can you tell us anything from the absence of skid marks coming from that opposite direction?

SHEETZ: Yes, I can.

FIRESTONE: What's that?

SHEETZ: I can tell you that the driver of that oncoming car never braked, never tried to stop or even slow down.

To Jaywalker's way of thinking, it would have been a powerful moment to stop. But Firestone wanted even more. Why settle for a mere kill, after all, when you can follow it up by ripping out your victim's bloody heart, and hoisting in the air for all to see?

In the days following Carter Drake's surrender, Firestone had obtained a search warrant for his Audi, and troopers had gone to the Manhattan garage where it was stored. Unlike Jaywalker's open-air, seventy-five-dollar-a-month parking spot in the middle of the Hudson River, Drake's spot was indoors. It was heated in the winter and air-conditioned in the summer. The spot had been purchased several years earlier for $128,500, a figure that included neither the monthly maintenance charge of $2,585 nor the additional *service fee* of $975. Tips, while not required, were encouraged, and were also extra.

The troopers had towed the Audi up to a more modest garage in New City, where William Sheetz and other investigators from his squad had spent five hours going over it.

FIRESTONE: What did you find?

SHEETZ: We found nothing out of the ordinary. There was no indication of external damage. The steering system was intact. The brakes were fully functional. The windshield was clean and unobstructed, and provided a good view of whatever was ahead. The headlights worked, both high beams and low. The horn worked.

FIRESTONE: In other words—

JAYWALKER: Objection.

THE COURT: Yes. Please don't summarize the witness's testimony.

FIRESTONE: Were you able to come up with any explanation as to why the driver might have failed to see the van?

SHEETZ: No.

FIRESTONE: Or why he'd been driving in the wrong lane?

SHEETZ: No.

FIRESTONE: Or why he never tried to slow down or stop?

SHEETZ: No. No explanation at all.

And that was where Firestone left it.

Jaywalker glanced at his watch before collecting his notes and walking to the podium. It was after four o'clock. William Sheetz would be the last witness of the day, and of the entire week, for that matter. Jaywalker loved nothing more than to send jurors off for the weekend on a high note for the defense. But given this particular witness's testimony, that was going to be a tall order. Still, he had a couple of points to make, and he did some quick thinking on how to save the best for last. And then, as he so often did, he started where his adversary had left off.

JAYWALKER: Is it fair to say, Investigator Sheetz, that you've investigated a number of accidents that included a leaving-the-scene component?

SHEETZ: Yes, sir.

JAYWALKER: Dozens?

SHEETZ: Yes, sir.

JAYWALKER: Hundreds?

SHEETZ: Yes, sir.

JAYWALKER: Thousands?

SHEETZ: I'd say so.

JAYWALKER: And you'd agree, would you not, that in most, if not all, of those cases, you were able to discover some evidence that the driver of the vehicle that left the scene at least slowed down before doing so?

It was vintage Jaywalker. He had no idea at all if that was true or not. But the way he'd worded the question made it almost impossible for the witness not to answer in the affirmative. First, by inviting him to agree with the very first question out of his mouth, Jaywalker was making it easy for Sheetz to do so. If he disagreed right off the bat, he risked coming off as overly argumentative. Next, by using the phrase *most, if not all,* rather than something like *almost all* or *the vast majority,* Jaywalker was looking for agreement on no more than a bare majority of accidents. But later on, the jurors would forget the qualifier "most" and remember the absolute "all." Then, by using the words *you were able to discover some evidence,* he was appealing to Sheetz's ego and prowess as an investigator. A negative response could be construed as damaging to either or both of those things, a positive one as reinforcing them. On top of that, the supposition underlying the question, that even a motorist who eventually decided to leave the scene would experience a moment of indecision before driving off, made sense. It was consistent with everyday human experience. You slowed down, even briefly considered stopping, before you panicked and sped off. And finally, by pretending to be reading the question verbatim from some learned treatise, rather than springing it ad lib from his own devious imagination, Jaywalker was warning the witness that if he disagreed with the premise, he risked challenging an authority in the field.

SHEETZ: Yes, sir.

JAYWALKER: You'd agree with that?

SHEETZ: I'd agree with that.

JAYWALKER: Good. So let's take a look at that extremely rare case where you could find absolutely no evidence that the driver who left the scene ever stopped or slowed down. Might that give you pause to consider that he might never have been aware of the accident that had occurred?

Sheetz realized too late the corner he'd put himself into. Sure, he could have backtracked and second-guessed his earlier answer. But John Wayne never did that, did he? So he did the next best thing, and gave Jaywalker as qualified a yes as he possibly could.

SHEETZ: That could be one explanation.

JAYWALKER: And does that explanation become more plausible with the fact that the accident, in this case the van's leaving the roadway and going over the embankment and out of view, occurred behind the driver who continued on, rather than in front of him or to one side of him?

SHEETZ: Yes, sir. I guess so.

JAYWALKER: And does that explanation become more plausible still if the incident occurred at night, in the darkness?

SHEETZ: Yes, sir.

JAYWALKER: And even more plausible if the driver who continued on did so at fifty or sixty miles per hour, and would quickly be out of both visual range of the scene and auditory range, as well?

SHEETZ: I suppose so.

JAYWALKER: And drawing your attention to this diagram of the scene. I'm sorry, tell us again who made it?

SHEETZ: I did.

JAYWALKER: Right. This bend in the road here… *(Pointing)* Continuing on after its near collision with the van, how soon would the Audi have rounded it and lost sight of the van altogether?

SHEETZ: It depends on how fast the Audi was traveling.

JAYWALKER: Let's assume it was going the speed limit.

SHEETZ: Maybe two seconds.

JAYWALKER: And if, as it's been suggested, the Audi was going five or ten miles an hour over the limit?

It was another of those win-win questions Jaywalker loved so much. Carter Drake's driving too fast was one of the things the prosecution was counting on to demonstrate recklessness and depraved indifference to human life. Yet here was Sheetz, about to admit that in terms of having been able to see what had happened behind him, Drake's speeding would actually work in his favor.

SHEETZ: A little less than two seconds.

JAYWALKER: I see. You don't know exactly how long it took for the van to go over the embankment, do you?

SHEETZ: No, sir.

JAYWALKER: Or to explode?

SHEETZ: No.

JAYWALKER: Or to burst into flames?

SHEETZ: No.

JAYWALKER: So you'd have to agree that it's entirely possible that the driver who continued on never saw, in his rearview mirror, the van leave the roadway. Wouldn't you?

SHEETZ: It's possible.

JAYWALKER: Never saw or heard the explosion?

SHEETZ: It's possible.

JAYWALKER: Never saw the flames?

SHEETZ: Possible.

JAYWALKER: Probably never saw other motorists pulling over and stopping?

SHEETZ: Probably not.

JAYWALKER: Certainly never saw troopers and EMTs at the scene?

SHEETZ: No, sir.

In the space of three minutes, Jaywalker had taken the witness from plausible to possible to probable to certain that Carter Drake had been totally unaware of the destruction he'd left in his wake. And if it was one part semantics and two parts sleight of hand, who cared? At least it would send the jurors home on a note of uncertainty.

JAYWALKER: By the way, those gasoline fumes you mentioned? Where did they come from?

It seemed like an innocent enough question, something that any third grader should have been able to answer. *From the gas tank.* But Sheetz didn't say that. In fact, for just a second, he didn't say anything. And that second was enough for Jaywalker to know that he had him on that, too.

Way back in the early weeks of the case, when Abe Firestone had bombarded him with three huge cartons of worthless duplicated nonsense, and Jaywalker had bitten the bullet and combed through every page of it, his reward had been a sleepless night, a sore back and four nuggets of gold. The first of those nuggets had been Moishe Leopold's mistaken belief that there'd been not one but two people in the Audi. The second had been the lack of any reference whatsoever to Amy Jo O'Keefe, the little redheaded firecracker who'd matched Carter Drake drink for drink before driving herself home safely to New Jersey. Right now, Jaywalker was about to cash in nugget number 3.

SHEETZ: The fumes?

JAYWALKER: Yes, the fumes. Where did they come from?

SHEETZ: They came from the van.

JAYWALKER: Can you be more specific?

SHEETZ: Some came from the van's gas tank.

JAYWALKER: And others?

SHEETZ: We found the melted remains of a five-gallon metal gasoline container.

JAYWALKER: Were you able to determine whether that was an approved gasoline container?

SHEETZ: I don't recall.

Jaywalker pulled a document from his file and had it marked for identification. Dispensing with the usual protocol of asking the court's permission to approach the witness, he walked up to the stand and handed it to Sheetz. Then he stayed right there. In the movies, the cross-examiner and the witness are often pictured together. It makes for what Hollywood calls a nice tight shot. In real courtrooms, lawyers aren't supposed to crowd witnesses. But Jaywalker had once had a client who told him it made him absolutely nuts when the prosecutor had "gotten in his face." So Jaywalker did it every chance he got, and showing an adversary's witness a document provided a perfect opportunity.

JAYWALKER: Take a look at that document, will you?

SHEETZ: Yes, sir.

JAYWALKER: Do you recognize it?

SHEETZ: I do.

JAYWALKER: What is it?

SHEETZ: It's a memo I wrote on May 31 of last year. A long time ago. I'd forgot about it.

JAYWALKER: And does reading it now refresh your recollection and help you recall that the metal gasoline container you found was an unapproved type?

SHEETZ: Yes, sir.

JAYWALKER: What made it unapproved?

SHEETZ: It could have been several things. It might have been unvented, which means it might have been prone to burst on impact, instead of expanding or contracting. Or it might have been the type that spill when turned over. Or it might not have been spark resistant.

JAYWALKER: Or it might have had all three of those defects?

SHEETZ: Yes, sir.

JAYWALKER: Was there in fact an impact to the van?

SHEETZ: There was.

JAYWALKER: Did the van in fact turn over?

SHEETZ: It did.

JAYWALKER: And is it your opinion that there was in fact a spark?

SHEETZ: It is.

JAYWALKER: The van's gas tank is by law constructed to withstand all of those things. Correct?

SHEETZ: Correct.

JAYWALKER: How about the unapproved gasoline can?

SHEETZ: It was apparently built without regard to those things. That's why I referred to it as unapproved.

JAYWALKER: What's an accelerant?

FIRESTONE: Objection. He's not an arson investigator.

THE COURT: He may answer if he knows.

JAYWALKER: Do you know what an accelerant is?

SHEETZ: Yes, sir. It's a highly volatile, and therefore inflammable, substance that's often used to get a fire started.

JAYWALKER: Is gasoline an accelerant?

SHEETZ: Yes, sir. One of the best. Or worst, depending upon how you choose to look at it.

JAYWALKER: And if you choose to look at it from the point of view of those eight kids in the van?

SHEETZ: One of the worst.

JAYWALKER: In your expert opinion, but for the presence of that unapproved gasoline can, which was prone to burst, spill or explode in the presence of a spark, might those kids be alive today?

The fact that Firestone's objection was sustained made little difference to Jaywalker. This wasn't some civil case he was trying, after all, in which the jury would be called upon to determine negligence and apportion fault among the defendant, the driver of the van, and the company that owned or operated it. But just as William Sheetz's earlier concession—that Carter Drake might never have been aware of the accident he'd caused in his wake—would give the jurors something to think about over the weekend, so too would Sheetz's implicating the exploding gasoline can, particularly when coupled with his dubious claim that he'd forgotten all about it.

So if Jaywalker hadn't actually succeeded in out-dueling John Wayne, at the very least he'd knocked him off his high horse just a bit. But still, he wasn't quite finished. He had a teaser for the jury, one last thing for them to take home with them and wonder about. Gold nugget number 4.

JAYWALKER: Let me draw your attention to this photograph, one of several you took of the interior of the Audi.

SHEETZ: Yes, sir.

JAYWALKER: I wonder if you can tell us what this is, right here on the console? *(Pointing)*

SHEETZ: This?

JAYWALKER: Yes, that.

SHEETZ: It appears to be a newspaper.

JAYWALKER: Appears to be?

SHEETZ: It's hard to tell.

JAYWALKER: Why?

SHEETZ: Because it's rolled up.

JAYWALKER: I see.

With the weekend upon them, Jaywalker relented and took Amanda up on her offer to follow her home. In the process, he rationalized, he was doing more than merely giving in to his libido, more even than falling in with the culture's *Thank-God-It's-Friday* attitude. This was one of the weekends Eric was due to come home from school. For some time now, despite Carter's insistence that his son be left out of things and not called as a defense witness, Jaywalker had insisted on at least sitting down with the boy and seeing what he had to say about his father's level of intoxication the evening he'd been sent in to fetch him out of the End Zone. And for some time now, Amanda had been promising to deliver Eric for that conversation. But each time, something would come up. Eric was behind in his courses and needed to stay at school to catch up. Or his ride with a classmate had fallen through. Or Greyhound had changed its schedule so that the bus to Manhattan no longer stopped anywhere near the school, which was in western Massachusetts.

Finally Jaywalker had put his foot down. He'd insisted that Amanda call Eric and extract from him a solemn promise that no matter what, he'd be at his mother's by noon this Saturday. After some hemming and hawing, Amanda had agreed and then reported back that it was a done deal. So Jaywalker would have to work on the weekend while on trial. What else was new?

That said, by midnight Friday, he was hardly regretting his decision. He and Amanda had enjoyed a memorable dinner at the Union Square Café, her treat, despite his protests. And afterward, they'd enjoyed an equally memorable follow-up in her bedroom. And while he'd surely needed the meal, not having eaten in the previous twenty-four hours, if asked to choose, he would have had no problem. No reservation required, no waiting for a table, no calories to speak of, and no check to fight over.

It was only the following morning that the ringing of the telephone brought the news that Eric had been prohibited from leaving the campus because he'd been placed on both academic and social probation. Was that, Jaywalker wondered, the equivalent of the *double-secret probation* that had threatened to ground an entire fraternity in "Animal House," his all-time favorite movie?

"Get up," he told Amanda, "and get dressed."

"Why? What for?"

"Road trip."

19

ROAD TRIP

The drive up to Massachusetts took the better part of three hours, even in Amanda's Lexus. Jaywalker had seriously questioned whether his Mercury was up to the task, so he'd volunteered his driving services if Amanda was willing to supply the wheels, and she'd grudgingly agreed. When he expressed surprise that she didn't exactly seem overjoyed at the prospect of seeing her son, she smiled knowingly.

"You haven't met Eric," she said.

"No," he agreed.

"Eric has issues."

"Issues?"

"Eric is a full-time, 24/7 rebel," she explained. "He lies, he steals, he drinks, he does drugs. But he does it all with great charm. He's very good at manipulating people."

"Me, too."

It was the truth. More than once, Jaywalker had referred to himself as a master manipulator. He'd earned the distinction back in his DEA days, when his success, and occasionally his very life, had depended upon his ability to convince dealers to accept him as one of their own, trust him fully, and sell him enough bulk narcotics to put them away for significant chunks of their lives. And he'd carried the skill over to his lawyering, where he made his living by manipulating adversaries, witnesses, judges and juries, also with considerable charm. In one dark moment he'd confided to his wife that he was no better than a jostler, a guy on the subway who bumped into you to distract you even as he picked your pocket, and afterward apologized profusely for his clumsiness.

"Well, don't let Eric con you," Amanda was saying. "He's not to be trusted, no matter how sincerely he looks at you. He's very, very good at it."

The Berkshire Academy for Boys and Youths, unaffectionately referred to by its inhabitants as "BABY," was a cluster of redbrick buildings scattered over a snow-covered, 240-acre campus that would have been the envy of many good-size universities. Constructed in the 1890s with state funds, it had originally served as a combination orphanage and home for the severely retarded, a warehouse of sorts for the hundreds, and at times thousands, of boys throughout Massachusetts who either had no other home, or had one but were unwelcome there. By the 1940s, the number of inhabitants had dwindled to the point where it was no longer economically feasible to continue funding the home, and it had closed down and fallen into decay. In 1951, it was put on the auction block and sold for what was at the time considered a handsome price, eight hundred and seventy-five thousand dollars. Over the next thirty years it changed hands several times, eventually bought by the Cabot Foundation, which rehabilitated it and turned it into an all-boys preparatory school. But rather than attract the sort of Ivy League–bound student population that Philips Exeter, Choate and Deerfield had, Berkshire gradually became a repository for the underachiever, the problem child and the downright delinquent. For many young men of privileged background—according to Amanda, tuition, room and board came to something in excess of seventy thousand dollars per year—it represented the last stop before reform school, juvenile detention or worse.

Eric Drake, it would seem, fit right in.

They met him at the main administration building after a half hour's wait. Jaywalker had brought along a subpoena, the Samoan penny type, in case it came to a showdown, but it didn't. In fact, none of the three administrators they spoke with knew anything about the academic and social probation that had prevented Eric from traveling to New York for the weekend.

"Didn't I tell you what he's like?" said Amanda. "He must have made that all up. Probably had a party he wanted to go to. Or a baseball game."

"It's January," Jaywalker pointed out.

"Whatever."

When Eric appeared, dressed all in black and escorted by a teacher's aide, he seemed genuinely surprised to see his mother, and totally confounded by Jaywalker's presence, once Amanda had introduced him as Carter's lawyer.

"Is everything all right?" he asked. "I mean, with the trial."

It was almost as if he'd never planned on heading to the city, and had no knowledge of being rebuffed in attempting to. And when Jaywalker made an oblique reference to double-secret probation, he drew nothing but a blank stare. Then again, the kid was only eighteen. But still…

"I need to speak with you," he told Eric.

"Sure."

"Alone."

Amanda protested, saying she'd traveled three hours to see her son, only to be told now to disappear, to sit once more on the courthouse bench, so to speak. But Jaywalker insisted. He'd learned over the years that you didn't interview young people in the presence of their parents, not if you wanted the truth from them.

The aide found them an empty office and closed the door on his way out. There was a desk in the room, and several chairs. Jaywalker motioned Eric to sit, and then chose a chair nearby. He didn't want the desk to act as a barrier between them. He figured thirty-some years and his own lack of either a nose ring or orange hair were sufficient obstacles.

"How's school?" he asked.

"Sucks."

So much for small talk.

"How's my dad?" Eric asked.

"Good," said Jaywalker. "Amazingly good, considering."

"What's going to happen?"

"He's going to get convicted on some of the charges. Drunk driving, reckless driving, vehicular manslaughter, maybe leaving the scene. I think we've got a shot on the murder count, but it's going to be uphill."

"What kind of time is he looking at?"

They were all normal questions, asked normally. What a psychologist might have termed *appropriate,* both in form and content.

"If he's lucky, ten or twelve years. If he's not…" Jaywalker found himself unable to finish the sentence. How did you tell a kid his father was in real danger of ending up with a sentence of twenty-five to life? Especially a kid who, despite the Halloween costume and the advance billing, seemed genuinely likable?

"I need to ask you a few questions," he said instead.

"Shoot."

"The evening you drove up to Nyack with your mother—"

"I didn't drive," said Eric. "My mom drove."

"Right," said Jaywalker. This kid would make a pretty good lawyer, he decided. "She drove. But you went into the bar, the club. Right?"

"Right."

"How did your father seem?"

Eric hesitated for just an instant. "What do you want me to say?" he asked, turning his palms up.

"The truth. There's no jury here."

"He seemed drunk. Drunk and belligerent."

Jaywalker nodded, his way of telling Eric that was fine, he just needed to hear it. "Tell me what happened," he said. "In as much detail as you possibly can."

"There's not much to tell," Eric said. "My dad was pissed, and pissed off. He felt like the bartender had snitched on him. But he followed me out of the place. Once we got outside, I asked him for the keys. He asked me if it looked like daylight to me. Meaning I wasn't allowed to drive. I was still seventeen then, and all I had was a learner's permit. I said no, it didn't look like daylight. And he said, 'No fucking way, kiddo.'"

"And?"

"And I said, 'Fuck it.' I walked over to my mom's car and told her to deal with him."

Jaywalker nodded, but said nothing. He wanted this to be a narrative as much as possible, not a Q and A.

"So my mom got out and walked over to where my dad was standing, or staggering, and the two of them started arguing. Nothing new, it's what they do. Me, I got tired of listening to them, so I got back into my mom's car. After a while, my mom came over and handed me her car keys. 'Go straight to your father's,' she said. 'And don't you speed, or we'll all end up in jail.' Then she walked back over to my father. The last I saw of them, they were shouting at each other, across the Audi. Him refusing to give her the keys, she calling him a stupid asshole. Stuff like that. So I drove home to my dad's."

"Whoa. *You* drove home to your dad's? In the Lexus?"

"Yeah. I do know how to drive, you know."

"Yeah, I know. But…" Again Jaywalker stopped mid-thought. Both Amanda and Carter had told him that she'd given up on Carter, gone back to the Lexus, and driven Eric to Carter's place before driving herself home. This was a totally different version, one that put Amanda in the passenger seat alongside her husband.

And then he remembered Amanda's warnings. *Eric has issues…he lies…he's very good at manipulating people…don't let him con you…he's not to be trusted, no matter how sincerely he looks you in the eye…he's very, very good at it.*

So who was telling the truth here, and who was lying? Did you give the adults the benefit of the doubt? Was it majority rule? Did you discount Eric's version because of the nose ring and the orange hair? Did you heed Amanda's warning, or had she been deliberately trying to undermine her son's credibility in advance?

"Had you ever been up to Nyack before?" Jaywalker asked Eric. It was something of an occupational hazard, resorting to cross-examination to test a story. But he needed to know.

"No."

"Did you know your way back to the city?"

"No, I didn't have a clue."

"Did you stop to ask anyone for directions?"

"No."

"Didn't you get lost?"

"No."

"So tell me," said Jaywalker, about to spring the jaws of the trap shut. "How did you happen to get home, in the dark, without getting lost?"

Eric shrugged easily. "My mom's car has a GPS," he explained. "I punched in my dad's address."

Okay, score one for the kid.

"You had to cross the George Washington Bridge, right?"

It was one of those crossings that had a one-way toll. You were free to leave the city, but once you did, it cost you a bundle to get back in. Not exactly a welcome mat, but it did cut down on the number of tollbooths needed.

"So tell me. How much was the toll?"

"I haven't a clue."

Jaywalker shot him his best *gotcha* look.

But Eric shrugged again. "EZPass," he said.

Okay, two for two. But wasn't three the charm?

"EZPass I know," said Jaywalker. "In fact, I sub-poenaed their records a few months back, and I have here a photograph of the Lexus going through the tollbooth." He reached into a file, withdrew a photo and studied it. "It's taken from behind, so you can't see the faces. But there are two people in the car, and it sure looks like a woman's driving." The photo actually happened to be the one of the rolled-up newspaper on the console of the Audi, but from where he was sitting, Eric had no way of knowing that.

"Nice try," said Eric. "But sorry. I was driving the Lexus. And I was alone. Whatever my parents may have told you, and whatever that's a photograph of."

And the way he said it wasn't plaintive or insistent or argumentative. It was matter-of-fact, take it or leave it. The way you said something that was true.

So Moishe Leopold had been only half-wrong. He

may have mistaken the Audi for a Porsche, which was understandable, given how closely the two resembled each other. And a moment later, when Julie Napolitano had asked him if it could've been just one person in the front seat instead of two, as he'd originally thought, he'd been willing to back off on that point, as well, and concede he was probably wrong. But he *hadn't* been wrong about that; he'd been right. It was Carter and Amanda who'd been wrong.

Not just wrong, *lying*.

They rode the first hour home in silence, Jaywalker driving, Amanda staring out the passenger-side window. The snow-covered hills along the Taconic Parkway drifted by. They saw deer, wild turkeys and a red-tailed hawk. There was little in the way of traffic. It was Saturday, and the skiers were off skiing, the shoppers were off shopping, and with gas prices climbing, nobody, it seemed, was out for a weekend drive.

"So why did you lie to me?" he finally asked her.

"Carter," she said. "Carter insisted. He's a control freak, a certified micromanager, in case you haven't noticed. He insists that Eric be kept out of things, and me, too. He's afraid that if I admit being in the car, they'll charge me as an accomplice or something. And that they'll arrest Eric for having driven home with only a permit. Carter says they can take away his license for two years for that."

"Bullshit."

"He says he looked it up."

"Let's assume he's right," said Jaywalker, who had no idea if he was or wasn't. "Who cares if Eric can't drive for a couple of years. He doesn't need to. He's at school, and he doesn't even have a car. And as far as you're concerned, there's no such thing as an accomplice to motor vehicle offenses. Meanwhile, Carter's looking at spending the rest of his life in prison." It was an exaggeration, but not by all that much.

"Well," said Amanda, "why don't *you* try telling him?"

"I will. But right now he's not here, and you are. I need you to start by telling me what happened, from the moment you got into the Audi until the time Carter dropped you off."

"Carter will kill me."

Jaywalker looked over at her, just to make sure she didn't really mean it. But she was smiling, sort of. If you wanted to call a wry, bitter grin a smile. He decided her words had only been that: words, an expression. "If you don't tell me," he said, "*I'll* kill you."

She spoke for the next twenty minutes, almost without interruption. Carter had refused to give her the keys. He'd gotten behind the wheel of the Audi, started it up, and begun revving the engine noisily. For several minutes she'd begged him to let her drive, but he'd refused. Only when Eric had driven off in the Lexus and Carter had threatened to leave without her had she climbed in. Even as he drove, they'd continued to argue, about his driving too fast, drinking too much, whoring around, and all sorts of other stuff. At some point, he'd begun to go even faster, warning her to shut up or he'd kill them both.

"When that didn't work…"

He waited for her to finish her sentence, but she didn't.

"When that didn't work, what?"

He looked over at her again. This time, instead of sort of smiling, she was sort of crying. At least, a tear was running down the left side of her face, the only side he could see. He put on the four-way flashers, slowed down, and found a place to pull over. The driver of a huge SUV leaned on his horn as he sped by, spraying gravel against the side of the Lexus. Jaywalker killed the engine and turned to Amanda. "When that didn't work, what?" he repeated.

"He pulled into the other lane."

"The lane of oncoming traffic?"

She nodded. Tears were coming down both cheeks now, he could see.

"Did you shut up then?" he asked her.

"Shut up? No, I screamed."

"And?"

"And you know the rest."

"No," he said. "I don't."

"A couple of cars managed to get out of his way. Don't ask me how. Then, all of a sudden, the van was right in front of us."

He waited for more.

"It was like a game of chicken. The van tried to stop. Then it pulled to the right, our left. And as we passed it, I turned and saw it go over and disappear."

"What did you do?" Jaywalker asked. He already knew what Carter had done.

"I opened my mouth to try to say something. But nothing would come out. By the time I was able to speak, to say we had to turn around and go back, we were miles away."

"But you did say it?" He was beginning to have second thoughts about the accomplice thing.

"Yes."

"And?"

"Carter said I could get out and walk back if I wanted to, but he was going home. And he did. And I've got to tell you, it was weird. It was like the whole thing sobered him up, just like that. He drove like a normal person the rest of the way. Slowly, but not too slowly. Carefully. Normally. When we got to the city, he dropped me off, and I went upstairs and cried myself to sleep, praying that nobody got hurt. In the morning, I turned on the TV, and found out otherwise. A little while later, Carter phoned to say that someone had gotten his license-plate number, or part of it, and he was going to turn himself in. I think I said, 'That's good.'"

"How about the business of the wasp?" Jaywalker asked her. "And the rolled-up newspaper?"

"He made it up sometime afterward. He *is* allergic. That much is true. So he figured his doctor would be able to back him up on that, and people would believe the story."

"Anything else?"

"No. Yes."

"What?" he asked.

She looked him in the eye. "You have to promise me," she said. "You can't tell Carter I told you any of this. He really would kill me if he found out."

Jaywalker studied her face, by now red and puffy from crying. And this time he decided they might not be just words after all.

"Promise me?"

Back in his DEA days, Jaywalker had learned how to write a C.I. out of a case. A C.I. was a confidential informant, a snitch who was trading information on bigger dealers for leniency on his own case or money, or sometimes both. Say a C.I. had told Jaywalker and his team that Vinnie Bug Eyes had forty kilos of pure heroin stashed in a warehouse on Columbia Street, over on the Brooklyn docks. The team would sit on the place for a couple of nights. They might see stuff, they might not. Then they'd go to an assistant U.S. attorney and say they'd observed known dealers coming and going at odd hours of the night, looking around furtively and lugging heavy-looking suitcases in and out. Stuff like that. One of them would sign an affidavit. The assistant would go before a judge or a magistrate and get a search warrant for the warehouse. They'd kick in the door, tear the place apart and find a shitload of drugs and money. *Stash and cash,* they used to call it. And the best part was, Vinnie Bug Eyes never found out there was a C.I. involved who'd given him up. Because they'd written him out of the search warrant, out of the case altogether.

Sure, it had involved a bit of perjury and a little making of false sworn statements, both felonies that could have landed Jaywalker and the rest of his team in federal prison for five or ten years. But in the process, they'd brought down the bad guy, gotten the drugs out of circulation, and kept the C.I. from turning up in some dark alley with a bullet in the back of his head, and his tongue cut off and shoved down his throat. So it was a matter of the end justifying the means, he'd rationalized at the time. And, he figured, if he could write a C.I. out of things back then, surely he could do as much for Amanda Drake now.

"I promise," he told her.

Having spent Saturday driving up to Massachusetts and back, Jaywalker was forced to spend a good chunk of Sunday pondering what to do about this latest development. Amanda's admission that she'd been in the passenger seat of the Audi when her husband had run the van off the road was the least of things. Far more important was how she'd put the lie to the fable about the wasp and the rolled-up newspaper. Jaywalker now knew he couldn't call her as a witness, not without blowing away the only chance Carter had.

But it got even worse than that.

A lawyer doesn't necessarily have to believe his client in order to put him on the stand and have him tell his story. If that were a requirement, even fewer defendants would end up testifying than they now do. But, as with most things, there's a limit to the rule. A lawyer who *knows for a fact* that a witness intends to lie may not let him do so. That limitation applies to prosecutors and defenders alike, and extends to *all* witnesses, not just defendants.

Jaywalker was anything but naive, and he knew plenty of lawyers on both sides of the aisle who ignored the limitation. But as much of a rule breaker as he was, ethics were a different matter to him, and he drew a bright line when it came to suborning perjury. He was willing to coach a witness on how to say something, but not what to say. And more than once in his career he'd thrown a phony-alibi witness out of his office, once so roughly that he'd been arrested for assault.

He now knew this much. Come Monday morning, he'd have to confront Carter Drake about the wasp business. He'd promised Amanda he wouldn't let her husband know she'd given him up on it, and he'd honor that promise. Years ago, when his daughter had grown old enough to ask him to promise her certain things, he'd learned never to do so unless it was within his power to deliver. So "I promise I'll always love you" was okay, but "I promise I'll always be here for you" wasn't. A promise was just that, a promise.

Lying, on the other hand, was occasionally permitted under Jaywalker's personal code of conduct. Back when his wife lay dying, her body reduced to skin and bones, her face ravaged and contorted in pain, he must have told her a hundred times that she was still beautiful. And when her breath was fouled from swallowing what little was left of her own blood, he'd assured her it still smelled sweet, though both of them had surely known better. So just as he'd lied to Eric about the phantom EZPass photo, so too would he lie to his own client, in order to protect Amanda but at the same time get her husband to come clean. And once he'd done that, Carter would be stripped of his own lie and the only defense he had. At that point, he'd be willing to talk about a plea, and all that would be left was twisting Abe Firestone's arm hard enough to get him to let go of the murder count.

But in the meantime, just in case he was wrong about any of that, there were Monday morning's witnesses to prepare for.

20

A GUEST OF THE COUNTY

On Monday morning, before the jury was brought into court, Abe Firestone rose and announced his intention to call a video technician named Landon Miller to the stand. Miller was employed by a company Firestone had commissioned. They'd created a video that, according to Firestone, would recreate for the jurors the view from the driver's seat of the Audi as it crossed over into the wrong lane, narrowly missed two oncoming cars, forced the van off the road, and continued on without stopping.

"Have you shared this with Mr. Jaywalker?" Justice Hinkley asked.

"Not yet," said Firestone. "I only saw it myself for the first time this morning. I contacted the company Friday, after court. The defense has done such a good job confusing the jurors that I felt they should have a chance to see what things really looked like from the defendant's perspective."

"Sit down, Mr. Jaywalker," said the judge. He'd been on his feet, ready to explode, ever since he'd heard the word *video*. Words like *ambush, surprise, improper* and *prejudicial* were on the tip of his tongue. Not to mention *joke, cartoon* and *bullshit*. But sit he did.

"Don't worry," the judge added. "You'll have plenty of time to be heard on this. Mr. Firestone, exactly when in your case were you hoping to call this witness."

"Now."

"How long is the video?"

Firestone looked over at David Kaminsky for a clue, got one, and replied, "Five minutes."

The judge sent word to the jury room that there would be an unavoidable delay before the morning session got under way. Then she ordered the courtroom cleared. As the rows emptied, Jaywalker overheard two reporters discussing going to the Appellate Division to complain. He wished them luck. The Appellate Division was in Albany, a good two hours away.

The technician, whom Jaywalker had expected to be geeky-looking but who turned out to be Madison-Avenue, button-down handsome, was permitted to enter the courtroom and, with the help of an equally attractive female assistant, set up several huge television screens, so everyone would be able to see without moving from their seats. Then the lights were dimmed, and the feature presentation came on.

Jaywalker hadn't known quite what to expect. He'd considered it quite possible that the company had gone out and gotten a hold of an Audi TT, mounted a camera on the dashboard or the driver's forehead, and recreated the route Carter Drake had taken, complete with a substitute white van and a couple of stunt drivers. What he found himself watching instead was a high-tech, full-color, professionally made, virtual-reality production. A sort of *Batman Driving Badly,* he decided. The windshield, the instruments on the dashboard beneath it, the hands gripping the steering wheel, and the road ahead, were neither real nor animated, but somewhere in between the two. The only thing missing was a Hollywood sound track.

Jaywalker was immediately reminded why he no longer went to the movies. There'd been a time when he'd been a lover of special effects. He could watch *King Kong* a hundred times over—the original one with Fay Wray, the mechanical ape, and the tiny lizards pretending to be dinosaurs. But he couldn't sit through the remake. *Star Wars* and its progeny had left him cold, and by the time *Harry Potter* came along, he hadn't even been tempted. Computerized effects had made the impossible possible, but to Jaywalker, none of it looked real anymore.

And so it was with this production. The guardrails lining the roadway weren't guardrails at all, but digitized recreations of them. The cars veering out of the way of the Audi weren't real. Even the van, slamming on its brakes as the Audi closed in on it, didn't look real. Furthermore, the five minutes Firestone had predicted was way off. From start to finish, it took less than a minute. And yet, when the van suddenly turned, fishtailed, took flight and disappeared off to the left of the giant screen, the effect was unmistakably powerful. And the Audi driver's calmly pulling back into his proper lane and continuing on without ever slowing down was nothing less than bone-chilling.

They watched it three times through, from start to finish, but it didn't get any better.

"Turn the lights back on," said Justice Hinkley. And when that had been done, she turned to the defense table and said, "Mr. Jaywalker?"

He spoke for ten minutes, citing the prosecution's breach of pretrial discovery, the dangers inherent in substituting a movie for actual testimony, and the unfair emotional impact the recreation would inevitably have upon the jurors. If they were vague about what the particular stretch of road in question looked like, let them go visit it as a group, under the court's supervision, the way that was sometimes done when one side or the other requested it. But don't show them a dumb *cartoon* of it.

But even as he argued he could sense, the way a good lawyer can always sense, that his words were falling on ears that, if not quite deaf, had certainly become hearing impaired.

"Don't you agree that the courts have to keep up with ever-changing technology?" the judge asked him.

"Not if it means depriving my client of a fair trial, I don't. This is nothing but an ambush. They had nine months to do this and give me a chance to hire experts to examine it. I could have made my own competing version. Instead, they slap it together over a weekend and spring it on us first thing Monday morning."

"Would you like a day's continuance?" the judge wanted to know.

"No. I'd like you to rule that whatever its probative value may be—and for the life of me, I think that's less than zero—is vastly outweighed by its prejudicial impact. I want you to keep it out."

"Would you like a *voir dire* of the witness, in the jury's absence?"

"No."

"Would you like the jury brought to the scene?"

"No."

"Would you like a limiting instruction?"

"Maybe I'm not making myself clear," said Jaywalker. "I want it out, period. I keep hearing what a strong case the prosecution has. Well, maybe they do. You want to take a chance and let this piece of—"

"Careful."

"—evidence in," Jaywalker continued, grateful that the judge had steered him away from the word he'd been about to use, "then go ahead. Give us an issue to appeal on. We should be thanking you." And with that, he sat down.

For a long moment, Justice Hinkley said nothing. She was too busy writing. When she was finished, she looked up and spoke in a measured, calm voice. "The court hereby holds defense counsel in summary contempt. Counsel is an experienced practitioner who knows full well that threatening a court with reversal is a breach of ethics. It is only because I believe that you've acted out of nothing but overzealousness on behalf of your client that I suspend sentence. Next time, I promise you, I won't."

Jaywalker nodded a silent thank-you.

"Now, let me ask you again," said the judge. "Would you like a twenty-four-hour continuance?"

"No."

"Would you like a limiting instruction?"

"Yes."

They spent a few minutes going over what the judge would tell the jurors when it came time for them to see the video. They would be instructed to use it only for clarification purposes, not as a substitute for the sworn testimony of eyewitnesses. But to Jaywalker, the distinction hardly mattered. This was the Age of the Video Screen, he knew, whether that screen happened to be on a TV set, a computer or what used to be called a telephone, in the old days. No matter what the judge told the jurors to do or not do, they'd get into their deliberations at the end of the case and pretty much forget who had said what. But they'd remember that white van on the big screen, veering off, fishtailing and leaving the roadway. How could they not?

The playing of the video for the jurors turned out to be every bit the horror show Jaywalker had expected it to be. They got to see it only once, but from the rapt attention they appeared to give it, once was enough. As he watched it from the defense table, the only thing Jaywalker could take comfort from was the dimming of the courtroom lights, allowing him and his client to hide in the semidarkness. But then the lights came back up, and there was no place to hide, literally or figuratively.

On cross-examination, he focused on the sources of information that Landon Miller and his team had relied on in putting the video together.

JAYWALKER: Did you interview the driver of the Audi?

MILLER: No.

JAYWALKER: Did you try to?

MILLER: No. There wasn't time.

JAYWALKER: Did you try to contact me?

MILLER: No.

JAYWALKER: Interview any of the other drivers or eyewitnesses?

MILLER: No.

JAYWALKER: So whom did you interview?

MILLER: May I check my notes?

JAYWALKER: Sure. I imagine Mr. Firestone will give me a copy of them sometime next year.

THE COURT: The jurors will disregard that remark.

MILLER: We interviewed Mr. Firestone, Mr. Kaminsky and Investigator Sheetz.

JAYWALKER: That's it?

MILLER: That's it.

JAYWALKER: Two prosecutors and one prosecution witness?

MILLER: I guess so.

JAYWALKER: Kind of like Fox News? Fair and balanced?

FIRESTONE: Objection.

THE COURT: Sustained.

JAYWALKER: Let me try to understand this, Mr. Miller. You made a movie version of what Mr. Firestone, Mr. Kaminsky and Investigator Sheetz told you. You spoke to not a single eyewitness. You didn't even attempt to speak with anyone from the defense. Am I correct?

MILLER: Yes.

JAYWALKER: Care to tell us how much you charged the taxpayers of Rockland County for this production?

FIRESTONE: Objection.

THE COURT: Sustained as to form.

JAYWALKER: How much did you bill for your services?

FIRESTONE: Objection.

THE COURT: Overruled.

MILLER: That's a proprietary matter.

THE COURT: Not anymore it isn't. Please answer the question.

MILLER: *(Inaudible)*

JAYWALKER: I couldn't hear that.

MILLER: One million, two hundred and fifty thousand dollars.

Which, judging from the collective gasp emanating from the jury box, was as good a time for Jaywalker to collect his notes and sit down as he was going to get.

The setting up of the video equipment, the previews, the arguing, the instructions to the jurors, the actual showing, the testimony and the removal of the equipment left no room for additional witnesses in the morning session. Which was just as well, as far as Jaywalker was concerned. He needed to talk to Carter Drake, in order to straighten out the business of Amanda's having been seated next to him in the Audi rather than driving the Lexus with Eric.

He did it locked in a holding cell with his client over the lunch hour. He even broke his no-lunch rule and accepted a cheese sandwich from a guard, as well as a cup of warm yellowish water he guessed was tea, though only after subjecting it to a repeated smell test.

For lack of imagination, he tried the same ploy with Carter that he had two days earlier with Eric. "I've got an interesting bit of news for you," he said.

"What's that?"

"Firestone has photos he subpoenaed from EZPass."

"Oh?"

"It seems you weren't alone in the Audi," said Jaywalker. "There's a woman sitting in the passenger seat, and from the back she looks very much like your wife. And the shot of the Loxus shows only a driver in the front, and he looks an awful lot like your son."

Drake finished swallowing a mouthful of stale bread and cheese. Velveeta must have somehow come in with the low bid for the concession, Jaywalker had already decided. A million and a quarter to piss away on a one-minute cartoon was okay, though.

"Why can't you keep my family out of this?" asked Drake.

"Why can't you tell me the truth?" countered Jaywalker. "Then maybe I can." He left it at that. This was neither the time nor the place for a lecture on trust, honesty and professional ethics.

"So what if she was with me?"

"Don't you see? It changes everything. For starters, the wasp story won't sell."

"Why not?"

"Because," Jaywalker explained, "if there had really been a wasp, your wife could have dealt with it. You already had enough on your plate, driving—"

"Drunk?"

"You said it. I didn't."

"Okay," said Carter. "You want the truth, here's the truth. My wife *was* in the car with me. That much is true.

But there was a wasp, and when it started flying around, I asked her to kill it. But she was angry at me, and she wouldn't do it. So I tried. I probably even made a bigger deal of it than I should have. You know, reaching way over to accentuate the fact that she wouldn't help me. You know the rest."

Did he? All Jaywalker really knew was that his bluff about the EZPass photos had worked, and that Amanda had indeed ridden home in the Audi. As for the wasp story, it was still up for grabs. Amanda had said it was a lie, but Carter was sticking with it. And Jaywalker couldn't very well confront him with Amanda's version, not without breaking his promise and giving her up.

Besides which, Carter's insistence that it was true provided Jaywalker with some ethical cover. Because he was in no position to say for sure who was telling the truth and who was lying, he could go ahead and put his client on the stand and have him tell his story. He could even tell Amanda that her husband was sticking with it. If she were to get the hint and remember it his way, she could bolster his defense. On the other hand, if she were to continue to insist that there'd been no wasp... Well, he'd cross that bridge when he came to it.

The afternoon session brought a woman named Lone Thanning to the stand. Thanning was the Rockland County medical examiner, and a witness Jaywalker had been dreading for some time. One of the elements the prosecution is required to prove in a murder case is that the victim died, and that some act of the defendant caused that death. In some cases, that cause-and-effect relationship is thrown into serious debate. Jaywalker had tried cases where cause of death was *the* issue before the jury. The guy with the .45 blood alcohol reading, for example, whose stepson had conked him on the head with a bottle. Had the blow really been the cause of death? Or had it been merely incidental to the victim's suddenly collapsing from acute and chronic alcohol poisoning? Or the nineteen-year-old who'd lost his balance after being punched in an alley fight, and had happened to land on a jagged piece of glass that severed his femoral artery? Had the defendant truly caused his death, or had it been a tragic accident?

But when it came to the nine occupants of the van, cause of death was hardly in issue. They'd died, Jaywalker was more than prepared to concede, because the van had rolled over, exploded and burned. Precisely when in the course of those events their deaths occurred, or exactly how, made no difference at all. So Jaywalker had repeatedly offered to stipulate that the medical examiner, if called as a witness, would testify that all nine deaths had resulted from the van's being forced off the road.

But Abe Firestone would have none of that.

Just as Jaywalker wanted to keep the gruesome details from the jurors, Firestone wanted to get as much mileage from those details as he possibly could. And because neither side can be forced to accept a stipulation in lieu of actual evidence, Justice Hinkley wasn't about to intervene. The most she would do was to warn Firestone—and David Kaminsky, who would conduct the direct examination of Dr. Thanning—to keep things as brief as possible and refrain from going into overly graphic details.

Still, Jaywalker knew, it wasn't going to be pretty.

Kaminsky asked Dr. Thanning about her title, training and experience. She described earning her medical degree, doing several internships and residencies, earning board certification in forensic pathology, and working as an assistant medical examiner in the county until her promotion several years ago.

KAMINSKY: What are your duties as chief medical examiner of Rockland County?

THANNING: I run the office and report to the county executive. Along with my staff, I investigate every violent or suspicious death that occurs in the county, as well as a large number of cases where the cause of death is unknown.

KAMINSKY: How do you go about investigating those deaths?

THANNING: Chiefly by performing complete postmortem examinations, commonly referred to as autopsies.

KAMINSKY: How many autopsies have you performed or assisted at?

THANNING: Thousands.

KAMINSKY: Did you have occasion to perform an autopsy on May 28 of last year?

THANNING: I did.

KAMINSKY: Who was the subject of that autopsy?

THANNING: A man by the name of Walter Najinsky.

Walter Najinsky had been the driver of the van, and had long been the forgotten victim in the case. But that was about to change. Najinsky was about to be remembered in death far more than he had been in life, except perhaps by his immediate family and friends.

KAMINSKY: Would you describe Mr. Najinsky's remains for us as you first encountered them?

THANNING: Yes. The entire body was charred black. The facial features were virtually unrecognizable. Almost all of the flesh had been incinerated, except where one shoe had partially protected one foot. Other than that, what I was looking at was essentially some very burned flesh and a skeleton.

Jaywalker pretended to be taking notes, but only because he didn't dare look at the jurors. The silence in the courtroom told him all he needed to know.

KAMINSKY: What did your examination reveal?

THANNING: It revealed third-degree burns of the entire body.

KAMINSKY: Would you please explain to the jury what third-degree burns are?

THANNING: We divide burns into three degrees, increasing in severity from first degree to third degree. First-degree burns are a reddening of the skin, the sort of thing you might sustain from getting your finger too close to a match, or touching the surface of a pot that's been on the burner of a stove. Second-degree burns involve blistering, where the heat and duration of exposure are enough to kill the outer layers of skin, and cause them to separate from the internal layers. Third-degree burns include charring, much the same way a steak will char if left on a hot open flame too long.

KAMINSKY: Did your examination reveal anything else?

THANNING: Yes. I was able to determine that there were several fractures to bones, specifically the right fibula and tibia, the pelvis, and both the left and right clavicles. In addition, there was a depressed fracture of the skull.

Kaminsky had the witness describe the various bones she'd mentioned. Then he asked her if she had been able to determine the cause of death.

THANNING: Not with absolute certainty. It was most likely the burns. But the skull fracture was also capable of causing death. And it's impossible to rule out internal injuries, which means bleeding from major organs. The body was simply too badly burned to make a determination.

KAMINSKY: Did you take photographs of the body?

JAYWALKER: You can't be serious.

Never mind that it was a line John MacEnroe used to get away with regularly. Jaywalker wouldn't be so lucky. Justice Hinkley banged her gavel once and declared a recess. Then, as soon as the last juror had left the courtroom, she held Jaywalker in contempt for the second time that day. "Only this time, I sentence you to one day in jail, and I do not, repeat, do *not,* suspend the execution of that sentence. Mr. Stephens," she called to a uniformed trooper assigned to guard the defendant and escort him to and from the courtroom. "Please make the necessary arrangements. Mr. Jaywalker will be a guest of the county tonight."

Then she asked David Kaminsky to show her the autopsy photos. Jaywalker had asked that she exclude them seven weeks ago, arguing that they were too inflammatory to show the jurors. In addition to the charred remains of Walter Najinsky, there were multiple photos of the bodies of the eight children, smaller than the driver's, but no less jarring. They ranged from moderately disturbing to truly hideous.

"Any probative value they might have," Jaywalker pointed out, "is far outweighed by—"

"Quiet," said the judge. She continued to inspect the photos for several minutes, gradually sorting them into two piles, before looking up. "These you may offer," she told Mr. Kaminsky. "These you may not. The defense's objection to them is noted and overruled."

Jaywalker noticed that somewhere along the line he'd ceased to be "Mr. Jaywalker" and had become "the defense." One of the prices of vigorous advocacy. He was permitted to see which photos had passed muster. They included five of Mr. Najinsky from various angles, as well as a close-up of the skull fracture, and one of a child, charred beyond recognition. Jaywalker had seen them all, having been furnished copies many months ago. Even he would have had to concede that Justice Hinkley had kept the very worst of them out. There was one, for example, of the eight children's bodies, arranged side by side, that reminded him of concentration camp photos he'd seen. And another of a small blackened skull framing tiny white teeth that seemed to be smiling out at the viewer.

Still, the ones the jurors were going to be permitted to see were ghastly enough.

And the thing was, by excluding the worst of them, the judge would no doubt be deemed to have forged an acceptable Solomonic compromise in the opinion of some appellate court, a year or two from now. Judges weren't asked to be perfect, after all, just reasonable.

Once the jury had been brought back into the courtroom, Kaminsky had Dr. Thanning identify the photos of Mr. Najinsky and describe what each one depicted. Then he moved on, out of the frying pan, as it were.

KAMINSKY: Did you conduct autopsies of the additional eight victims, the children?

THANNING: No, I did not.

KAMINSKY: Why not?

THANNING: I was able to tell from a gross external examination that all eight had suffered third-degree burns over just about their entire bodies, and that in all eight cases, they could not have survived those burns. Based upon that conclusion, I elected to use my discretion and yield to the wishes of the families, who are all orthodox Jews opposed on religious grounds to invasive autopsies. Also, they wanted to bury their children without further delay, in accordance with their beliefs.

Which didn't stop Kaminsky from introducing eight additional photos, one for each of the children, and then having them *published*, passed among the jurors. Jaywalker watched out of the corner of one eye as each juror in turn physically recoiled from the images.

He asked Dr. Thanning no questions.

* * *

The afternoon's final witness was another doctor, this one a forensic pediadontist named Oliver Landsman Jacoby. Dr. Jacoby, so far as anyone had been able to ascertain, was the only person on the planet who made his living and spent all of his professional time identifying dead children by comparing their teeth to their previous dental records or, if no such records existed, to dental characteristics they shared in common with their parents or siblings. It was, one might say, a niche industry.

Because the eight children had been so thoroughly burned, and because the religious beliefs of their parents forbade intrusive procedures to their bodies, the Rockland County authorities had decided against attempting to draw tissue samples for DNA typing. With no cheeks left to swab, skin to scrape, or hairs from which to collect follicles, that likely would have required extracting bone marrow, something that Lone Thanning had been understandably reluctant to do.

Enter Dr. Jacoby.

Again it was David Kaminsky who did the honors. Again Jaywalker rose to stipulate that the bodies were indeed those of the eight children named in the indictment. Again Firestone and his team rejected the offer. And again Justice Hinkley admonished Jaywalker for grandstanding in front of the jury. Though she did refrain from adding to his contempt sentence.

This time, the prosecution's inflexibility backfired just a bit. Kaminsky had Dr. Jacoby produce a series of packets. The first such packet contained multiple photographs and X-rays taken after the incident, and showing the teeth of the dead children. Each photo bore a number, 1 through 8, as well as the letter X, for "unknown." The rules of spelling, it seemed, were going to yield to the conventions of algebra. Next, Dr. Jacoby identified eight more packets, each containing not only photos and X-rays that had been taken during the lives of the children, but those of close relatives, as well. Each of those items bore the letter K, for "known." But here the numbers ran into the hundreds. And even though Kaminsky had taken the trouble to have all of the items premarked, it still took a good twenty minutes for them to be offered, remarked, and received in evidence. During those twenty minutes, the jurors got to sit on their hands. Jaywalker made a point of yawning several times, and noticed that a few of the jurors caught the bug and followed suit. Never a good sign for the prosecution.

Then Kaminsky began the tedious process of drawing out from Dr. Jacoby the evidence upon which he'd been able to match the teeth of each child with a name, through either prior photos, X-rays, or comparisons of *markers,* or unusual characteristics, with the teeth of known relatives. At one point Kaminsky got so confused trying to match up the Xs with the Ks that he offered to give up trying and accept the defense's offer of a stipulation.

"Objection," said Jaywalker. "Grandstanding."

Once it had gotten the desired effect of a couple of grins from the jury box, he withdrew the objection and agreed to stipulate. But before sitting down, he made sure to make a point of looking at his trusty Movado knockoff and shaking his head from side to side in mock exasperation over the waste of the jury's time.

But if a handful of jurors had noticed and smiled, Kaminsky remained oblivious. Finished with his direct examination of Dr. Jacoby, he insisted that the photos and X-rays, all 216 of them, be published to the jury. Justice Hinkley complied, but it was a mistake. There were simply too many exhibits, and unlike the video and the previous photos, these were in black and white. The jurors barely looked at them. Could it be that they were beginning to become desensitized to the horror?

Jaywalker could only hope.

Jaywalker half expected Justice Hinkley to relent and let him go for the night, but she didn't. She did permit him to turn his valuables over to Amanda for safekeeping. These included his identification, his keys, his watch and his money, which, assuming the overnight rate of exchange with Samoa hadn't changed, came to $17.42. Then he was escorted into the pen area by an apologetic trooper.

"Any chance I can double bunk with my client?" Jaywalker asked him. "I need to prepare him for testifying."

"I'll see what I can do," said the trooper. "But…"

"What?"

"Nothing."

"What?" Jaywalker repeated. And when that didn't work, he pulled out his trump card. "C'mon," he said. "I used to be on the job." The words might not have meant anything to a civilian, but to anyone in law enforcement, they were the way you said you were one of them, that you, too, had once carried a gun and a shield for a living. They were words he'd learned back in his DEA days, when he'd been out on the street undercover, carrying a bad-guy gun but no shield. And when some gung ho cop would stop him, give him a toss, and discover a .380 Browning semiautomatic shoved down his belt, with one in the chamber and eleven in the clip—which happened more than once—and was about to crack him over the head with it to teach him a lesson, Jaywalker would mutter the words just in time to save his skull.

On the job.

"Okay," said the trooper. "Just make sure you keep your food straight from his."

"Ten-four," said Jaywalker.

Which was his way of saying he got it. What the trooper was telling him was that Carter Drake wasn't much liked, and there was the outside but nonetheless distinct possibility that things were ending up on his meal tray or in his coffee that didn't exactly belong there. Not that the advice came as a total shock to Jaywalker. He'd once been warned by a court officer never to pour himself a cupful of water from the pitcher of a particular judge who was known to be discourteous toward his staff.

After a pat-down and some processing, including fingerprinting and photographing, Jaywalker was placed in solitary. He caught a nap on a bare steel cot, using his jacket as a blanket and his shoes for a pillow. It wouldn't be the first night he'd spent in jail, and it probably wouldn't be the last, so he figured he might as well make the best of things. After an hour or so, he was awakened and handed a pen through the bars, along with a printed form. He read just enough of it to understand that he was forever surrendering his right to sue the state, the county, the city, and their agents and employees in the unlikely event of assault, rape, death or dismemberment. He signed with his left hand, illegibly enough so that if more than three of those things were to happen, his daughter could claim that the handwriting wasn't his. Then his earlier wish was granted, and he was led down the corridor to a two-bunk cell, where Carter Drake took one look at him, smiled broadly and said, "Hey, it's my cousin Vinny!"

Whatever *that* was supposed to mean.

21

IN MY SLEEP I CAN TELL YOU

Spending a night in jail may actually have a positive effect on some people. It can serve as a warning to mend one's ways. It can provide an educational experience, even a humbling one. Gandhi is said to have emerged from imprisonment more determined than ever, Martin Luther King more revered. In modern times, at least one politician used his five years as a prisoner of war as a springboard to some degree of political success.

That said, jail does little for one's personal hygiene. Even though Jaywalker had been careful to keep his food—to use the word loosely—separate from that of his cell mate, he emerged the next morning looking like he'd slept in his suit and, well, smelling pretty much as might have been expected. The one-night rate, it turned out, hadn't included shower privileges. And unlike even the cheap motels he was used to on the rare occasion when he traveled, there'd been no cute little soaps, shampoos and conditioners arrayed on the bathroom sink. In fact, there'd been no bathroom. There'd been a sink, a steel thing with a single faucet producing cold water, and a matching toilet, no seat, no lid.

With no mirror in sight, the best he could do was to

run a hand through his hair and over the stubble on his chin. He had to tie his tie three times to get the ends right. His shirt was badly wrinkled, but that was nothing compared to how it smelled.

So when Jaywalker walked into the courtroom Tuesday morning to find Amanda waiting for him with a fresh suit and shirt, clean undershorts and socks, a toothbrush and toothpaste, a comb and—most welcome of all—a stick of deodorant, he was beyond grateful. She'd found his address among his identification, she explained, and used his keys to let herself into his apartment. Security had been no problem, there being none.

Justice Hinkley allowed him ten minutes to use a public restroom to change and defumigate. By the time he reappeared, he looked pretty much himself, give or take a day's stubble. Not that *pretty much himself* was ever going to land him on the pages of *GQ* magazine. But at least he smelled good, thanks to a generous underarm and overbody coating of Old Spice Original Scent.

Most murder cases involve a single victim. Yet prosecutors invariably feel compelled to offer not one but two witnesses when it comes to identifying the body for the jury. The first is typically a police witness, often a detective or officer who viewed the victim at the crime scene and later at the medical examiner's office, to assure the jurors that the bodies are one and the same. Chain of custody, so to speak.

In Carter Drake's trial, that had posed a problem, but only a bit of one. By the time the police arrived at the scene of the crash, the victims were already unrecognizable. But between the testimony of Lone Thanning and Oliver Jacoby, all nine of them had been fully identified for the jury.

The second identifier at a murder trial is generally a

next of kin or other close relative of the deceased. The avowed purpose of this exercise is to have someone who knew the victim in life, and subsequently saw him or her in death, vouch for the fact that the now-lifeless body is indeed the person named in the indictment. So much for the avowed purpose. What's really going on, of course, is that the prosecutor wants to humanize the victim, wants to bring in a grieving mother or father, son or daughter, to take the long walk to the witness stand and, choking back tears, describe having to see an only child or beloved parent laid out on a cold slab in the morgue.

Abe Firestone had weeks ago signaled his intention to call eight family members, one per child, in order to make civilian identifications of their loved ones. Jaywalker had immediately screamed foul, pointing out that because none of the eight could in fact identify the remains of their children, the tactic was nothing but an appeal to emotion. And when Justice Hinkley had wavered, he'd threatened to test each of the witnesses by displaying a huge blowup of the photo showing the eight charred bodies, and seeing if the parent could truly pick out his or her child.

Not that he would have done it, of course. But with Jaywalker, you never knew, and the specter had evidently been too much for the judge. For once, she'd sided with the defense. But at the same time she'd invited Firestone to come up with an alternative, some less inflammatory way of personalizing the victims. A week later, Firestone had unveiled his plan B. He intended to have a single parent stand in for the others. She—and the choice of gender was a pretty good indication that the prosecution was still hoping to maximize the emotional impact—would describe her own child, and then go on to name and say a little bit about each of the other seven. Again Jaywalker had objected. If the names of the children were what needed mentioning, surely some school official was in a better position to say who'd been on the van and who hadn't been, as opposed to some mother who might have been forty miles away, getting her hair done while the kids were climbing aboard.

In the end, the judge had agreed once again with Jaywalker, though not before scolding him for his sexist remark and warning him about his cavalier attitude. But there'd been no jurors around, and no members of the media. Still, she'd been right, and he'd apologized. He should have used a working mother in his example, rather than a well-coiffed one. So Firestone and his team had reluctantly moved on to plan C, eventually reporting that they'd taken the defense up on its suggestion and enlisted someone from the school to do the job.

Now, once the spectators had been allowed back inside the courtroom and the jurors led in, Julie Napolitano stood and announced that the People were ready to call their final witness, Rabbi Mordecai Lubovich.

Oy.

All eyes turned to see a small man, not much more than five feet tall, flanked by a pair of uniformed troopers, enter the courtroom. To Jaywalker, he looked to be in his seventies, maybe even his eighties. Then again, maybe it was the sadness he seemed to carry in with him that added to his years. The deep lines in his face gave him an uncanny resemblance to Edward G. Robinson. Not the early tough-talking one, though. More the weary warrior, the one who'd seen too much and wanted out. The one from *Soylent Green*.

NAPOLITANO: By whom are you employed, Rabbi Lubovich?

LUBOVICH: I'm employed by the Ramaz Yeshiva, here in New City.

NAPOLITANO: In what capacity?

LUBOVICH: I'm the equivalent of the principal.

NAPOLITANO: For how long have you been so employed?

LUBOVICH: For thirty-two years.

NAPOLITANO: Do you recall the day of May 27 of last year?

LUBOVICH: How can I forget?

But there was no glibness, nothing the least bit clever about the way he said it. With those four little words, he was telling the jurors what his life had been ever since that day, and what it would be until the day he died. And even as Jaywalker's heart reached out to the poor man as it hadn't done to any previous witness, he found himself thinking *Shit, I should have let them bring in the parents.*

NAPOLITANO: Did there come a time that day when a number of children from your school boarded a van to be taken somewhere?

LUBOVICH: Yes. Eight of my children, from different classes, had been selected to attend the groundbreaking ceremony for a new *shul,* a synagogue, in Haverstraw.

NAPOLITANO: How were they selected?

LUBOVICH: They were among my most promising students. They were the best and the brightest, you could say.

NAPOLITANO: Who loaded them onto the van?

LUBOVICH: I did, along with another teacher. I made sure they were each buckled into their seats. The seats they would die in.

NAPOLITANO: Can you tell us their names and ages?

LUBOVICH: In my sleep I can tell you.

And he proceeded to list them. Not reading from some list, but staring off into space. "Michael Fishbein, eleven. Sarah Teitelbaum, also eleven. Anna Moskowitz Zorn, ten. Andrew Tucker, nine. Sheilah Zucker, nine. Steven Sonnenshein, eight. Beth Levy-Strauss, seven. Richard Abraham Lubovich, six. He happened to be my great-grandson, my only great-grandson."

There comes a moment in every murder trial when the victim or victims cease to be a name and suddenly come to life. Up until that moment, Jaywalker had thought the moment had occurred when Adam Faulkner, the first trooper to arrive on the scene, had described the tiny charred bodies he'd encountered, some of them still smoking. Or when the veteran EMT Tracy D'Agostino had told how she'd climbed out of the van, walked twenty yards away, and vomited her guts out. But he'd been wrong. The prosecution, foiled by Jaywalker's own objections, had been forced to go to plan C and recruit an official from the school. They'd come up with what might have seemed to be an unlikely candidate in Rabbi Lubovich. He was a man, for one thing, less likely than a woman to stir emotions. And he was old, far too old to be looked upon as the parent of a young child. But in their selection, Firestone and his staff had stumbled upon the perfect witness, and right now that perfect witness had created The Moment.

Mordecai Lubovich had done his crying long ago. He had no tears left. But suddenly everyone else in the courtroom did, and had enough to make up for what the rabbi could no longer do.

Julie Napolitano should have left it right there, having not only choreographed The Moment, but having done so at the perfect time, with what should have been the very last words to come from the mouth of the prosecution's final witness. But she evidently had more on her notepad, so she forged ahead.

Not that what she followed up with was all that anti-climactic. What she did was hand Rabbi Lubovich a set of photographs, each one a glossy, full-color, sixteen-by-twenty-inch portrait of a child, and ask him to match a name to each face. As he did, she took the photo back from him, stuck it onto a large piece of white oak tag she'd earlier propped up on an easel, and affixed the name of the child just beneath his or her photo. By the time she'd finished the exercise, the jurors had two rows of four photos, eight in all, right in front of them. Having earlier been supplied the names of the young victims, they now had the children's faces staring directly at them, begging for justice.

"The People rest," said Julie Napolitano.

It was barely eleven o'clock, but Justice Hinkley excused the jurors for a long lunch break, telling them that they wouldn't be needed for another three hours. Once they'd filed out of the room, Jaywalker rose and formally made the obligatory motion to dismiss the charges against his client. He didn't bother arguing the point or citing cases. He knew better. And so did Justice Hinkley, who quickly denied his motion, ruling that if anything, the People had presented far more evidence than they'd been required to.

Out in the hallway, he found Amanda and used her cell phone to call Nicky Legs. "Get a hold of Drake's doctor," he told him. "Let him know we may be needing him as early as tomorrow afternoon, or maybe Thursday morning."

"What's going on?" Amanda asked.

"The prosecution's case is finished," he told her.

"Finished? Like *fell apart?*"

In her dreams.

"No," he said. "More like *completed.*"

"What's next?"

"Carter, at two o'clock."

"Wow," she said. "How does it look?"

"You don't want to know. And by the way, thanks for going to my apartment. That was really very sweet of you."

"Anytime."

"I've got to go," he said, pointing to a door that led to the pen area and turning toward it. But she caught his arm.

"You didn't tell him?" she asked. "Did you?"

"Tell him what?"

"You know. That I admitted I was in the car with him."

"No," said Jaywalker. "I kept you out of it. And Eric, too."

"Thank you. And the wasp business. Is he still sticking with that?"

"I'll let you know," said Jaywalker.

"The defense calls Carter Drake."

Drake rose from his seat at the defense table and made his way to the witness stand. The trooper who'd been sitting directly behind him stayed put, a silly gesture intended to disguise the fact that the defendant was in custody. As if the presence of another trooper, seated by the witness box, didn't give it away. Or the stories about the five million dollars' bail he'd been kept from posting, that had made the front page of the *Rockland County Register* for weeks and been mentioned regularly on local talk-radio shows.

Jaywalker spent twenty minutes on background, establishing that Drake was a husband, a father and a gainfully employed resident of the state. He did these things not only to introduce his client to the jurors and to attach a few positives to him, but to give Carter a chance to get used to the business of testifying.

Not that they hadn't practiced. Counting the three hours over the lunch break and the six they'd spent the evening before, even after "Lights out!" had been called, Jaywalker had devoted at least a dozen sessions to fleshing out Carter's story and getting him ready for the worst Abe Firestone could throw at him. For there was no doubt in his mind that Firestone would conduct the cross-examination himself. There was simply too much ego in him, and far too much publicity value in it, for him to pass the job off to David Kaminsky or Julie Napolitano. No, it would be Firestone's show, and Jaywalker had mimicked him in mock cross-examinations, right down to the gruff voice and heavy-handed theatrics.

From talking about his background, Jaywalker brought Drake forward to May 27 of the previous year, and established that he'd spent the day working hard with a client, right over in Nyack.

JAYWALKER: Did you take time out for lunch?

DRAKE: No, we worked right through.

JAYWALKER: You did finally finish, though?

DRAKE: Yes, we finished about four-thirty or so, as I recall.

JAYWALKER: What did you do then?

DRAKE: Gilson, the client, suggested we get a bite to eat and something to drink. I agreed, and told him to pick the spot. I followed him in my car so he wouldn't have to take me back to his office when we were done.

JAYWALKER: And where did you go?

DRAKE: Not far. To a place called the End Zone. It's what they call a sports bar, I guess.

JAYWALKER: Had you ever been there before?

DRAKE: No, never.

Jaywalker allowed himself a peek at the jury box. Things seemed to be going well, so far. It had taken a lot of coaching, but Drake had managed to develop what passed for a pleasant, earnest way of speaking. He was good to look at, well dressed without being showy, and likable. Then again, he hadn't gotten to the part about drinking yet, or killing nine people.

JAYWALKER: What happened once you got to the End Zone?

DRAKE: We found a table and ordered some food. Hot wings, or buffalo wings, I think they call them there. And drinks.

JAYWALKER: Drinks?

DRAKE: Martinis. We each ordered a martini.

JAYWALKER: And what happened next?

DRAKE: The drinks came, the food took a little longer. So we drank the martinis, and by the time the waitress brought the wings to the table, she saw our glasses were near-empty, and asked if we wanted refills. And we said, "Sure." And when those came, we drank them, too. And much too fast, as I now know. At the time, though, I didn't notice. Honest, I didn't.

JAYWALKER: Did you order more food?

DRAKE: No, the wings weren't very good. They were deep fried, and I keep reading about how bad fried food is for you.

Great. In a dozen practice sessions, the answer had always been a simple "No," or at very worst a "No, I wasn't all that hungry." Now, all of a sudden, Drake had felt the irrepressible need to ad lib, and in the process had not only managed to insult the quality of food at a local establishment, but had also offended any KFC aficionados on the jury. And if their waistlines were any indication, there were several likely candidates.

So much for being likable.

JAYWALKER: But I gather the martinis were good?

DRAKE: Unfortunately, they were very good. So I quit after round three.

Another ad lib. By throwing in the part about quitting after round three—which wasn't even responsive to the question Jaywalker had asked—Drake had managed to jump ahead in time, leaving out important events. In spite of all the work the two of them had put in, he was proving to be a very difficult witness.

Jaywalked tried to glide him back a bit without being too obvious about it.

JAYWALKER: Was it still just the two of you at the table?

DRAKE: No. Frank Gilson had called his girlfriend. He's not married. And he'd told her to come join us. And a while later she showed up, along with two of her girl-friends. So it was the five of us at the table. Frank, me, and the three young ladies.

He'd done it again. It was supposed to be *friends,* not *girlfriends.* And *young women,* not *young ladies.* There were women who took offense at certain expressions. Jaywalker's wife had been one of them. She'd made him be the first lawyer in the city to stop calling jurors "ladies and gentleman."

"What am I supposed to call them?" he'd asked her.

"*People,*" she'd told him. "They're *people.*"

"You've got to be kidding. 'Good afternoon, *people?*' Give me a break."

He'd settled on *jurors.*

Where was he? Jesus, he told himself. Concentrate.

JAYWALKER: Did you drink anything else after you stopped drinking martinis?

DRAKE: Yes. The ladies wanted to do shots of tequila.

They insisted that everyone at the table join in. I protested a bit—

Drake, the victim.

—but then I said okay. And I stayed in for two rounds, I believe. Three at the very outside. But I'm ninety-nine percent certain it was just two.

JAYWALKER: You've listened to the testimony of previous witnesses at this trial, have you not?

DRAKE: I have.

JAYWALKER: Specifically, the witnesses Frank Gilson, Trudy Demarest, Amy Jo O'Keefe and Daniel Riley. Did you hear what they had to say about their estimates of how much you had to drink?

DRAKE: Yes, I did.

JAYWALKER: And while their estimates varied widely—

FIRESTONE: Objection.

THE COURT: Sustained. Strike the word *widely.*

FIRESTONE: And I don't like the word *estimates,* either.

JAYWALKER: Well, isn't that special.

FIRESTONE: It wasn't their *estimates,* it was their *recollections.*

THE COURT: Quiet, both of you.

(*Laughter*)

THE COURT: It was their *testimony*.

JAYWALKER: Perfect. And while the testimony of those witnesses varied, with some guessing—I'm sorry, *testifying*—that you had as many as six or seven tequilas, you sit there and tell us it was only two, and under no circumstances more than three. How can you be so certain?

DRAKE: Because I was the one who was drinking them. I kept count. I knew I had to drive home, so I cut myself off. I'm not saying the other witnesses lied. I'm sure they testified to the best of their recollections. But I dropped out, I really did. Though I must admit I kind of pretended I was still in.

JAYWALKER: Why did you do that?

DRAKE: I guess I didn't want to come off as a wuss.

JAYWALKER: A what?

DRAKE: A *wuss*. It's what we used to call a *party pooper*.

JAYWALKER: And was there any special reason why you didn't want to be perceived as a wuss?

DRAKE: Well, for one thing, nobody wants to be perceived as a wuss.

JAYWALKER: And?

DRAKE: And I guess maybe I was trying to make an impression on the ladies.

JAYWALKER: What is the present status of your marriage, Mr. Drake?

DRAKE: My wife and I are separated.

JAYWALKER: For how long now?

DRAKE: For about a year.

JAYWALKER: So then by the time you went to the End Zone with Frank Gilson, you'd already been separated some five or six months. Is that correct?

DRAKE: That's correct.

Jaywalker brought him to the point where Riley the Bartender had asked him to call home. He'd put up a fuss, Drake readily admitted, but only because he'd stopped drinking about an hour earlier, was already sobering up, and considered himself fully capable of driving.

JAYWALKER: So why hadn't you left?

DRAKE: Because I was having a good time. And because I wanted to be on the safe side, and give myself a little more time before getting behind the wheel.

JAYWALKER: But you did make a call?

DRAKE: Yes. I mean, I wasn't about to get into a fight about it, or anything like that.

JAYWALKER: Whom did you call?

DRAKE: I called by wife. She was the only person I could think of who lived close enough to me and would be willing to do it. And I figured she'd be able to bring our son along.

JAYWALKER: Even though you and your wife were separated?

DRAKE: We still loved each other, and cared about each other. We'd separated because we'd begun to argue too much, and too often. It was supposed to be a trial thing. We'd started seeing a marriage counselor, in fact, working towards resolving our issues.

Jaywalker established that Drake had had no more to drink while waiting for his wife to show up, and that he'd left the End Zone as soon as Eric had walked in. But once outside in parking lot, he'd insisted that he was going to drive himself home.

JAYWALKER: Why did you do that?

DRAKE: Several reasons. First of all, I remembered that my son only had a learner's permit. He wasn't allowed to drive alone or after dark. Second, I was convinced I was fine. And third, the Audi takes some getting used to. It's very fast, very responsive. And again, it was night, it was dark out. Amanda—that's my wife—wasn't really used to it. All things considered, I felt it was safest for me to drive it, and for her to follow me in her car.

JAYWALKER: Did Amanda agree to that?

DRAKE: No. She started arguing with me, and I argued back. We started yelling at each other. At some point, Eric, who'd walked back to her car and gotten into it, drove off.

JAYWALKER: What happened next?

DRAKE: I got into my car and started it up. I told my wife it was up to her. She could get in or stay there in the parking lot. She got in.

JAYWALKER: And?

DRAKE: And I began driving home.

JAYWALKER: How did that go?

DRAKE: At first, it went fine. I had absolutely no trouble driving. No trouble at all.

JAYWALKER: But at some point, I gather that changed?

The question was deliberately open-ended. Even at this point, an hour into his client's direct examination, Jaywalker had absolutely no idea what to expect next. Would Drake tell the wasp story, banking on the fact that his wife would have no choice but to back him up on it? Or would he abandon it and go with the argument narrative, and then try to come up with some other way of extricating himself from responsibility? It was truly weird not knowing, absolutely bizarre. Jaywalker—the compulsive, driven, overpreparer, the dotter of all *i*'s and crosser of all *t*'s—was totally clueless. Here he was, suddenly at a fork in the road where he had to turn left or right, and he had absolutely no idea which it would be. He was about to follow his client's lead, the last thing in the world he ever wanted to do. But what choice did he have?

It didn't take long for him to find out which fork they were taking.

DRAKE: Yes. I noticed a wasp flying around in the car.

JAYWALKER: A wasp?

DRAKE: Yes, a wasp. You know, like a hornet.

JAYWALKER: And why did that change things?

DRAKE: I'm very allergic to insect bites. I've ended up in the emergency room several times.

JAYWALKER: What happens when you get stung?

DRAKE: I get what's called an anaphylactic reaction. My throat closes up, among other things, and I'm unable to breathe. Each time it happens, it gets worse. I've been told that the next one could kill me.

FIRESTONE: Objection.

THE COURT: Come up.

Up at the bench, Firestone, prompted by David Kaminsky tugging at his elbow, argued that what Drake had been told was hearsay. "It's an out-of-court utterance," he pointed out. "And whoever supposedly told him this, even if I were to believe him, isn't here for me to cross-examine."

"It's not hearsay at all," said Jaywalker, who for all of his idiosyncrasies, knew his evidence. "It's not being

offered for the truth of the statement. It's being offered
only to show his state of mind, and to explain why he
did what he did next."

He could have added that he'd be calling his client's
doctor to the stand later on—Drake had made certain of
that by choosing the wasp fork—but he decided not to
tip his hand. Better to let Firestone blunder into that by
accusing Drake of making it all up.

THE COURT: Overruled. Step back. The answer will
stand.

JAYWALKER: Who told you the next reaction could
kill you?

DRAKE: My doctor. The doctors and nurses in the emergency room. All the reading I've done about it. I have to
be very, very careful.

JAYWALKER: So what happened when you noticed the
wasp flying around inside the car?

DRAKE: I opened the windows, and I asked my wife to
try to get it out or kill it. But she wouldn't. She was still
angry with me, and she refused. At one point, it landed
on the windshield. There was a newspaper on the console, between the seats. I grabbed it, rolled it up, and tried
to swat the thing.

JAYWALKER: And?

DRAKE: I missed it, and it began flying around again
like crazy. I must have made it angry or something, because all of a sudden it was like it was trying to get me,
buzzing all around my head, trying to get at my eyes. I

tried to slow down, but I must have had my right foot on the gas pedal instead of the brake, because the more I tried to slow down, the faster we went. And at some point I must have lost control, because all of a sudden I looked up and we were in the wrong lane. I tried to downshift, to force the stick shift into second or third, but I couldn't, I couldn't.

And here Drake gestured with his left hand, showing how hard he'd tried to slam the thing into a lower gear. And his demonstration was so convincing, and his voice so anguished, that Jaywalker nearly missed it.

He'd used his left hand, instead of his right.

Jaywalker had been standing back by the railing, the *bar* that separated the *well* of the courtroom from the spectator section. He tended to do that when he wanted his witness to speak louder, to project his voice. Now he walked to the podium and pretended to be studying his notes while he tried to figure out the significance of what had just happened. But a rushing noise and a pounding at his temples made concentrating all but impossible. Had he been the only one to notice Carter Drake's error? Was it possible he'd only imagined it? He turned toward the audience section so that his own body would be facing the same way the witness's was. No, Drake had definitely gestured with his left hand. But as he'd sat in the driver's seat, the gearbox would have been to his right.

Unless he *hadn't* been in the driver's seat.

JAYWALKER: Tell us, if you can, what prevented you from getting the car into a lower gear.

And suddenly there it was, a flash of panic in Drake's eyes. It lasted less than a second before vanishing, and the only reason Jaywalker saw it was because he'd been looking for it.

DRAKE: I don't know.

JAYWALKER: Don't you?

DRAKE: *(No response)*

JAYWALKER: Maybe I can help. Was it by any chance because you didn't have your left foot on the clutch pedal?

DRAKE: I don't remember.

JAYWALKER: How do you downshift in the Audi TT?

DRAKE: The same way you downshift with any man-ual-transmission car. You depress the clutch, move the stick into a lower gear, and release the clutch.

JAYWALKER: And the stick—the gearshift selector—is mounted on the floor, between the seats. Just as it's shown in this photograph that Investigator Sheetz took.

(Hands exhibit to witness)

JAYWALKER: Right?

DRAKE: Right.

JAYWALKER: Yet a minute ago, in demonstrating how you tried to force the stick shift into a lower gear, you used your left hand, and reached to your left with it—

FIRESTONE: No, he didn't.

THE COURT: Yes, he did.

JAYWALKER: Didn't you?

DRAKE: If I did, it was by mistake.

Jaywalker let the answer hang in the air for a few seconds. Technically, the judge had been wrong to state her own recollection of the gesture. She should have told the jurors it was up to them to decide. But now, with her vote cast in Jaywalker's column, several jurors were nudging their neighbors, as if to say they'd picked up on it, too. And Drake's "by mistake" had by now taken on an absurd quality, somewhere the far side of plausible.

JAYWALKER: Let me ask you again. Isn't it a fact that the reason you couldn't downshift was because you didn't depress the clutch pedal with your left foot?

FIRESTONE: Objection. He's trying to impeach his own witness.

JAYWALKER: I ask that the witness be declared hostile.

It was a shot in the dark, he knew. For starters, he doubted there'd ever been an instance where a lawyer had succeeded in having his own client declared a hostile witness. But that sort of minor detail didn't bother Jaywalker. What worried him was that all a declaration of hostility triggered was the right to ask your own witness leading questions, in which the questions themselves contained or strongly suggested the answers, which could then be as limited as a simple yes or no. It didn't give you the right to impeach your witness, to attack him and try to show he was lying.

Fortunately, almost no one besides Jaywalker knew the rule or appreciated the distinction. Not even Justice Hinkley. "Overruled," she said.

JAYWALKER: You didn't step on the clutch, did you?

DRAKE: I, I, I guess not.

JAYWALKER: Yet you're an experienced driver, aren't you?

DRAKE: Yes.

JAYWALKER: How long had you had the Audi?

DRAKE: I don't know. Eight months.

JAYWALKER: How long had you been driving standard-shift cars?

DRAKE: Since I was seventeen.

JAYWALKER: So what happened? Why didn't you step on the clutch before trying to downshift?

DRAKE: I don't know.

JAYWALKER: Yes you do.

FIRESTONE: Objection.

THE COURT: Sustained.

JAYWALKER: You didn't step on the clutch because you couldn't reach it. Right?

DRAKE: *(No response)*

JAYWALKER: And you couldn't reach it because you weren't in the driver's seat at all. You were in the passenger seat, weren't you?

DRAKE: No.

JAYWALKER: And the reason you were in the passenger seat is that your wife was driving. Wasn't she?

The collective gasp from the jury drowned out Carter Drake's response, and Justice Hinkley had to ask him to repeat it.

DRAKE: Leave her out of it. It wasn't her fault. It was my fault.

JAYWALKER: Maybe it *was* your fault. But you weren't behind the wheel, were you?

DRAKE: Yes, I was. It was all my fault, every bit of it. So leave my wife out of it, and leave my son out of it. They had nothing to do with it. I'm the one who's responsible here. I'm the one who killed those kids. Me, me, me. I was driving. I was driving. I was…

Whatever else he might have wanted to say was lost in his sobs, drowned out by huge body-racking convulsions that completely overcame him. It was almost as though Carter Drake had suddenly regressed right there in front of their eyes and become a boy, a ten-year-old version of himself. A boy who believed that by shutting his eyes as hard as he could, clapping his hands tightly over his ears, and continuing to say over and over again that it wasn't so, he could somehow blot out the truth.

But Truth can have a funny way of revealing herself, and to everyone else in the courtroom, with the possible exception of Abe Firestone and his two assistants, she'd suddenly and unexpectedly laid herself bare, for all to see. Carter Drake had no doubt gotten it half-right. In large measure, he *was* responsible for what had happened. Had he not had too much to drink and needed help getting home, those eight children and their driver would still be alive. But he hadn't killed them. He hadn't driven their van off the road. He hadn't even been driving.

"I have no further questions," said Jaywalker.

But Firestone did.

For a full two hours, he took Drake back over every detail of what had happened in the car. The easy part was getting Drake to say he'd been driving. But when it came to explaining away his having gestured with his left hand reaching for the gearshift, or his left foot's not having been able to reach the clutch pedal, Firestone made no headway at all. And that fact must have been as obvious to Drake as it was to everyone else, because at one point, when it had become clear that his insistence that he'd been driving was ringing hollow, he looked away from Firestone and toward Justice Hinkley. And turning both of his palms upward, he asked, "Can't I just plead guilty?"

"No," said the judge, "you cannot. Your job is to answer the questions."

Firestone finally gave up trying and sat down, but his frustration and anger never once ebbed. Even after the jurors had filed out of the courtroom for the evening, and Jaywalker was packing his files and notes into his briefcase, the D.A. was in front of Jaywalker, spraying a fine mist of spittle as he delivered his unsolicited opinion.

"He's lying!" he shouted, his face crimson, the veins in his forehead bulging. "He's goddamned lying, and you know it. You put him up to this. They warned me. They told me you were one clever son of a bitch. But this…this is fucking criminal! This is an outrage! The guy goes out and kills nine people, and you twist things around to make it look like he was nothing but an innocent passenger! Well, fuck you! I'm still going to get him. You watch. And I'm going to get you, too, before I'm done."

Jaywalker finished packing his briefcase and snapped it shut. "You flatter me," he said. "And I suppose I appreciate your calling me clever. But I'm not *that* clever. Nobody is."

Amanda was waiting for him in the corridor, but she was hardly alone. A swarm of reporters had her surrounded, snapping pictures of her, shoving microphones into her face, and outshouting each other demanding her comments on the latest development. Jaywalker walked right past her, afraid that if he were seen talking with her, it would smack of collusion.

Sitting behind the wheel of his Mercury, he waited until he saw her reach the parking lot, get into her Lexus and pull out onto the street, before he began following her. He finally managed to catch up to her on the Palisades Parkway, no mean feat for the Merc. As he drew alongside her, he motioned her to follow him. They pulled over at a scenic overlook, where he killed the Mercury's engine, got out and joined Amanda in the Lexus. Unlike the Merc, it had a heater that actually worked.

"What was all that about?" she asked.

"I wanted you to follow me."

"No," she said. "Back in court."

"Oh, that," he said. "Carter told the truth."

"The truth?"

"That you were driving."

People developed *tells,* Jaywalker had learned long ago, almost imperceptible giveaways that they were lying, or hiding something, or bluffing at the poker table. Some would break off eye contact and look away or down at the floor. Others would raise a hand to the mouth, or the tip of the nose, or one ear or the other. Jaywalker would bite the inside of his cheek. And it was always his left cheek. He had the scar tissue to prove it. But he couldn't help it; for the life of him, he couldn't. Which was why they called it a tell.

Amanda had just bitten her lower lip.

"Why didn't you let me know?" he asked her.

She looked away, out the side window. "Carter," she said. "He insisted. He wouldn't have it any other way. From the day it happened, all that's ever mattered to him is keeping Eric and me out of it. It's his penance, I guess. But I can't believe he changed his mind."

"He didn't, exactly."

He told her what had happened. She nodded grimly several times, but didn't interrupt. When he was finished, she asked, "What's going to happen to me?"

"Not too much," he said. "You certainly weren't drunk, or anything like that. Nobody's going to accuse you of acting with depraved indifference, the way they'd been able to accuse Carter. It was an accident. But it was a bad one, and you did leave the scene."

"What happens tomorrow?"

"Tomorrow," said Jaywalker, "I put you on the witness stand."

"And what am I supposed to do?"

"Tell the truth," he said. "Tell the absolute truth."

22

THE LADY AND THE TIGER

Before they began Wednesday morning, Abe Firestone asked to approach the bench. There, he indicated that not only did he want David Kaminsky and Julie Napolitano to flank him at the prosecution table, but he wanted a fourth chair added.

"And who is the guest of honor?" asked Justice Hinkley.

"Investigator Sheetz."

Jaywalker objected, but the judge ruled that since Sheetz had already testified, she saw no reason to exclude him. And appellate courts had long approved of the policy of having "case agents" or other members of law enforcement sit with prosecutors to help out with technical matters. "But this means you won't be permitted to call him as a rebuttal witness," she said.

"Fair enough," Firestone grunted.

They stepped back, and as the jury entered, so did Sheetz. But instead of being dressed in a dark suit and tie, as he had been during his own testimony, now he was wearing his trooper's uniform, and even carrying his Mountie hat.

This time it was Jaywalker who asked to approach,

complaining that Sheetz's sudden presence, accompanied by his change in clothing, was nothing but a thinly veiled attempt to intimidate the next witness.

"Who is the next witness?" she asked him.

"The defendant's wife."

"I didn't know that," said Firestone. "I figured you were putting on the allergy doctor."

"So *that's* who you wanted to intimidate."

"Cut it out, you two," said the judge. "I've got a jury waiting to get started."

"Listen," said Firestone. "If he's putting the wife on the stand, I'm going to ask her if she's been sleeping with her husband's lawyer. Go get that photo," he told Julie Napolitano.

She darted back to the prosecution table and began leafing through a pile of stuff. *Jesus,* thought Jaywalker, *they really do have a photo of us in bed.* A moment later, Napolitano returned to the bench and held up a photo for the judge to see. But it was the same one that had appeared on Page Six of the *Post,* showing Amanda and Jaywalker in the diner, her leaning toward him and looking for all the world as though she was about to kiss him.

"Even if what you say is true," asked the judge, "how is that relevant to anything?"

"Credibility," said Firestone, repeating whatever Kaminsky was whispering in his ear. "Bias. Conflict of interest." It was like watching a ventriloquist at work, with an overstuffed dummy.

"I'm going to reserve judgment on that," said Justice Hinkley. "Step back and call your next witness."

"The defense calls Amanda Drake," Jaywalker announced.

All heads turned to watch Amanda enter. All but Jaywalker's, that is. His eyes were on the jury box. What he saw were nods and a bit of nudging with elbows. Just as he'd planned, the jurors had been seeing Amanda for a week and a half now, passing her in the corridor and wondering just who the tall, pretty blonde was. A few of them, the elbow-nudgers, had evidently figured it out, and were now eager to trot out their *I-told-you-so's*. Jaywalker had more than a passing interest in identifying them. When deliberations began, those same jurors would take over, talking about things they'd spotted in the evidence, stuff they'd figured out from the testimony. They'd be the leaders, the ones Jaywalker would have to focus on and win over.

He began gently with Amanda, getting her to talk about her career as an interior designer, her marriage to Carter Drake twenty years ago, their teenage son, and her separation from her husband about a year ago. Despite having spent a lot of time with her—a fact that Abe Firestone had already signaled he hoped to explore in detail—Jaywalker had for once underprepared a witness. Part of that had been his indecision over whether to call Amanda at all. Part had been his fear that she'd come off as too rehearsed. But most of it had been because of the impossible position the facts had conspired to put her in. As a result, up to this very moment, he still had no real idea what she'd say. Would she invite being arrested and charged herself in order to save her husband? Or would she protect herself by burying him? He knew this much: if Amanda were to lie and insist that Carter had been at the wheel, Jaywalker would have to go after her and, if need be, destroy her. It wouldn't be pretty and it wouldn't be fun, but he'd have no choice. Yes, she'd hired him, paid him generously, and even slept with him. But she wasn't his client. Carter Drake was, and it was to him that Jaywalker owed his undivided loyalty.

It was a tough rule, but a good one. Just as it was

whenever parents retained him to represent their child. The parents often didn't like hearing it, but it was the child who became the client. So no, he wouldn't tell them what the child had confided to him. And no, he wasn't going to help put the kid in rehab when he could beat the case altogether, no matter how much the parents pressured him that it would be best for the child. It was why he'd largely stopped taking juvenile cases, and prostitution cases, too. Well, that and the stairwell episode. No pimp or madam was going to tell *him* to make sure one of the girls got a few days in jail just to teach her a lesson. And it was the same reason why he'd long ago stopped representing Mafia members and wannabes, because back when he had, he'd found himself answering to all sorts of their friends and associates, guys with bent noses and funny nicknames like Johnnie Knuckles or Vinnie Ice Pick. So Carter Drake was his client, and Amanda was only a witness. And if it came to choosing between them, there was no choice; there couldn't be.

She answered his preliminary questions flawlessly. She was just nervous enough to make her answers come off as real. She was earnest and thoughtful. And she was likable. Likable counts, Jaywalker knew. Then again, he hadn't gotten to the hard part yet. But he was about to.

JAYWALKER: Did there come a time in the early evening hours of May 27 that you received a phone call from your husband?

AMANDA: Yes.

JAYWALKER: And in response to that phone call, did you do something?

AMANDA: Yes. I called my son, Eric, who was staying

at his father's at that time. And I told him to meet me downstairs in ten minutes, that we were going to pick up his father.

JAYWALKER: And did you in fact pick up Eric?

AMANDA: Yes.

JAYWALKER: And did the two of you go somewhere?

AMANDA: Yes. We drove—I drove to Nyack, to a place called the End Zone.

JAYWALKER: What happened when you got there?

AMANDA: I sent Eric in to get his father. I waited in the car. I was very angry, and I didn't want to cause a scene in the place.

JAYWALKER: What happened next?

AMANDA: Carter and Eric came out a few minutes later. I could see them arguing. I could also tell that Carter had been drinking, and had probably had too much. He gets like that sometimes. After a while, Eric came back over to my car and said, "I give up. You deal with him." Or something like that. So I— So I—

It was the first sign that she was about to lose it. Jaywalker looked at her hard, tried to will her to calm down. *You can do this*, he told her silently, hoping that his assurance could somehow take flight, travel the twenty paces between them, and reinforce her.

JAYWALKER: Are you okay?

AMANDA: Yes. No. I don't know.

JAYWALKER: Would you like a few minutes?

AMANDA: No. I'm all right.

JAYWALKER: Okay. So what did you do after Eric came back and told you to deal with his father?

AMANDA: I got out of my car and walked over to Carter. By that time he was standing next to his car, the Audi. He was fumbling with the keys, trying to unlock the door.

JAYWALKER: What happened next?

AMANDA: *(No response)*

JAYWALKER: Can you tell us what happened next?

AMANDA: We—we argued. I told him he was too drunk to drive. He refused to let Eric drive my car because he only had a learner's permit that wasn't good after dark. We yelled and screamed a lot.

JAYWALKER: And?

AMANDA: And then at some point, Eric just drove off in my car. I figured that ought to settle things. You know, the permit no longer mattered. Now I could drive the Audi. But Carter wasn't finished arguing. And we started fighting over the keys.

Knowing that the moment of truth was coming, Jaywalker paused for a moment to signal the jurors that something big was coming. When finally he asked his next question, he asked it softly, almost sadly.

JAYWALKER: And who won the fight over the keys?

AMANDA: *(No response)*

JAYWALKER: Who won the fight over the keys?

AMANDA: I did. I knocked the keys out of his hand. They fell onto the pavement. I picked them up before he could.

JAYWALKER: Did there come a time when the two of you got into the Audi?

AMANDA: *(No response)*

JAYWALKER: Mrs. Drake?

AMANDA: Yes.

Her voice was so faint that it was barely audible. Only the total silence in the rest of the courtroom allowed it to be heard.

JAYWALKER: Who got behind the wheel?

AMANDA: *(No response)*

JAYWALKER: Mrs. Drake?

Which was when it happened.
A tiny movement at the prosecution table caught Jaywalker's eye. He looked over and saw Investigator

William Sheetz lean forward ever so slightly, reach behind him, remove something from the back of his belt, and place it on the table in front of him.

Later on, in the internal investigation that would follow the trial, Sheetz would insist under oath that he did what he did only because the item had been digging into his lower back and causing him discomfort. He'd also claim that he wasn't even aware that seconds later he began idly playing with it, the way one might play with a paper clip or a pencil, without even realizing it. The administrative judge conducting a hearing in that investigation would accept Sheetz's explanation and clear him on charges of official misconduct, obstruction of justice, and intimidation of a witness.

But everyone in the courtroom knew better.

Because the thing about it was, the item made a sound as soon as Sheetz began playing with it. And nothing, absolutely nothing, makes quite the sound that a pair of handcuffs does when one slides the business end of one cuff into the receiving end, over and over again. It's a ratcheting sound, metal teeth being drawn over metal teeth. It's a sound…well, it's the sound of an arrest about to take place.

And Amanda, who heard it along with everyone else in the room, suddenly couldn't take her eyes off the source of the sound. So hard and so long did she stare, her eyes wide, her mouth open, that Justice Hinkley was finally forced to intervene.

"Are you able to continue, Mrs. Drake?"

But Amanda couldn't answer. She couldn't even nod, or shake her head. All she could do was to continue to stare at the handcuffs.

Her handcuffs.

The judge banged her gavel once, harder than usual. "We'll be in recess," she announced.

As soon as the jurors were out of the room, she made a record of what had happened, describing it in detail for the court reporter to take down. Then she turned to the prosecution table. "Investigator Sheetz," she said, "remove yourself from my courtroom immediately, and don't come back. Ever. And you should expect to face criminal charges."

"For what?" It was Firestone's voice.

"For trying to intimidate a witness."

"A witness," barked Firestone, "who was about to lie."

"Careful, Mr. Firestone. Consider this your warning." Then she turned to the witness stand. "Mrs. Drake, do you realize the position you may be about to put yourself in?"

All Amanda could do was shake her head slowly from side to side. The judge evidently took it as a no. "Do you have a lawyer?" she asked.

Amanda managed to point vaguely in Jaywalker's direction.

"No," said the judge. "What I mean is, do you have your *own* lawyer, other than Mr. Jaywalker?"

"No."

"Well, before we go any further, we're going to get you one." She scanned the audience for volunteers, settling on a young man in the second row whom she apparently recognized. "You, stand up. What's your name again?"

"Mermelstein," said the young man. "Judah Mermelstein."

"Right," said the judge. "Have you been following this case?"

"Very much so. As a matter of fact, I—"

"Good. I'm assigning you, for today only, to represent the witness. You're to sit down with her and explain to her the potential jeopardy she's in, advise her of her rights, and represent her through the end of her testimony. Do you understand?"

"Yes, but—"

"There are no buts about it. I have a trial going on, and a jury waiting. Can you do as I say?"

"I can, only—"

"Then do it. We'll reconvene in twenty-five minutes." And with that, she stormed out of the courtroom.

No doubt Mermelstein had been trying to tell the judge that having represented the defendant, however briefly, he was in no position to now represent a witness in the same case. But whatever it was, Justice Hinkley hadn't wanted to hear it.

And Jaywalker? Was he supposed to run after her and try to explain the problem to her? Or should he sit down, let things unfold and, if it should come to it, have an issue nicely preserved for appeal?

He sat down.

It was almost noon by the time they resumed. Amanda was led back to the witness stand and reminded that she was still under oath. Judah Mermelstein was provided with a chair, placed directly to one side of her. It was the same chair Investigator Sheetz had occupied earlier, before he'd felt compelled to play with his handcuffs. Needless to say, he was nowhere in sight right now.

THE COURT: Mr. Mermelstein, have you had an opportunity to confer with the witness?

MERMELSTEIN: Yes, Your Honor.

THE COURT: Are we ready to proceed?

MERMELSTEIN: Yes, but—

THE COURT: Good. Bring in the jury.

Even as the jurors entered, they took in Sheetz's absence and Mermelstein's presence. Jurors don't miss much, Jaywalker had come to learn. They got things wrong every now and then, for which he was mostly grateful. But they didn't miss much.

The judge apologized for keeping them waiting, and instructed them to refrain from speculating about the cast change. Then she told Jaywalker to continue his examination.

JAYWALKER: Right before the recess, Mrs. Drake, I asked you which one of you got behind the wheel of the Audi, and which one of you got into the passenger seat. Do you recall that question?

Before answering, Amanda looked over at Mermelstein. Only when he nodded did she look back at Jaywalker.

AMANDA: Yes.

JAYWALKER: I ask you that same question again now, Mrs. Drake. Who was driving the Audi that evening, you or your husband?

Just as there can come a Moment in a trial when everything changes, so too can there come a Question upon which everything hinges. This was such a question. If Amanda were to say, "I drove," the entire direction of the trial would change. She would tell a story totally different from the one Carter had. There would be no wasp, no accidental loss of control of the car, no desperate attempt to steer it back into its lane or force the stick shift into a lower gear. Instead, she'd take full responsibility for everything that had happened. Then Abe Firestone would do his best to expose her as a liar, intent on saving her husband. What the jury would do was anyone's guess. And if they saw fit to acquit Carter, Amanda would probably end up wearing handcuffs as a reward for her honesty.

On the other hand, if she were to say, "He drove," that declaration, combined with Carter's earlier insistence that he had been behind the wheel, would likely be the nail in her husband's coffin. No left-handed versus right-handed slip, no why-he-couldn't-reach-the-clutch theory was going to be enough for Jaywalker to pull the rabbit out of the hat at that point.

So which was she going to do?

Way back in grammar school, a million years ago, a young Harrison J. Walker and the rest of his class had been assigned to read a famous short story, compose their own endings to it, and read them aloud. The story was called "The Lady and the Tiger," and it was set thousands of years ago, back in the time of gladiators. A young man has been imprisoned in a dungeon and told that it will be his fate to be thrown into the ring for the king's amusement. During the fortnight while he waits, a princess comes to visit him, and over time the two of them fall in love. On her final visit, she tells the prisoner that on the very next day he will be led into the ring, where he will find two solid doors. Hidden behind one door will be a ravenous tiger, starved for weeks. Should he choose that door, he'll be ripped apart and devoured alive. Behind the other door will be a beautiful lady. Should he be lucky enough to choose that door, he'll be freed to wed her, go off with her, and live happily ever after. The princess then confides that she's learned which door holds the lady, and which holds the tiger. "Choose the left door," she whispers.

What the prisoner must decide, of course, is whether to trust the princess. Has her love led her to save his life, or has it been trumped by her jealousy? In the end, he decides to trust her, and chooses the left door. The last two lines of the story read: "So I leave it up to you, dear reader. Which came through the door, the lady or the tiger?"

Jaywalker was the author now. By posing the question *"Who was driving the Audi that evening, you or your husband?"* he was forcing Amanda to choose a door. And in doing so, she would once and forever reveal her true self and seal her own fate. Either she was Amanda the selfless, who would save her husband at her own expense, or she was Amanda the selfish, who would doom her husband in order to save herself.

Which would she be, the lady or the tiger?

And the funny thing was, he could still remember the ending he'd composed to the story, almost word for word. Even as his seventh-grade classmates had taken sides, most of the girls writing that true love would prevail and it would be the lady who'd come out, and most of the boys opting for envy and the tiger, young Jaywalker had refused to do so. *Why did it have to be one or the other?* he'd asked himself. *Why did he have to follow the rules?* So at the moment of truth, right before the prisoner would be forced to make his choice, Jaywalker had had the princess gather up her skirts, leap over the barrier that separated the spectators from the ring, and make her way to the door on the right, the one that she knew held back the tiger. Just as she reached for the lever that would spring the door open, the king rose, shouted, "No!" and declared the spectacle over, as well as all future gladiator events, slavery, war, famine and homework. And the princess's reward for her bravery was that she, and not the lady hidden behind the other door, would be permitted to wed the prisoner, go off with him, and live happily ever after.

The teacher, whose job it had been to judge the endings and grade them, had given Jaywalker a failing mark, citing not only his sarcasm, but his refusal to ultimately answer the question. Still, judging from the spontaneous outburst of applause as he returned to his seat, Jaywalker knew he'd won something more important: the approval of his classmates. And in that split second, a trial lawyer had been born, a trial lawyer willing to break rules, flout convention and defy judges, all so that he could convince those whose votes really mattered. *Peers*, they were called. As in *a jury of one's peers*.

And just as he'd managed to figure things out back then, it suddenly dawned on Jaywalker that history was about to repeat itself. His question had presented Amanda with a choice, what sounded like an either-or proposition. But it was a false choice. And just as the young Jaywalker had refused to commit to one door or the other, so too was Amanda going to refuse.

She wasn't going to choose.

She wasn't going to save her husband, but she wasn't going to sacrifice herself, either. She didn't have to.

He asked her again.

JAYWALKER: Who was driving the Audi?

AMANDA: On the advice of counsel, I refuse to answer on the ground that doing so might in—in—in—

MERMELSTEIN: Incriminate.

AMANDA: Might incriminate me.

FIRESTONE: Objection! Objection! She can't do that!

THE COURT: Jurors, I hate to do this, but I'm afraid I'm going to have to confer with the lawyers. It seems we have some business to attend to.

Once the jury had been led out, Justice Hinkley cleared the rest of the courtroom, as well. A lot of reporters grumbled, but the judge was in no mood to argue. "Sue me," she told them.

As soon as the last of them had left, the judge announced that, having been warned earlier, Abe Firestone was now being held in contempt for his outburst, and would be spending the night in jail. "Now," she said to him. "Suppose you tell me why the witness cannot invoke her Fifth Amendment privilege."

"Because she started answering questions, and then stopped when she didn't like the question." The voice wasn't Firestone's, but David Kaminsky's. "She can't pick and choose."

Instead of asking Jaywalker to respond to that, the judge turned to Amanda's new lawyer. For once, Jaywalker was to be nothing but a bystander, albeit a very interested one.

"She's not picking and choosing," said Judah Mermelstein. "You asked me to confer with her, and I did. I determined that she's in real jeopardy of incriminating herself, however she testifies. You asked me to advise her, and I did. I advised her to refuse to answer all questions that go in any way, directly or indirectly, to the issue of who was driving."

"This is a fraud!" shouted Firestone. "A fraud!"

"You've got one day already," the judge reminded him. "Want to try for two?"

Apparently not.

"Mr. Mermelstein," said the judge. "May I assume that if your client is asked additional questions along this line, she will continue to invoke her privilege and refuse to answer them?"

"You may."

"Upon that representation, the court is satisfied that it would be useless, and therefore improper, to have the witness asked any more questions on the subject and be forced to invoke her privilege. Now, Mr. Firestone, as district attorney, you have a remedy. You can grant the witness immunity from prosecution. If you do that, I'll compel her to answer, since her answers will no longer incriminate her, except for perjury if she lies."

"Immunize her?" Firestone shouted. "If she *was* driving, I'm going to prosecute her for murder. Why would I want to *immunize* her?"

"Very well," said the judge. "It's your call."

"If Your Honor please?"

"Yes, Mr. Kaminsky?"

"The witness has already testified on direct examination. If no further questions may be put to her, the effect will be that the People will be denied the right to cross-examine her. That's unfair."

"So it is," the judge agreed. "Therefore, you have a choice. You can ask me to strike her direct testimony altogether and tell the jury to disregard it. Or you can let it stand as is. Or, if you're very careful about it, you can cross-examine her on other areas."

Firestone, Kaminsky and Napolitano went off to the corner of the room to confer. When they broke their huddle and returned, Kaminsky spoke for them. "We'd like to cross-examine her," he said. "And we intend to ask her about her relationship with Mr. Jaywalker."

"Her relationship?"

"Yes. We want to try to show that there's been collusion between the two of them."

"I'll let you ask relevant questions," said the judge. "If I feel you're crossing the line, I'll rule accordingly. Now, Mr. Jaywalker, are you through with Mrs. Drake?"

"In exactly what sense do you mean?"

"I mean do you have any further direct examination of her."

"No."

"Good. Your wisecrack is contemptuous, and you'll be joining Mr. Firestone in jail tonight. Mr. Clerk, bring the jury back in."

"And the spectators?"

"Them, too."

While David Kaminsky might have had a better handle on how to cross-examine Amanda Drake within the boundaries Justice Hinkley had set, Abe Firestone's ego was again too big to assign the task. He began innocently enough, asking her to describe her husband's condition when she'd first seen him emerge from the End Zone. She stated, as she had on direct, that he'd appeared drunk.

FIRESTONE: Too drunk to drive?

AMANDA: Certainly too drunk to drive safely.

FIRESTONE: No doubt about that in your mind?

AMANDA: No doubt about that.

FIRESTONE: And yet he insisted he was fine. Right?

AMANDA: I don't know if he used the word *fine*. But he insisted he could drive.

FIRESTONE: And you disagreed.

AMANDA: That's right.

FIRESTONE: And you then fought over the keys.

AMANDA: Yes.

FIRESTONE: Who won?

MERMELSTEIN: Objection.

THE COURT: Sustained.

FIRESTONE: Tell me, Mrs. Drake. Do you love your husband?

AMANDA: I would say we have a love-hate relationship.

FIRESTONE: So you do love him?

AMANDA: In part, I do.

FIRESTONE: Would you help him out if he was in trouble?

AMANDA: If I could. I helped him out by driving up to Nyack.

FIRESTONE: Would you lie to help him out?

It was a question prosecutors couldn't resist, Jaywalker knew. So it was a question he'd made sure to prepare Amanda for. And not to just say no; common sense dictated that a wife would lie to help her husband out, and jurors were smart enough to know that.

AMANDA: I'm not sure. I might, I guess. But I haven't had to decide. I haven't lied up till now, certainly, and I don't expect to. Besides, I'm very bad at lying, and you'd know as soon as I tried.

(Laughter)

FIRESTONE: How about your relationship with Mr. Jaywalker?

AMANDA: I wouldn't characterize that as a love-hate relationship, if that's what you're driving at.

(Laughter)

FIRESTONE: How would you characterize it?

AMANDA: I was asked by my husband to find him the best criminal defense lawyer I could. I found Mr. Jaywalker. Because he's my husband's lawyer, I've developed a professional relationship with him. I've also come to consider him a friend.

FIRESTONE: Have the two of you discussed the case?

It was another area prosecutors loved. And therefore another area Amanda was ready for.

AMANDA: Of course.

FIRESTONE: A number of times?

AMANDA: Naturally.

FIRESTONE: Were some of those conversations, shall we say, beneath the bedsheets?

THE COURT: Sustained, we shall say.

FIRESTONE: Well, you and Mr. Jaywalker have been intimate. Have you not been?

THE COURT: Sustained. Move on, Mr. Firestone.

FIRESTONE: By "intimate," I mean—

THE COURT: And by "Move on," I mean "Move on." Is that clear enough for you, Mr. Firestone, or do I need to explain myself further?

FIRESTONE: It's clear enough, Your Honor.

God bless.

FIRESTONE: Well, Mrs. Drake, did Mr. Jaywalker ever tell you what he wanted you to say when it came time for you to testify?

AMANDA: Yes, several times. He told me to tell the absolute truth, no matter what happens.

Nicely done.

FIRESTONE: Did the two of you discuss strategy?

AMANDA: Strategy?

FIRESTONE: Yeah, trial strategy. In other words, how he intended to get your husband off.

AMANDA: No, we didn't.

FIRESTONE: Never?

AMANDA: Never.

FIRESTONE: And he never told you what to say? Not even once?

AMANDA: Only to tell the truth. He said that would be good enough, once the jury heard it.

Firestone didn't quite give up there, but he might as well have; it got no better for him. After another fifteen minutes of dancing, he finally quit, and Amanda was allowed to step down.

"The defense rests," said Jaywalker, in a voice meant to sound both soft and self-assured. And just like that, the trial testimony had ended, not with a bang, but a whisper.

With the testimony completed, the lawyers spent the afternoon in conference with the judge. First, perhaps exhibiting a measure of buyer's remorse, Abe Firestone asked her to strike the testimony of Amanda Drake, as she'd earlier offered to do. Jaywalker objected, naturally.

"No," she told Firestone. "I gave you your choice, and you made it." Then she spent the better part of an hour explaining how she intended to charge the jurors. Only when she'd finished did she turn to her clerk. "Are the accommodations for Mr. Firestone and Mr. Jaywalker ready?" she asked.

"Won't you reconsider?" Kaminsky pleaded. "I'm sure they're both sorry."

Jaywalker said nothing. *Sorry* had never been a big part of his vocabulary.

"Certainly," she said. "Very well, I've reconsidered. And I'm not changing my mind. Take them away."

So that night, the two of them doubled up in the same cell that Jaywalker had shared with his client two nights earlier. Firestone was livid; he kept complaining that he was supposed to be home, working on his summation. Jaywalker, who'd been working on his summation for six months, couldn't have cared less. He used his one phone call to ask Amanda to bring him another change of clothes.

"I don't have the key to your apartment this time," she pointed out.

"Look under the doormat of the apartment across from mine," he told her.

"The one *across* from yours?"

"Yeah. The little old lady's, 4-G. We keep each other's spare keys. Only this way, anyone who happens to discover one under the mat will find it won't unlock the door it's in front of."

That night Jaywalker gallantly insisted on taking the upper bunk. The truth was, there was no way he was going to sleep directly beneath the two-hundred-and-fifty-pound Firestone. The good news was that around midnight, Abe stopped complaining. The bad news was that a few minutes later, he started snoring.

23

A SUPERSTITIOUS ATHEIST

"Michael Fishbein, eleven. Sarah Teitelbaum, eleven. Anna Moskowitz Zorn, ten. Andrew Tucker, nine. Sheilah Zucker, nine. Steven Sonnenshein, eight. Beth Levy-Strauss, seven. Richard Abraham Lubovich, six. Walter Najinsky, forty-three." One by one, he recited their names and ages. He did it slowly, and as gravely as possible. And he did it from memory. He knew that if he didn't do it, Abe Firestone would.

"None of them should have died, not one of them. And but for the actions of my client, every one of them would be alive today. Because we can all agree, every one of us, that it was Carter Drake who set into motion the chain of events that took them from this life, and took them from you. In a very real sense, he bears responsibility. He will go to his grave bearing responsibility. He will meet his Maker bearing responsibility. Knowing full well that he would have to drive home that evening, he drank too much, perhaps far too much. That was an incredibly selfish act on his part, an act that neither you nor I, nor even this court, has the power to forgive.

"But we are a nation of laws, and a trial is an inquiry into whether our laws have been broken. Nothing more, nothing less. And under our laws, selfishness—no matter how blatant and how repugnant it may be to us—is not a crime. Search for it in the indictment. Read all ninety-three counts. You will find no mention of selfishness, no charge of arrogance, no accusation of ultimate responsibility. What you will find are the names of ninety-three specific crimes alleged to have been committed by my client at about nine o'clock on the evening of the twenty-seventh day of May, some eight months ago. And as it turns out, despite his insistence that he is guilty of every one of those crimes, Carter Drake is guilty of none of them."

He let that hang in the air a moment. He'd woken up during the middle of the night, Jaywalker had, totally disoriented, with no idea where he was. Only the sound of Abe Firestone's snoring had jarred him back to reality. Then, as he lay on his back on the upper bunk, the ceiling only inches from his face, a flood of panic had washed over him. Had the jurors caught Drake's left-handed blunder? Did they understand the significance of his inability to downshift? Or had those things gone right over their heads? He hadn't slept after that, had instead spent the rest of the night fighting off the sensation that the cell was filling with water. The rise and fall of Firestone's breathing beneath him became a giant bellows-driven pump, gushing out invisible gallons of seawater that would eventually rise and engulf him. He had failed, he knew. In his inability to get Drake to finally come out and admit he hadn't been driving, he'd left the jurors with too little to go on. They were going to convict.

That had been last night.

Now it was today. And if they were going to convict, they were going to do so over Jaywalker's dead body.

"You and I came into this trial," he told them, "absolutely certain of two things. The first thing we were certain of was that nine people, eight of them very young children, had died horrible, horrible deaths. Needless deaths. The second thing we were absolutely certain of, or at least thought we were absolutely certain of, was that it was my client who'd been driving the Audi when it ran the van off the road and caused those nine deaths. I was every bit as certain of that as you were. And for much of the trial, nothing happened to cause us to question that certainty. After all, hadn't the defendant turned himself in? Wasn't it his car? Didn't Concepción Testigo point him out, remembering him from his yellow hair? And most of all, didn't the defendant himself tell you that he was driving? And even now, doesn't he continue to insist that he was?

"Well, it just so happens we were wrong, you and I. Carter Drake turned himself in because he wanted to protect his wife from getting into trouble, just as he'd wanted to drive home that evening because he wanted to protect his underage son from getting into trouble. And because he turned himself in, and because it was his car, nobody ever gave it a second thought. Not the police, not the prosecutors, not even I. So you're in pretty good company. And as far as Concepción Testigo is concerned, the driver of the pickup truck, don't blame him. What did he tell you? 'I only got a quick look at the driver, but I did get his license plate.' 'Which plate?' Mr. Firestone asks him. 'Front or rear?' 'Rear,' says Testigo. 'Do you see the driver in court?' Firestone asks. 'I *think* that's him, over there,' says Testigo. 'I remember his *yellow hair*.'

"*'I remember his yellow hair.'*

"Who else in this case just happens to have yellow hair?" Jaywalker asked them. And he saw the name *Amanda* on sixteen pairs of lips. So he simply nodded.

"How did we discover, you and I, that it was Amanda Drake who was driving? We discovered it purely by accident, Carter Drake's accident. He was trying to demonstrate how he tried to jam the stick shift into a lower gear. And then he was *so* intent on showing you that he made a mistake. And when you stop to think about it, it was the most natural mistake in the world. Because it was the truth. Carter Drake used his left hand, the one he actually used that night. Had he been behind the wheel, surely he would have used his right hand. There can be absolutely no doubt about that. If any of you aren't sure, look at Investigator Sheetz's photo of the interior of the Audi, and you'll see." He held up the photo. "Carter Drake used his left hand in the demonstration just as he used it in real life. And his doing so proves conclusively that he was in the passenger seat. There can be no other explanation. None."

At least four jurors—now five, six—were nodding in agreement. They weren't happy about it, but they were nodding.

"But there's even more," he told them. "Why couldn't he get the Audi in a lower gear in order to slow it down? You saw how hard he tried. Well, we know there was nothing wrong with the car. Sheetz told us that. They checked it out thoroughly, inside and out, no doubt because they didn't want Drake coming in here and saying there had been some sort of mechanical failure that had caused him to speed up and swerve into the wrong lane. So we know we can rule that out.

"Once again, there's only one possible explanation. In order to change gears, you first need to do something else. You first need to use your left foot to step on the clutch, the pedal on the far left." He turned his back to the jurors so he was facing the same way they were, and gestured from right to left. "Accelerator, brake, clutch. Carter Drake couldn't depress the clutch because he couldn't reach it. And he couldn't reach it for one reason, and one reason only.

"He was in the passenger seat.

"I'd love to add one other thing, to talk about Amanda's refusal to say whether or not she was driving. But Justice Hinkley will tell you that you may draw no conclusion from that."

Firestone objected, and the judge instructed the jurors to disregard the comment, but they were both too late. A lot of cases are won by putting something in evidence. Every once in a while, though, a case is won by putting something in the ear. Amanda's having taken the Fifth, invoking it at the precise moment when she would otherwise have had to incriminate herself, was simply too important to leave out. It would be worth another night in jail, if it came to that. It would be worth a week of nights, if only they could find him a no-snoring cell.

"So you can convict Carter Drake if you want to, as I'm sure Mr. Firestone will ask you to. He even told you in his opening statement that he would, back before any of us knew what we now know. If not for the admitted fact of Carter Drake's drinking too much, his wife never would have had to drive a car she was unfamiliar with, in a place she was unfamiliar with, in the dark, and in the midst of an argument, and this tragedy never would have occurred. So there'd even be a kind of poetic justice were you to convict him.

"But you're not here to impose poetic justice. You aren't poets. You are jurors, and you're here to impose *real* justice. And real justice, no matter how unpleasant and distasteful it sometimes becomes, requires us to ask ourselves one question, and one question alone. Are we convinced—convinced *beyond all reasonable doubt*—that it was Carter Drake, and not Amanda Drake, who was behind the wheel of the Audi at that fateful moment? Or do we have at least some hesitation when we get to that issue, some lingering doubt that leaves us less than convinced beyond all reasonable uncertainty? There can be only one answer to that question, jurors. And that answer is no, there's no way we can be convinced, not beyond all reasonable doubt. So it's up to you. If you do your duty, follow the law and impose real justice, you *must* find Carter Drake not guilty, and leave how he is finally judged in other hands."

And with that, barely twenty-five minutes after he'd begun, Jaywalker sat down.

Abe Firestone spoke for twice as long, but not half as well. Despite Jaywalker's having done so, he, too, listed the names of the victims, though he read them from the captions beneath their photos on the oak tag exhibit. He accused Jaywalker of orchestrating the "mistake" with the stick shift and the clutch, and of getting Amanda Drake to invoke her privilege so that both husband and wife would evade responsibility.

But Firestone was off his game. Apparently the same night in jail that had first panicked and then enervated Jaywalker, had simply exhausted Firestone. He lost his train of thought, repeated himself, backed up, and repeated himself again. Only toward the end of the hour did he seem to regain his composure, finishing strong as he demanded justice for the nine victims.

"If ever anyone was guilty of murder," he told the jurors, "it is this defendant. If ever anyone acted in a reckless manner, exhibiting a depraved indifference to human life, it is this defendant. And then for him to pull the kind of stunt he pulled and pretend he wasn't even driving… The nerve of him, the gall, the *chutzpah*, to try to blame it all on his wife. Shame on him, shame on him."

Firestone ended as Jaywalker had begun, reciting the names of the victims once more. Had it not been for the fact that his passion was misguided, devoted as it was to asking the jury to convict an innocent man, it would have been an extremely effective closing, at least the last part of it. But from the looks on the jurors' faces, they weren't buying it.

Then again, Jaywalker had been wrong about such matters before. The thing about jury verdicts was that you never knew.

Never.

Justice Hinkley's charge to the jury took exactly an hour, and it was just before one o'clock in the afternoon when the twelve regular jurors retired to deliberate. The four alternates, rather than being discharged, were led off to a separate room, just in case one of the regulars became sick or otherwise incapable of continuing.

As for Jaywalker, he became both sick and incapable of continuing. Exhausted from a night spent listening to Firestone's snoring, to fighting off claustrophobia, and to tweaking his summation to fit the trial's latest twists and turns, he'd gotten through the morning on adrenaline and caffeine. While his summation had been short, far shorter than he'd originally planned, it had been emotional, and had taken a lot out of him. Listening to Firestone for an hour, and then to the judge for another hour, had been an ordeal, and at times he'd had to bite the inside of his cheek or pretend to be taking notes just to stay awake.

He found an empty stall in the men's room and tried to throw up, but he'd eaten so little over the past four days that all he could do was gag. *Dry heaves,* they used to call it back in college, when they'd come back to the dorm, knelt before the porcelain god, and paid the price for having been stupid boys trying to act like stupid men.

He left the stall and caught a glimpse of himself in the mirror. Amanda had come through once again with a pressed suit, a clean shirt and a new tie. She'd brought a razor and comb this time, both of which he'd used in the twenty minutes the judge had allowed before summations started. But none of it had helped much. He looked as if *he'd* been on trial for three weeks. His eyes were dark and sunken, his skin pale, his clothes loose from the fifteen pounds he'd no doubt lost.

He glanced upward toward the heavens, but spotted only a bare lightbulb, protected by a wire cage. *Oh, Lord, God of Rockland Light and Power,* he began silently, *grant me an acquittal in just this one case and I'll never ask you for anything again. I'll eat regularly. I'll quit the business and take up writing full-time. I'll clean my apartment. I'll go to the dentist. I'll have that colonoscopy I keep putting off, and that PSA test. I'll even stop seeing Amanda, if you want me to. Just don't let me lose, not this one.*

It was pretty much the same prayer he always offered up around this time, to whatever deity might be listening in and have a spare moment for a humble nonbeliever with a shoddy history of following up on his pledges once his wish had been granted. But old habits died hard. He continued to put his left shoe on before his right because, at least since his wife's illness and death, things had more or less worked out for him so far. He threw a little salt over his shoulder if he'd happened to spill some. He folded his towels as they came out of the dryer, even though a moment later he'd unfold them so he could hang them on the hooks in his bathroom. And he always remembered to say thank-you after each acquittal. Always.

He was an atheist, but he was a superstitious atheist. Just in case.

Back in the courtroom, the jury had already sent out a note. Jaywalker felt the sudden surge of adrenaline, the pounding of his heartbeat at his temples. Notes were clues, valuable indications of what the jurors were focusing on and which way they were leaning.

But not this one.

They wanted to know how long the judge would make them deliberate tomorrow if they couldn't arrive at a verdict today. Tomorrow was Friday, and for many of them the Sabbath would begin at sundown.

With no objection from Firestone or Jaywalker, Justice Hinkley sent them back a note assuring them that under no circumstances would they be required to deliberate on the Sabbath. What she didn't tell them was that under no circumstances could she permit them to return to their homes, either. This was a murder case, and the law required that they be kept together, even when they weren't deliberating.

But even with their innocuous request, Jaywalker wondered, had the jurors been telegraphing that they were in for a long ordeal? Why else would they be thinking ahead to tomorrow? And what did "lengthy deliberations" mean in this case? Surely there was reasonable doubt as to who'd been driving the Audi, and if there was, the case should end right there. The fact that the jurors didn't seem to be seeing it that way couldn't be good.

After he'd gotten his clothes and toiletries from Amanda in the morning, Jaywalker had sent her packing, even before the jurors had begun arriving. He didn't want them seeing her anymore, especially in his company. He'd expected Firestone to make the collusion argument in his summation, and he hadn't been disappointed. So even though it might have been nice for the jurors to see a devoted wife each time they filed in and out of the courtroom, Amanda's presence, coupled with the fact that she might well have been the one who'd

killed the nine victims, could have proved troublesome
for the jurors, to say the least. And while they couldn't
take their anger out on her, they *could* take it out on her
husband.

But Amanda's absence left Jaywalker with basically
no one to pass the time with. Even when he wasn't complaining or snoring, Firestone was hardly the best of
company. Kaminsky was bookishly smart, but awfully
nerdy. And to paraphrase an old saying, Napolitano was
cute but young. And the media, as always, was off-limits
to Jaywalker. That left the gawkers and the courtroom
staff, good for five minutes' banter now and then, but not
much more. So he sat in the courtroom by himself, going
over what he'd said in his summation and how he might
have said it just a little bit better.

Vintage Jaywalker.

The second note didn't come out until three-thirty.

The jurors wanted to know if they could find the defendant guilty on counts eighty-six and eighty-seven on
the theory that he'd committed them earlier in the day,
when he'd driven from New York City to Nyack, and
then again from Frank Gilson's office to the End Zone.

Jaywalker knew the indictment by heart, all ninety-
three counts of it. Counts eighty-six and eighty-seven
charged Drake with driving without a valid driver's license and without insurance. Both were violations of the
Vehicle and Traffic Law that paled in comparison with
the more serious charges. In fact, even if Drake were to
be convicted of both of them, he'd already spent enough
time in jail that his sentence would have to be the equivalent of time served, or perhaps a fine.

But far more important than the jurors' interest in
those charges was what their question meant: that they'd
decided, or were on the verge of deciding, that Amanda

had been driving the Audi at the fateful moment, or at least that there was reasonable doubt as to whether Carter had been. What they were asking now was whether they could nonetheless convict Drake of *something*. And they'd seized upon the two counts they were asking about knowing that when Drake had driven up to Nyack that morning, and later to the End Zone that afternoon, he hadn't been licensed or insured.

This was good. This was *very* good.

Justice Hinkley asked the lawyers for their reactions.

"Sure they can," said Jaywalker. He'd be giving up virtually nothing. And by tossing the jury a bone, the payback would be enormous, an acquittal on the remaining charges. The ones that counted.

"Mr. Firestone?" the judge asked.

"I don't give a rat's ass," said Abe. He might not have been the sharpest tack in the toolbox, but he, too, could see where this was going.

Justice Hinkley pulled out her copy of the indictment, thumbed to the two counts in question, and studied them. "Both of these counts specify a time," she said, "'at or about nine o'clock in the evening.' It's clear to me that the grand jury had in mind the time of the accident. For me to tell the jury yes, they can nevertheless convict the defendant on those counts based upon his driving earlier in the day, would constitute both an amendment and an enlargement of the indictment, something I have no power to do. Accordingly, I'm going to tell them no, they cannot do that."

Jaywalker protested, offering to waive any appeal on the issue, but the judge refused to change her mind. And she was right. Having voted the indictment in the first place, only the grand jurors had the power to amend it. And they'd been discharged months ago.

"Bring in the jury," said the judge.

* * *

Just as he could read a lot more into a note than the words it contained, so too could Jaywalker read the faces of jurors in the midst of deliberations as they entered the courtroom. Any trial lawyer learns to do that. At least any good one.

It's a good sign if they're willing to look at the defendant and his lawyer, a bad sign if they're not. A smile is to be treasured, as is any sort of laughing, joking or looking relaxed. Even the way they make their way to the jury box is telling. Jurors who are leaning toward acquittal will think nothing of walking close to the defense table; those in the conviction camp will steer clear, favoring the prosecution table.

This jury was angry.

They didn't smile, they didn't joke, they didn't relax. They avoided both the defense and the prosecution tables. And the only eye contact they made was with the judge.

Hearing that they could convict the defendant of driving without a license or insurance only if they were convinced beyond a reasonable doubt that he'd done so at or about nine o'clock on the evening in question seemed to make them angrier. Their faces grim, they filed out and returned to their deliberations.

The buzzer sounded twice at 4:46.

A single buzz meant the jurors had a note.

A double buzz meant a verdict.

The courtroom filled up almost immediately. Carter Drake was brought in through a side door. Jaywalker said a final prayer to a God he didn't believe in and took his seat next to Drake.

"What do you think?" Carter asked him.

"I have no idea."

He had all sorts of ideas, of course, and they were all banging around furiously in what was left of his brain. But they were drowned out by the pounding in his chest and at his temples, and by the rushing noise in his ears. And even were he to admit his hunch to himself, that they were about to hear the words *Not guilty,* he would never say so out loud. Not in a million years.

When the jurors filed in for the last time, they seemed as angry as they had been before, and as unwilling to make eye contact as ever. And studying them, Jaywalker hoped he understood that anger. *Let them be angry,* he prayed. *Let them be angry at Carter Drake, but only for setting in motion the chain of events that hadn't ended until nine people lay incinerated beyond recognition. Let them be angry at Amanda for whatever she'd done to cause the Audi to wander into the wrong lane, and to fail to get it back where it belonged. Let them be angry at the prosecution for being so stupid as to indict the wrong person. Let them be angry at me for being the one to show them they had to acquit. Let their anger be the anger of frustration, not the anger of retribution.*

"Will the foreperson please rise?"

Juror number one stood. She was a pleasant-looking woman, a teacher's aide with two young children of her own. She was thirty-four, she'd told them during jury selection a thousand years ago, and an orthodox Jew who wore a wig in public and kept a kosher home. And to look at her face, she was very, very nervous. But Jaywalker wasn't looking at her face. He was looking at her hands. They were empty. They held no verdict sheet, no note, no written breakdown of how the jury had voted on each of the ninety-three counts in the indictment.

Which could mean only one thing.

Either the jury was about to convict Carter Drake of everything, or they were going to convict him of nothing.

"Will the defendant please rise?" said the clerk. And as Drake stood, so did Jaywalker. He'd been second-guessed for that a couple of times, accused of showboating, even asked once if he was prepared to share the defendant's sentence in the event of a conviction. "Sure," he'd said, having already seen the jurors' smiles. The point was, he didn't care what others thought. It was his verdict as much as his client's. If the jury was about to reject his client, then they'd rejected him, too, and he'd take it standing up. What warrior ever chose to sit before his firing squad?

"Madame Forelady, has the jury reached a verdict?"

"Yes, we have."

"As to all ninety-three counts?"

"Yes."

"On count one of the indictment, charging the defendant with the murder of Walter Najinsky on the theory of recklessness evincing a depraved indifference to human life, how do you find the defendant, guilty or not guilty?"

24

It would have taken an hour, perhaps more, for the clerk to read each of the counts contained in the indictment, and for the teacher's aide to recite the words *Not guilty* ninety-three times. Graciously, if perhaps a wee bit testily, Abe Firestone rose to his feet after five such recitals, and suggested that the court might wish to inquire whether the news on the remaining eighty-eight counts was going to follow the pattern suggested by the first five.

"Thank you," said the judge. Then, turning to the forelady, she said, "Please answer this question 'Yes' or 'No.' Has the jury found the defendant not guilty on all ninety-three counts of the indictment? Just 'Yes' or 'No,' please. Nothing else."

"Yes."

25

A VERY DEAD BATTERY

It was May, three and a half months after the verdict. A lot had happened in that time. Carter Drake had been released from jail. His Audi had been returned to him, minus a few parts, and his bank accounts unfrozen. His civil lawyers had reached settlements with the families of seven of the nine victims, and were said to be on the verge of settling with the remaining two. The combined value of the settlements was reported to exceed twenty million dollars, and to cover Amanda, as well as Carter. Because of the not-guilty verdict, and because the evidence now strongly suggested that Amanda had been driving the Audi, her insurance company was contributing significantly to the settlement pool. The defenses the company had originally asserted—namely, that Carter Drake had been unlicensed, uninsured and intoxicated—had ceased to apply once it had been determined that he hadn't been the driver.

Abe Firestone had tried to indict Drake for perjury and obstruction of justice, on the theory that he'd lied by saying he'd been driving. But two separate grand juries had refused to vote true bills. There's long been an unwritten rule that bars bringing charges against a defendant who takes the stand and, in the face of overwhelming evidence to the contrary, testifies under oath that he's innocent. In the event of a conviction, a second prosecution for perjury looks a lot like overkill. And in the event of an acquittal, it smacks of poor losing. When a defendant insists he's *guilty,* in the face of overwhelming evidence of his *innocence,* no grand jury in the world is going to indict him for perjury, especially if he was trying to take the blame for a crime committed by his wife.

Firestone hadn't stopped there. Next he'd tried to build a murder case against Amanda. But there'd simply been too many obstacles standing in his way. First, there'd been no indication that she'd been drinking. Then there'd been Concepción Testigo's identification, however weak and however based upon "jello hair," of Carter as the driver. Firestone had even gone so far as to do what Jaywalker had only pretended to, subpoenaing photographs from EZPass. But when the photos arrived at his office, they'd showed only the license plates of the Audi as it went through the tollbooth, not the occupants. With little to go on but Firestone's own anger and sense of justice, his case against Amanda had never even made it as far as the grand jury.

By mid-April, Carter and Amanda had not only both escaped prosecution and settled most of the civil cases against them, they'd resolved most of the personal differences between them, too. Amanda still kept her own apartment, but only because the lease wouldn't be up for another three months. For all intents and purposes, she'd moved back in with her husband, making Jaywalker's pledge to stop seeing her an easy one to carry out. He hadn't done quite so well in terms of visiting the dentist or scheduling a colonoscopy or a PSA test, but he was getting ready to clean up his apartment any day now.

So it came as something of a surprise when he got a phone call from Amanda, wondering if by any chance he wanted to take another ride up to Massachusetts with her to pick up Eric, whose semester was ending the following day. "Carter's stuck out of town," she said, "and my car's in the body shop, recovering from a fender bender. So we'd have to take yours."

"Sure," he said. "Why not?" He'd actually taken the Merc in for its annual oil change not too long ago, and it was running pretty well, all things considered. So he figured it might just be up to the task. Besides, when all was said and done, he was still the same old Jaywalker, and the thought of seeing Amanda again, with her husband out of town, was impossible to resist.

He picked her up at nine, and they were on the Taconic forty-five minutes later, heading north on a beautiful spring morning. Sitting beside him on the front seat, Amanda looked terrific, and Jaywalker kept both hands on the wheel, lest one of them wander toward her of its own volition. They talked little about the past, and barely mentioned the trial. She asked how his other cases were going, he asked about her design jobs. They listened to old favorites on the Merc's AM radio, oblivious to the static.

At Route 23 he turned right, and they stopped to get gas and lunch at a diner. He liked the way she didn't wait for him to come around and open her door, hopping out on her own instead. As he watched from the driver's seat, she bent over to stretch her back muscles. The unexpected view of her rear, which might have had forty years under its belt but sure didn't look like it, was worth the trip right there.

They ordered sandwiches and Cokes, and ate outside at a picnic table, underneath a huge white umbrella. It was nearly eighty degrees in the shade, and the cold days of New City in January seemed light-years away.

Only after they'd climbed back into the Merc, and Jaywalker had turned the key in the ignition, did he realize he'd left the headlights on. He'd developed the habit of driving with them on even in the daytime after reading somewhere that it cut head-on collisions by sixty percent. But being old, his car didn't have one of those annoying little chimes that reminded you to turn the lights off when you got out.

What that added up to now was a very dead battery.

He had no jumper cables, his last set having mysteriously disappeared from the trunk long ago. He looked around for help, and even asked a couple of people sitting inside if they had cables. But if anyone did, they weren't admitting it.

"Do you have AAA?" Amanda asked.

"No," he said, not bothering to add that the closest he'd ever gotten was AA.

"So what do we do now?"

"You get in the driver's seat," he told her. "Turn the key to the On position, but not Start. Put the car in first gear, and keep your foot on the clutch. I'm going to push, and when it gets moving, pop the clutch."

But instead of getting in, she just stood there, looking away from him. And when he asked her what the matter was, she turned and walked a couple of steps away.

It didn't take much effort for him to catch up to her. "You can do this," he told her.

"No, I can't."

"What do you mean, you can't?"

For a long moment she said nothing. When finally she spoke, it was with eyes still averted, and in a small, tentative voice, the sort of voice a child might use when owning up to breaking a good lamp or an expensive piece of pottery. "I've never driven a standard-shift car," she said. "I don't know how."

He found a couple of guys to give them a push, and they got back on their way. He said nothing to Amanda, not a word. But sometimes silence can be more deafening than rage, and just after they'd crossed over the New York–Massachusetts line, she asked him to pull over and turn off the engine. He did, this time remembering to turn off the lights, as well.

"You think I'm horrible," she said.

"I don't know what to think," he told her. It was the truth.

She took a deep breath. "I sought you out," she began, "because everyone kept telling me you were the best. Even if you were suspended. You're going to think I'm a complete wacko, but I followed you, trying to make it look like an accident."

"I know."

"You know I followed you?"

He nodded. "For two days."

"Three," she said.

"I guess I must have been out of practice."

"Then, when the revolving door got stuck—"

"It didn't get stuck," he said. "I stopped it."

She smiled. It had been a while. "It was all Carter's idea," she said. "He said if either of us, or even both of us, said I'd been driving, nobody would believe us. That it would just look like I was trying to protect him because I had a license and I hadn't been drinking. He said the only way it would work was for him to take the stand, say he was driving, and then somehow slip up. But he said he needed me to find a lawyer smart enough to catch the slipup, and clever enough to know what to do with it. So I found you."

"And played me."

She nodded.

"*Jesus,*" was all he could say. Here he thought he'd pulled off a miracle, won an absolutely unwinnable trial, a Tenth Case. When all he'd really done was to play the part of the village idiot, and play it to perfection. Between them, Carter and Amanda had done all the heavy lifting. The left-handed mistake had been nothing but Carter's invention, the inability to reach the clutch a fallback measure, just in case Jaywalker had been asleep at the switch and missed the first cue.

"And our…"

"That was real," she assured him, her hand reaching out and finding his forearm. "All of that was real."

But how could he possibly believe that? How could he not think that their lovemaking had been just another part of the Grand Plan? A part that Amanda had kept her husband apprised of in minute detail, no doubt.

"I feel like an absolute idiot," said Jaywalker, drawing his arm back from her grasp.

"An *idiot?* You were *brilliant.* Everyone was right about you."

"And you?" he asked. "Suppose Judah Mermelstein hadn't been sitting in the courtroom? Suppose he hadn't been smart enough to tell you to take the Fifth? What would you have done then?"

"He didn't tell me to take the Fifth," said Amanda. "I told him I was going to. He wasn't even sure I could. But Carter had looked it all up, and checked it out. He knew."

"You barely needed me," said Jaywalker. It was the truth, and it was hard to swallow. "You paid me all that money to be, to be… I don't know what I was. I was like the magician's assistant. You know, the dope he pulls up from the audience, the one who stands on the stage while they pull rabbits out of his ears."

"You were nothing like that," said Amanda. "You were wonderful. You were the best."

But her words were just that.

Words.

26

DEUS FEDEX MACHINA

After that, there was only one more twist left to the story. It took place the following January, almost a year to the day after Carter Drake had walked out of court a free man.

Jaywalker had nothing to do with it this time, not even a bit part. Nor did Amanda or Abe Firestone or Judah Mermelstein, or any of the other players who'd had roles in the earlier performance.

It happened on a Tuesday, a weekday, when Carter Drake was at his office in midtown Manhattan. A package arrived, delivered by the FedEx man. Not the regular one who stopped by almost every day, but a substitute whom no one could remember seeing before or after. The package was a fairly large one, approximately three feet by two feet by eight inches high. It was marked PERISHABLE—DO NOT FREEZE, and the shipping label indicated it had been mailed from a well-known purveyor of fruit and gifts called Harry and David, out in Bear Creek, Oregon. But according to the investigation that followed, neither Harry nor David nor anyone else had any record of having shipped it, and the professional-looking tracking label it bore turned out to have been created on a home computer.

Carter Drake must have used a letter opener to pry it open, because they found one on the carpet of his office. Inside the box he'd discovered oranges, grapefruits, clementines, and an assortment of little jars of honey, marmalade and fruit preserves. There even appeared to be a small branch, sprouting green leaves and snow-white orange blossoms in full bloom. But upon closer inspection, the branch turned out to be a cutting suitable for planting, complete with its own tiny root system encased in peat moss and wrapped in a clear plastic bag. And attached to the branch and tucked in among the orange blossoms was a small object, pretty much the size, shape and color of a well-used Ping-Pong ball. But it wasn't a Ping-Pong ball. It was a hive.

They found Drake an hour later, doubled over on the carpet. The paramedics pronounced him dead at the scene. An autopsy was conducted, and the cause of death was determined to have been suffocation brought on by an acute anaphylactic reaction to insect venom. That insect venom appeared to have been introduced to Carter Drake's body by exactly nine separate bee stings. Nine.

In a way, many agreed, it was an appropriate ending. But perhaps no one summed it up more cleverly than the *New York Times* reporter who likened it to a *Deus FedEx Machina*.

To Jaywalker, it was an ironic final chapter to a strange, sad story. To his way of thinking, Carter Drake's drunken and reckless driving might not have added up to murder. But if you were to throw in the cavalier way in which he'd gone on to manipulate his wife, his son, his own lawyer, the jury, and the entire criminal justice system, there was probably no better way to describe his conduct than by using the words the grand jury had settled on a year earlier, back when they'd handed up the indictment.

Depraved indifference to human life.

There came a time when Jaywalker cranked up the Merc and took one last drive up to Rockland County. He waited until fall came, and even when fall came, he waited for a clear day, knowing how the sun would light up the brilliant colors of the changing leaves along the Palisades Parkway.

He found the eight memorials by the side of Route 303. They were neat and well tended, but the number of artifacts had dwindled. There were fewer photos, cards, stuffed animals and items of clothing. Even the tiny baseball mitt was gone. But there was a forwarding address of sorts. Propped up against a small Star of David was a funeral announcement someone had encased in plastic, evidently to protect it from the elements. Following the service, it said, interments would take place at the Beth El Cemetery in Valley Cottage.

He located it without too much trouble, and parked inside the metal gates. He told an old man wearing a yarmulke what he was looking for, and the man smiled and pointed to a rise, a small hilltop in the distance.

"You can drive up there, if you like."

But Jaywalker preferred to walk.

He found them beneath the shade of a huge maple tree that he guessed had to be older then he was, older even than the man with the yarmulke. They were in a single row, small rounded mounds marked by smaller headstones. It had been eighteen months since the accident, half a year since the unveilings would have taken place, and the grass atop the mounds had taken root, sprouted, grown and filled in. And as they had been in both life and death, the children were still together.

All eight of them.

From there he drove over to New City, where he spent the rest of the afternoon. He walked the streets, sampled the shops and exchanged small talk with anyone willing to share a few minutes of time with him. They talked about nothing in particular. The weather, the fall colors, the price of gasoline. What they didn't talk about was the case, not unless he pressed them to. And when he did, they surprised him. Where Jaywalker had fully expected to find lingering anger, bitterness and frustration, he found only a readiness to move on. A few people even mentioned that they recognized him as the lawyer for the accused, but none seemed determined to hold it against him. One went so far as to tell him he was a good lawyer and a *mensch*.

Driving home, he couldn't help but marvel at the way the community had managed not only to survive, but to come together and heal. The eight families had opted for a single funeral service, he'd been told, and then buried their children shoulder to shoulder beneath the same tree on the same hill in the same cemetery. Somehow they'd gotten past all of it—Carter Drake's initial responsibility for all that had happened, Amanda Drake's unwillingness to implicate him or herself, and Abe Firestone's ultimate inability to place blame upon either one of them.

They'd moved on.

To Jaywalker, that sheer depth of resilience, that capacity of the families and the community to survive, was nothing less than astounding. It was enough to make him drive the rest of the way home with a wry smile on his face. It was enough, he realized at some point, to make a guy wonder....

ACKNOWLEDGMENTS

Once again I find myself deeply indebted to my literary agent Bob Diforio, who claims he's deluged with other writers but continues to treat me as though I'm his only one, and to my fabulous editor Leslie Wainger and the rest of the gang at MIRA, who do pretty much the same. I would be totally lost without either one of them.

For some reason, I always seem to have great difficulty persuading my wonderful but terribly overcommitted wife, Sandy, to find time to read my latest manuscript. But eventually the sheer force of my nagging prevails. Warning me in advance that she's going to absolutely hate it, she disappears into the den for the better part of the day. Sometime that evening, she emerges and tracks me down, a broad smile on her face, to pronounce the work my very best yet. That's the moment when I know it's okay to send it off.

An enthralling legal thriller by

JOSEPH TELLER

Criminal defense attorney Harrison J. Walker, aka Jaywalker,
has just been suspended for receiving "gratitude" in the
courtroom stairwell from a client charged with prostitution.
Convincing the judge that his other clients are counting on
him, Jaywalker is allowed to complete ten cases. But it's the
last case that truly tests his abilities....

Samara Moss stabbed her husband. Or so everyone believes.
Having married the billionaire when she was an 18-year-old
prostitute, Samara appears to be a gold digger. But Jaywalker
knows all too well that appearances can be deceiving.
Has Samara been framed? Or is Jaywalker just driven by
his need to win his clients' cases?

THE
TENTH
CASE

*Available now
wherever books are sold!*

MIRA®

www.MIRABooks.com MJT2605R

AN INTENSE NEW THRILLER FROM

JOSEPH TELLER

One phone call changed Jaywalker's
life forever....

Criminal defense attorney
Harrison J. Walker, better known
as Jaywalker, receives a call from
a desperate mother. Her son,
Darren, has been arrested for
raping five white women in a
long-forgotten corner of the Bronx.

A young black man, Darren is positively
identified by four of the victims as the fifth
prepares to do the same. Everyone sees this as
an open-and-shut case—everyone except Jaywalker.

As he looks deep into the characters involved in the crime
and the character of our society, what he finds will haunt him
for the rest of his career.

BRONX JUSTICE

Available wherever books are sold.

P.D. MARTIN

IN KUNG FU TARGETED STRIKES
CAN KILL INSTANTLY...
BUT HOW?

Aussie FBI profiler Sophie Anderson is settling into her job in the L.A. bureau when she's pulled into a case like no other—the victim has had his throat literally ripped out. But what weapon could have caused such devastating injuries? And who is the John Doe?

As L.A.'s underworld rears its ugly head, Sophie will have to draw on her experience and her developing psychic skills to find a brilliant killer who's carved a trail of death in organized crime across the U.S. He leaves only one thing behind him—horrifying murder scenes.

The Killing Hands

Available now wherever books are sold.

MIRA®